RICHARD LIVETH YET

A HISTORICAL NOVEL SET IN THE PRESENT DAY

BY

JOANNE R. LARNER

Copyright ©2015 Joanne Rosalie Larner

All rights reserved.

This book or any portion thereof may not be reproduced or used in any manner whatsoever without the express written permission of the publisher/author.

The right of Joanne Rosalie Larner to be identified as the author of this work has been asserted by her in accordance with the

Copyright, Designs and Patents Act of 1988

This is a work of fiction. Any depiction of real people living or dead is the author's own creation

DEDICATED TO JOHN LARNER
MY LONG-SUFFERING HUSBAND,
WITHOUT WHOM THIS BOOK
WOULD NOT HAVE BEEN POSSIBLE
AND TO THE STAR OF THE BOOK,
RICHARD PLANTAGENET,
DUKE OF GLOUCESTER,
BY THE GRACE OF GOD,
KING RICHARD III OF ENGLAND AND FRANCE
AND LORD OF IRELAND.

Table of Contents

ACKNOWLEDGEMENTS	9
INTRODUCTION	11
CHAPTER ONE - JUNE 1485	**15**
Alone	15
CHAPTER TWO - JUNE 2014	**18**
Bring Me To Life	18
Baby What A Big Surprise	21
Drive By	30
Soap (I Use The)	32
Rude	38
Try	46
I Vow To Thee My Country	55
Finding Beauty	57
Don't Know Much	64
Somebody That I Used To Know	66
Feels Like Home	68
Amazed	72
Grenade	76
CHAPTER THREE - JULY 2014	**84**
Everything I Own	84

Strong	87
True Colours	93
I'm Too Sexy	98
Heart of Gold	102
The Best	107
Handy Man	109
Hero	113
Read All About It	120
Music	126

CHAPTER FOUR - AUGUST 2014   132

An Englishman in New York	132
Need You Now	140
It's All Coming Back to Me Now	143
The Armed Man	148
Glorious	149
What Doesn't Kill You (Stronger)	155

CHAPTER FIVE - SEPT 2014   160

Little Arrows	160
My Prayer	167
Only Love Can Hurt Like This	173
I Don't Want to Miss a Thing	175

CHAPTER SIX - OCTOBER 2014   180

Thank You For the Music	180
Hot Stuff	186
Mars, The Bringer of War	189
Locked out of Heaven	195

CHAPTER SEVEN - NOVEMBER 2014 — 198

Requiem for a Tower	198
Hazard	201
Remember	207
Poison	212
Lady Eleanor	221
Kings	224
Senses Working Overtime	227
Fantasia on Greensleeves	233

CHAPTER EIGHT - DECEMBER 2014 — 237

Hocus Pocus	237
Dream A Dream	241
DNA	244
I Wish It Could Be Christmas Every Day	247

CHAPTER NINE - JANUARY 2015 — 254

Red Red Wine	254
Kiss From A Rose	260
If You're Not the One	262

CHAPTER TEN - FEBRUARY 2015 — 265

The Riddle — 265

Unfaithful — 270

The Silence — 272

Torn — 274

Road To Hell — 278

CHAPTER ELEVEN - MARCH 2015 — 282

Bad Things — 282

Don't Speak — 284

Requiem — 290

Fire — 302

CHAPTER TWELVE - APRIL 2015 — 308

Weight of the World — 308

The Proud One — 311

Bad Boys — 318

CHAPTER THIRTEEN - MAY 2015 — 321

Flying Theme (E.T.) — 321

Norwegian Wood — 326

That Thing You Do — 329

Mountains — 333

Earth — 339

Dancin' Away With My Heart — 342

CHAPTER FOURTEEN - JUNE 2015 — 346
Kissing You Goodbye — 346

CHAPTER FIFTEEN - JUNE 1485 — 350
Wind of Change — 350

CHAPTER SIXTEEN - JULY 2015 — 354
You Ruin Me — 354

CHAPTER SEVENTEEN - AUGUST 1485 — 358
Past the Point of Rescue — 358

CHAPTER EIGHTEEN - AUGUST 2015 — 364
Halo — 364

AUTHOR'S NOTES — 370

RICHARD'S PLAYLIST — 376

BIBLIOGRAPHY — 379

Acknowledgements

I would like to thank:

My lovely husband, John, without whom this book could not have been written - he took over much of the housework and walking the dogs whilst I worked on it and calmed me down when I thought I had lost it all on the computer!

The members of Making Fifteenth Century Re-Enactment Glorious, Destrier, Ricardian, Blanc Sanglier, Murrey and Blue, and B.O.A.R.s Facebook Groups, who helped me in my research, especially Tim Eagling, Stephen Lark, Judy Thomson, Janet Reedman, Karen Griebling, Maire Martello, Christine Smart, Sandra Heath Wilson, Dom Smee and Andreas Wenzel.

Viv Taylor and Helen Thomson who read the first draft and provided feedback, my sister, Lynne, who meticulously proof-read it for me (her grammar and spelling are impeccable) and Jane Orwin-Higgs for her valuable advice on style and her encouragement.

Jostein Lostad, my Norwegian best friend and his family; Laura Conboy, my best English friend, who helped me research the Major Oak; Maria Ball and Dalia Mikneviciute, my personal trainers; my dogs, Jubilee, Jonah and Hunter; Kieran, the archery instructor at Center Parcs; all of whom make an appearance in the novel.

NaNoWriMo (National Novel Writing Month), who provided the impetus and the deadline to give me a kick up the bum.

The ladies of the Women In Business Network for their enthusiasm. Anyone else I have forgotten, I'm sorry!

Introduction

This is a work of fiction, a historical fantasy novel, which started as an idea I had after reading numerous novels about Richard III. I loved them and couldn't get enough, but there was one problem: I always knew how they were going to end! So I decided to write one with another possible ending, and while I was at it, why not make it even more different by exploring how Richard III or any mediaeval person might react if they were summarily transported to the present day? I had read a couple of novels where time travel had occurred, but I wanted to go a bit deeper and try to think how strange everything would be to a Mediaeval man.

Although I have tried to make the historical parts as accurate as possible, I have taken a few liberties with areas which are unknown or unclear (these are many when it comes to Richard III) and I have also invented a few scenarios. Please don't be offended if I have portrayed Richard or any other historical character differently from your image of them. This is my own personal version of Richard.

Talking of which, the cover is a painting of my fantasy Richard, depicted in the story as Rose's work. The crown is from John-Ashdown Hill's commission which was part of Richard's re-interment ceremony.

In the story Richard is given a gift of an iPod with an eclectic mix of music on it - I have used over seventy of the many songs from this playlist as scene titles. Please note, the lyrics of the song are irrelevant, it is just the titles that relate to the scene content. They are listed in chronological order in the Author's Notes at the end of the book, with their artists, in case you want to look them up, download them or create your own copy of Richard's playlist! (OK, it's my playlist - but it is from my actual list of music on iTunes!)

The title, 'Richard Liveth Yet' comes from a 1456 listing of the descendants of Joan of Acre and Gilbert de Clare, known as the Clare Roll. It ends with a list of the children of Richard, Duke of York, and the only mention for Richard is 'Richard Liveth Yet'. This caused many to believe he must have been a sickly child, but this has since been disputed, experts now believing that he was merely being contrasted with his unfortunate siblings who had died:

"Sir, aftir the tyme of longe bareynesse,
God first sent Anne, which signifyeth grace,
In token that al her hertis hevynesse
He as for bareynesse would fro hem chace.
Harry, Edward, and Edmonde, eche in his place
Succedid; and after tweyn doughters cam
Elizabeth and Margarete, and aftirward William.
"John aftir William nexte borne was,
Whiche bothe he passid to Goddis grace:
George was next, and after Thomas
Borne was, which sone aftir did pace
By the pathe of dethe into the heavenly place.
<u>Richard liveth yet</u>; but the last of alle
Was Ursula, to him whom God list calle."

Joanne R Larner

Chapter One - June 1485

Alone

June 22nd 1485

Richard felt alive and at one with nature as he rode his noble steed across the clearing after the enormous white boar which had suddenly appeared as if from nowhere at the far edge. The others would be unable to keep up with his courser; Royal Rebel far outclassed theirs in speed and dexterity, but he didn't mind. He rather enjoyed being alone to witness the peace of the summer's day, bringing the forest to life.

Although most gentlemen would not wear armour for hunting, Richard was wearing his cuirass as he rode through Sherwood Forest. He often wore his harness beneath his clothes, especially if he went hunting for more than an hour or two. He found it helped to support his back, which bore a deformity – an S-shaped curve. It had begun to develop when he was a child of about eleven or twelve and had gradually worsened with age. The armour gave him some ease, in fact he was more comfortable wearing it and seated in the saddle than he was sitting on his elaborately carved throne. And not just physically.

So he was glad to get away from everyone for a few precious minutes. He wished he could get away forever. Being alone in nature was the only time he could find peace these days, ever since he had lost the three people in the world who had meant the most to him: first his brother Edward, then his son, little Ned, a year later, followed by his wife, Anne. He often felt alone now, even when he was surrounded by others, flattering and praising him; he was never really certain whether or not they were sincere in their words. It was too easy for them to say whatever they thought he wanted to hear just to flatter him. There were others who, he suspected, had their own advancement in mind, who would lie and fawn quite deliberately in order to achieve their ends. That was just one of the many disadvantages of being King of England.

He had had no idea how difficult it would be. He had had the greatest admiration for Edward, who had been king for so many years and had enjoyed, for the most part, a very successful reign. But he now realised Edward's reign had been based on favours, corruption, power mongering and injustice. Edward had got away with it for so long because he was charming and affable, as well as being handsome and kingly in appearance, and the people had loved him. Richard would have to be a different kind of king altogether and root out all the weeds of corruption that were choking the England he loved so much. Of course even he, Edward IV, had had a few teething troubles before establishing himself on the throne. Perhaps that was all that was happening to him now – teething troubles.

And one particularly troublesome tooth was called Henry Tydder. He was on the point of invading Richard's realm – the nerve of the upstart! He was not only Welsh, but he was of bastard stock on both sides of his family and had no valid claim to the throne. However, he had managed to gather enough support in France to launch an invasion and now Richard had to defeat the Bastard. He sighed, shaking off the thought of the battle that was to come – he had an odd feeling about it. Perhaps it was because it would be his first real battle as king – yes, that was probably all it was. He was confident in his ability to plan and execute warfare successfully. After all, he had had a great teacher in his brother, Edward. 'The Kingmaker', Richard Warwick too, his cousin and guardian while he was training to be a knight in Yorkshire, had taught him to be swift and skilful in the mêlée from an early age.

But enough of thoughts of war, it was time for the relaxation and exhilaration of the hunt – now where was that boar? It was still ahead of him, disappearing over a hillock to his right and he followed swiftly, spurring Royal Rebel forward eagerly. He almost wished he could escape his life forever and just be free to do whatever he wanted to do, instead of having the burden of his duty as King to weigh him down. As he topped the brow of the small hill and they galloped down the other side, Rebel suddenly stumbled and went down, neighing in panic, his fore legs buckling beneath him. Richard was catapulted over Rebel's pricked ears and landed head first among the roots of an old oak tree. He blacked out as he hit the ground.

Chapter Two - June 2014

Bring Me To Life

June 22nd 2014

Rose Archer had come to the Major Oak, because it would have been there in his time. Anything that was over five hundred years old had suddenly become attractive to her, since she had seen that TV documentary. It was amazing, incredible how one TV programme could have changed her life and given birth to an obsession with somebody who had died over half a millennium before. She couldn't explain it, but something about the story it told had called to her, moving her spirit and entering her heart, lying snugly there like a wayward kitten that had come home and curled up to sleep in a drawer. It had left her forever changed.

She had watched the programme over twenty times and still wasn't bored by it, unusual for her. Each time the part that chance had played in the outcome had left her feeling astounded and thrilled. No, actually, it wasn't chance, it couldn't have been – it was fate, pure and simple: it was meant to be.

It had told the story of the last Plantagenet King, Richard III, the last English king to die in battle. She had known nothing about Richard before this. At school, the Tudors were the subject studied in History, and Macbeth and Coriolanus the Shakespeare plays she had read, so she hadn't even The Bard's famous interpretation of him as a starting point – thinking about it, perhaps that was just as well. She had heard of the infamous mystery of the Princes in the Tower, but she remembered it vaguely as something her mother had once mentioned and which she had assumed had happened much more recently than five hundred years before.

The programme had asked even more questions than it had answered and she had begun to read, as only she could – every spare moment, absorbing all the hundreds of diverse versions of Richard's life, both fiction and nonfiction. Clearly, it was not only she who had become entranced by the enigmatic King, whose life held so few facts and so many mysteries that each novel written about him was unique and different, each Richard changed slightly from the last.

She'd read novels told from the point of view of his friend, Francis Lovell; his mistress (whose identity changed in each novel); his fool; his armourer; his lawyer; his betrayer Buckingham; his niece; his wife and countless other friends and acquaintances. Each story was different, but they were all spoiled because she knew how they were going to end! It made her feel sad and empty, the terrible waste of a life that could have been so positive and influential for England. If only he had won at Bosworth, if only he had been allowed to rule as he had wanted, how would England have changed?

And now his remains would be re-interred at Leicester Cathedral next year and she had decided to be there. She had even decided to book into the Travelodge Hotel that stood on the spot previously occupied by the Blue Boar Inn – the inn where Richard was thought to have stayed on his final night before leaving for the battle. After all, it wasn't every day you got to see a Medieval king reburied! She felt that she had to go, that there was an invisible thread drawing her inexorably there to pay her last respects. Would that finally lay to rest the obsession she felt about him? She wasn't sure whether she hoped it would or not…

She was in Nottingham visiting her friend, Laura, for a long weekend, combining it with the Earth & Fire Ceramic Fair at Rufford Abbey at the weekend. She had decided to go and see the Major Oak – she had been to the area many times, but had somehow never made it to the iconic, ancient tree before. It was humid and she had waited until the late afternoon, hoping that the heat would lessen by then. She preferred rain or snow to heat. Her fair skin was so pale, it would never tan enough to be noticed by anyone other than herself. She remembered going on holiday to Kos, the Greek island, for two weeks, and returning whiter than those going out there! She had finally given up and accepted she would never have that sun-kissed, golden honey-coloured skin she so desired, just like she would never have long, shiny hair. Hers was so curly, even when she grew it, it looked shorter than it really was because the hair curled up so, lifting the ends up. She used to hate it but she had become accustomed to it now and it was really handy to just wash it and go, leaving it to dry by itself.

She walked slowly up to the fence surrounding the oak tree, resting her hand on it while she finished the apple she had brought with her. She tried to imagine the many thousands of people who must have seen this ancient tree, admired it, climbed it and sheltered under it. What tales it could tell if only it could speak! She stood still, thankful for the shade of the fluffy clouds passing in front of the fierce lion sun and transfixed by the power of this old soul of a tree, enjoying the solitude and imagining she was travelling back in time through all the centuries the tree had witnessed.

Baby What A Big Surprise

Suddenly she was startled out of her reverie by an incongruous sound, a deep groaning coming from the other side of the tree. Were its branches protesting the weight of the years, giving up the ghost at last? No, it was a human sound, but how could it be? No one else had been anywhere near. The sound came again and she realised it emanated from the far side of the tree and leaned over the fence to try and see who or what was on the other side of the gnarled, crusty, old trunk. There appeared to be someone lying on the floor, entangled somewhat in the roots; a man, dark and slim and wearing clothes that belonged to the very age she had been thinking of. She remembered that there was a re-enactment of some battle or jousting tournament, something of the kind, going on in the area. Suddenly, a movement way off in the trees at the other side of the clearing, caught her eye. Before she could see what it was, it had disappeared.

The man wore a long scabbard at his side with the ornate hilt of a very real-looking sword protruding from it. He was also carrying a bow and arrows – it looked like a long bow, no less! Yes, that must be it – he had somehow strayed away from the re-enactment and got lost here – he was probably drunk. She shrank back a little when she realised that she was alone here with this strange man, who might very possibly be a dangerous mugger, rapist or even murderer! Then he suddenly became aware of her gaze and glanced up, his blue-grey eyes meeting her green ones. He frowned in confusion and quickly and gracefully found his feet, brushing off his clothes which were made of richly decorated velvet of a dark green hue and his boots looked to be hand stitched soft leather. He vaulted easily over the fence and walked quickly towards her, his bearing upright and naturally graceful.

"Who art thou, sir.....er, lady? And what is this strange apparel thou wearest?" he asked. Then: "What is this place? I know not this tree – how came I out of the forest so suddenly?" His eyebrows were drawn together in confusion, his expression wary.

She couldn't help laughing at that formal mode of speech – she awarded him points for keeping in character! Her fear disappeared without her knowing why. Well, she would string him along a little.

She held onto the edges of her T-shirt and lowered her right knee towards the ground as she attempted a curtsey. "Good day, good knight!" she laughed, intending to follow this with the well-worn, old, jokey punch line, only to scream and overbalance, heading straight for a patch of dirt! In an instant, he had grabbed her arm to steady her - ouch! His grip was painful. She was grateful for his timely intervention but stared at the bejewelled hand which was still holding her elbow firmly – she felt as if a current of electricity was passing through her arm; the hairs on the back of her forearm were standing up.

He released her and stared at his own hand – had he felt it too? He backed away a few paces along the fence, his eyes narrowing and ran his hand through his hair, brushing it away from his face. He had a pale face; fine, high cheekbones, a bold nose and a prominent jutting chin: stubborn, she thought. His lips had a slight downturn at the edges but his lower lip was quite full – more so than the upper - and his expression was serious, even sad or maybe worried. Two small lines were drawn between his dark eyebrows and there were several more lines of care around his eyes and mouth and the beginnings of frown lines on his broad forehead. His eyes were deep and blue-grey and she found she couldn't look away, they held her gaze like the magnetic North holds a compass needle.

The man looked around him, as if searching for something in the woods behind him.

"Lady, hast thou seen my trusty steed? When I swooned I had just tumbled from his back - he is wont to stand if his rider is unhorsed, unless affrighted. I fear lest he hath been stolen. He is the colour sable, black as pitch with a white blaze down his face, and I fain would find him."

"I thought I saw something black moving a way over there." Rose pointed to a stand of trees about one hundred metres behind the man. "I can't see it any more though - it was going quite fast in the opposite direction."

The man turned and ran off at a trot into the trees.

"No, wait! You'll never catch it. Why don't you come with me and we can take the car and look for it from the other side?"

The man stopped and peered through the trees, trying to make out his horse in the shadows. He looked even more worried. After a few fruitless minutes' scrutiny, he sighed, his hands on his hips, and turned back towards Rose.

"Very well. How canst thou aid me? And what is this 'car' thou speakest of?"

Rose frowned - he was obviously more than half crazy.

"You know what a car is!" she said, incredulously. "It's over there." She gestured behind her towards the car park, where she had parked her old Vauxhall Astra Estate, even though it was too far away to be seen from where they were.

He peered suspiciously in the direction she pointed, passing his right hand through his long, silky hair to push it right back off his face, and she saw the blood in the hair line of his left temple for the first time.

"Oh, you've hurt yourself!" she cried. "Come on, we should get you to Casualty immediately," she said, taking his arm, concerned that the blow might have caused a concussion. His soft blue eyes changed in an instant to cold ice, his teeth gritted.

"Unhand me, wench! Dost thou dare lay hands on the person of thy Sovereign Lord!?"

He hadn't raised his voice, but spoke with such authority and covert menace that she dropped her hand as if it had been burnt by the touch of him.

The man was obviously mentally unbalanced, which was unnerving enough, but the sudden flash of cold anger in his eyes was terrifying.

"OK, OK, I'm sorry if I offended you. But please stop mucking around! You've cut your head and I only wanted to help you. You can stop using that fake Mediaeval accent now as well, the joke's wearing thin. I don't even know why I'm bothering!"

At that she turned on her heel and stalked off towards her old car, otherwise known as Griselda, and left him standing alone at the tree. A good few seconds passed before she heard his footsteps running behind her.

"Hold, lady, I spoke out of turn. The wound is but a scratch and need not concern thee. But I appear to be lost in this place and I am most confused. Wilt thou aid me? Thou shalt be rewarded right richly, certes, once I find my steed and my path back to Beskwood Lodge."

"Do you mean Bestwood Lodge? That's about fifteen miles away. I could drive you there if you like, just don't growl at me again!"

"Fifteen miles! It seems I have strayed much further than I intended from my companions. Mayhap they will be concerned for my welfare. I would thus be most grateful for thine assistance, my lady."

He walked alongside her, his face still showing signs of worry. As they approached the car, he suddenly recoiled and took a couple of swift steps backwards, drawing his sword in a single fluid movement. He pulled her back with him as his breath hissed between his teeth.

"Sweet Jesu, 'tis a dragon! – I have wandered into a land of nightmares! Get thee behind me lady, I will protect thee!"

"What are you doing, it's just my old car!" she laughed.

"This monster belongs to thee? Art thou a witch, a sorceress?" he whispered, now backing away from her. His lethal looking sword was now pointing directly at her heart.

She stood stock still, frozen in fear, suddenly aware that he was serious; she wasn't laughing now – maybe he had damaged his brain.

"Yes, it belongs to me - but it's not a monster, it's a machine and, no, I'm not a witch or a sorceress," she said simply. "I'm just an osteopath."

He looked at her levelly, as if testing her honesty and re-sheathed his sword.

"Thou speakest a strange dialect – I recognise it not. Osteo – path – that is Greek is it not? Bone – disease?" he asked.

She was impressed. Not many people had that level of classical knowledge these days.

"Yes, that's right, that's where the name comes from. Basically we give hands on treatment to anyone with a musculoskeletal problem – backache, neck pain, headaches, shoulder problems, that sort of thing?"

"Backache, didst thou say? And are thy ministrations effectual?" He was suddenly interested, his face hopeful, blue eyes revealing interest and intelligence. Then a sudden shadow darkened his even features. "Thou employest not sorcery?" he asked, suspicion again clouding his expression.

"Only for very difficult cases!" she laughed, then saw his look of horror. "Hey! Don't worry - I'm only joking!" she said hurriedly, before he had time to unsheathe his sword again.

She stepped up to Griselda and patted her on the bonnet. Then she pressed the remote, which made him jump. He was certainly a nervous guy!

"My name's Rose – what's yours, by the way?" she asked, as she opened the door.

He inclined his head gracefully, glancing suspiciously at the car. "Enchanté, Lady Rose, I am Richard Gloucestre, King of England and your Sovereign Lord."

"Hmm!" she snorted. "Has Laura sent you here as a practical joke? She knows how fascinated I am by Richard III. Look, just get in the car, will you?"

She opened the car door and gestured for him to get in. He did so gingerly, feeling the cloth of the seat as he did and staring, amazed, at the car's dashboard. She closed the door as quietly as she could and went around to the driver's seat. He tensed when she reached over to help him put the seat belt on, flinching as if he thought she was going to stab him. Boy, he sure was stand-offish.

"I'm just making sure you'll be safely secured in the seat – cars go a little faster than horses!" she said, going along with his deception.

She stopped suddenly as she noticed he was wearing some kind of armour underneath his clothes. Was he so afraid of being attacked?

"I thank thee, Lady Rose. I am indebted to thee for thy kindness. Verily, though I am king, I know not rightly what to do, all is so strange and fearful. I am also sore tired, for I have ridden more than three hours whilst hunting for an uncommonly large white boar, which, it seems, has led me a merry jape into this strange country." He stopped abruptly as she turned the ignition and he felt the car's vibrations, then looked quickly around.

"Whence comest this celestial music?" he asked in wonder, and she realised the radio had come on when she had started the car. "The sound is strange, but verily 'tis beautiful!" he said. It was Classic FM and luckily one of the more gentle classical pieces. Thank goodness she hadn't had her Viking metal CD on! She reached over to turn it off, in case a more alarming piece of music started. When the music was cut off he turned to her with a frown and put his hand on her forearm.

"Why dost thou stop the heavenly melody? Wouldst thou allow it to play again? I pray thee? Oft do I listen to melodious music. 'Tis a soothing balm to the troubled spirit."

She smiled and slowly and gently took his hand, noticing that his skin was warm and a little calloused. She moved it to the on/off button of her radio and pushed his index finger against the switch. The music began again. She pushed his finger on the button again and it stopped, again to start it once more.

"You can control it yourself here," she said. "The other buttons can change the kind of music that's playing – it's hard to explain. Feel free to play about with them, but note that we have many different types of music – some of which you might not even recognise as music at all." She was thinking of 'Rap'. He pushed the button again a few more times, turning the radio on and off and then pressed one of the preset station buttons. It was Heart FM and the song was "The Glory of Love" by Peter Cetera. He was singing the line about a knight in shining armour. How appropriate!

Richard turned and looked at her, a broad smile lighting up his face which up until then had had a constantly worried expression. The smile transformed his whole persona, his blue-grey eyes softening, showing small laughter lines at their edges, a dimple appearing on one side of his mouth. He looked incredibly handsome.

"Never have I heard such strange, yet beautiful, music. This is indeed an extraordinary land."

She put the car into gear and slowly, carefully drove out onto the road, gradually accelerating, so as not to alarm him too much.

She drove around to the other side of the wooded area, as close as she could to where she thought she had seen a flash of black in the undergrowth. They got out of the car and Richard jogged into the wood, calling and clicking his tongue, but there was no response and they could see no trace of Richard's mount. They spent about an hour searching, but it was starting to get dark and eventually Richard conceded that they must wait until daylight and try again then. Rose offered to take him to Bestwood Lodge and promised to pick him up early the next day and bring him back to try again.

They returned to the car and she reached into her bag for her Sat Nav. As she got it out, the book she had been reading came out with it and fell open onto the floor. It was a book about how the "Looking for Richard" team had found the remains of Richard III and it was open at the picture of his reconstructed face. She picked it up, glancing at the man sitting beside her and almost dropped the book again in shock. Oh my God! His face was so like the reconstruction of Richard III it was uncanny! His eyes were bluer and his hair not quite so dark, but....In her shock she had gasped aloud and he tilted his head a fraction to look at her, a questioning look in his sad eyes. He suddenly looked very vulnerable, confused and lonely.

As they drove through the darkening landscape, Rose tried to bring her rationality to the fore - just because he bore a passing resemblance to the reconstruction and was called Richard (or so he said!) and wore mediaeval style clothes and jewellery and spoke in an olde worlde way, didn't mean anything. He must be playing the role of Richard III in a re-enactment, got separated, hit his head and lost his memory, thinking he was really Richard III. Or he was just a great actor, sent by someone as a prank to wind her up. Yes, that must be it. But who would do that to her? Of course: Laura! She had been laughing at how obsessed Rose was with Richard III just the other day. Maybe she wanted to get her own back for all the long chats she had had to endure about a King who died over five hundred years before. Well, she had to admit, if it was a prank, it was a brilliant one! She might as well enjoy it - what the hell!

Drive By

After about twenty minutes they arrived at the Bestwood Lodge Hotel. It was a large brick built building with several different sections and large grounds. She pulled up in the car park, got out and opened the door for Richard. He looked at her suspiciously, two small lines appearing between his eyebrows as they narrowed into a frown.

"What meanest thou by halting at this place, Lady Rose?"

"We're here. This is Bestwood Lodge. Come on, out you get!"

He took a deep breath, sat up straight and carefully got out of the passenger seat. He looked around him and his eyes scanned the Hotel, passing right across it and sweeping onwards, until he had looked through the whole three hundred and sixty degrees. Then his eyes turned back to Rose, dark and puzzled, the frown still evident.

"Thou art mistaken, Lady Rose. This place is not Beskwood Lodge. The Lodge is a smaller, wooden structure and 'tis surrounded by deep forest, not this…..strange terrain." He stared down at the tarmac he was standing on.

"Yes, it is! Look at the sign over there!" She pointed towards the hotel's name sign swinging gently in the breeze.

He looked. Then he shook his head, setting his hair moving in waves like a dark ocean. What wouldn't she give to have such beautiful dark brown hair? - she had always been envious of those with long, dark hair - the opposite of her blonde curls. She watched him blinking in the light pouring from the hotel's windows, a slight touch of fear in those sad, blue eyes.

"Thou art mistaken, I say! I have never set eyes on this place before!" And he turned on his heel and began walking away from her.

"Wait, Richard," she cried. "Look, if this isn't the right place, why don't you come back to the B & B where I'm staying. You can get a room there instead and we can sort this out tomorrow."

He stopped and looked over his shoulder, a lock of his wavy, brown hair falling over his brow and covering one eye. He looked like he was peering round a curtain. He paused a good few seconds and then sighed, brushed the stray lock of hair back from his face and lowered his head momentarily before giving a quick nod and walking back to her.

"Very well, Lady Rose. I do thank thee for thy help."

She helped him to do his seatbelt up again and they drove back in the direction of West Bridgford.

The evening was becoming more and more strange. He seemed genuinely certain he didn't recognise the Lodge, but surely he couldn't really be....?

"What year is it, Richard?" she asked.

"'Tis the second year of our reign," he replied immediately. She looked puzzled, trying to work out his meaning. "The year of Our Lord, one thousand, four hundred and eighty five."

She was silent as she took this in, not sure whether to trust his apparent sincerity. Then she said: "Well, if that's what you think the date is, you have come forward in time more than five hundred years; this is the year 2014."

He looked stunned - he had gone even paler than before and she could see droplets of sweat beading on his upper lip. He was a good actor!

"Are you sure you don't know Laura?" she ventured, suspicion suddenly returning. The other option was pure fantasy!

"Nay, lady, I do not" he replied. He stared, wide-eyed at the scenery whizzing by, then gradually began to relax a little.

"Rose, wilt thou help me get home? I am sore needed there."

He looked like a lost little boy for a moment, then he gained control of himself again, staring at her levelly.

"Yes, of course. We can try to get you back tomorrow," she suggested, already feeling like a fool. "Maybe you should find your horse first, though?"

He nodded, then shifted in the seat, stretching his legs out in front of him, the fingers of his left hand, bearing three rings including one with a large ruby, drumming rhythmically on the side of the car door. The music had changed to The Overtones – Gambling Man.

He continued to watch the changing landscape, as he listened to the radio, his head nodding slightly to the rhythm of the song, whenever it was a quicker piece.

"So, obviously you haven't met Henry Tudor at Bosworth yet?" she asked after a few minutes. She turned to look at him but he had fallen asleep, his dark head resting against the side of the door.

Soap (I Use The)

She smiled to herself and drove on, into Nottingham City and then to West Bridgford, where Laura and Andy lived with their lovely family, and where she was staying in a nearby cottage. When they arrived, Richard woke with a start, his hand automatically reaching for his sword, which he had had to remove to get inside the car. She had placed it, with his bow and arrows, in the back seat area, diagonally so that the bow would fit in.

"You're very jumpy," she said with a rather embarrassed smile. What was she doing bringing a stranger home with her? Her sensible head had now once more convinced her romantic one that the stranger was just a clever King Richard 'double' from a re-enactment in the locality. It was too weird otherwise.

He looked at her, his fine brows knitted together and she again noticed the two small vertical lines that had been etched between them. Just like that famous portrait of Richard! She mentally scolded herself – "Don't be silly, Rosie, of course he's not really King Richard, you're just projecting your own wishes and fantasies onto a stranger who bears a passing resemblance to him," her sane persona told her crazy one, sternly.

"Have we come safe to our journey's end, Lady Rose?" he murmured, still half asleep.

"Yes, but I shall have to ask the owner if she has a spare room for you – I think she might - it doesn't seem too busy." She went round to his side to help him with the door, which he was pushing and pulling. He got out of the car very carefully, retrieving his sword from the back seat.

"Er, I advise you to leave that locked in the boot!" she said, wondering what the owner of the B & B would make of him if he went blithely in waving his sword about, even if it was just a replica.

He hesitated, then said "What meanest thou by 'boot', my lady?" He glanced down at his own boots, a quizzical look in his intelligent, blue eyes.

"No, not that kind of boot!" she laughed. "Here, give it to me – I'll put it in for you."

He offered her the sword, still in its scabbard and, expecting to stagger under its weight, she was amazed at how light it was. She managed to get it into the boot but had to leave the bow inside the car as the boot was too small for it. He followed her along the garden path and stood at her side, silently, taking everything in as she invented an explanation for his predicament for the lady of the house. He was obviously wise enough to realise he would be better served by keeping quiet and he let Rose do the talking.

Luckily the landlady didn't ask too many nosy questions and happened to have another room free right next door to Rose's. Rose wasn't sure if she was pleased or worried that he would be sleeping in the room next to hers. She took him upstairs and opened the door to his room and then her own. He went in and just stood in the middle of the room, staring at everything. He went over and felt the bed, then sat on it, bouncing gently.

"Why, 'tis as soft as a wet nurse's paps!" he exclaimed, his expressive eyebrows shooting up in amazement. "Of what is it fashioned?"

She was a little shocked at the language coming from so courtly a man, but then remembered reading that words which were considered coarse today were merely normal and everyday in Mediaeval times. It was apparently religious curse words which had more power then. But of course, an imposter would know these little details too! Before she could answer his question, he had pulled off the duvet and sheets and was examining the mattress and bed base with undisguised interest.

"I'm not sure," she replied. "Look, let me look at your cut and then you should get cleaned up. After that maybe we could go and find something to eat, I'm ravenous!"

He nodded and she slipped into her room and found her small, portable first aid kit. She gently swabbed his temple with saline, finding that he was right: once the dried blood had been cleaned away, it was only a small scratch. He sat very still as she worked, still frowning slightly and glancing at her occasionally from the corner of his eyes. When it was clean, she patted it dry with a clean pad and smeared a little petroleum jelly on it.

"I won't put any dressing on as it is too close to your hairline and it has stopped bleeding anyway," she said.

"What is this grease thou hast administered? 'Tis not dragon's blood, is it?" he asked, suspiciously.

"No, it's an everyday remedy here," she said, at a loss to explain where it came from.

"Very well. I thank thee for thy care, lady. Mayhap thou wouldst be so kind as to draw water for me? Indeed I would be glad to rid myself of these soiled vestments and soothe my aching bones in a hot bathtub. Yet verily t'would be a mercy if thou wouldst first direct me to the privy?"

Alarmed at his frankness she said: "Follow me, I'll show you the bathroom. We are sharing it, but it's only we two, so you don't need to hurry too much. Oh! I don't suppose you have a change of clothes, do you?"

"Thou art correct, my lady – alas I have only the raiment I am wearing."

"I'll look in my case and see if I can find something that would fit you – we are about the same height. In the meantime, here is the bathroom."

He looked at her with eyebrows raised.

"I will not wear lady's attire," he said. "The King hath a reputation to keep, even here."

"It's alright, Richard. Men and women wear very similar clothes these days; you needn't worry about your reputation." At least not as regards your clothing, she thought, remembering the battering his reputation had received once the Tudors were in power.

She opened the door of the bathroom and stood back to allow him to go in. He did so, moving easily despite his protested tiredness and aching bones. Then he stopped in the middle of the room, staring helplessly around. She went over to the loo and lifted the lid – he peered in and hesitated before kneeling down in front of it and plunging his hands into the water at the bottom.

"This basin is right awkward to use – I am not accustomed to kneeling to wash!" he muttered. "And the water is cold!"

"No, no!" she cried. "That is the loo – the privy! You use it – you can sit on it if you need to – and then you flush it, like this!" she said, pushing the handle down, blushing at the thought of what she was describing to him.

He raised his eyebrows as the water flowed noisily into the toilet bowl.

She went on. "This is the bath. You put the plug in, here, and turn on the taps to fill it up. Here is soap, shower gel, shampoo and conditioner." She saw his puzzled expression. "Or you can use the shower – just press this button and water comes out of here. Press it again to stop it. I'm sure you'll work out the details of the soap and shampoo. And there's a gown that they've provided for you."

He walked into the shower and pressed the button, soaking himself and her, as the door wasn't closed. He gave a surprised grunt and pressed the button again, turning it off. He touched the tiled walls, his long, strong fingers tan against the stark white, then fingered the shower head.

"Do you think you can manage?" she queried, wondering what she would do if he said "No"!

To her relief, he nodded.

"Just call me if you need any help or...anything," she finished lamely, her blush flaring again as his eyes, the colour of a darkening sky and with a twinkle she hadn't noticed before, seemed to bore into her. His mouth gave the slightest twitch as if he was desperately trying to suppress a smile. She turned and fled, closing the door firmly behind her and retreating into her own room, where she flung open the wardrobe and searched through her clothes for something suitable for him to wear.

Eventually, she found a blue T-shirt and a pair of jogging bottoms, a fleece, a pair of socks and trainers that were a little large for her and a pair of her knickers. On second thoughts she discarded the latter – she just couldn't imagine him wearing ladies' underwear. She waited until she heard the loo flush and the shower flowing, the hiss of it sounding like an angry adder woken from a snooze in the sun. It seemed to go on a long time. Then it stopped, just a soft dripping sound and, in the comparative silence, his voice singing. It was surprisingly deep and very pleasant: a melodic tenor although she didn't recognise the tune. She ventured out into the corridor again with the bundle of clothes and heard a vigorous rubbing sound – she guessed it was him drying his hair. She knocked on the door intending to leave the clothes outside for him but it opened immediately to reveal him dressed only in the gown, which was quite short. His hair was still wet, tousled from the towelling it had received. His eyes were soft and he smiled as he saw her, but not enough to show the dimple. He didn't seem the least bit bothered or embarrassed by his lack of formal dress.

"'Twas verily a marvel, Lady Rose! The water was right hot as it burst forth from the pipe and yon liquid has a delicious aroma. Are these the vestments thou hast procured for my comfort? I humbly express my gratitude to thee once more." He reached out and took the clothes, striding confidently past her into his room. "I shall be out, directly!"

Rude

When he was dressed (he had needed a little help with the fastenings of the trainers) and she had also showered and changed, she took him downstairs and outside. She thought they might go to the pub where she had dined previously with Laura and Andy. She made sure she had the keys before she closed the front door.

When she looked up from her handbag, she saw him standing a short distance in front of the house staring up at the sky. His hair was still a little damp and curled very slightly at the tips. It was thick and long and sleek. His profile in the twilight was fine, somewhat haughty, the prominent cheekbones emphasising his firm chin and straight nose. She again noticed his lips and for some reason she recalled a silly girls' magazine article which said that a man whose lower lip is fuller than the upper lip is outwardly quite reserved and strait laced, but actually very sexy in bed. He was chewing the bottom, fuller, one and his brows were drawn together again in a slight frown. He turned to her.

"Whither have the stars gone, Lady Rose? I can but see ten or twenty, when I am accustomed to seeing manifold stars at home."

"It's called light pollution. We use electricity, a kind of energy, to light our homes and workplaces and at night the brightness masks the light from the stars – they are still there, just not so obvious. In places that are less well lit, you can still see the stars."

"That is well, Lady Rose. The stars are a beautiful miracle of Our Lord and should be admired, thinkest thou not?

"Yes, I love looking up at the stars, and in the daytime at the clouds too! I like to make pictures out of them – dragons and giants and horses."

He smiled fully then, his blue eyes warming and softening, the dimple reappearing. "Hast thou seen dragons? Or giants?"

"No, I don't really believe they exist! But I like to imagine they do sometimes. Maybe I spend too much time imagining the impossible. Look, are you hungry? Let's get going shall we?"

"'Tis late and yet we have not attended Vespers. Should we not worship our good Lord before we contemplate feasting?"

"Ah, yes, Richard. I should have told you that nowadays we don't really worship very much. Even very devout people only usually worship once a week in church. Does it bother you? Perhaps you could pray privately in your room later on and I will find out later where the nearest Catholic Church is so that you can visit. Religion is quite a complicated subject these days - I'll explain later. Meanwhile, let's go and have some dinner, shall we?"

He inclined his head gracefully, one finely arched eyebrow raised in curiosity as he allowed her to lead the way. He looked odd, somehow, in the modern clothes, although the blue T-shirt gave his eyes a slightly different cast, making them seem a much brighter blue. She realised with a slight shock that she had begun to think of him as a real Mediaeval king – she'd explained light pollution to him! And about the churches! If he was just a skilful actor, she would be the butt of endless jokes later!

He moved easily and quietly along the country lane, and was not nearly so jumpy now. He seemed to be getting used to being in the situation he had found himself in. As if he had read her mind, he suddenly said: "Knowest thou how I came to be lost in this time, Rose? Dost thou think I shall be able to return to the time whence I came? I have a realm to govern, after all!"

She noticed that he had called her plain Rose, omitting the "Lady", for which she was glad.

"I have no idea, I'm afraid," she said. "But my friend, Laura, lives nearby and she might know something. I'll give her a ring later."

"Wherefore must thou give thy friend a ring?" he asked, puzzled again.

"I'll show you what I mean in the restaurant - at the ale house," she smiled. "It is a way of communicating over long distances instantly!"

"Verily I find thy speech nigh impossible to fathom!" he said. "Wouldst thou teach me the rudiments of it, I pray thee?"

"With pleasure, Richard! I was going to suggest it would be a good idea for you to learn how to speak the way we do.

Do you speak any other languages?" she added, testing him, knowing that Richard III did indeed speak French and Latin.

"Indeed I do, Rose. I am fluent in French and Latin of course, but I am also acquainted with Portuguese, though its charms are new to me. I have sent suit to Portugal to seek the hand of the Infanta Joana in marriage and my Portuguese friend and henchman, Edward Brampton hath been coaching me in the rudiments of the tongue. 'Tis devilish hard!"

"Well, then, I'm sure you won't have any trouble with English - modern English, I mean." she said.

They had reached the outskirts of West Bridgford now and there were more houses and roads leading off the one they were following, walking in a companionable silence.

The bistro-pub was only a couple of hundred yards away now, its glowing lights shining a welcome to hungry and thirsty travellers.

She walked into it and Richard followed her, his eyes wide with curiosity. She led the way to a table at the side and they sat down opposite each other. The lighting was quite dim, but Richard had screwed his eyes up as if blinded.

"By what device are the lights so bright?" he said.

"That's the electricity I was telling you about," she said. "In fact, these lights are not very bright at all compared to some we have."

He looked incredulous. She picked up the menu, but found she couldn't read it, her mind was racing so much - the idea that she was actually entertaining the man she had read about so avidly was preposterous. He couldn't really be Richard III, but if he wasn't, then who was he? Richard picked up his own menu and scanned it, his eyes shining with delight as he saw the lines of print on the page.

"This bill of fare is printed, is it not, Rose?" he asked.

"Yes, it is. We have many things printed nowadays." She cleared her throat; her voice was shaking! "What would you like to eat?"

Before he could answer, a waiter appeared at their table and, looking down his nose at them, said: "Are you ready to order yet, Sir, Madam?"

Richard set the menu down and asked: "Dost thou have lamprey or pike?"

The waiter's eyebrows shot up.

"He's only joking!" Rose put in swiftly and laughed. "He's just got back from a Mediaeval re-enactment. He's still in character."

The waiter smiled condescendingly. "I'm afraid not, Sir. We do have Roast Salmon or Trout Meunière, if Sir would like fish."

Richard had noticed the waiter's reaction and said quickly: "Yes, those sound delicious."

"Which ONE would you like, sir?" the waiter sneered, looking down at Richard. Richard's eyes changed, growing instantly harder and colder. He opened his mouth to speak, but Rose cut in quickly: "We'll have one of each – then we can share."

She glanced at Richard questioningly.

"Yes – that is what I meant," he agreed, his tone clipped and his eyes still icy cold and fixed on the waiter, who had suddenly started sweating.

"Would you like any vegetables with your meals, Sir…Madam?" he said in a politer tone.

Rose ordered a selection of fresh vegetables to accompany their fish and some rosé wine. The waiter left hurriedly.

"That serving man was unutterably rude, Rose, dost thou not agree? He would be horsewhipped for his insolence if this were my court. There is no need for such contumelious behaviour!"

Rose nodded and said: " I have been here a few times and he is the only rude one - you seem to have put him in his place though!"

Richard smiled, his good humour restored.

When their meal was served, he looked in confusion at the cutlery, then at Rose and copied her as she picked up the knife and fork. He looked very awkward as he began cutting the food, but said nothing as he took the first bite.

"'Tis right delicious! I do enjoy a fine fish meal – 'tis well, as meat is not permitted on so many days. I must confess I am used to sampling more dishes than this, but I suppose I must try to learn the ways of this strange world. Methinks I should attempt to learn thy manner of speech as swiftly as possible. I pray thee – I mean please, wouldst thou start to instruct me, Rose?"

"I was thinking the very same thing!" she smiled. She poured them each a glass of wine and raised hers. "Cheers, Richard – here's to the English vernacular!"

He raised his glass as well and took a large swig, repeating the words back to her. She noticed that his slight northern burr disappeared as he mimicked her own accent perfectly, but before she could comment on it, he winced as the ice cold liquid passed his lips. Then he swallowed and smiled appreciatively.

"'Tis a fine wine – I have never seen one of this clarity and colour. 'Tis surely a costly vintage. But so cold it fair freezeth my mouth!"

"Did it hurt your teeth, Richard?" she asked, suddenly remembering that the skeleton they'd found in the Greyfriars Church choir had shown signs of tooth decay, apparently. Wait, what was she thinking – yet again he had her almost believing in this elaborate deception! It was just like Laura to prime him about these little details!

"Aye, I find that of late I have some pain from certain foods – if they be too sweet, too hot or too cold. I find that willow bark helpeth – dost thou know of such a thing in this land?"

"Yes, we do!" she said. "By the way, we don't use 'thee' and 'thou' any more, it's 'you' and we say 'it's' rather than ''Tis'".

He nodded as she groped for her handbag and opened the side pocket where she kept some paracetamol.

"Here, try this!" she said, offering him the pack. He took it carefully and turned it over several times, with a confused look on his face.

"I wot not how to use this. Must I chew it?" he asked, about to put the edge in his mouth.

"Here, let me show you," she said and opened it, taking out two caplets and pouring him some of the water which was on the table between them. "Put them on your tongue, one at a time, and swallow them with the water."

He did as instructed without too much mishap and then said: "Rose, I am sore ashamed, but I have not any means of making restitution to thee - to you, for your help and care, not even for this meal. I mislike being obliged to anyone and feel quite helpless. Think you that I am trapped here for the remainder of my life?"

"I have no idea," she replied. "But, as I said, I will contact my friend, Laura, and see if she has ever heard of anything like this happening before - maybe she has some local knowledge." She was privately wondering how Laura would react if it was indeed she who had orchestrated this elaborate hoax!

She took out her smart phone and rang Laura's number, but it went straight to voicemail. She left a message asking her to call her back ASAP, while Richard stared at the phone, fascinated.

She turned her attention back to the man sitting opposite her. She might as well enjoy his company anyway – he was definitely a sight for sore eyes. It had been a long time since she had felt so attracted to a man – a real flesh and blood man at any rate! But of course she would do, as his looks were so similar to her fantasy knight in shining armour – Richard III!

Suddenly everything fell into place. Of course! Laura had kept on at her to find a new man after her marriage had ended in divorce and tears six months ago, after seven years. It must be a ploy to get her to start dating again – what a sly one that Laura was! But it was a brilliant plot, she had to admit. All the detail that was involved and the elaborate speech and authentic clothing – even the weapons looked real! It must have cost her a fortune. And how did she get this actor guy to agree? Was he paid or perhaps he was a friend of Laura's – otherwise what would be the point of trying to get her to fall for him? Yes, he must be one of her friends who was single and willing to go along with her plan. She was surprised a man like this was desperate enough to agree to a blind date though. Surely he must have plenty of women ready and eager to fall into his arms, as handsome as he was.

Try

Richard squirmed a little in his seat, hunching his shoulders up and down.

"Are you alright?" she asked.

"Yes, thank you, 'tis – I mean it's - just an affliction of mine that I have borne for many years. I am accustomed to it now, but betimes it plagueth me somewhat."

"What is it, then?" Rose asked, professional interest now overriding her suspicions about Richard's motives.

"I have a stiffness in my back that began when I was but ten or eleven years of age. I'd as fain not talk of it, please. 'Tis shameful to be so afflicted and deformed."

"Deformed?! You don't look deformed to me!" she said, trying to lighten the mood.

"Yet should you perceive me unclothed, would you know it to be true," he said, frowning once again.

"Would you let me take a look at it, Richard? You know my work is as a specialist in bone and joint problems? I have my portable couch in the car; I brought it in case Andy, Laura's husband, needed a treatment - he often suffers with his back. Perhaps I could help you. It would be worth a try – and no charge for you, of course!"

He didn't reply, just met Rose's gaze with those deep blue eyes, looking up without lifting his head, then gave a short nod of acknowledgment. "I will consider your offer," he said.

He thoroughly enjoyed the desserts, when they arrived. He had strawberry meringue and also tried Rose's crème caramel. He wasn't so sure about the coffee, it seemed, pulling a face at its bitterness and leaving most of it.

When they got back to the B & B, his mood had lightened again – he obviously thrived on activity. When he was still, he seemed to be poised ready to spring into action again at the drop of a hat. He had a few little nervous mannerisms, too. For example, he would pull at the pocket of the joggers (which was roughly where his dagger had been, although it was now hidden inside his clothes – he refused to leave it behind). He would also occasionally twirl his hair between his slender fingers, push it back off his face or tap his fingers on the edge of the table. It was as if he was so full of energy, it had to come out somehow. It made her all the more determined to try to help him to relax more thoroughly if he allowed her to treat his back problem. She was well aware of the effect too much stress had both on the physical body and the mind.

"If you are still willing to minister to my back, I will allow it," he said. "But you must take an oath that you will reveal nothing about it to anyone at all, on pain of death."

"On pain of death!" she squeaked. "Now you're being ridiculous! But I am bound by patient confidentiality in any case – that means that I must keep anything that concerns your medical history and treatment private – so no-one else will find out anything about it, I promise you. You don't need to threaten me!"

"I beg your forgiveness, I meant not to menace you, but it would be treason to reveal it – and treason is punishable by death."

"Luckily, not in this day and age!" she snorted.

She took the portable couch and treatment bag out of the boot and he took the couch from her, carrying it up the stairs as if it were as light as a dandelion wish. He was obviously a lot stronger than he looked...a veritable enigma.

She set up the couch in his room, which was a little larger than hers. She also had massage wax and a vibro-massager, which she plugged in. Then she remembered her electro acupuncture machine – a small hand-held, battery operated gadget which had no needles, just a small tip, like a ballpoint pen nib. It delivered a tiny electric current which stimulated the acupuncture points and was similar in effect to traditional acupuncture. Just in case it was needed!

She had a case history sheet, which was hilarious to fill in as most of Richard's answers made little sense to a modern osteopath:

Name: Richard Gloucestre, aka Ricardus Tertius Rex

Date of birth: 02/10/1452

Age: 32/561

Address: Middleham Castle, Middleham, Wensleydale; Crosby House, London; Nottingham Castle, Nottingham; Windsor Castle, Windsor; and many others.

Occupation: King

Phone number: (Puzzled frown)

Name of Doctor: Dr Hobbys

Marital Status: Widowed

Previous illnesses: None of note

Previous injuries: Deep cut to left shoulder received at Battle of Barnet, 1470, from sword.

Accidents: Numerous falls from horses while an adolescent and a few as an adult, no broken bones.

Road Accidents (e.g. whiplash): Was whipped occasionally as child!!!!

Operations: None

Presenting complaint: Chronic mid and low back pain and stiffness, with associated headaches, twenty years' duration, getting worse.

On a scale of 0-10 (where 0 is no pain at all and 10 is the worst you could imagine): 3-6

Aggravated by: Movement after inactivity
Eased by: Keeping moving, stretching.
Medication: Willow bark
She didn't ask him if he smoked!

She then explained to him what she was going to do – he should disrobe down to his underwear and she would then ask him to do various movements and examine how his spine performed them. She would also feel certain areas of his spine and he should let her know if anything was painful. She would then give some treatment, which would probably include massage and articulation (moving the joints through their natural range of movement) and maybe some electro-acupuncture. She showed him the little machine and let him feel the tiny electrical pulsations. He recoiled a little but then allowed her to touch him with it again.

"'Tis very strange," he said in wonder. "Like a vibration of a lute string, but prickly."

He took his clothes off and laid them on the bed, turning to her, his arms spread in a resigned gesture. He was completely naked. She belatedly remembered that she hadn't given him any clean underwear and swiftly offered him a towel to wrap around his waist, averting her eyes in embarrassment.

"You are sure you are forbidden to reveal my disfigurement?" he enquired anxiously, his habitual frown on his face. His nakedness hadn't seemed to bother him as much as his concern about his 'deformity'!

"I swear", Rose said and, after a long pause during which he regarded her sternly from beneath his furrowed brows, he turned his back to her.

She couldn't help the gasp of astonishment as she saw his spine. In a flash she remembered the recent 3D reconstruction of Richard III's spine, published by Leicester University, showing the curve accompanied by a twisting: Richard's spine was identical, the curvature quite extreme. It was not the traditional 'hunchback' as portrayed in Shakespeare's wildly inaccurate 'history', but a sideways curve, a scoliosis. This is not usually visible when the sufferer is clothed but obvious when unclothed, as Richard's was now.

Because of her profession, she knew that this degree of curvature was extremely rare nowadays in an adult, as most would have been operated on as children, rods being inserted to hold the curve straight. And this man had not only an identical spine to Richard III, but identical facial features, height and similar mannerisms. There was only one conclusion she could reach: Richard III had indeed somehow travelled through time and was standing there in front of her right now, alive, real and semi naked!!

She was aware that her heart had started thumping in her chest so loudly she wondered if he could hear it. Thoughts of some of the disrespectful retorts she had said to him ran through her mind. He was a KING! She remembered how nervous and proud she had been when she had treated a C list actor a few years before. And now – well, this was a major step up from that! She thought she might faint, but managed to take a few deep breaths and calmed down a little.

"You're a professional, Rosie," she told herself, sternly. "So act like one!" Then she said, aloud: "I'm going to touch you now, to feel what is going on with your spine. Is that alright, Richard...er...Your Grace?

He turned his head to look at her over his left shoulder, an eyebrow raised quizzically.

"So you begin to confer on me my rightful title now? 'Tis a little late, is it not?" And his serious eyes held hers, steadily.

"I apologise, Your Grace, but I only now realise that it is indeed you – it is incredible that you are here, I hope you can understand that I didn't intend any disrespect."

"Well, as you are now witting of the truth, should you not give obeisance to your king?"

She stood there, shaking, her mouth open in confusion.

"A curtsey, perhaps?" he explained, with a warning tilt of his head, his eyes as cold as steel.

She took a deep breath and, trembling, lowered her knee to the ground, dropping her gaze and aware at the same time of how ridiculous it was to curtsey wearing jeans. Then she remembered that - she thought anyway - people were supposed to stay on their knees before the king until told to rise and hastily lowered the other knee as well. She kept her eyes down, feeling suddenly a little afraid, she wasn't sure why.

Then she heard a strange sound, coming from Richard's direction. She glanced up to find him with his hand over his mouth trying to stifle his laughter. When he saw her looking, he removed it and his chuckle exploded out, his shoulders shaking with mirth.

"I'm sorry, t'was but a jest. I think we are well enough acquainted now to dispense with any formality. Also, I realise that here I have not the power and status I had in my world. I would be pleased if you would continue to call me Richard."

Now she was indignant.

"You bastard!" she shouted. "I was terrified of you!"

He grinned. "Am I so formidable, then, Rose? And, actually I am absolutely not a bastard!"

She began to laugh as well then as, turning his back again, he said: "Shall we continue?"

She placed her hands on his hips and her thumbs on the small dimples on each side of the base of his spine. She asked him to slowly bend forwards. He did so, and she noted that his pelvis was quite well aligned, but that on bending forwards, his right shoulder blade and upper right back area became much more prominent as his spinal twist was exaggerated. Just as must have happened after Bosworth, when his poor, naked corpse, bloody and battered, had been slung face down over the back of a horse for its journey into Leicester. Surely that was when the rumours of his "hunchback" must have begun.

Oh Richard! Her mind called out to him, as he stood there unaware of what she knew was destined to happen to him should he manage to return to his own time. He was completely ignorant of his terrible, cruel fate! He had placed himself in her hands, trusting his royal body, with its terrible secret deformity, to her discretion. On pain of death, of course!

The responsibility of it hit her again suddenly and her usually sure fingers began to shake uncontrollably. She cleared her throat and asked him to bend sideways to right and left, and then backwards, noting restrictions which were typical of scoliosis sufferers. She held his pelvis fixed and asked him to twist his torso left and then right, noting that one way was much easier and freer than the other. Finally she asked him to turn his head this way and that, backwards and forwards, noting that again one direction was less restricted than the other.

She had treated scoliosis before, but none with such an extreme curvature. Well, she could only try her best – hopefully she would at least be able to alleviate some of his pain and improve his mobility. She had him lie on the couch, face up first of all, covering him discreetly with a large towel, and checked the mobility of his peripheral joints, the hips, knees, shoulders, elbows. She checked the motion of his ribcage, while instructing him to breathe deeply, noting that there were restrictions in this too.

Poor thing! He must be in constant discomfort and with only willow bark to help with it – no wonder his face showed signs of strain and worry. She determined to help him. Asking him to turn over, she did a few more tests and then began to massage his back, using the sweet orange-scented massage wax. Her hands warmed the wax until it was liquid in her palms and she spread it over his shoulders and upper back, down to his lumbar spine and up as far as his skull. She had a sudden, horrific vision of his skull with huge holes in it, as it was when found in the Leicester car park, and felt sick.

She mentally shook herself, resolving to concentrate again on her patient. She kneaded his tight muscles, smoothing and soothing, breaking down adhesions and causing him to emit the occasional groan or gasp, but she hoped any pain she caused him would be a "good pain" as some of her patients described it. She moved his shoulders so that his tight shoulder blades were loosened a little and then showed him the vibro-massager and got his consent to use it, gently at first, then she increased the speed and depth. Hopefully, it would speed up the relaxation in his muscles and put a small vibration through the joints of his spine, helping to loosen the restrictions there. Then she got him sitting up on the edge of the couch and used a muscle energy technique, holding him in a position of restriction and asking him to push away from it, then gently moving the joint a little further into the restriction. She preferred these techniques which, she felt, helped the muscles adapt more quickly to any changes she was initiating. Of course, the curvature could not be corrected just like that, but every journey begins with a first step. Finally she used the electro-acupuncture machine. She suspected Richard was one of the top twenty per cent of subjects who are good responders to acupuncture, as he seemed to relax and go into a slight trance-like state during this.

She explained to him what she was trying to do, how exactly his spine was twisted and asked him if it affected his breathing.

"Yes, it does!" he said, impressed. "I notice it when I practise in the tilt-yard or in swordplay, but most of all in battle. I tire more quickly than I should and then I find it difficult to take a deep breath; my chest feels tight."

"You can get dressed again," she said. "I will give you some exercises to do, but I just want to check something on the Internet. Why don't you come and watch? – I expect you will find this fascinating!"

Richard certainly did find it fascinating and asked astute, intelligent questions, to most of which Rose didn't know the answer. Electricity seemed to be a major stumbling block and she wasn't really sure how to explain it to him. Instead, she showed Richard how to "Google" and demonstrated by Googling "scoliosis exercises and treatment" and showing him what she had found. There were some great videos demonstrating exercises which normalised the curvature of the spine in scoliosis patients, and Richard tried them immediately, picking up the idea very quickly and vowing to perform them religiously. They involved taking out the sideways curve of the spine by bending to the opposite side and then, simultaneously, eliminating the twist by rotating the opposite way, the feet in certain specific positions. Richard said he could feel the stretch and Rose felt his spine as he did them, making sure they were going to be effective.

"Already, it feels slightly looser and there is a lessening of the pain – and my headache is gone!" he said, delightedly. "You are an angel of mercy!"

I Vow To Thee My Country

"I'm glad the treatment has helped, Richard. We must do more sessions over quite some time, to get a permanent change," she said.

"Then 'tis a pity I will not be staying longer for I must get back tomorrow. The Tydder bastard's expected invasion is imminent. I am the KING! I cannot be absent in my country's hour of need, I cannot. It is my duty to return and settle this rebellion once and for all. There is much to do - I have to muster the army, send to my noble lords to bring their men to me and prepare the battle strategy. Tydder is likely to come in the summer and June is already nearly over. I have to defend the crown and the realm. The oath I took requires it. My companions whom I left in the forest will be seeking me and if they find me not, they shall believe I am unmanned and have fled through cowardice. I cannot have my reputation defiled so! You will keep your word and help me, will you not, my Lady Rose?"

Rose couldn't help but think of the battering his character would get, even after showing his valour on the battlefield.

His courage was the one virtue that even his enemies granted him. How ironic it would be if he failed to attend the battle because he was stranded here in the 21st Century, and had his reputation ruined again because of it. How unfair!

"Of course I will try to help you, Richard. But I'm not sure it will be so easy to get back again."

"We must return to the strange tree where we met and try to find the way back."

"OK, if that's what you want to do - but what about your horse?"

"I must find him first and take him back with me."

"Do you know how it happened that you arrived in this time so suddenly?"

"No, I do not. I did nothing to cause it - I am baffled as to the reason and the means. I sense that I must needs return to the tree though. There was some power around it. I felt…when first I touched you…a strange sensation…"

"You felt it too!? I thought perhaps it was just me."

She reached out her hand to touch him again, experimentally. He automatically leaned away from her.

"It's alright - I only want to see if it happens again," she said, forgetting she had already touched him while treating him.

He extended his hand imperiously, palm down, and she instinctively knelt before him, taking the proffered hand and touching it to her lips. She wasn't sure if that was the correct etiquette, but he seemed to be OK with it. As she did this, she noticed the rings on his hand. There were two on the one hand, a large plain gold band with a sapphire in it on his thumb and a gold ring with a ruby inset in it on his little finger. A third ring was on his other hand, she noticed, another gold ring with a prominent dark stone in it shaped like the end of a bullet. His skin was not soft, as one might have expected of a king, but hard and calloused. She noticed the soft, dark hairs on his forearm as she kissed his hand. This time there was no electric-like jolt, no tingling, just a sense of warmth and strength. He put his other hand on her shoulder and raised her from her kneeling position.

"You see? I believe 'tis the tree that gives off the power that tingles."

"Well, if you want to get there before the worst of the tourist crowds, we had better get some sleep," Rose said.

So Richard bade her goodnight, kissing her lightly on the cheek and thanking her for the treatment. He strode over to the door and she watched it close after him, sighed and turned away, getting her nightclothes ready and heading for the bathroom before he got there first.

Later, lying in bed and thinking of Richard just on the other side of the wall, she was half afraid to go to sleep in case she awoke to find it was all just a dream. What on earth had she got herself into?

Finding Beauty

Rose insisted they eat before their quest so, over an early breakfast, Richard asked Rose many questions about osteopathy, stating that he had had the best night's sleep he had had in years after Rose's treatment. He asked also about history and the monarchy. She managed to fob him off about that by giving him certain information, whilst withholding other things which she had no idea how to broach with him, in particular that he had lost the battle of Bosworth to Henry Tudor, along with his kingdom and his life. He was interested in Queen Elizabeth II and how a woman had come to rule England. She managed to skirt round the question of the first Queen Elizabeth and the Tudors. She hurriedly changed the subject, suggesting they left for the Major Oak to search for his horse, Royal Rebel. After passing the Sherwood Visitor Centre, they made their way to the Major Oak area and walked around to the north of it, where Rose had seen the flash of black the previous night, and split up in order to cover more ground. She could hear Richard making a soft, clicking sound interspersed with calling out "Rebel! Hey boy!"

She followed his lead and also called out the horse's name as she squinted between the trees.

After about ten minutes, she heard a soft thud up ahead and something that could have been a snort. Then she saw a dark shape far off in the trees. She'd found him! She moved forward cautiously and saw the horse standing between two large bushes. As she approached, he gave a shrill whinny and he moved backwards and forwards, his forelegs prancing up and down. His glossy flank quivered and his eyes were rolling in his head, with…was it fear? She became wary as she stared at him - he looked panicked and a bit crazy! But she didn't want him to escape again, so she couldn't very well shout for Richard in case it spooked him even more. She took a few tentative steps forward, stooped and picked a handful of grass, holding it out to him. The horse whinnied and reared up - his hooves came crashing down again a few feet from her. It seemed as if he was trapped there somehow, as he hadn't managed to reach her although he had lunged forwards slightly.

"Be still!" came urgently from behind her left shoulder. "Back away slowly - he is a highly strung stallion and could mayhap be a danger to thee, Rose, if thou approach too closely."

Richard stepped forwards confidently and firmly put Rose behind him as he went right up to the great horse. He clicked his tongue and the courser pricked his ears at the familiar sound. "Art thou trapped, boy?" She noticed he had modified his accent - it sounded somewhat like a Yorkshire accent, and he almost crooned the words.

The horse nickered softly, already calmer at the sound of his master's voice. Richard stepped towards him from one side, moving slowly and surely, but not making direct eye contact. He gently took the rein which dangled down onto the soft earth, patted the strong black neck and rubbed down the horse's nose. The other rein had got completely tangled in a bramble bush, which is why Rebel had remained stuck there, between the trees. It meant he couldn't move far either backwards or forwards. And Rose realised that she might have had a lucky escape, if he had intended to beat her to the ground with his flying hooves.

Richard slowly and carefully untangled the rein and then led the magnificent animal forwards, still crooning gently to him. His ears were alert and twitched this way and that and he nickered again.

"Rose, thou mayst approach him now - he is calm enough! Come and meet Rebel, my faithful courser. Is he not a beauty?! He is one of the best bred horses in the realm - from Jervaulx Abbey stud. He is rather headstrong and wilful, but intelligent and powerful - and agile as a destrier, almost. I trained him myself. I am right glad that he is found - he must have been affrighted by something which caused him to run off in such an uncharacteristic fashion."

Rose had got nearer to the horse and Richard held out his hand and took hers in it, bringing it up to caress Rebel's soft muzzle. The horse jerked his head a little, lifting his lip and showing a row of dangerous looking, large teeth. Her other hand was in her jacket pocket and she suddenly realised there was an old packet of sweets in there! She pulled them out and saw that they were polo mints - she remembered that most horses like polos, so she took one from the pack and offered it to Rebel. He snuffed gently at the unfamiliar smell, and then his soft mobile lips nibbled at her hand and hoovered up the mint.

Richard smiled. "What is that thou gavest him? He clearly enjoyed it! But certes, he must be hungry by now - I must see if I can return to my own time immediately and inconvenience thee no longer. Where exactly was it that first thou saw me last night?"

"Let's go back to the tree and I'll try to remember," she said, so they walked back, Richard leading Rebel and crooning softly to keep him calm.

"Well, you were quite a long distance away, you know, so I can't be sure," Rose said, when they had arrived back. "But I think I saw you first just behind the tree and to the right."

Richard immediately tied Rebel's reins to a stout tree branch, then vaulted over the barrier and began to walk towards the tree.

"Hey, what about me?!" called Rose. "How am I supposed to get over there?"

"Just stay there a moment and guide me to the exact place thou saw me, please?" asked Richard. "Thou shalt ascertain the angle and distance more accurately from there."

"OK," said Rose, resignedly, calling out "Left a bit, back a little, no, right a bit more..." until finally she was satisfied that he was in the same place he had appeared.

"Can you see anything helpful on the tree or anything?" she called out as Richard peered at the tree and prodded the trunk.

"Not a thing!" said Richard, pursing his lips in annoyance. "And I do not even feel the tingling sensation."

He hit the trunk and felt all around it and between the two halves of it. He walked a little way away and looked from there, kicked the leaves away and stamped on the ground, but found nothing at all out of the ordinary. Rose clambered awkwardly over the fence, nearly slipping off. Then she, too, searched the vicinity of the tree, without really knowing what she was looking for.

Eventually after prodding, running at, tapping and rubbing the ancient tree trunk they had to admit defeat and clambered back over the fence.

"Maybe we should go back to the B & B and see if we can come up with a plan."

"I agree, Rose. But first let me take thee riding," he said, as if that were the most natural thing in the world. Rose was panic stricken! Ride on that huge beast?! OK, he was beautiful and the polo mint had seemed to please him but nevertheless, it was a long way down to the hard ground from that height! Richard pre-empted her protest by simply lifting her in one smooth motion up onto the horse's back, towards the front of the large, high, mediaeval saddle. Then he sprang up behind, pressed right up against her, because of the constraints of the saddle. Luckily they were both very slim.

"Art thou comfortable?" he asked. Then without waiting for her reply, he squeezed his knees and Rebel sprang forward like a huge cat. Rose let out an involuntary squeal of fear, but Richard just chuckled.

"I love this, I feel more at home already!" he smiled, and she knew he was being facetious. He must have found it next to impossible to really feel at home in this world which was so foreign to him. Even woods that were large and thick by our present day standards must seem small and crowded to Richard, who had known England when most of it was covered with impenetrable forest. Equally, the most dangerous things they were likely to encounter here were cyclists and skateboarders. He began to tell her about the creatures which populated the forests of his England - large deer, wolves, bears and, of course, wild boar. As her train of thought shifted, she asked him why he had chosen the white boar as his personal emblem.

"The boar is an animal I identify with because it is an honest and courageous creature - it is the only game animal that turns and fights to the death. It will continue to charge even when pierced with a spear."

She swallowed, thinking of the Battle of Bosworth, where he himself, the human representation of the white boar, had also charged and fought to the death, bravely and fiercely.

Richard continued: "It was already a royal emblem - for the honour of Windsor - so I thought it a suitable one for a royal duke when I became Duke of Gloucester. The white is for the white rose of York, of course - and when I associated the boar and York I suddenly realised that the Latin for York was Eboracum, often shortened to EBOR, which is an anagram of B-O-R-E.

"But boar, the animal, is spelt B-O-A-R," she cut in.

"Oh, not in my day," he said. "Spelling was quite, shall we say 'free' then. Anyway, I enjoy word play such as this, so I knew the white boar had to be my cognizance."

"I love word play too!" said Rose, pleased to find something they had in common. "And talking of the boar, they were hunted to extinction here in England, I think in the Tu-," she broke off, glancing at him over her shoulder, but he hadn't noticed her slip. "Well, after your time anyway. BUT, they have been reintroduced, so there are now a few places in England where they live wild again. It was a similar story with the beaver."

Richard raised his eyebrows and smiled. "Well, if there are any in this wood, I will be sure to protect you, My Lady!"

Rose giggled. They rode on, discussing the flora and fauna of the woods, comparing the present day with Richard's era. After a half an hour or so, Rose really began to appreciate the smooth gait of Rebel and his fantastic agility. He side stepped bushes and other obstacles as gracefully as a ballet dancer and responded instantly to Richard's slightest touch or command. She couldn't help but be impressed.

She suddenly realised that Rebel would have to be left at a stables, so she told Richard she would arrange it as they rode, if he would keep Rebel at a sedate walk for a time. She Googled the closest stables and then telephoned them, booking Rebel in. If she could have seen Richard's eyes, she would have smiled at the astonishment and suspicion in them as she tapped a small shiny box and then talked as if to herself, while holding it against her ear! He said nothing, however, deciding to simply observe the strange customs of this world and learn from them. They rode Rebel straight to the stables and left him in their care, then got a taxi back to the car and drove to the B & B.

Don't Know Much

As they arrived, Rose's phone rang. It was Laura.

"Oh, hi Laura!" she said. "I was wondering whether you could give me, well, a friend of mine, some advice. Have you ever heard any weird stories about the Major Oak - any mysteries, or...?"

She paused, listening as Laura told her all the spooky, paranormal and mysterious stories she had heard about the Oak. Nothing seemed relevant to Richard's situation.

"I was thinking more sort of, sudden manifestations of people, or time slips?"

Laura hadn't heard of anything like that, but invited Rose over to have lunch with her and chat a bit more, after she had researched it at work - she was a part time librarian and had the afternoon off. Rose wasn't sure whether to take Richard with her or not, since she now knew Laura had had nothing to do with his sudden arrival in modern England. She wasn't sure what she should tell her about Richard either. She finally said: "Thanks, but actually, I have a friend with me - maybe we could meet in Town somewhere?"

"Ooh! Is it a man friend?" Laura said. "About time too!"

Rose rolled her eyes.

"No, it is a male friend, but he is just a friend, Laura! I'm not even sure he'll be free to come along." She looked at Richard and mouthed: "Do you want to go and meet Laura with me?"

He nodded eagerly. "I would be very interested to meet this lady whom you thought was an associate of mine!" he said, so it was decided.

They met in the Olde Trip to Jerusalem, the oldest pub in England, apparently. Rose had thought it might make Richard feel more at home. He was delighted that the pub was still there, although dismayed at the demise of Nottingham Castle, which in his time had been a huge fortress up on the top of the hill above. Richard had said he was happy for Rose to reveal his identity - if Laura believed her!

It turned out that Laura had been unable to find out anything about the kind of weird events they were interested in, so Rose explained to her what had happened to Richard. She seemed to accept it without any problem at all. Rose was impressed. After they discussed possible reasons for Richard's predicament, Laura finally said:

"Why don't you call Lynne, back in Essex? She has always been interested in the paranormal, hasn't she? Maybe she would know."

"Of course!" Rose cried, wondering why she hadn't thought about Lynne, another childhood friend of hers, at once. She supposed she was too preoccupied with how to act towards an authentic mediaeval king! So, while they were waiting for their lunch to arrive, she gave Lynne a call. Would you believe it? Straight to voicemail again! So she left a message and they ate their lunch and chatted. Laura seemed to take a real shine to Richard and asked him about his life in Mediaeval England. It was only after they'd left her in the City and were on their way back to the B & B that Rose suddenly realised Laura hadn't believed a word of their fantastic tale the whole time, and had just been humouring them!

They spent the rest of the day sourcing a horse-box so they could bring Rebel back with them to Rayleigh in Essex, where Rose lived.

Somebody That I Used To Know

The next day Rose took Richard back with her to her home in Rayleigh, the small horse box (containing a genuine mediaeval steed) being pulled along behind them. Richard was astounded at the numbers of cars on the motorway and the speed that they travelled.

"It is not only faster than a horse, it is also more comfortable!" he exclaimed in delight. "I would dearly like to learn how to control such a machine. Can you teach me, Rose?"

"Well, you have to have a licence to learn to drive and for that you need a birth certificate – it isn't so easy to do things these days with all the paperwork involved. You may have to be content with being a passenger. Hey, could you pass me one of those mints out of the glove compartment please?"

As they were driving down to Essex, she explained to him her situation at home: That her parents had died when she was twelve, in a car accident, and she had been brought up by an aunt until her marriage to Matt, when she was twenty two. Matt, had left her for another woman and they were divorced now, after seven years of marriage. He asked if they had any children and she shook her head sadly. That was the one thing she regretted. They had waited and waited and then when she finally felt she was ready to start a family, it was too late, he had already met Penny.

"Is that why your husband put you aside?" he asked. "Because you are barren?"

"He didn't 'put me aside' – it was a mutual agreement! I couldn't forgive him and he didn't really want me anymore. He's with her now," she said. "And I'm not barren! At least I don't think so. We used contraception – we have reliable ways of preventing a pregnancy these days," she said.

"Why would you want to?" he asked. "Isn't that a natural part of marriage? And it is against God's law to prevent a pregnancy anyway!"

He had been practising speaking in modern English ever since he had requested her help with it and he was extremely quick at picking it up. He sounded almost 'normal' already. And he obviously enjoyed a bit of debate.

She explained about modern ideas of marriage and children, but he didn't seem convinced. However, he didn't pursue the matter, he just pursed his lips, raised his eyebrows and sighed. She felt he was biting his tongue out of politeness, but at least he hadn't lectured her. It was understandable that he would have old fashioned ideas about relationships, marriage and family life, being from a society that was more than five hundred years old!

Finally, as they entered Rayleigh, she asked him what he thought of it and to her surprise he said he had been there before! He remembered the church of Holy Trinity, which, in his time, had not long been built (it had impressive stained glass windows then) and he had hunted deer in the vicinity on a couple of occasions with his brother, Edward.

"I think there used to be a bull baiting site here in mediaeval times," she said. "Do you remember that?"

"No, I don't remember one in Rayleigh in my day, but in any case I have never really enjoyed seeing helpless animals tortured. Only humans!" he joked. She rolled her eyes, shaking her head. At least she hoped he was joking!

Feels Like Home

It was about three hours later that they drew up onto the gravel driveway of her home. Her small bungalow had an almost mediaeval 'feel' itself, as it had beams, a wood burning stove and mediaeval style light sconces on the walls. This might make him feel at home, she thought. However, she also had fourteen solar panels on the roof! She pointed out the white rose for York and the "Planta genista" - the broom shrub from which the Plantagenets got their name - in her front garden and he smiled, shaking his head in bemusement.

He walked into the bungalow and looked around curiously. In the hallway was a display of Rose's photographs of Norway, her favourite country. In the corner was a huge, round fish tank with three fantail goldfish. It was illuminated by an internal light which changed as the hours passed and in the evening became 'moonlight', a softer, bluer light. There were a couple of chairs there which formed a waiting area for her patients. Richard sat down and watched the fish for a while in fascination. Rose didn't tell him they were called Ned, George and Dickon after the three York brothers! He picked up a "Readers' Digest" from the small table and leafed through it - there were about a dozen copies there for her patients to read.

"What a beautiful book! You must be very wealthy to have so many!" he said.

"Unfortunately not, no! Those books are quite cheap – printing is easy these days. In fact most people have their own printer. If you like those, you'll love these!"

She unlocked her treatment room and switched on the light. He blinked at the brightness and she dimmed it slightly. He watched as she turned the dimmer switch.

"May I try, please?" he asked.

"Of course, please be my guest."

He reached for the switch and very carefully turned it this way and that in delight. "What a cunning device! Quite marvellous!"

Then he saw the two large bookcases at the other side of the room. One was full from top to bottom with fiction of all genres and the other held all her non-fiction books on subjects as diverse as Norway, osteopathy, the Vikings, Mediaeval castles and dog training. There were both hard- and paper-backs. He stared at them open mouthed.

"You must have two or three hundred books here! A priceless collection! It makes my own library seem poor in comparison."

"Well, perhaps by the standards of your time, but most people have lots of books at home these days. I have more in the lounge and even more up in the loft!"

"What a fabulous thing! Do you mean that most people can read and write? Even peasants?"

She laughed. "Yes! Everyone is taught to read and write these days. Children attend schools from the age of about four or five until they are fifteen to eighteen. It is compulsory. They also learn science, languages, history, geography and many other subjects."

"What about chivalry and warfare?"

"No, I'm afraid chivalry is dead. And only people who want to make a career in the army, navy or air force learn about warfare."

"Air force?"

"Ah yes – you wouldn't know about aeroplanes. There was a man, an Italian called Leonardo da Vinci, born the same year as you, who believed that a machine could be built to enable people to fly. He never actually built one, but eventually people mastered the science of it and now anyone can fly, in huge metal machines. We can fly from here to Scotland in an hour and to America in as little as five hours."

"America?"

"It is a huge land mass lying west of Europe – it was discovered in 1492 by a man called Christopher Columbus. He was also about your age - a year older, I think. He was Italian, but was financed by Ferdinand and Isabella of Spain. He had also asked the King of Portugal, but he refused."

"Mean you Isabella of Castile? She was once proposed as a possible match for Edward, my brother, but he rejected her in favour of Elizabeth Woodville Grey."

The name sounded like a swear word on his lips.

"Yes, that's right. I believe Columbus' brother, Bartholomew, came to England to beg for financial backing also, in 1489."

"Really? I shall look out for him," he said. Rose was silent. She couldn't very well tell him that the King of England at that time wasn't Richard, but Henry Tudor! She supposed, if he remained here long enough, he would find out, but she hoped to break it to him gently.

"Mmm," she said. Then, changing the subject: "Look, let's get the bags in, eh?"

They got their luggage in and then she made him a coffee (he wanted to try it again and managed to drink it all this time, though he still made a face at the bitterness). A little later she gave him another treatment, using her adjustable couch, and checked that he was doing the exercises correctly. He was doing pretty well and he announced that he was pleased with her ministrations so far and was hopeful of a permanent improvement. She was too – he was still young after all, and had the chance to make a change if he persisted with the regime.

"Are you hungry?" she said, changing the subject.

"Certes, yes!" he said.

"I think I'll order a pizza. I'm a bit too tired to cook tonight."

A half an hour later the bell rang and Rose brought the brightly coloured pack into the kitchen.

They sat at the dining room table and Rose found a bottle of rosé wine in the fridge. Richard had spent the half hour while they awaited the pizzas' arrival exploring the wonders of a modern kitchen. He was curious about everything from the hob to the freezer, the microwave to the dishwasher. Rose found it difficult to explain the way they worked to him. It made her realise how much she, and all modern people, took technology for granted.

He relished the pizza, saying that they had a similar dish - a kind of flat bread with different toppings on it. He thought the wine was "like the nectar of the gods." She laughed.

She told him he was welcome to stay as long as he wanted or needed to, but that she had only one bedroom (the second was used as her treatment room). She did have a good quality sofa bed, which he could use, but she also had two dogs - they were staying with a friend at the moment, but she would pick them up the next day. She also told him she would have to work some of the time, but that she would help him with his modern English and mastery of the Internet and other technical innovations, so that he could explore how to get home. He was no longer suspicious or afraid of this strange world and was keen to learn more, both information and how to use the technology. They planned to research the known facts and theories about time travel. Through this research, they hoped to develop a strategy to return him to his own time.

Amazed

The next day she wasn't very busy with work and she left Richard at home while she went to pick up Jonah and Jubilee, her two dogs. Jubilee was a twelve year old yellow Labrador and Jonah an eighteen month old black Labrador cross. When they got back, the dogs ran around Richard, and Rose was afraid Jonah would jump up, but he seemed to recognise Richard's aura of authority and gave him space, approaching him calmly and wagging his tail when Richard petted him. Rose was amazed - Jonah was usually so boisterous.

"They're beautiful dogs," Richard said, smiling, and sat down, a dog on each side, gazing up adoringly at him. They had a cup of tea and then took the dogs out for a walk in the nearby woods, laughing at Jonah haring around like a mad thing and jumping over logs and bushes to chase squirrels.

Later that day, after Rose had seen a couple of patients, she took Richard to the local library and then the supermarket.

In the library he felt awed by the sheer number of books and other media available to borrow. He thought it was an inspired idea to lend books to those who couldn't afford to buy them. He was even more enthralled when Rose showed him the sections on history, where his own name was rather prominent, and the historical fiction, where there was a whole shelf of books about him! She wouldn't allow him to read any yet, though, for fear of how he would react when he found out about his own early demise at Bosworth Field and swiftly steered him outside again.

"I have the best books about you at home. I will let you read them at your leisure, but there are a few things you need to know first."

"What are they?" he asked.

"All in good time, Richard. Let's go to the supermarket now and get the shopping." And they set off to the car park.

He found it rather overwhelming, the dazzling lights and crowded aisles. The bright colours and printed word on everything delighted him, however, and he was beginning to be able to decipher the pronunciation of most of the words, even if they meant nothing to him – words like: Yoplait, Hovis and KitKat!

He picked up different items, studying them intently, reading the labels and occasionally putting something into the trolley. He had the job of pushing it around.

"Rose, if your civilisation is so advanced that it can, if you are to be believed, fly men to the moon and people around the earth, make life-like pictures move and teach everyone to read, how can it not design a wheel that travels in a straight line?!" he burst out, exasperated with the errant trolley.

She laughed. "It's one of the great mysteries of supermarkets," she said. "Along with 'Why do they move everything around just when you've got to know where it all is?' and 'Why does the queue you're in always move much more slowly than the others - until you change!?'"

She asked him what fruit and vegetables were available in his day and he showed her, although he didn't at first recognise the beetroot and carrots because they had changed colour since his time - the beetroot had been yellow and the carrot, purple! Of course, some of the main ones missing from his diet had been potatoes and bananas, both of which he soon came to adore. He actually wasn't particularly hard to feed. He might be a king, but he was quite content to eat whatever was available, although he did prefer to eat a lot of protein foods. That wasn't a problem as Rose was the same - she had always preferred the meat and fish to the vegetables. They both also loved desserts. Richard especially liked strawberry trifle and shortcake. Rose preferred raspberry, but neither were fussy eaters. She was finding that they had more and more in common the more she got to know him. She had had certain preconceptions about him. Her idea of Richard had been rather romantic and idealised, but she now realised that this was real life and that he was a man, just like any other. Well, not exactly like any other, true, but he seemed to be rather enlightened and forward thinking for a man of his era. For example, he had had his laws published in English, she knew. She asked him about it as they wandered around.

"Yes, I felt it was important that as many people as possible understood the laws, else how could they be expected to obey them?" he said.

"What else were you planning to do, before you were whisked away to the future?"

"I want to create more bodies such as the Council of the North that I presided over as Duke of Gloucester. I want the same standards of justice and fairness to be upheld over the whole realm. I want local issues to be dealt with locally but with equal justice everywhere. I want every person in the realm to feel that they can be heard if they have a grievance, to know that their King will intercede for them if they do not get a fair hearing locally. I am intending to found a Chancery chapel at York Minster and I am also finishing a new chapel for the dead of Towton that Edward started. But of course most of this has to wait until Tydder is defeated and the realm is at peace again. I need to secure my throne and the succession - that is a priority now. I have no heir of my body…" He lowered his head, hesitated, then continued. "My son, Edward was ever a sickly child, but I held so much hope for him." He hesitated, his eyes misting over, then continued: "Anyway, I urgently need to marry and produce another heir - it is a vital task for a king."

"There was talk that you were intending to marry Elizabeth of York, your niece."

He sighed. "I publicly denied that scurrilous rumour! But I was partly to blame for it. I allowed her to wear the same style and colour of dress as Anne last Christmas. I thus encouraged the rumour at first because I wanted Tydder to hear of it. If he thought I was bedding or intending to wed Elizabeth, he might be pushed into invading before he was fully ready. Because he has sworn to marry her when he is king! 'WHEN', he says, the insolent devil! He shall never lay his filthy hands on my crown!"

Rose went pale, but ignored his words and steered the conversation back to Elizabeth.

"So you never intended to marry her then? Wouldn't it have solved the problem of those lords who were loyal to Edward and his line? You would have united the two sides of the house of York."

"Yes, but think, Rose! I had become King because Edward's children were bastards. That included Elizabeth. A king cannot marry a bastard, whoever her father may have been. Secondly, the supporters of the House of Neville in the North would have been alienated because their sympathies lay with my consort, Anne, so recently deceased. So I would lose as much support as I gained. Thirdly and most importantly, she was my brother's child! That is incestuous and I could not countenance that before God. However, Elizabeth unfortunately developed a youthful attachment to me. To be honest, I think a part of her - the Woodville part - simply wanted to be a queen. But I have now settled this matter. As I mentioned, I have sent to Portugal to seek the hand of Infanta Joana for myself and Manuel for Elizabeth. Who knows, she may even end up Queen of Portugal!"

Grenade

A few days later, Lynne called Rose back. She had just arrived back from holiday, which was why she hadn't returned Rose's call earlier. Rose was sure Lynne would probably laugh and laugh at her, believing it was a hoax of some kind, But she could at least ask her if she had heard anything about such occurrences. Lynne was very into the occult, psychic phenomena and the paranormal. She wasn't sure if Richard would approve of that, though. He was known to be very religious. Rose explained the situation as convincingly as she could and asked Lynne's opinion about how Richard had got here in the twenty first century and whether he would be able to get back again. She also told her they had found nothing at the Major Oak site which gave them any help in getting Richard back to the Middle Ages.

Lynne was, understandably, very sceptical at first, but finally Rose managed to, if not convince her, at least persuade her to suspend her disbelief long enough to give an opinion about "time slips" and other such phenomena. She asked Rose and Richard many questions such as what they were thinking about when it happened, what the date and time of day was in each world, where exactly Richard had landed (he didn't know as he had been half unconscious) and many others.

"It's very weird that the person who 'appeared' through time is none other than Richard III, who is your pet obsession, isn't it?" she commented. Rose squirmed at that, glad that Richard was not listening to Lynne's side of the conversation!

"Do you think that has anything to do with it, then?" she asked.

"Yes, I do," Lynne confirmed. "You know about the Law of Attraction, don't you?"

"Yes, I think so. Isn't that where basically you attract whatever you're thinking about?...Oh! I see what you're getting at! You think I manifested him here because I'm so obsessed with him?!"

"Obsessed with whom?" asked Richard who was leaning over, trying to hear what was being said.

Rose felt a wave of heat infuse her cheeks.

"Lynne is talking about you, Richard, although I wouldn't call it an obsession, exactly. I have been interested in your reign for a while, because there are so many mysteries surrounding your time on the throne and very little surviving evidence."

She didn't say that her 'interest' had started when she had seen his bones dug up from the car park!

Lynne continued: "Not only that, Richard was apparently thinking about how he'd like to be able to get away from his life and not have to be a king, bound by duty. And you were both thinking those thoughts while you were at the same place, and on the same date and time, although different years, of course! The universe decided it could provide both your needs at once!"

"Yes, but I think he really wants to go home again now. That was only a transient thought - he doesn't really want to give up being King."

"Really? Even after what happens at Bosworth?" Lynne added.

"He doesn't know about that yet", Rose said.

"About what?" he asked.

"Nothing, it's not important," Rose replied.

"Rose! Don't you think he has a right to know?" Lynne said, appalled.

Rose lowered her voice: "Of course he does, I just don't really know how to break it to him. Any suggestions?"

"Not really," said Lynne. "I'll have a think about it and call you back, OK?"

Rose hung up and went over to join Richard on the sofa. He had, in just a few days, learned how to use the TV. It was an intriguing wonder to him and he had once again succumbed to its lure and switched it on. As with most men, he loved having the power of the remote control! There was a quiz show on and Richard watched attentively, his eyes glued to the box in the corner of the room.

She glanced at the TV - it was a repeat of her favourite quiz, Pointless.

They watched it together, Richard asking questions after every round, but seeming to enjoy it, despite not having the requisite knowledge to join in, simply because he was born (and died) before most of it had happened!

Then, amazingly, in the 'head to head' round, there was a question on Richard III, himself. Rose stared at the screen in horror, unable to move or do anything, feeling the blood drain from her face as the questions came:

'Where was Richard III born?'

'At what battle was he killed?'

'Which town was it where his skeleton was found under a car park?'

'Who played him in Blackadder?'

'Who wrote the play about him in which he says the line "A horse, a horse, my kingdom for a horse!"?'

She sensed Richard tense as he sat beside her. She didn't dare look at him. She wanted the proverbial earth to open up and swallow her. Damn! Why hadn't she thought he might see something like this! She had wanted to try and break it to him as gently as possible, not have it thrown at him like a grenade, with no prior warning.

He continued to watch in silence, but she could feel that the atmosphere had entirely changed and didn't know what to do, so she just sat there, inwardly cringing at every answer given to the questions. Finally when all the answers had been revealed, Richard turned to her quietly, his face ashen, his mouth tight and those frown lines apparent again between the fine eyebrows.

"Why did you keep this from me? I died at Bosworth?! It can't be true! That Bastard Tydder can't have beaten me! He is untried, a green youth, and I am a tested general, a successful one too! And my bones have been disturbed from their resting place – under a car park??? I don't understand. And what's all this about a horse – are they suggesting I was trying to run away? I would never do that. I ran away with Edward once and we spent several months in exile – I vowed then I would never live like a homeless beggar again, I'd rather die!"

"Well, you did die, Richard, I'm sorry, but it's true! And Henry Tudor – Tydder- he founded a dynasty that lasted over a hundred years and is probably the most famous royal family in British history. His son, Henry VIII, was a bloody tyrant, but was the most memorable and most written about king in our history. Only one other is now written about more than he – and that is you, Richard!"

His eyebrows shot up.

"Me!? Am I remembered even though I only reigned for - Christ's bones! - just two years? I must have been loved then. At least that is a small comfort."

Rose glanced at him from under her fringe. She wanted to cry.

"Richard, you WERE loved, by many – especially those from York and the North, but, I'm so sorry, you were written about mainly because you were hated. You have the reputation of being the most evil king in the whole of British history."

Richard paled but said nothing. Rose then told him about Shakespeare and his famous play, Richard III, in which he was accused of murdering most of his own family and scheming to gain the throne for years - the archetypal ruthless tyrant.

He opened his mouth to speak, his expression one of complete dismay. His lovely eyes shone with unshed tears. She longed to go over and hold him tight to comfort him, but thought he would be unlikely to thank her for that, being a man who was so private and who didn't like to show his emotions. Finally he shook his head, pressed his lips together and lowered his gaze, too upset to say anything.

"I'll explain the whole story, but please understand that it is not so clear cut," said Rose. "That evil version of you originated from the Tudors and their historians, such as Thomas More. There were barely any contemporary records left in existence to give your side of the story - the Tudors destroyed them all. But later on, some historians began to question the Tudor view and see it as propaganda. There have been hundreds of books written about you, both fact and fiction. Some support you and some support the Tudor view. There is even a Richard III Society – I'm a member! The Society is dedicated to restoring your tarnished reputation and portraying a fair picture of you and your achievements. I wanted to try and tell you all this in a careful way, a gentle way. I knew it would hurt you and I didn't know how to begin. I'm so sorry you had to find out about it like that."

Richard sat in silence still. He closed his eyes and pinched the bridge of his nose momentarily with his slender fingers. His chin wobbled slightly but he didn't break. Then he clenched his fists, his knuckles white he was squeezing them so hard.

Finally he turned to her.

"So," he said, his voice husky with emotion. "Not only did Tydder rob me of my crown and my life, but my good name too! Everything I tried to do was in vain. My reputation, that which I treasured and protected above all else was despoiled, my realm stolen from me and my family, by that upstart! I cannot believe it! How did it happen? The duty that I took upon myself for England, at great cost to my conscience and my very soul, to return her to a fair, just realm, to protect her people rich and poor alike, all in ruins!"

"But wait! It hasn't happened yet – from your point of view I mean. Bosworth hasn't happened yet. Perhaps if we find out what went wrong you might be able to change it!"

"Aye, if I ever get back there! Perhaps it would be better for England if I never went back at all. Even if I did, is it possible to change history? From here, all of that happened over 500 years ago, mayhap it can't be changed."

"You can only try."

"That is true. I do not like giving up. I have never been happy to accept my fate, have always struggled to do what is best, what is right. But I can't decide if I want to go back to that corrupt, evil place or stay here. It is right strange here in your world but there are also many marvels to behold."

"Well, I suppose you don't have to decide right away, do you? Stay awhile, learn what history has to say about your reign and your death so that you have as many facts as you can. Then you can decide if you want to try again to go back to sort it all out. It doesn't seem as if it will be easy – you might not be able to get back at all. Or you might go back to a completely different time. But in the mean time you can learn about this time and have a break from being King for a while. What do you think?"

He considered her suggestion and then he smiled, the lines disappearing from his forehead, the dimple showing again. "Yes, you're right; why not stay here for a while? I am certainly curious about all the new inventions you have these days. I might as well enjoy being a common citizen for a while."

"Hardly a common citizen, Your Grace!" she laughed, dropping him a swift, but wobbly curtsey. He raised one eyebrow, a half smile on his face.

Chapter Three - July 2014

Everything I Own

Richard had insisted on seeing Shakespeare's Richard III and Rose decided to show him the Olivier version, of which she had a DVD. Richard had started by scowling at the screen, but ended up laughing as the depiction of him was so ludicrous. For a start, he was portrayed as much older than his proper age, so that Shakespeare could have him taking part, in another work, in the first Battle of St Alban's, when in reality he was only about two years old at the time! The withered arm, limp and hunchback were so extreme, Rose had worried he would become upset at this mocking of his spinal deformity, but he said it made his actual problem seem minimal by comparison. At the end, he had decided that the character was quite a charismatic fellow, even though he bore no resemblance to himself at all. He was portrayed as so evil that it was completely unbelievable. But he could see that, as a morality tale, it was impressive and the writing was marvellous.

"I am not surprised that Shakespeare is thought of as the world's greatest playwright," he said. "I am quite honoured that he wrote a play bearing my name, even though it seems it has been at the root of most of the misconceptions surrounding my reputation."

Richard felt uncomfortable not being able to pay his way and persuaded Rose to help him raise some cash by selling his jewellery: his rings, hat brooch and chain. So Rose enquired around on the Internet and eventually took some of the items - one ring and the brooch and chain - to show one of the experts at the British museum. She said they had discovered the 'hoard' in her back garden when using a borrowed metal detector. Rose had taken the precaution of rubbing some earth around the pieces to make them look older. To their delight, the experts valued the "hoard" at a huge sum - an amount which could easily have bought a substantial family home, even in the expensive south east! This meant that Richard now had his own means of support and he insisted on paying rent to stay with Rose.

One of the main problems he had, which might be important regarding the battle, was that he could not train as he normally would in preparation for it. He had ever struggled to keep up with other stronger boys and men, but refused to give in to the physical limitations caused by his scoliosis and slight build. In his youth, he had been so determined and trained so hard that he had become better than almost all of his peers in fighting, archery, riding and war-craft.

"I will soon start to lose condition if I can't train – this must be rectified. Otherwise how will I be able to best Tydder? It is especially important for me because I am at something of a disadvantage owing to my physique - I tire more quickly."

"Yes, you're right. Perhaps I should take you gym training with me? But I don't know whether that would provide the sort of training you need. What did you use to do before?"

"When we were in intensive training, we would ride a lot, practise archery, swordplay and be in the tilt yard for hours, often in full armour to get us accustomed to fighting with weight - tournament armour is much heavier than combat armour, you know. But what is this 'gym' you mentioned?"

"Well, many people exercise to keep fit these days as everyday life often doesn't provide enough physical activity - they use machines with weights and other equipment. I normally go to the gym twice a week and Pilates once a month, but I have let it lapse this summer as I have been too busy. But we could go to see my personal trainers and you can try out the equipment and see if it would help you in any way. I see Maria for gym training - she has her own private gym at the end of her garden - and Dalia, who is a Pilates teacher, in her special studio."

"What is Pilates?"

"Oh sorry, I keep forgetting you don't know about these things. Pilates is a method of exercise, using special equipment to help you tone up your core muscles and improve physical strength, flexibility and posture - it would probably be great for you, actually, now I come to think about it. It could complement the exercises you are already doing for your spine. And Maria's gym could help with your cardiovascular fitness - your heart and lung efficiency. Plus, you can still ride - Rebel is here in Rayleigh. He is only a short distance away too. I can take you there to show you exactly how to get to the stables and then you could walk there whenever you want and take him out."

"Yes, but it's not much fun riding alone," he complained. "And I would like to experience training at a gym and Pilates - they sound interesting. But I also need to practise fighting, hand to hand combat and battle situations, everything I will need at the battle of Bosworth."

Rose looked thoughtful. "Hmm, I might have thought of just the thing you need!" she said.

Strong

She rang both Maria and Dalia later that day and told them she had a friend who might like to train with them. She said he was in training for a battle re-enactment, but had been out of action for a while and now wanted to get back into it. She also said he had moved here from Yorkshire to forestall any questions about his mode of speech. The two trainers were happy to meet Richard and help him with his fitness regime.

They were very different in almost every way, except their commitment to fitness and health. Maria was a bubbly, pretty girl of thirty. She had a young family and worked from home as a personal fitness trainer, which she could fit around school hours. She was petite but perfectly proportioned and very toned. Her gym, in an outbuilding at the end of her garden, was equipped with several cardiovascular fitness machines: treadmill, cross trainer, rowing machine and static bike, as well as free weights, fitness balls and other assorted items like boxing gloves, skipping ropes and mats, which meant she could provide a varied workout. Rose always enjoyed her sessions with Maria, as no two were the same and they were tailored to the individual. She was quite a hard taskmaster but had an infectious giggle and a great sense of humour.

Rose and Richard were outside her door on a sunny Monday afternoon in July and Maria led them inside. She wrote down various health details and the aims of her new client before doing a taster session. Rose was set to work on the rowing machine while Richard answered the questions and allowed himself to be weighed and measured. Rose had warned Richard that women of today wore clothes that might be considered revealing in his day, so he wouldn't be too shocked by the tight clothes Maria wore. He had said nothing so she wasn't really sure what he felt about that.

"Well, you are a good weight for your height, Richard, slightly under, if anything," Maria said. "I think we will try out your cardiovascular fitness on the treadmill and then see how you are with a few weights."

Richard stepped onto the treadmill and almost fell off as it started moving, but quickly regained his balance and started walking and then jogging as Maria gradually increased the speed. He was doing pretty well, Rose thought, until Maria put in the hill climb and then he started to struggle with his breathing.

"It's my back, you see," he said. "My scoliosis affects the rib movement, so my stamina is not as good as I would like".

"That's fine, I'm sure we can get an improvement for you - let's see how you are with the kettle bells."

Maria positioned Richard in a space and demonstrated how to swing the kettle bell around his head and then the other way, which was aimed at improving his flexibility as well as toning up his arms. When she got him lifting the free weights she was surprised at his strength.

"You're quite slim, but you are much stronger than you look. I'm impressed!" she said. "Let's try some boxing."

She gave Richard two boxing gloves and herself put on the large pads.

"OK, jabs for thirty seconds," she said, bracing herself for his efforts.

He stood there, a puzzled frown on his face, saying: "I'm sorry, I don't understand what I'm to do, Maria."

She explained that he must hit the pads one at a time with alternate hands.

"You want me to hit you?" he said, incredulously.

"No, not me, hit the pads - don't worry, I'm used to it," she said.

He took up a wider stance and swung his fist at the pad in a rather half-hearted fashion.

"That's not hard enough Richard - I barely felt it!" she laughed.

He frowned again and took another attempt, with little improvement.

"Is that the best you can do?" she sighed.

"I'm not in the habit of hitting women," he said. "I can't help holding back,"

"Imagine she's Buckingham!" called Rose helpfully.

Finally he managed to deliver a proper punch and Maria encouraged him to continue in that vein.

The whole workout was just half an hour but quite intensive and Maria played rhythmic music encouraging them both to work hard. Richard pushed himself to the limit and felt his muscles protesting at this new type of exercise. They finished the session out of breath and perspiring. Maria said they'd do some other exercises next time and they paid her fee and left.

Richard was exhilarated.

"I'm not sure about the boxing - I still don't like the idea of hitting a woman. But I love those machines! How marvellous to be able to run and yet stay in the same place!"

"I'm glad you enjoyed it because I have booked you in for twice a week for the next month," Rose said. "And Maria is great, isn't she? She encourages and brings out the best in you without any shouting or nagging. She has helped me get fit, I'm sure she will be able to help you too. It could make all the difference in the battle, couldn't it?"

"Yes, the fitter I am, the better. And you are right about Maria. I try to be like that as a leader in battle too - it is better to encourage and praise, inspiring loyalty, than trying to force someone to obey against their will."

"I know that Richard. You are well known to value loyalty. But be careful - some people see that attitude as weakness. By the way, in two days' time we will go to see Dalia - she is quite different from Maria."

"In what way?" asked Richard.

"Wait and see!" she grinned.

Dalia's place was in Southend and they arrived there promptly at one o'clock two days later. When she opened the door to them, Richard found himself staring directly at her bosom - she was the tallest, thinnest woman he had ever seen! She was six feet two and had not an ounce of fat on her. Her legs were long and elegant: she was an ex-high jump champion from Lithuania.

"Ah! You must be Richard," she said, her strong Eastern European accent apparent. "Well, come in and see my torture chamber, Dahling!"

Richard turned to look at Rose in astonishment, his eyes wide. Dalia was wearing a skin tight pair of black leggings and a black Lycra top, with a pair of bright purple skimpy Lycra shorts over the leggings. She wore red lipstick and her eyelashes were long and dramatic. Her almost white-blond hair was piled glamorously on top of her head. She looked like some kind of Wonder Woman figure.

"Have fun! I'll pick you up in an hour," Rose said, her eyes twinkling in amusement, and turned away before Richard could protest. Dalia's hand shot out and grabbed Richard by the front of his T-shirt, pulling him inside.

She ushered him downstairs into the basement and he began to wonder whether it was indeed a torture chamber she had down there. He was sure that was a whip leaning against the wall at the bottom of the staircase! To his relief the room downstairs was light and airy, but he swallowed in dismay as he saw what must be a modern day rack in the middle of the floor, complete with ropes and strange metal attachments.

"Come on now, Richard - are you going to be a good boy?!" she said, licking her lips.

He gave her the 'look' which had quelled noble lords and high born churchmen alike, but she simply returned his stare, one immaculate eyebrow raised in amusement.

"Don't look so worried, Dahling - I don't bite! Well, not much anyway," she said, putting her hands on her hips and drawing herself up to her full height. She towered over him. "Now we are going to have fun!"

She proceeded to instruct him in the use of the Reformer Pilates machine - the 'rack' in the middle of the room. He had to lie on it and put his feet on the end plate, pushing the platform he was lying on away by straightening his legs.

"Engage your core, Richard. And don't go so fast - slowly, with control! Twenty times - one, two, three…!"

He found, once he had got the hang of it, that it supported his back while he was exercising and the machine was so versatile. She had him standing up on it, pushing his legs apart, 'slowly, with control', pulling himself to and fro using the strong cords, and bending forwards and slowly backwards again, one vertebra at a time. This was impossible for him to do perfectly, but he found, after a few repetitions, his flexibility did improve. And by the end he found he was thoroughly enjoying it - he could feel it was benefiting his spine and core strength.

"Well, Richard, you have done a really good workout - I'm very pleased with you, Dahling!" Dalia said. He couldn't believe an hour had gone already - it really had been fun!

Then the bell rang and it was Rose, come to pick him up. Dalia kissed them goodbye on both cheeks and waved to them as they left.

"What did you think of Dalia?" asked Rose, glancing at Richard's flushed face, as they crossed the road to the car.

"She is…formidable," he said. "She reminded me a little of my mother."

Rose glanced at him in astonishment.

"I don't mean physically. Although my mother is taller than average and quite slim, Dalia is more so, but it's her attitude that's similar - the same authority and self-assurance. I'm not sure about her revealing attire and she kept calling me 'Darling' - very forward of her! But I really enjoyed the Pilates. Can we come back next week?"

Rose laughed. "Yes, if you like - I'll text her when we get home. She is larger than life, but very funny, isn't she? She told me that many of the Lithuanian women are tall and slim like her and the men are even taller, but stockily built and very strong - in fact one Lithuanian man, Zydrunas Saviskas, has won the World's Strongest Man competition several times. And don't worry - she calls everyone 'Dahling'"

"Remind me never to consider invading Lithuania," he said.

True Colours

To help with Richard's battle readiness, Rose had made enquiries on Richard's behalf about joining in with re-enactment training and actual re-enactments by simply searching on Facebook. She found a great group called 'Making Fifteenth Century Re-enactment Glorious' and discovered that one of the Group's Admins, Tom Falconer, actually lived in Rayleigh. They arranged to meet in the Costa Coffee one lunchtime. She went alone, as she wanted to surprise Richard after she had found out everything she could. She told him she was going shopping and left him listening to choral music.

On the way to the rendezvous she suddenly realised that Tom didn't know what she looked like, as her Facebook profile picture was of her dog, Jonah! She hoped she would find him, as she was hopeless at facial recognition. There had been countless times when a patient she had only seen once or twice knocked on the door and she had been surprised when she saw them because she had had a totally different mental 'picture' of them! And woe betide if she met a patient in a different context! She had on more than one occasion been tempted to say "Sorry, I didn't recognise you with your clothes on!" Perhaps she was suffering from prosopagnosia or 'face blindness'!

Anyway, Tom's Facebook pic was very distinctive as he had extremely long hair and a beard.

"Let's hope he hasn't had a haircut and shave recently!" she thought.

She needn't have worried, as she spotted him - complete with resplendent hair and beard - waiting outside the Costa, looking like a pirate in denims. She went up to him and introduced herself and they went inside. She ordered a large cappuccino and he had an Americano. After they'd found a table they chatted for a short while about Rayleigh and other general topics. Then she told him that she had a friend who used to do re-enactments on the continent, but had now moved to England and wanted to keep his hand in.

"Oh, which group did he belong to?" Tom asked, smiling.

"I've no idea, I'm sorry. I only know he was pretty good and used to play some of the major roles. He's an excellent horseman and very knowledgeable about Mediaeval battles," she added.

"Oh, he's a mounted re-enactor?" asked Tom. "And does he want to ride over here or just join in with the foot soldiers?"

"Oh no, he definitely wants to ride. He wants to keep in practice for when he goes back. He needs to keep his skills sharp and stay fit."

"Well, in that case he needs to get in touch with Destrier."

"Destrier? What's that?" asked Rose.

"Destrier - it's a group named after the mediaeval war horse - that's what they were called - destriers."

Rose remembered now, she had read about the large, powerful horses who fought as courageously as their riders, biting and kicking at the enemy.

Tom continued: "All the mounted re-enactors in England come from that group now. They're the best and most authentic when it comes to mounted battles, charges, jousts, all that sort of thing. They have a group on Facebook. You should get in touch with them."

"Thanks, I will. By the way, what's your opinion about what went wrong for Richard III at the Battle of Bosworth? What should he have done to win the battle?"

"Well, he should have imprisoned Thomas Stanley - or topped him - and not allowed him to be there at the battle."

"Yes, that would work, I suppose! I read a theory that William Stanley, Thomas's brother, had seen Richard kill Tudor's standard bearer, saw it fall, and must have thought Henry was lost, so he joined the battle on Richard's side. But Richard's knights were so suspicious about Stanley's treachery that they assumed he was trying to help Tudor and they ended up fighting each other. What do you think about that?" asked Rose.

"It's possible. It happened before, at Barnet, that allies were mistaken for the enemy and they started fighting and killing each other."

"Hmm!" said Rose pensively. "That's given me something to think about! I am a bit of a Ricardian myself, you see! Well, thank you so much for your help. It's been most enlightening!"

She walked back to the bungalow and rang the bell, as she couldn't find her key. Richard opened the door, smiling at her and held it wide. He was wearing a pair of blue jeans, smart brown shoes and a blue T-shirt that bore the legend: "Don't Believe The Hype!" She smiled back at him.

"I've got some news for you! I've just been having a chat with a fifteenth century re-enactor! Apparently, if you want to ride in a re-enactment, you have to join Destrier. That's a group that specialises in training and providing knight riders for anyone who wants to put on a show, re-enactment or entertainment with mediaeval knights. They have a group on Facebook, so I'll try and contact them today and see whether you can join in with them."

They went inside and he made her a cup of tea while she went on line. She found the group straight away and messaged the Admin.

"Right! Now all we have to do is wait for a response!" she said cheerily. "So what have you been doing while I was away?"

"Well, I have been browsing and I found a group on Facebook that promote art forms dedicated to me! It's called B.O.A.R.s - the Benevolent Order of Artful Ricardians! Some of the artwork is stunning. That is wonderful, is it not?!"

"I know it", she said. Then added, quietly: "I belong to it, in fact!"

"You do?" he exclaimed. "And have you created any works of art or literature about me?!"

"Ye-es!", she replied, cagily. "I've done a short story and a few pictures. But they're not very good."

"Let me see!" he cried. She didn't reply, but looked at him appraisingly, trying to ascertain whether she should show him or not.

"I don't know," she said, finally. "They're not really up to a good enough standard for a king…"

He narrowed his eyes and pouted his lips, just a little.

"Now, Rose, you know that while I'm here I am but a normal man, not a king and I would verily like to see them?" he wheedled. "I pray thee?"

She couldn't resist that. She loved mediaeval speak.

"OK, as long as you swear not to laugh," she said.

She went to the cupboard in her treatment room and got out a bag containing all her artistic Ricardian efforts. There was a short story which she'd printed off from the computer and five pictures - three paintings and two sketches. She let him read the story first; it was a spooky tale about William Stanley seeing scary visions while about to be executed by Henry VII, à la Scrooge in 'A Christmas Carol'.

The pictures were all of Richard, most of them her attempts at doing a portrait of him. The last painting was of him kneeling, holding a rosary and weeping, mourning his Queen, Anne, whose ghost stood behind him with her ethereal hand on his shoulder.

Rose thought it rather crudely done and a bit out of proportion. She had meant to do another one on canvas (this was only on paper) that would be more detailed and larger. She moved to take it from Richard's hand, but he snatched it out of her reach. She opened her mouth to say something but stopped when she realised the picture was shaking in his hand. She looked at his face and was shocked to see that there were bright tears in his eyes. He raised his gaze to her, his expression half of wonder and half of distress. As he did so one tear escaped from the corner of his eye and ran down his cheek. He blinked and another one trickled down, from the other eye. He put the picture down and pulled her roughly to him hugging her tightly, She was bewildered, not understanding why he was so moved, but she put her arms around him and hugged him back.

"Richard?" she ventured. "I'm sorry if it's upset you. I didn't mean to…"

"No, not at all, Rose. I'm not upset, I'm…moved. It's not the best painting I've ever seen, but you've captured exactly the emotion I felt the day Anne died. I almost experienced it all over again. And, strangely, I did sense she was around me at that time because just when I thought I couldn't go on, I suddenly felt comforted. May I keep it, please?"

"Of course you can! I consider it an honour that you would even want it!"

He smiled, brushed the tears away and gave her another quick hug, before rolling up the picture and spiriting it away into the section that Rose had allocated to him in the living room sideboard.

"I've bought some steak," she said. "Does that sound OK for dinner tonight?" She had popped into the under-cover market, The Lanes, in Rayleigh town and visited the butcher - Richard was an avid meat eater.

"Mmm! Yes, please!", he grinned, the tears forgotten as he savoured the anticipation of a well-cooked piece of beef, served with jacket potatoes and salad. He had fallen in love with potatoes of all types, cooked in any way.

I'm Too Sexy

A few days later Rose got a reply from one of the organisers of Destrier - if Richard wanted to take part in any of the re-enactments he had to do at least two days' training with them. Richard had no objection to that, in fact the training was exactly what he wanted and so it was that a few days later, Rose was driving Richard to their training ground.

Richard was excited. Rose could tell by the way he was fiddling with his remaining rings, tapping his foot and being generally fidgety. His eyes looked greyer today as he was wearing a grey sweatshirt whose colour was reflected in them, but they were shining and he was talking non-stop about what the trainers would be like, whether he would be expected to wear armour, or harness as it was properly called, and what the training would entail. Each re-enactor had to provide their own armour, as it was made to measure.

Rose had found out that a full set of a high quality harness such as this would cost twice as much as a saloon car, and it would also be easier if he had his own horse. Luckily Rebel would fit the bill and they were bringing him with them in his horse-box. True, he was not the kind of horse Richard would use in a real battle, but he would be quite adequate for a re-enactment as he responded perfectly to Richard's expert touch and they fully understood each other. The other lucky chance was that Richard did have his main body armour, which he had been wearing when he came through to this time and was wearing now under his sweatshirt, as well as a completely authentic mediaeval saddle, so only the leg and arm pieces and helmet would have to be made.

They arrived to the sound of clanking and grunts as two mounted 'knights' engaged in mock battle with each other in the nearby paddock. Rose was suddenly concerned that Richard would actually hurt someone.

"Richard," she said. "You won't actually try to kill anyone, will you? Don't forget they are not really experienced in proper battle, they have never killed anyone and are only using blunted swords and weapons and trying to make it look real, without the real bloodshed."

"Of course I won't, Rose," he replied, scowling. "Do you take me for some kind of savage?!"

And he stalked off towards the paddock as a large man with tousled hair and dust-covered clothes came out to talk to him.

"Well," she thought. "You were known as a warrior king. You did have a reputation of being fierce and strong in battle and you certainly knew how to kill!"

She got out of the car and wandered over to the paddock, where Richard and the man were deep in conversation. There was, a little way away from the paddock, a tilt yard, with it all set up for a jousting competition and she wondered whether Richard would be doing any jousting today. That would be a sight she'd like to see!

The man talking to Richard was nodding and pointed in the direction of the stables. Richard shook his hand and turned back to the car and horse-box, from which he led Rebel towards the stables, marching off eagerly. A few minutes later he emerged, wearing a padded jacket under his armour and mounted on the large black horse. He couldn't hide the small smile on his face and his eyes were brighter than she had ever seen them before. He guided the horse through into the paddock and the man who had greeted Richard called out something she didn't quite hear. Richard immediately started the horse trotting, looking relaxed and confident in the saddle. The man said something else and Richard turned the horse diagonally across the paddock and then the other way so that they were going the opposite way around the circle. The man called another instruction and Richard responded by squeezing his knees so the horse started into a canter. They continued like this for a while with the man calling out instructions and Richard following them to the letter.

"OK," the man called finally. "You're obviously comfortable in the saddle. Have you taken part in any jousts before?"

"Yes, I have done, though not recently," replied Richard.

"Let's see you gallop down the lists a few times, holding a lance," the man said, opening the gate leading to the other enclosure. The quintain, a shield-shaped target which spun around when hit was already set up.

He handed Richard a helmet and gauntlets, finally passing him a long metal lance, which would normally have a balsa wood tip. This was designed to break on contact, scoring points for the contestant according to where it hit, but minimising any injuries to the jousters.

Richard wheeled Rebel around and paused, taking a deep breath. Then he closed the visor, nodded shortly and squeezed the horse forward into a gallop. As he approached the target, he lowered the lance and caught the target on its outside edge. At the end, he turned the horse, galloped back down the other side and around, immediately charging again towards the quintain. This time he scored a direct hit and let out a whoop of triumph. He turned again and again, charging up and down, scoring hit after hit for about twenty minutes.

Rose grew quite breathless watching him. She could hardly believe how it excited her to watch his prowess in the lists. She could really see how mediaeval ladies might have swooned when their champions rode out, dressed in their shining armour, bearing their 'favour'. Phew!

After a few more charges, he began tiring and his hits became less accurate.

The man called out: "OK, that'll do for today! That was impressive. You'll be a great addition to our team. Can you come back next week for another session? We insist on at least two training sessions before we allow you to take part in any re-enactments or shows. What were you interested in doing? Anything in particular?"

"Well, I'm keen to join in with anything, I really miss it. But my preference would be for re-enactments. Especially Bosworth - that's a special interest of mine."

He was panting as he spoke, his chest heaving with the effort of breathing.

"OK, we'll discuss it next week, alright?"

Richard nodded, dismounted and handed back the helmet and gauntlets, then covered the sweating horse with a horse blanket and led him back to the horse-box. He returned to Rose a few minutes later, his face glowing red and still breathing heavily.

"How was it?" Rose asked.

"Marvellous!" he laughed. "It was great to be back in the saddle riding the way I am used to and practising for battle again. But I am much too out of breath for comfort. I will have to improve my fitness if I'm to defeat the Welsh Bastard!" And he marched off to the car, a spring in his step.

As they drove home he asked, suddenly: "Would you like to come riding with me? I need to keep up my riding practice as well as the battle training, but it would be nice to have some company for the rides."

"I'd love to, though I'm not much of a rider," Rose replied. "I suppose I could hire one of the horses at the stable."

"No, Rose, I will get you your own horse. Can you source the best place to buy one?"

"You don't need to do that - a hired one would be fine."

"I would like to, please," he said. "And in any case, you will need a faster horse than average if you are to keep up with Rebel and me!"

Heart of Gold

So it was that a few days later they visited a horse auction to see if he could find a suitable mount for her. Once she had her own horse, they would be able to ride every day and he would get back to his usual fitness in no time.

Richard had wandered around the auction house, inspecting the horses. Rose watched him, still feeling that it was unreal that he, a Mediaeval king, was actually here, large as life and her friend. Her heart swelled as she watched him look at the animals' teeth, lift their feet to inspect their hooves and feel their flanks. She could watch him all day. He moved so easily and fluidly, his body lithe and supple. He had tied his hair back and it revealed his strong jaw, proud chin and broad cheekbones. She sighed. Why did he have to be so charismatic? The more time she spent with him the more attracted to him she became, but she was afraid to say anything in case he didn't feel the same and because she was frightened of losing his friendship.

He returned to her and said he had found three horses that were broadly suitable. He would see how they looked in the ring. She liked to see him so alive and enthusiastic and smiled up at him.

"What colour are they?" she asked, realising as she did that she was doing the typically female thing. If ever she were to be asked to give a description of a car, she knew the colour would likely be the only part she would be sure of. She wondered if ladies in Mediaeval times did the same with horses.

Richard grinned at her. "I'm not worried about the colour, but as you ask, there is a black, a grey and a piebald."

"I like the palominos best," she said. He looked at her questioningly, not recognising the name. She pointed out a beautiful palomino in the pen along to the left of them. It had a glossy golden coat and its mane and tail were a shining silvery colour.

"It is beautiful," he agreed. "But beauty isn't the main quality you need. Still, we'll have a look at him in the ring. That's certainly a lady's horse, he should be easy for you to control," he added, gesturing towards the palomino.

As they stood and watched the various horses being paraded around the ring, he put his hand on her nearest shoulder and squeezed, pointing with his other hand.

"See that one. The black. That's one of the ones I like the look of. The others are…" he scanned the arena and pointed out two other horses. One, the piebald, was being led around outside the enclosure and the grey was snorting and stamping the floor in his pen, his white flowing mane quivering. Richard turned back to the ring. The black was prancing around, resisting the efforts of his handler to calm him down. He seemed to glare at everyone and his eyes were wild. He wouldn't walk forwards, but insisted on prancing sideways, whinnying loudly, shaking his head to try to get free from his handler.

"Well, he certainly looks spirited," Rose said, a little worried at how unruly it seemed.

"He's perfect!" Richard enthused, his eyes shining.

"But he scares me Richard, can we please look at the palomino?"

So they waited and watched until the pretty horse was led in. He was quite spirited too, but not as large as the others. Rose looked at Richard, wondering what he was thinking. His eyes were fixed on the little horse but he didn't show any reaction or interest. He didn't bid at all, simply sizing up the other interested parties, but when the bidding slowed down and the auctioneer's hammer was just about to fall, he made his move. He ended up buying the palomino for a bargain price and seemed very happy with his deal. He asked Rose if she would mind fetching the car with the horse box and she left him to talk to the auctioneer and pay.

"It'll cost a fortune to stable them both. Your cash won't last forever you know! Don't forget, you can't just levy some taxes to pay for everything - the money will run out in no time," she said.

"Don't worry, I have two more rings, you know. And hopefully it will be temporary because I plan to be back in my own time in about six months."

She nodded, lowering her head at the thought of losing him. God! How she would miss him! Then she felt a hand on her shoulder and looked up.

"You look sad. What's on your mind?" he said, a concerned frown on his handsome face.

"Oh, it's nothing really. I just…I mean…oh, Richard! I'm going to miss you so much!" Just saying it made hot tears prick her eyes and she turned away towards her new horse, patting him on the neck in order to avoid looking at Richard.

"Oh Rose!" he said. "Don't worry about that yet. Let's enjoy the time we have left to spend together, eh?"

And he pulled her hand from the horse and turned her into him enfolding her in his arms, holding her tight and stroking her hair. That was it - she just burst into tears. She hated being so weak, especially since she knew she looked repulsive when she cried! But she clung to him, sobbing, and he rocked her gently, shushing her and whispering in her ear.

"Rose, sweeting, please stop crying. I hate to see you so upset."

"I'm sorry!" she burbled. "I can't help it! I can't bear that you'll go back and I'll never see you again, I can't bear it!"

"There's no point in thinking about that yet. We don't even know if I'll be able to get back, do we? And whatever happens, I'll never forget you. You are, and always will be, special to me."

She clung onto him, wetting his shoulder with her tears, not knowing whether to be cheered or devastated by his words. After a few minutes her sobs settled and he rubbed her shoulder, then put her to arm's length and looked into her face. He smiled a half sad, half happy smile and she gave a wobbly smile in return.

"Come on," he said. "Let's head home and get your horse settled into his new place. What are you going to call him?"

"I don't know. Do you have any suggestions?"

"I've been thinking about it," he replied. "What do you think of Heart of Gold - he is a beautiful golden colour and his owner has a heart of gold!"

"That's just right, Richard! And Goldy for short! Thank you so much for him! I have never had a horse before."

"You haven't?! That seems so strange to me! Because we ride almost as soon as we walk and it's so natural. Will you be up to riding with me, do you think? Maybe hunting?"

"Not hunting! We don't hunt these days - except foxes. And I like foxes and don't approve of hunting them. But, yes I can ride, though certainly not as well as you! I'm a bit rusty as well. I hope Goldy's not too rebellious!"

"He's a perfect horse for you - very biddable and willing and not too skittish! And OK - no hunting!"

They travelled back to Essex, Rose driving very carefully so as not to spook the new horse too much, and went straight to the stables. They had already been advised that there would be an extra horse and, thankfully, they had the space. The stable was only ten minutes away from her bungalow and she was already looking forward to 'riding out' with Richard. What a blessing it was to even know him! When she had seen that documentary, little did she know that within the space of only just over two years, she would be spending time with the man himself! Sometimes she had to pinch herself to make sure it wasn't all a dream. It was selfish of her to weep because he might be leaving - she resolved to be thankful that she had come to know him at all.

The Best

Anders, the Destrier organiser, was even more pleased with Richard's performance at his second training day. He didn't let on to him, but he was extremely excited by the way Richard handled both himself and Rebel, and the horse was poetry in motion. He had never seen a horse and rider so in tune with each other and he wondered whether Richard actually lived in the saddle! He was already planning to use him in some of this year's displays and re-enactments, even though it was generally Destrier's policy only to permit new members to join in as ground crew for their first year. Richard was too good to waste doing that! He would be a splendid addition to their team.

He had Richard practising at the quintain and manoeuvering Rebel in ever more complicated patterns – Richard could control the big horse with no hands as Rebel responded to subtle signals from his legs and feet. The only thing Anders could compare it to was a video he'd seen of a bullfighting horse called Merlin. The horse had seemed to skip just out of reach of the bull's horns, sidestepping, pirouetting and turning at just the right time and with such grace it seemed to be dancing. Rebel was similar, but he knew Rebel's skill was equalled by his rider.

When Richard had finished, Anders invited him to take part in some of their events, including Bosworth at the end of August. Richard accepted graciously but admitted to Anders that, although he had his own body armour, which would be suitable for a re-enactment, he would have to have the helm, leg and arm portions of his armour made urgently so that they would be ready in time (he told Anders that he had borrowed them previously). He desperately wanted to take part in the Bosworth re-enactment and so Anders suggested that he order the other parts of his armour from three separate armourers to save time. Richard concurred, but decided that he would also find out which armourers were considered the best in the world and try to engage their services. He couldn't very well ask Anders, as he might wonder why Richard himself didn't know this already, since he had said he had done re-enactments before.

He was wondering whether he might be able to take the armour with him if and when he got home and he wanted the best. That was what he was used to, so why not? He also wanted to look well on the field at the Bosworth re-enactment. He still had the natural pride and royal bearing he was born to - if he was going to be seen in public he was determined to acquit himself well and look the part. He knew he would be unlikely to be allowed to play King Richard in the re-enactment, as a newcomer, but he would hopefully play a leading knight and thus be able to observe the way the battle panned out and learn something to his advantage.

Handy Man

Richard explained to Rose that he needed to have some armour made and that because it was needed quickly, he had decided to order the separate parts of it from different armourers. He would also need to be measured so that it was an exact fit. They researched it on the Internet and apparently the three best armourers came from three different countries: England, Germany and Sweden. If he wanted to use them, two of them would have to come to him, as he had no passport and was unable to travel abroad. Richard also did a Google image search and found a set of harness that was very similar to his own body armour, and a helmet that he was happy with.

"What can I do to help?" asked Rose immediately.

"I need you to make an appointment for me with the English armourer, Bill Best, and to explain that it is urgent and that I will pay well to obtain it. It would normally take about six months for an armourer to create a whole harness, but that's with one man doing it. Because of the time constraints, Anders suggested three different armourers make a section each. They will all produce different parts of the harness, but it must fit together seamlessly. I have the main body already, as I was wearing it when I entered the present time, so one armourer must make the two leg sections, one the two arm sections and the last one, the helm. The helmet is the most important. I want it to look authentically fifteenth century, but the straps holding it on must be impervious to a blade and fitted on as firmly and snugly as possible. I think that Bill Best is the 'best' man for that job."

He smiled at his own joke.

"I understand. I can organise the English appointment, and I think I'll ask my Norwegian friend, Torstein, to help with the others. Though he won't be too happy about the Swedish one."

"Why not?" asked Richard.

"Because he is Norwegian, of course! You know Norwegians hate the Swedes in the same way that the Scots hate the English. They were ruled by them for many years, so now that they are independent they don't like to be reminded of that time."

Richard looked at Rose curiously.

"Do the Scots really hate the English? I thought you were all one country now?"

"Well, hate is rather a strong word, but many do still harbour resentment towards the English because of the history between the two countries. In fact there is going to be a referendum - a vote - in Scotland soon, to see if they want to remain as part of the United Kingdom or not. They probably feel antagonistic because some English King in the Middle Ages sent his little brother to conquer them and said he could keep any of the land he took. Naming no names!"

Richard frowned, taking Rose's comment seriously. "I was neither the first nor the only conqueror of the Scottish borders, you know. Nor was I the least merciful - in fact you might argue I was the most merciful. I took Berwick by siege and then Edinburgh capitulated without any blood spilled. I forbade my men to burn any villages or to rape or kill any of the occupants who surrendered to us. Unlike the Bitch of Anjou, who let her troops rampage through northern England before luring my father and brother out of Ludlow and ambushing them dishonourably, humiliating my father by placing a paper crown on his head and murdering my brother, Edmund, who was only seventeen, AFTER he had surrendered."

His voice was getting more clipped, though no louder, as his anger increased. She saw that steely coldness in his eyes as he spoke of Margaret of Anjou and she could really sense what it must be like to have Richard Plantagenet as an enemy - not good! Of course, he had only been nine years old when his father and brother had been executed, so he hadn't been able to exact his vengeance at the time. He had a fierce, ruthless side, a fiery temper at times and occasionally acted impetuously. He also had a natural authority that he exercised when required and he was an unrepentant killer in the heat of battle, by his own admission.

Conversely, she also knew him to be gentle, honest, loyal, empathetic, fair, tolerant and generous. He had both good and bad character traits. He was just a man, after all - if a pretty special one.

So Rose enlisted Torstein's help and, of course, they had to request that the foreign armourers came to England, as Richard had no passport. She told Torstein it was for a friend who had a problem with getting his passport renewed, but who was well off enough to pay the fares of the men concerned. Luckily Torstein was not a nosy person and accepted this explanation. He was very helpful and communicated with the German and Swedish armourers, efficiently arranging for them to travel first class to England urgently for a meeting with Richard. It was lucky he spoke both languages fluently, as this helped to overcome their suspicions at such an unusual request.

Richard met them both together several days later and they were happy to co-operate and make matching leg pieces and arm parts similar to Richard's photo. They measured him in detail and confirmed they would return with the finished armour within the month.

When the English armourer, Bill Best, met Richard he was expecting a jumped up rich guy who assumed money could perform miracles and wanted to dress up and play at being a knight in shining armour. He was surprised to say the least when he came face to face with an unassuming, knowledgeable and accomplished fighter who knew exactly what he needed and the difficulties faced by the necessity for speed in the armour's making. Richard showed him the photo of the armour and the helm he wanted. If he managed to take the helmet back with him it might be another way to change the result of the battle. If, as many thought, his helmet had been either knocked off his head or the strap securing it had been cut, he wanted to try to prevent this happening. He couldn't tell Bill why he needed the added security just for a re-enactment, but invented a story that he had had a previous head injury (he didn't explain that it was over five hundred years before!) and therefore needed the added protection for his already damaged skull. Luckily, Bill bought his explanation and said he thought he could create a suitable helm.

"But, Richard," he added. "If you have injured your head before, having a helmet fixed onto it might be counterproductive, if you understand me."

"How so?" asked Richard, intrigued.

"Well, suppose you accidentally got hit on the top of the helm with a pole axe or mace during the re-enactment - something heavy? The shock waves passing through a rigid helmet would be tremendous and if your skull is that vulnerable it might cause a concussion or worse!"

"You're right, of course," said Richard. He hadn't heard the word 'concussion' before, but intuited the general meaning. And of course his possible injuries were unlikely to happen 'accidentally' in the real battle.

"Any suggestions, then, Bill?"

"Yes. Suppose I made a double skinned helm, a bit like a motorbike helmet only in metal rather than plastic. If the outer layer was of a softer metal, it would crumple when hit thereby absorbing most of the force of the blow. It would at least give you a chance to get out of there before any further damage."

"Brilliant!" grinned Richard. "Let's do it!"

Hero

Having ordered the armour sections, Rose and Richard had a little breathing space and rode out together for the first time. Rose had obtained all the equipment she needed, primarily from the trusty EBay: saddle, bridle, blankets, boots, hat, grooming equipment and all the paraphernalia that was needed to keep a horse happy and well looked after. Richard had also obtained a modern spinal belt which Rose had ordered and bought for him. It was made from a stiff, padded material and was adjustable by a Velcro fastening. Richard loved Velcro! When he tried it on, he announced that it was supportive and comfortable and would be tremendously helpful when riding - he thought he might even be able to dispense with wearing his armour under his clothes for hunting, if he used the belt.

Rose felt excited and not a little nervous as she waited for Richard to bring out their horses. He looked excited too, although it was a little disconcerting to see him wearing a modern riding hat - he had also a tweedy type jacket with beige jodhpurs and black boots - he looked fit and athletic as he marched over to Rose, and helped her to mount Goldy. He expressed some surprise that she rode like a man instead of side saddle, but admitted it was more practical. Both Goldy and Rebel looked amazingly well groomed and shining, their manes and tails flowing tangle-free and beautiful. She asked the stable hand to take their photo for her when she and Richard were both seated on their horses. She always took lots of photos so that she would have as many as possible of Richard, in order to remember him when or if they had to part.

"Shall we take them for a few turns around the paddock first, just to get used to them?" she asked, realising she was trying to delay the moment when her lack of riding talent might become apparent to Richard.

"If you wish, Rose," Richard agreed, his lips twitching in amusement. He obviously realised she was uncomfortable on the, still strange, horse.

They walked their horses into the enclosed paddock and Richard led the way, starting at a walk and glancing behind him frequently to make sure Rose was alright.

"Ready to trot?" he called, his voice echoing around the indoor paddock, as he urged Rebel into a trot without waiting for Rose's reply. "I'll trot round 'til I'm behind you, then you trot round behind me, OK?"

Rose was starting to feel a bit more comfortable on Goldy now and, when Richard and Rebel had completed their circuit, she squeezed with her knees and Goldy sprang forwards into a proud trot, his head up and alert. She had ridden a little as a teenager, but never a horse as responsive as Goldy. He seemed to anticipate what she wanted and his gait was comfortable and steady with none of the erratic sideways shying that she had come across in other horses. She reached her desired destination behind Richard and he immediately trotted off again. Rebel was obviously more spirited than Goldy, tossing his dark mane and snorting in protest as Richard controlled him expertly. After a few circuits, they progressed to a canter and Rose was starting to enjoy it, relaxing into the saddle and using her legs to signal her instructions to Goldy.

"Shall we go outside?" Richard said, widening his eyes and emphasising the word "outside" as if it were somewhere dangerous and spooky.

Rose rolled her eyes and said: "I think I'm ready to brave the wild outdoors! Come on then!"

And she squeezed her knees, putting Goldy into a canter and riding out of the paddock ahead of Richard. He said nothing, just grunted in annoyance and suddenly Rebel had gained on her and was about to overtake Goldy. She panicked a bit then, as many horses she had ridden had hated other horses overtaking them but, despite her tension, Goldy was as solid as the earth beneath their feet and happily gave way to Rebel and Richard. He led the way then, slowing a little to allow Rose to keep pace and they headed into Hockley Woods.

"Richard, don't forget that there will be walkers and dogs and cyclists and things in the woods - it isn't as isolated as it used to be."

"I know, I know! It's a shame as I will have to modify Rebel's speed, I would love to let him have his head and gallop, but that will have to wait for another time and place. How are you finding Goldy?" he called back over his shoulder.

"He's fantastic! I love him!" she cried, her exhilaration clear in her voice.

"I'm glad to hear it. You chose well - he's perfect for you. As Rebel is for me - a bit of a challenge, but worth the effort - he's a great ride. The belt is supporting my spine well too, Rose; very satisfactory."

They spent a happy hour and a half riding through the woods, exchanging banter and eventually found their way back to the stables. They dismounted and saw their horses were properly stabled, fed and watered before leaving for home. Rose's legs were shaking terribly, because it had been so long since she had ridden and they had been mounted for about two hours in all, a long time for her. Richard laughed as she groaned at her aching muscles.

"I'll have you at home in the saddle in no time, Rose!" he chuckled and she had to admit he had been a gentle and patient teacher, understanding her trepidation and taking things slowly in order to help her.

After that, they rode out often, fitting it in around her patients at home and the endless research they were doing regarding his return and plans for Bosworth. Rose came to adore those times, alone with Richard, gradually getting to know more about him. They often went quite slowly and chatted comfortably as they went.

"Did you go riding often with Anne?" she asked him one day.

"Yes, of course. And little Ned, too. He was just beginning to show promise as a horseman and he had a natural, instinctive way with his falcon - he would have been an excellent huntsman."

His eyes were focused on the distance as if he saw something there that was invisible to Rose. She supposed he was thinking of his poor, dead wife and son and immediately felt guilty for bringing up the subject and spoiling his mood. What a sad life he had had!

Abruptly, he urged Rebel forward cursing under his breath and leaving Rose behind. She was both shocked and alarmed at his reaction. Was he angry with her? Maybe he was distressed and needed to get away. Then, all at once, she saw the reason for his sudden move. Up ahead was a junction of two wide paths with one coming in to join with theirs at an angle of about forty five degrees. The trees were sparse in that part of the woods and only short, stubby bushes formed the area between the two paths. She could see another rider coming along the one about to intersect with theirs, galloping hard and Rose swore softly as she realised there was a man with a dog directly in the strange rider's path!

"Why isn't she slowing down to a walk?" she thought, as that was the unspoken rule when a rider came upon a pedestrian or dog. All at once, she realised what Richard had already seen - the rider was a tiny girl and her horse was bolting, completely out of control. Richard was already halfway to the junction, ahead of the galloping horse and terrified rider but she didn't see how he could help from where he was. By the time he reached the junction, the hapless pedestrian and dog would have passed it and the runaway horse would be upon them.

Then Richard suddenly turned Rebel, who reared up and leapt over the stand of bushes between the two paths, as easily as a cat jumps a garden wall. Richard wheeled him around in a tight circle, dust billowing up around Rebel's hooves as he slid a little and ended up facing the rogue horse. The horse was smaller than Rebel, but had clearly been spooked by something, as his ears were flat and his eyes were rolling in his head, the whites showing even from that distance. Rose put her hand to her mouth in horror as she saw what must surely happen. It was now Richard who was directly in the speeding horse's path - a crash was inevitable! She was afraid to watch, but couldn't tear her gaze away.

Richard turned Rebel again so that he was sideways on to the galloping runaway, and with the horse only about thirty feet away from him now, raised his arm, his palm towards the oncoming horse, in an instinctive 'stop' signal. At the same time he hissed a loud "Sshhh!" sound. To Rose's amazement and delight, the other horse immediately slowed to a trot, Richard smoothly moved Rebel to one side and, as the horse trotted by, reached out and grabbed the bridle, gradually slowing it still more until they both came to a stop about ten feet from the dog. The frightened horse was quivering and his flanks heaved as he panted after his exertions.

"Are you alright, little lady?" Richard asked the pale, petrified rider.

She nodded and promptly slid off the horse, landing on the ground inelegantly. Richard dismounted too and leading the two horses in one hand, put his arm around the child's shoulders.

"That was pretty frightening, wasn't it?" he said, softly. "And you were very brave to hang on for so long. Where is your mother, little one?"

"She's back there," the girl said, and immediately burst into tears, in shock.

By this time, Rose had managed to guide Goldy up to the path's junction and took Rebel's reins from Richard as he held them out to her wordlessly. He led the child and her horse back the way they had come while Rose waited. The dog walker looked up at her as she passed.

"Bloody hell!" he said. "That was a close shave! Thank goodness your bloke was quick thinking enough to act like that, otherwise poor old Bruno would have been a goner!"

Rose nodded dumbly as Bruno came up to his owner, wagging his tail, quite unaware of how close he had come to being toast! She could hear Richard saying something to the girl's mother, whom she now glimpsed up ahead on the path. She couldn't make out the words, but heard a woman's voice, sounding a little peeved. Immediately Richard cut across her and she heard him say, his voice uncharacteristically raised:

"Madam! Your daughter could have been killed or badly injured. She shouldn't have been riding that horse - it is much too large and strong for her! I suggest you hold your tongue and show a little gratitude! And ensure you take better care of your child in the future!"

He stalked back along the path to Rose and mounted Rebel smoothly. "Ignorant witch!" he muttered, glaring angrily back at the mother.

The dog walker called up to him:

"Hey! Thank you, mate. That could have been very nasty. Here, let me shake your hand." Richard offered it to the man, dumbly. The man pumped it up and down. "I'm grateful, truly mate, thanks again!"

He walked off finally with Bruno trailing along behind, still wagging his springy tail.

Richard and Rose looked at each other. She was still trembling and he was very pale. He took a deep breath, letting it out in a deep sigh, releasing his pent up tension.

Richard had behaved exactly as she would have expected; he had shown courage, presence of mind, chivalry and selflessness. And his precise control of Rebel was awesome! He was a true hero knight. And his shining armour would be ready soon!

Read All About It

Richard had become enthusiastic about the Internet, especially after seeing it work so well with the armour project. Having already discovered that he had lost the Battle of Bosworth, Richard insisted he wanted to explore more of what had been written about himself on the Internet, stating that he wished to know the worst. Rose said that she ought to be present when he did, in order to explain anything he found on there (and because she was worried he would get upset again – there was such a lot of nonsense written about him, by idiots and those who just liked stirring up trouble).

The next day there wasn't enough time first thing, as she had quite a busy day ahead of her seeing patients in her home practice. She asked him to wait until she was free, telling him she would help him search the Internet that evening after her last patient. However, when she returned to the living room after finishing her final notes for the day, she found him in front of the PC, leaning forwards with his head in his hands. He had managed to work out how to get on-line by himself, from having seen Rose do it before, and had found an article about the Looking for Richard Project that had discovered his bones in the Leicester Social Services car park. He looked up as she entered and his face was pale and blotchy. His beautiful eyes had a desolate look, haunted and defeated.

"Rose, I have read exactly how they think I met my death at the battle. They describe each injury as if they were there – can they really know how a man died by looking at his bones? Even worse, they say I was subjected to humiliation wounds after my death, that my body was insulted and despoiled, that I was thrown naked over a horse and taken into Leicester. That my corpse was thrown into a grave that was too small and that I may not even have been given proper Christian burial rites. My life has been hard, God knows, but my death seems to have been even harder! This must be a nightmare, surely it can't be true? It is not right for a man to see his own skeleton, his own skull, bearing the injuries that killed him! It is too much to endure!

"But that isn't the worst – the article has comments from ordinary people below it. What they say is…shocking! They say I deserved such an end, mocking my deformity, insulting my name, cursing me! Such hatred!"

And he collapsed into muffled sobs, burying his face down onto his arms, the terrible choking sound of his suppressed cries piercing her heart. She didn't know how to help him, but instinctively did the only thing that could have at that moment. She didn't try to explain anything or give any words of comfort or consolation, she just sat down beside him and embraced him, moving his head onto her shoulder, stroking his hair and rocking him as if he were a small child who had fallen over and hurt himself. She could feel the heaving, silent sobs, convulsing through his body. Somehow, the fact that he was suppressing the sound, trying to hold his emotions in even through this, touched her more than if he had just let go completely. They remained there for several minutes and despite her sympathy for the despair she knew he felt, part of her felt a strange joy also, that he needed her at this moment; that she had the power to bring him some small comfort, comfort for a lost king.

She remembered how much he had borne over the last couple of years of his life – he had barely mentioned to her how he felt about the deaths of Anne and the two Edwards, but she guessed he had been holding that in too, as many men do. This had been the final straw, the trigger which opened the floodgates that he had kept shut for so long.

Eventually, he pulled back from her, turning his face away, ashamed at his emotional display. She passed him a box of tissues in silence.

"I am sorry to act in such an unmanly way before thee, Rose. You must think me a puling child to weep so. Verily, I am ashamed."

She noticed absently that he reverted slightly to his mediaeval mode of speech when he was feeling emotional.

"Don't be silly! I only wish I could offer you better comfort. If only you hadn't seen that while you were by yourself – you were right, it is a terrible thing to find out. But know that there are many who do love you still, even in this time and age. They won't rest until your reputation is restored and your body finds repose in a sanctified place. I am one such."

"It is my own fault, I was ever impatient. I should have waited for you, as you requested. I said I wanted to know the worst. Is this the worst or is there more?"

And Rose began to try to explain to him all she knew about his life and death and details of what the Tudors did to his reputation and his family afterwards. At times it made him angry, at times indignant or confused. He wept at some parts, like when she told how it was thought his illegitimate son, John, had been executed by the Tudors, and also his niece, Margaret, as an elderly lady.

"My strong, healthy son? And poor Margaret! How can God allow such evil to happen? I thought he was on my side; I was sure I was going to win the battle and that it would prove I had had the right to take the throne. Does this mean I was wrong? Would it have been better to leave England in the hands of the Woodvilles controlling Prince Edward as King Edward V?" he cried hoarsely, his voice anguished and tortured.

Rose hesitated. The subject matter was getting uncomfortably close to the fate of the princes and she wasn't ready to broach that yet.

"To be honest I don't know. Maybe God has nothing to do with it. Maybe it's all just luck and chance. All I know is that time and again evil flourishes in the world and good people just have to do their best to stamp it out. We can only do what we feel is right, Richard. But sometimes it's a struggle."

"You speak the truth there. My whole life has been a struggle. Do you know, when I was a young boy, I decided that I would like to be a lute player, a troubadour, as my profession? I had no idea that I might ever be a prince, let alone King, although my noble family would never have let me be a simple troubadour. But I did enjoy playing and singing. Perhaps I might have become a churchman - that is what most younger sons ended up as, but then everything changed when Ned became king and we were suddenly royalty. And then he died. I was so proud when I was crowned King: God's anointed, chosen one. Yet it hasn't made me happy. I was happier when I was doing simple things like playing music, riding in the forest, spending time with my children. I wish I could have kept to my childhood ambition!"

"I think you were chosen by God to be King because you are strong enough to bear that particular burden. Not many are."

"Then why did he take it away from me? If I was meant to do some good...?"

"I don't know. But you're here now – maybe that's something to do with it. Maybe you're meant to be here so you can find out what went wrong and go back and fix it. Maybe you are meant to get a second chance!"

He looked at her, frowning and chewed his lower lip, mulling it all over in his mind.

"Well, if that is the case, I must learn as much as I can so that I can guard against the same things happening again. Even if it pains me I must find out why I was betrayed at Bosworth and I need your help. Will you help me? You are my best friend in this strange world."

"Of course I'll help you; it would be an honour!"

He squeezed her hand and gave a rueful smile.

"It is I who am honoured to have so trusty a friend. I feel a little better now. Could we have a cup of tea, do you think?"

They spent a lot of time after that researching the Internet, books and articles, trying to piece together what really happened at Bosworth. In this he wasn't much wiser than Rose as he had come forward in time before Bosworth took place. Rose showed Richard her library of Ricardian related books, both on her bookshelves and on her Kindle – he was astonished by how many she had and wanted to read them all. She suggested he only read the non-fiction ones, or a lot of time would be wasted. She did let him read The Daughter of Time though, as it was such a positive view of him, for a change. It was pleasant to see him smiling and chuckling as he read.

"I like this book – there is a wonderful description of the Tydder; they say he is 'shabby' and compare him to a crab! The facts are not all quite right though…"

Regarding the non-fiction works, he could correct some of the background to his reign and disputed much of what had been written by the Tudor historians, as she had expected. There were a number of questions that needed to be answered, such as: Where did the actual battle really take place? Was the fatal charge Richard made at Bosworth planned or an impulsive decision? Did his horse stumble, was it killed or did Richard dismount deliberately? Was Richard betrayed by both the Stanley brothers or just one of them? Did Northumberland also betray him or was he just unable to join the battle for some valid reason? Did Northumberland deliberately fail to call York to arms on the King's behalf, was it an oversight, or was there genuinely plague in York at the time? Some of these things were within Richard's control and some were not. He could make educated guesses about a number of them but not all.

And, of course, there was that other important question that he had not yet addressed and that she hadn't felt able to ask him about directly. Perhaps she was afraid of what his answer would be – many of his ideas were quite alien to her and she had to admit that she didn't really understand some of his mediaeval ways. On the one hand, she didn't want to believe that he might have ordered his own brother's sons to be put to death to make his own grasp on the crown more secure. And yet, she knew his motivation was duty above all else. What would he do if he thought his duty lay in securing the throne in order to end the strife of the previous thirty years, and the princes were obstructing this? Was he capable of murder if he thought the ends justified the means? She finally decided not to think about that for the time being. She should just concentrate on their urgent research - how to get him back to 1485 and how to avoid his death at Bosworth. She couldn't help wondering, though, why he hadn't brought the question up himself - he had come across it in the books and on the Internet, for sure. Did his silence indicate a guilty conscience?

Music

July 21st 2014

As a surprise and to help Richard feel a little more at home in the twenty first century, Rose had booked tickets for a special treat in London. She refused to tell Richard where they were going, but advised him to dress "smart casual".

He looked at her, puzzled, his fine eyebrows raised.

"Isn't that a contradiction in terms?" he asked, amused.

She explained the principle to him and he went off immediately to sort out an outfit. He was quite a smart dresser anyway, Rose had noticed, and he decided on a grey pair of slacks, a pale blue shirt and his new black leather jacket. She had to admit it suited him. On his feet he wore Italian leather shoes, black and well polished. He didn't wear a tie, but asked her if he should take one – he hated them, as most modern men did, and preferred an open neck. However, he was intrigued by zips as well as Velcro and always had a look of fascinated amusement on his face when using either of these fastenings. He liked the neatness and functionality of them and the fact that they were so quick to use. It had taken her at least ten minutes to get him away from the first item of clothing he had seen that had a zip – he just kept zipping it up and down again, chuckling softly to himself.

She took him down to the station at Rayleigh and they got their tickets and waited for their train.

He had seemed a little subdued over the last few days – she wondered if he was feeling daunted by the task ahead – winning Bosworth. Or perhaps he was missing his wife and son and the friends he'd left behind in the fifteenth century. It wouldn't be surprising if he felt somewhat depressed after all he had been through in the last few years, and then being catapulted willy nilly into the twenty first century, not knowing whether he would be able to get back home again...

He enjoyed the train journey, remarking on how smooth and comfortable it was. He was becoming accustomed to twenty first century life and was now rarely shocked by anything in this strange new world. They arrived at South Kensington station and Richard immediately became more animated and interested. He pointed out anything that still survived from the times he knew.

Then: "That wasn't here in my time," he said firmly, pointing to the Royal Albert Hall.

"That's where we're going," Rose replied. His eyebrows shot up and he opened his mouth to ask something, but she forestalled his questions by saying simply: "Don't ask me anything yet – we'll be there soon and all will be revealed – it's a surprise, so just wait and see!"

His eyebrows came together into an exaggerated mock frown, his lips pursed, but he said nothing, following her meekly across to the impressive building. Rose told him about Queen Victoria and her Albert, after whom the building was named and he listened attentively – he was always fascinated by anything regarding his royal successors.

As they approached the iconic venue, Richard was obviously interested in the people who were also on their way there and the colourful posters and advertisements which were displayed everywhere.

"It is marvellous that there are printed words everywhere and that everyone can read! That was my dream – to bring education and reading – knowledge - to everyone, not just the clergy and the wealthy. It is so exciting to see it in practice – to know that it is possible to achieve! Did you know that William Caxton was a friend of mine? He was an incredible man, so advanced in his thinking! I loved seeing those books that he printed!"

As he spoke, his eyes shone with passion and enthusiasm for the subject. Rose noticed that his whole demeanour had changed and he had become much more animated and talkative – she liked it.

"Yes, I did know you knew Caxton. Did you have many books yourself?"

"Not enough!" he laughed. "And not as many as you have. I have seldom seen so many books in one place – astonishing!"

"What about the library?" she said.

"Ah yes, but that is a communal resource, isn't it? Yours is the best private collection I've seen."

Rose felt irrationally proud. "Did you have a favourite book?"

"Hmm! That's a difficult question. Of course I had a hand written Book of Hours that I used all the time, but that wasn't printed. I think that's the book I've missed the most since I've been here, though. But I loved also some of the Arthurian tales – anything chivalric!"

"I thought as much!" she smiled. "Actually, your book of hours still exists – well part of it at least. Apparently Margaret Beaufort took it after you...I mean, after the battle and it survived down the years."

He looked wistful, his sad eyes lowered for an instant.

"Maybe we could get you a copy," she said. "Or at least copies of some of the content."

"Really?" he said eagerly. "I do remember part of my personal prayer, but it would be lovely to be able to read the others again."

"Will you tell me it, Richard? I would love to hear your personal prayer."

He smiled, closed his eyes and recited:

"Lord Jesus Christ, deign to free me, thy servant King Richard, from every tribulation, sorrow and trouble in which I am placed...hear me, in the name of all thy goodness, for which I give thanks, and for all the gifts granted to me, because thou made me from nothing and redeemed me out of thy bounteous love and pity from eternal damnation to the promise of eternal life."

"That's so beautiful." she said. "Thank you."

They had arrived at the entrance they needed and she guided him inside and up the stairs, giving the tickets to an usher and helping him to find their allocated seats.

"Is it a Mystery Play?" Richard asked.

"No, it's not a play. I'll tell you now: it is a special music show. We have a season of different classical music concerts all through the summer, called the Promenade concerts – Proms for short. They are very famous and celebrate all the great composers, but this one I chose for you as it is chamber music, which I think is more like the music of your time – I thought it would make you feel at home and cheer you up a bit!"

The music was by Rameau, performed by Les Arts Florissants and titled Pièces de Clavecin en Concerts. It included a harpsichord as well as violin and Rose felt it had the spirit of mediaeval music, more than any of the other Proms that year. She knew it wasn't the correct time period, but it had the right 'feel'. She hoped Richard would like it.

At the moment, he was gazing around in rapt amazement at the famous concert venue, asking questions about the lighting, the seats, the decor and countless other aspects of the place. She did her best to explain everything to him – it was amazing how difficult it was to talk in depth about twenty first century technology to a fifteenth century king!

When the lights dimmed a little and the musicians appeared, his attention was fixed on them and when they began to play, a gentle smile softened the contours of his face. As the Hall's acoustics amplified and purified the notes, he was transported by the music, as if hypnotised. He didn't say a word for the entire performance and, as she sneakily took a peek at his face, she saw his eyes were bright with emotion. She looked away, allowing him his private thoughts and, when the performance finally ended, he stood up and applauded enthusiastically with the rest of the audience, shaking his head in wonder. He turned to Rose, beaming, and then suddenly hugged her to him, whispering: "Thank you so much. I never enjoyed a music recital so much in my whole life. What an experience!"

"I'm glad you enjoyed it," she smiled back.

"I certainly did. The only other time I have been so moved and impressed by music was when Anne and I started bringing the best singers in the country to Middleham to join our choir. After a year or so, it had become the best choir in England, maybe Europe - at least I think it was - and I loved to listen to their renditions of various pieces. We used to have some great feasting and entertainment at Middleham."

He looked wistful and Rose suggested visiting Middleham and York the following month as part of their research.

"But remember that it won't be the same as you remember it - Middleham is in ruins now and York has changed. A lot," she said.

He nodded gravely. "I would still like to go there. I want to show you where I live - lived," he said.

Chapter Four - August 2014

An Englishman in New York

They managed a visit to Yorkshire in early August and stayed at a lovely B & B about six miles from Middleham. But on the drive there they took a slight detour and dropped in to Richard's birthplace, Fotheringhay.

Fotheringhay, in Northamptonshire, was only a couple of miles from the main road leading North, but it felt like the middle of the countryside. The castle was all but destroyed, nothing remaining but the large mound or mott and a chunk of masonry from the castle itself. Richard was pleased with the plaque which was mounted on the railing commemorating his birth at the location in 1452. Someone had recently left a white rose there and he smiled softly on seeing it.

"You are right, there are still people alive today who believe in my memory," he murmured, gently stroking the rose's petals and smiling ruefully.

He glanced at Rose, who returned his smile. It was still a lovely location, very peaceful and the river Nene at the bottom of the mound was beautiful with the sunlight sparkling along its surface. There were a couple of boats moored beside the remains of the castle and a small, white dog belonging to one of them was racing back and forth along the bank. Rose's dogs had been left with a friend for the weekend, but this one, too, approached Richard as if he were its natural leader. It's funny how dogs can recognise authority, she thought.

They walked up a steep diagonal path, with steps cut into the mound, until they got to the top. Sheep had obviously been grazing here, from the droppings visible everywhere. It was warm and bright but a little breezy at the top. The site was now privately owned, but the public were allowed free access to wander over the remains and the views from up there were stunning.

"Was it like this in your day, Richard?" Rose asked.

"Not really, there was a castle here then!" he teased. "No, the river was similar, but the countryside was more forested then. So much of the old forests are gone now, aren't they?"

They went down into the village of Fotheringhay and visited the church where he was baptised, to pay their respects to his parents and brother, Edmund, who were buried there. It had a lovely ambiance and there was a whole exhibit devoted to Richard and his family. There was even a window showing his family's coats of arms.

As they had entered the church, a man was playing the piano, practising for a concert, they supposed. It created a warm, welcoming atmosphere and Richard's mood, which had been, she thought, a little sad to see that the castle was no longer there, became more buoyant, as it always did when he heard good music, helped by the reminders that his family was still remembered and honoured in the twenty first century.

Having cheered up, he pointed out different areas that he had known. He showed her the impressive pulpit that his brother, Edward, had gifted to the church, saying the colours had been a little brighter when he knew it and showing her his own device of the White Boar on it. He described the grand re-interment service that they had had for their father and brother, whose bodies had originally been buried in Pontefract, near to where they had been killed. The York brothers had had their family's bodies brought back to Fotheringhay in a great progress in 1476 during which

Richard had acted as the chief mourner. After the solemn and sacred ceremony, they had held huge festivities giving thanks for the deceased's lives. About twenty thousand people were present and partook of the celebrations. There had been fields full of tents, and feasting and drinking that went on for days.

Rose asked him what he thought about all the arguments which were going on about where his own remains were going to be re-interred. Had he intended that his body should be buried in York Minster after his death?

"I hadn't completely made my mind up, but I was leaning towards that, yes. I had decided to commission a chantry chapel and I had paid for one hundred holy brethren to say masses for Anne and Edward, and myself when I passed, for all eternity. York is a place I have grown to love and I believe they love me too. I felt more at home there than London, certainly. And I was intending, after the Tydder matter was resolved, to re-inter Anne there and Edward too. I was going to make it our family tomb. Anyway, I suppose she is still in Westminster Abbey, then?"

"She is, although the actual tomb has been lost."

He frowned and sighed. "My lovely Anne, lost?"

"I believe so, but the Richard III Society has put up a nice plaque to commemorate her. We can visit it another time if you wish?"

"Yes, I would like to pay my respects, and to my son, as well."

"Nobody knows where he was buried, Richard. They thought it was at Sheriff Hutton but that was apparently discredited later," she said.

"He was buried in Jervaulx Abbey, quite near to Middleham, where he died, but I would have had him re-interred in York as well, with his mother."

He gave another great sigh and then knelt before the altar in the church, paying his respects to those of his family who were at their eternal rest there. She knelt beside him, praying for him, that he would find the strength to do whatever was right for him and the country.

When they arose, she continued the conversation she had begun before their prayers.

"So, do you mind that Leicester Cathedral is going to have your remains, as it seems it will do? There are many who strenuously object to it."

"Do you know, Rose, I just can't find any enthusiasm about those bones, since I am alive and my bones are actually here in my body. I feel no attachment to those remains at all. It is a very weird feeling to be discussing where I should be buried when I am yet breathing!"

"Of course, it must be," Rose said. "I'm sorry; we can consider the subject closed."

He smiled.

"Thank you!" he said, with obvious relief.

"But that reminds me of a famous quote about you: 'Richard Liveth Yet!' - that's from a poem written about your family - your parents and their children, and it gives all their names, including those who died in infancy. For you, Richard, it just says 'Richard Liveth Yet'. It's why many people thought you must have been sickly as a child."

"Well, they're wrong - I was as healthy as a horse. At least until I was about ten or eleven, when my back started to curve."

They stopped speaking for a while, just enjoying the calm, welcoming atmosphere of the Church.

"This is a lovely church, isn't it? Did you know, well of course you wouldn't, that a couple heard strange martial music coming from this church, years ago? It was summer 1976, exactly five hundred years after your father and your brother, Edmund, were re-interred here."

"Hmm!" he said. "Mayhap there was another time slip apart from mine, then!"

They left the church at Fotheringhay after donating some money in the box located by the entrance.

Then they drove on towards York and Middleham. They didn't arrive at the B & B until after dark, as the roads had been at a standstill for much of the way, because of road works.

"We would have been quicker travelling by horse! I thought you said modern transport was more efficient." he said, deadpan.

She was about to argue with him when she saw him wink and break into a broad smile, and she laughed along with him. She was only just beginning to get used to his dry sense of humour and she really enjoyed it.

The B & B was lovely – they again had adjoining rooms although this time he had several changes of clothes (which he'd bought with her guidance) and knew how to use the bathroom properly. He had also left his sword in her bungalow in Rayleigh, although he had insisted on bringing his dagger, keeping it concealed in his trouser pocket.

They rose early for breakfast and, as the B & B was very near Jervaulx Abbey, they went to see if they could find his son, Edward's, grave. Richard located it immediately although there was only a small slab that remained there, without an inscription, and they left some white roses on it, while Richard knelt and prayed. His face was pale with suppressed grief and of course this was quite understandable, if not inevitable, as from his viewpoint it had only been just over a year since he had lost his beloved son. Rose wasn't sure how to respond to his obvious emotion and finally just gave his shoulder a little squeeze to show her support.

After that they travelled into York and he showed her some of the old places he knew there. He was delighted to find that Barley Hall was still extant and laid out as it was, more or less, in his era. He had once or twice visited the owner, William Snawsell, while on business in York and had dined in the great hall there. He was also interested in the Viking village exhibition, Jorvik, especially since he realised the Viking settlement must have been there when he knew York, right under his feet.

He remembered the Shambles and told her what kinds of shops had been there in his time. Then they visited York Minster. He smiled nostalgically as they entered the great Cathedral, staring up at the amazing stained glass windows, as everyone who visited it did.

He explained some of the more obscure depictions to her and described his son, Edward's, investiture as Prince of Wales, which had taken place in York. His eyes shone as he told of the pageantry, the colours, the clothes they wore and how their crowns glowed like fire in the sunlight. He relived it for her, vividly bringing to life that magical day when being king had seemed a blessing and not a curse. He described the mass held in the Minster itself and then the actual investiture in the Archbishop's Palace, where there was great feasting afterwards. He smiled to himself as he described his son, Edward's, rapt face when he first saw his father and mother dressed in their regalia and how their son had made his oath of allegiance in a clear, childlike voice, with no hesitation. Richard, his father and King, had girded on a sword of state, placed a ring on his son's finger, a golden garland on his head and a staff in his hand. Then Richard's eyes were bright with unshed tears as he said, his voice breaking with emotion: "I was so proud of him; I loved him so much!"

Then he smiled again, sadly, as they walked to the far end of the cathedral.

"I'm not sure I like all these tourists swarming around. This is meant to be a place of worship and yet they are charging a fee to enter it. And what on Earth is that!?" he exclaimed, pointing, as he caught sight of the great grey pod, as Rose called it, in which one could discover more about the stained glass windows and see a panel or two close up. It was there to create the right kind of lighting to highlight the panels at their best. But it did look very incongruous and modern in such an ancient Mediaeval cathedral. She explained what it was and they went in and had a look. He was interested in seeing the panels close up and marvelled at the colours of the glass, but stated that the pod itself was an eyesore!

Finally they visited the Richard III Experience at Monk Bar. Rose was slightly concerned that someone would recognise him as he stood facing his own portrait, but no-one seemed to notice the uncanny resemblance! Richard was both flattered and dismayed by the exhibition. Flattered that there was an exhibition devoted entirely to him and dismayed that a lot of the information was inaccurate, notably the "Horrible Histories" part of it.

"And why do they have a film about the Battle of Towton here?" he asked. "I didn't even take part in that!"

"Well, I suppose they think it's relevant because it's how the Yorkists finally got the throne," she replied.

He raised his eyebrows but said nothing. He had a long wander around the gift shop in the downstairs part of the Experience, and bought quite a few items, including a replica portrait.

"Being here in York is...strange," he said. "This is no longer the old York I knew, it is all new to me, yet much of it does still remain."

They decided not to bother visiting the Henry Tudor Experience.

"I might do something I'd regret!" said Richard. "Like get arrested for vandalism!"

They did, however, walk to the site of the exhibit, as it was being held at Micklegate Bar, where the heads of Richard's father, the Duke of York, and brother, Edmund, were supposed to have been displayed by Marguerite of Anjou after they had been killed at the Battle of Wakefield. Richard stood there gazing up at the old remains of the Bar, his eyes serious and distant, his hands clasped together and his lips murmuring a heartfelt prayer. She wondered what was going through his mind. Although to her it all seemed so distant in time, it wasn't to him. Was he picturing how it would have been to look up and see the severed and bloody heads of his own father and brother?

"Is it really true that your father's and brother Edmund's heads were impaled on spikes here?" she asked.

"Yes, it is. I was not permitted to see it, of course, as I was only eight years old at the time it happened. But I think, in a way, what I imagined must have been even worse that the actuality. My dreams were haunted by terrible images of their heads, still moving and talking, but disembodied and bloody, my father's head crowned with a paper crown. I used to awaken nightly, sweating and terrified, for months afterwards.

"Sometimes I would dream of Edmund's death. It was said that he was caught fleeing the battle and was murdered by that butcher, Lord Clifford. I dreamed that I was there when it happened, I could hear him crying out for mercy and yet he was shown none. He was but seventeen.

"At other times, I dreamed myself in his place and felt the cold steel of the dagger that was used to murder him, slide between my ribs and up into my heart, a strange, empty, hollow feeling, not painful but terrible and frightening. I would see the blood come spilling out of the hole left as Clifford withdrew the dagger, my knees buckling as I fell to the ground. Then I would wake up."

"My God! How terrible, Richard," Rose gasped.

Need You Now

"Do you think it has affected you through your life?"

"No doubt it has. I find that sometimes I cannot feel pity for the dying, it has hardened my heart, inured me to bloody and brutal acts. I think I could not have survived otherwise. It's as if my heart now has a wall of iron built around it to protect it from ever feeling the pain of loss again. It is a rare few who manage to break down its barrier and know the deepest secrets of my heart, even fewer who have been able to elicit those feelings I have shielded so thoroughly. Anne Neville was one such, and Edward, my son, of course.

"When little Ned died, I thought I might go mad with grief. I couldn't eat, drink or sleep. My friends were concerned for my well-being and forced me to eat; else I fear I might have succumbed to the sin of self-murder by starvation.

"The grief affected Anne just as much, hastened her own demise and brought me again to my knees before God, praying for relief from my pain. Although our marriage was partly a matter of property and politics, I did love her well. Perhaps not with the same kind of passion that Edward loved the Woodville woman, but I loved her in a gentler way, as she loved me. We were good friends and as close as family – I had known her almost all my life as far back as I can remember. We used to play by the river in Middleham, trying to catch fish and eels when we were children. She was such a gentle lady, a little frail but strong of spirit. She had resisted the illness that took her for several years before she finally succumbed. She didn't reveal how she suffered, but fought it tooth and nail. She only gave up after little Ned died. She felt her reason for living was gone.

"I tried to tell her that I needed her still, that I was a reason to carry on, but I was obviously not enough. There was an eclipse the day she died, as if heaven itself mourned her passing. Of course, many said it was an evil omen, but I don't believe that. No, it was heaven mourning her. Afterwards, the only thing that forced me to go on was the duty I had to my other love, England, to protect her and heal her of the corruption which had corroded her heart for so long."

Rose was silent for a while after this long, impassioned speech. What a tragic life he had had. Why did one man have to suffer so much grief and bloodshed? Of course,

Richard wasn't the only one in those times to endure his share of death and battles. Many a young lass had lost her true love in the Wars of the Roses, many mothers had lost their sons.

"Do you know the expression 'Wars of the Roses'?" Rose asked, curious because she had heard that in those days it wasn't known as such.

"I have seen it mentioned on the Internet, but I knew not anything about it before," said Richard.

Rose explained that the battles and wars he had lived through were now known by that famous title, because of the white rose of York and the red of Lancaster.

"We just knew the separate battles," he said. "And, yes, the white rose was a major emblem of the house of York, but I hardly ever saw the red rose used for Lancaster."

"Maybe it was a later Tudor invention to make Henry's rule seem more as if it were meant to be - they combined the roses and brought peace to the land - that was their propaganda."

"I, too, wanted to end all the civil strife along with the corruption. Perhaps, after all it was impossible to do it."

He glanced over to her, shrugged resignedly and they turned back, heading towards a restaurant where they had made a reservation for an evening meal. Richard was much more assured at ordering from the menu now and instinctively took charge, easily catching the waitress's eye and seemingly unaware of the girl's nervous blush as he asked her to recommend a dish. She wondered if he was actually so naïve that he was unaware of the magnetic attraction surrounding him or if he was just playing it cool. He wasn't easy to read.

That evening they participated in a Ghost Walk, reluctantly on Richard's part, but Rose persuaded him they weren't going to be conjuring up the dead or doing anything sacrilegious and he finally agreed to tag along. The stories were mostly old and silly but the guide was amusing and had a spellbinding voice, which added to the atmosphere. Everyone seemed to enjoy it, even Richard, who was heard chuckling at one rather bawdy story involving a grave robber and a not-quite-dead lady corpse! He was enthralled by the story of Guy Fawkes as well.

"You actually celebrate someone who tried to destroy Parliament?" he asked Rose, amazed.

"Well, we're supposed to be celebrating that the Gunpowder Plot was foiled," she explained. "Although I think there are quite a few people today who sympathise with old Guy!"

It's All Coming Back to Me Now

The next day was earmarked for spending at Middleham, which had been his favourite home. Richard was very quiet as they drew up to park in the road beside the ruins of the old castle. He bit his lip and frowned as they passed into the courtyard and bought their tickets at the shop that sold gifts and refreshments. There was a small exhibit about the Middleham Jewel, that had been found in recent years, but was reckoned to be of Mediaeval origin. A replica of it was displayed there.

"God's teeth, that's the pendant that Anne lost years ago!" he exclaimed delightedly. "Do you think they'll give it back to me?" he joked. "I was the one who gave it to her after all! She was so mortified when it disappeared. She thought I would be angry and tried to conceal from me that she'd lost it. We had only been married a short time and I think she had heard that George had created a terrible fuss when Isabel had lost a piece of jewellery and was afraid I was as petty as he was. You did know that George married Anne's sister, Isabel, didn't you? Well, I pretended to be cross with Anne for a short time, but her little face was so upset that I didn't have the heart to tease her for long. She was so relieved when I said it mattered not a jot to me. I promised I would get her another one, but I could never find one quite the same. I think I got her a new arras instead in the end. Oh well, I'm glad it's been found at last and many people will be able to admire its beauty."

They sauntered out of the shop with the guide book Rose had bought.

"Why did you buy that?" he asked. "Don't you think I'm better qualified to guide you than a book?" His blue eyes were twinkling again and she smiled at him.

"Well, you are of course, but there are some parts of the castle that were changed after your time, so I thought you might be interested in them, that's all," she said.

"I'm only teasing you, Rose!" he laughed and put his hand lightly on her shoulder, giving it a short squeeze.

He looked up at the ruined castle, shaking his head ruefully.

"It's quite hard, you know, seeing my home like this," he sighed. "It makes me feel…old!"

"Well you are nearly five hundred and sixty two!" Rose replied. He chose to ignore that.

"Do you see up there?" He pointed to one of the corners of the main keep. "That was where my private rooms were. There was a sleeping chamber there with a privy, although I used to sleep with Anne mostly, unless I had been working very late and didn't want to disturb her. Her rooms were just across the courtyard – there was a bridge joining the two sections. Do you know some actually thought I stopped lying with her through personal choice, after she became ill? But it almost killed me not to be able to hold her. It was the doctors who said her illness might be transmitted to me if we continued to lie together."

"That's a lovely phrase – 'to lie with someone'. It's much nicer than our expressions today. I like 'being with child' too – much more beautiful than 'pregnant'," said Rose.

They wandered about and he pointed out various rooms and explained their functions. He was quite proud of the renovation work he'd had done to add a second floor to the keep and bring more light into the great hall. It no longer survived, but he showed her where it would have been. They climbed the tower and admired the view, which he said hadn't changed so very much – less forest of course! It was windy that day and she screamed as a gust tore at her clothes just as she let go of the rail to take a picture of him. Cameras and photography were yet another wonder to him and he enjoyed having his photo taken and then scrutinising the results. The gust was so strong she feared she would be blown away and ended up kneeling on the stone floor in panic! Suppressing a chuckle, he lifted her up and held on to her firmly.

"Don't worry, I've got you!" he said, hugging her to him in a sudden and surprising show of affection. She supposed it was all the emotion evoked by being back at his old home.

She wasn't going to complain though, and enjoyed the warmth of his firm body, feeling the strong, steady thud of his heart before he released her carefully and, keeping hold of her hand, helped her down the tower again. What a miracle it was, having him here in person! She suddenly realised how lucky she was to be the one who had found him that day. There were many people who had been Ricardians for much longer than she had, who would probably contend that they had more right than she to know him, but so what? It wasn't her fault that she had found out about him only recently. She knew for sure that none of them could possibly love him more than she did. As much perhaps, but not more.

He was pensive on the way back and she kept quiet herself, allowing him to process all the conflicting emotions he must be feeling. Finally, he said: "Can you imagine how unnerving it is to see your home in ruins and ravaged by time and destruction? To me 'twas only a matter of months since I stayed at Middleham Castle and now it seems to have aged overnight!" He was starting to fidget agitatedly and she could feel the tension in his body, see the tautness in his muscles and the strain around his eyes.

They had bought a bottle of wine in York and shared it in her room back at the B & B and he talked to her about his life in Middleham five hundred years before. He was a brilliant raconteur and she could picture it all as she listened, rapt, to his low, resonant voice. He described what they did every day, going hunting with birds and dogs, his work acting as judge to disputes in the area, investigating breaches of the law and sorting out grievances.

Those days had been simple in comparison to the period after he had become King. Suddenly, he was responsible for the whole realm and had to juggle the demands of several different factions. Many of the richer nobility resented his championing of the common people. He remembered how he had tried to prevent the rich monasteries and estates setting fish garths in the rivers, because they caught most of the fish before the ordinary people got a look in. He mentioned how he had sacked a scribe who had gained promotion by buying his way up the ladder. He had given the post to one more deserving. Rose said she thought that might have been part of the reason he had been betrayed at Bosworth – personal grievances of the Stanleys and Northumberland.

"You're possibly right!" he said, "But it's too late to change that now."

"Had Stanley requested leave to go home to his estates when you left your time?" she asked. "Only, if not, he will do."

"Did I let him go?" he asked, curiously.

"Yes, but only if he left his son, Lord Strange, as a hostage for his loyalty."

"Sounds sensible," he replied. "To request to go home just when Tydder is about to invade, that's rather suspicious, don't you think?"

"Yes, but what if taking his son hostage had the opposite effect, angering him enough to change sides? Perhaps he wasn't intending to betray you until then."

"It's possible, I suppose."

"Well, look, taking Lord Strange hostage didn't work anyway, so if - when - you get back try a different way. It can't make it any worse, can it?"

"I will consider it," he said.

They left Middleham the next day and returned to the bungalow.

The Armed Man

Soon after they arrived home in Rayleigh, Richard got word that part of his harness was ready and had been sent by the German armourer, Hans Gallingen. It arrived a couple of days later. The cuisses, poleyns, faulds and tassets, the proper names for the leg and foot armour, Richard told her, were all decorated with gilt designs of Yorkist roses. He tried it on with his own body armour and it was a perfect fit and match - now it was just a case of waiting for the arm pieces and the helm. Rose could only remember a few of the strange names, the pauldron, gardebrace and vambrace. And finally, the sallet and bevor: the helmet. This arrived within the next week from Bill Best - at last he had a complete harness and he put it on to show Rose - parading proudly around. The helmet was amazing and he pointed out all the intricate workmanship which made it worth the exorbitant sum of money he had paid for it! She had to admit he looked awe-inspiring while wearing the whole thing and he soon arranged to have another training session with Destrier to test it out.

Rose went along of course, as chauffeur, and she couldn't help tears coming to her eyes when she saw him gallop around the lists with his shining armour on and Rebel clad in the special armour made for a war horse and brightly caparisoned, the armour and colours borrowed from Destrier. Richard looked so natural and easy in the mediaeval saddle, his lance in one hand and his battle-axe at his side. His helmet shone in the sunlight - he was dazzling in more ways than one. She was imagining how he would have looked leading his army into battle at Bosworth - so courageous, so alive and so determined, but all to no avail! Oh, if only he could change history and defeat the bloody 'Tydder'!

After about an hour, he returned to Rose, flush with the exhilaration of a rewarding training session. "Guess what, Rose!" he said. "Anders has asked me if I would help to train some of the other Destrier members so they can ride the way I do!"

"That's fantastic! So when are you going to do this, then? You said their training sessions are mostly in the winter months, didn't you?"

"That's right, they don't want me to start until October. But that will be alright, won't it?"

He looked so happy, his eyes twinkling and his soft lips turned up in a smile.

Glorious

Anders had given permission for Richard to practise privately at Destrier's training ground every day in order to prepare for the Bosworth re-enactment, which was the weekend of the 18th and 19th of August. He had told Richard that, because of his skill and horsemanship and his offer of help with training in the autumn, he would recommend that Richard take part on horseback, as a knight in the Yorkist army, even though new Destrier members usually had to spend the first year serving on foot.

As the weekend of the re-enactment approached, he became more and more excited. On the Saturday, straight after breakfast, they set off in Griselda for the Battlefield site in Leicestershire, pulling Rebel, in his horse-box, behind them.

They arrived at the Bosworth Battle site about 12.30 pm and were directed to a pavilion bearing the Yorkist colours of murrey and blue. Rose had been told she was to play a serving wench and Richard, a Yorkist knight, since he had proved he could use a lance and had taken part in similar 'battles' before. However, as they entered the tent, the organiser, Martin, came scurrying out and said: "Oh, thank goodness you're here. Anders tells me you're an excellent rider. Richard, isn't it?"

"Yes, I can ride, though I am only a new member of Destrier," said Richard.

"Well, would you mind taking over one of the lead roles? Someone has gone off sick right at the last moment! I'm stuck for a replacement as everyone else has already got their role."

"Very well, which part am I to play?" Richard asked and then looked aghast at Rose when Martin said, happily: "Henry Tudor."

They stared at each other in shock.

"No, I'm sorry; I really can't play that part," Richard said.

"Of course you can, I know you haven't rehearsed, but really it's the easiest role of all – basically Tudor does bugger all! The hardest part is King Richard – now, I would never have suggested you, as a relative beginner, could play that role, but Tudor? Piece of cake!"

Richard's eyes were dancing with suppressed amusement.

"Well, if it's that easy, I'm your man," he said, giving Rose a surreptitious wink.

He was taken off and dressed in Henry Tudor's colours over his own armour. He held his helm in his hand and Rose burst out laughing when she saw the exasperated expression on his face. When he caught sight of her, he raised his eyebrows and shrugged. He was now mounted on Rebel, his black courser, and surrounded by a group of pike men. He had been told to keep well to the back. He looked curiously over at the man playing King Richard, and smiled ruefully.

'Richard' was mounted on a pure white steed with his shining armour covered by a surcoat bearing the royal standard. On his head, surmounting his brilliant helm was a circlet of gold – the royal battle crown, marking him out as the King. In the real battle, it had been a double edged sword for Richard because, although it inspired his own soldiers and knights and was an indication of his right to wear the crown of England, it also marked him out to the enemy and made him an easier target.

Rose was luckily in a position to get a good view of the action and she was torn between watching the real Richard and the fake one. She could sense that, even though he was playing Tudor and was only meant to skulk around behind his defending pike men, he really wanted to surge forward and engage with the enemy, in this case 'himself', just as he would have done in real warfare! She could see him prancing his horse up and down and shouting out orders which everyone ignored, as they all knew their own roles. She noticed he controlled the horse easily, scarcely using his hands, but guiding the beast with his legs. She thought he looked splendid and very dashing, although she obviously would have preferred him to have been playing himself!

She watched in breathless awe as the man portraying Richard led his cavalry charge straight at Tudor/Richard. 'Tudor' managed to play his part, sneaking away and avoiding 'Richard's' challenge. The man playing the King also played his role brilliantly, a grimace of rage on his face as he cut down Tudor's standard bearer, William Brandon and the giant, John Cheney, before succumbing to the treachery of William Stanley's army and going down fighting, bellowing "Treason! Treason!"

Afterwards Richard was exhilarated, but restless. He had experienced all the adrenaline of a real battle, but had been unable to dissipate it in action. However, he said he was impressed with the King's charge, even though it had failed.

"If I have to die in battle, that is the way to go, with courage and fighting to the end like a true chivalrous knight, not trying to flee like that snivelling coward, Tydder!"

"That's as may be but we don't want you to die at Bosworth at all! We will have to collate all the possible versions of the Battle that we can find and you can then see which you think is the most probable scenario of the way events actually panned out – I think you are the best placed to judge, as you actually know the people involved and what kind of strategy you might have employed, don't you think?" Rose asked.

"Yes, you are right. I have also noticed that you, yourself, have several books dealing with the battle and the story behind it – I shall have to read them all and let you know how I think the tableau really unfolded."

They visited the new Richard III Visitor Centre in Leicester, which had only been open for about a month, before returning to Rayleigh. He seemed to find the whole concept astounding, shaking his head in puzzlement at some of the exhibits. Rose was appalled at the depiction of him as a Nazi in Ian McKellen's film version of Shakespeare, but it meant nothing to Richard. He laughed at the white suit of armour which was meant to be similar to the armour he would have worn at Bosworth.

"That is not the kind of armour I will wear...wore," he said. "My harness was made by my Italian armourer who also made plain harnesses for over six hundred of my knights."

He refused to go near the open pit where his remains had been found. Rose went in and watched a hologram of Richard's skeleton projected into the grave, with a feeling of mixed fascination and dismay. She was pleased that at least the actual grave was surrounded by a see-through box, as opposed to the rest of the excavation area, which was covered by a transparent floor that tourists could walk on. Perhaps it was for the best that Richard hadn't come in here. They wandered outside and went over to the statue of Richard, which was just a few yards away. He liked the heroic depiction of himself, holding a sword in his right hand and the crown of England in the other. It had been commissioned by the Richard III Society and had previously been sited in the park near where the old castle had been.

"Another castle in ruins!" Richard sighed. Leicester had moved the statue to the vicinity of the Cathedral, where Richard's remains were going to be re-interred on March 26th 2015.

"Richard, I've just had a thought!" said Rose excitedly. How would you like to attend your own re-interment ceremony!?"

"Are you serious?" he said, his face a picture of distaste.

"Well, I know it sounds a bit morbid, but it does seem as if they are going to treat your remains with the utmost respect. It might be quite a good thing to see how many people still care about you and how your earthly remains are venerated. The Richard III Society will be there – you can meet some more of your fans! And just think – you'll be the only person, ever, to have attended his own burial without actually being present in the coffin. Or rather you will, as well, but...oh, you know what I mean!"

"I'll think about it," he said.

"If you want to do it, we should book our accommodation – I think it will fill up rapidly now the date is known. We could stay at the Travelodge, which is thought to be on the site of the inn where you actually stayed before the Battle! It used to be called the Blue Boar Inn in your time."

"It never was! It was the White Boar Inn!" said Richard, indignantly.

"Well, maybe the landlord changed the name after the battle, in fear of the Tudor," Rose replied.

"Hmm! He would have done too, he was another craven, obsequious, little coward!" snorted Richard. "Alright, then - book the hotel. I suppose we can always cancel it if I change my mind, can't we?"

"Yes, of course we can," said Rose. "That's settled then." So they reserved two rooms for the nights of 24th and 25th March. Rose wanted to pay her respects to Richard's remains, which were going to lie in state in the cathedral for three days before the funeral service. "We won't actually get into the cathedral on the day, of course, but they will have it televised live on a big screen."

"Rose, you are quite morbid aren't you?" he said. "I don't understand why you want to view my bones, when you can view them right now, along with my living flesh and blood! And I'm not sure I want to pay respects to myself – it seems a little perverse."

"Humour me, will you. Don't forget, I have been obsessed, er...thinking about the King Richard who died at Bosworth for a long time now and I somehow feel I need to just...say 'goodbye' to him. I can't really explain it properly, but it will give me closure, I think."

He shook his head in bemusement at her.

"Well, I'm not promising anything," he said finally.

What Doesn't Kill You (Stronger)

Back in Rayleigh a couple of days later, Richard awoke at dawn (which was about six in the morning in late August), as he always seemed to do, much to Rose's chagrin, as she was most definitely a night owl. Although he had told her he was quite happy to amuse himself for a few hours, she didn't like to leave him alone for too long in case he got himself into any trouble with the modern technology (once she had just caught him before he put his clothes into the dishwasher by mistake). In any case, it was rather rude to sleep late when you had a guest, especially one of such high status! So she got up at around seven and started making breakfast. They were having poached eggs on toast and beer. At least Richard was having beer – he insisted that it set him up for the day and was how he had always broken his fast.

When she had argued that these days it wasn't considered a normal breakfast he had retorted: "I am not a "normal" man – I am a King and although I understand that my reign was over more than five hundred years ago and I cannot now act in the way I was accustomed to then, I think I can at least decide what to have for breakfast!"

She had opened her mouth to protest, but he'd tilted his head, firm chin jutting forwards, his eyes changing to that ice cold warning stare and she had remained silent.

She had decided it was easier to just humour him – he wasn't particularly demanding on the whole, considering his proud royal blood!

They had fallen into a comfortable routine. She had shown him where the local Catholic Church, Our Lady of Ransom, was located and he went there at least once a day to pray, usually first thing in the morning. He knew he was welcome to stay with Rose as long as he needed to and he was grateful to her and always very courteous and gracious, despite the fact that he was living in very much less opulent conditions than he had been accustomed to. The area comprising his living quarters was a great deal smaller, for example, and the decorations were not as rich and sumptuous, however he did point out that the plumbing, heating and general conveniences were better in Rose's little bungalow than in any of his fabulously wealthy and spacious castles. In fact, he told Rose, he had never before felt so comfortable generally. The bed was better, the clothes softer and the ambient temperature more controllable. In addition, Rose's regular osteopathic treatments had definitely improved his back problem.

In between her normal clients, she treated him every other day, and in her free time she helped him research the Battle of Bosworth and his reign. They always had breakfast together and he hadn't ventured out in public without her yet, except to the church – she had insisted he should wait a few weeks to get used to the various aspects of modern life that were still so strange to him. They had become comfortable in each other's company and he had even allowed her to call him by his pet name, used only by close friends and family – Dickon. She had in return said he could call her Rosie, but he had said he preferred Rose, if she didn't mind, as he thought she was as beautiful as a rose.

"A white rose, of course!" he had added, his blue eyes twinkling.

As they chatted over the poached eggs, he suddenly dropped his knife and fork and pushed his seat back abruptly from the dining table. At that moment a loud clap of thunder was heard, causing the dogs to bark. He had gone deathly pale and his eyes were panic-stricken.

"What's the matter, Dickon?" Rose asked anxiously. "Do you feel ill?"

"Uuuuh!" he groaned. "My head! My head! Rose, I can't see properly, my sight is blurred. It just came on me of a sudden. I was feeling quite well a few minutes ago."

He stood up, gasped and put his hands over the back of his head, his fingers linked together, his elbows pointing forwards and he wavered to and fro, moaning in pain, before he suddenly dropped to the floor, unconscious.

Rose had gone to him immediately and her first aid training kicked in. She lowered her head to be level with his chest to check his breathing and felt the soft movement of air on her cheek. She felt for the pulse in his wrist and sighed in relief when the steady pulsations were there beneath her fingers. He didn't seem to be injured or having a fit; perhaps it was just a faint. She carefully moved him into the recovery position, lowering his head down gently so it rested on his own hand and gently stroked his hair away from his face. Her heart was racing - what could be wrong with him? After only a minute or so, which seemed like hours to her, he stirred and pushed himself into a sitting position on the floor, looking dazed. She was concerned, but relieved he had recovered consciousness, as she had no idea what she would have told an ambulance crew if she'd had to call them. She crouched down and put her arm around his shoulders, guiding him to the sofa, where she got him to sit down.

"How are you feeling?" she asked, worriedly. "Did you faint?"

"I know not," he mumbled, his eyes still slightly unfocused. "May I have some water, please? I have a great thirst."

She fetched a glass of water and he gulped it greedily. After a minute or two he seemed more himself, although he still had a rather vacant, spaced out look.

"I feel most peculiar – I could swear I was about to die, yet it wasn't the pain that made me think that, just a strange feeling. My heart was racing, suddenly for no reason and I felt like I wasn't really present. I don't know; I am talking nonsense."

He glanced at Rose who was looking concerned and worried, stroking his hand comfortingly.

"It sounds like a panic attack," she said. "I had a few some years ago. It is a very weird sensation. I didn't have a headache though. Or faint."

"I was not panicking!" he exclaimed, affronted. "I never panic!"

"No, it's not a very good name for it really. But you feel like you are about to die, for no particular reason. When I had mine, I found out it was caused by drinking strong coffee too quickly – the caffeine was the culprit. Maybe with you it's the beer for breakfast!" she joked.

He gave her a stern glance out of the corner of his eye, but said nothing. He made her feel like a naughty child when he did that – slightly nervous and a little bit excited too! She supposed it came naturally to him – he was used to quelling rebellious bloodthirsty knights and soldiers with a glance, so one twenty first century woman was no problem.

"Well, the headache is gone now – I feel back to normal again. Thank you for your concern, Rose. I don't know if it was a panic attack but I certainly felt like someone had walked over my grave."

He got up and returned to the table. As she rose to follow him, his last words made her realise the probable cause of his discomfiture.

"Dickon, I know what it is!" she cried. "Today is the anniversary of the Battle of Bosworth. It wasn't a long battle and they suppose you were killed after only a couple of hours fighting. I think you "felt" your battle wounds and experienced your own death in some way. It must have happened at about this time of day."

"Sweet Jesu, you could be right! It certainly felt as swift as a blow to the head would be, several blows actually, and the thirst I felt was like that felt after a gruelling fight. Doesn't that coincide with the way I was supposed to have died?" he asked.

"Yes, they believe you were cut down fighting in the midst of the enemy and the back of your head took the killing blow or blows, probably from a halberd. That was right where you were clutching your head just now. And your visual disturbance makes sense too - the back of the brain is the area that controls sight."

"Well, now I definitely want to avoid it happening again!" he said, earnestly.

Chapter Five - Sept 2014

Little Arrows

They were driving along, heading to Suffolk, the dogs with them in the back of the estate car.

"So where are we going, Rose? And for what purpose?" Richard asked for the umpteenth time.

"Center Parcs – it is a holiday village. Holidays are times that people take away from their jobs. Most employers give their workers about four or five weeks off that they can take when they wish. They can spend it doing whatever they enjoy. Center Parcs is great for families but anyone can enjoy it there as they have many different activities you can try. There are art classes, dancing, indoor sports such as bowling and badminton and outdoor ones, like riding, archery and golf. Or if you want to be pampered you can have a massage, a facial or a wax."

"I don't know what half of those items are," Richard said, "And I don't need a massage as I have my own personal osteopath, don't I?" he teased, his grey eyes twinkling. "But I am willing to try the rest, if you do the riding and the archery."

He grinned, showing his even white teeth. She had taken him to her dentist and he had needed one extraction and a few fillings.

The extracted tooth had been replaced by a dental implant and the result was impressive. He had also had his teeth cleaned and had taken to using the electric toothbrush the hygienist had recommended. His smile was thus even more attractive than before. He had loathed the visits to the dentist, though. He had especially hated the fillings and the cleaning and had remarked: "I think the dentist is your modern equivalent of a torturer. I do swear that undergoing tooth cleaning must be yet more excruciating than being put to the rack!"

She was glad he had suggested they do archery, as she was already a practised archer and hoped to impress him. Her ex-husband, Matt, had booked the Center Parcs holiday before their marriage had hit the rocks and she had decided to go anyway, as he had said he would be away in Ibiza with his new girlfriend. Well, they were welcome to Ibiza – she preferred an active holiday rather than lying on a crowded beach. And now she had someone to take with her.

"Lucky I brought my longbow and sword, Rose," he added. "Perhaps I might use them there."

"Hmm! I'm not sure that is allowed, Dickon. They do have their own equipment. I suppose the bow might be OK, but I doubt they'd let you use the sword, it'd be too dangerous."

"Of course it's dangerous," Richard laughed. "Of what use is a sword that isn't dangerous? How do they learn proper sword play if they don't use real, lethal swords?"

"Well, they don't really. They don't need to – swords aren't used in war any more. Most battles are fought from a distance with guns or missiles. The sword fighting – fencing - is more of a skill contest, with points scored for 'hits', I think – rather like the jousting contests you had in your day compared with a real battle."

Richard looked thoughtful but didn't reply further. She got the distinct impression that he thought a lot of our modern ways were quite ridiculous – and some of them were, she had to concede!

As they drove up to the Arrivals hut, Richard seemed quite excited and looked around curiously at the surroundings. There were a lot of trees at Center Parcs – so many that mobile phone networks were not always reliable as the trees blocked the satellite signal.

She told the staff that Richard was Matt – it was less complicated – and they were given two keys to villa number 212, situated in Pine area. This was one of the areas allocated to dog owners, and her two in the back of the car were waiting and eager to get out and stretch their legs.

Jonah and Jubilee had now progressed to open adoration of Richard and he was able to get them to do almost anything for him. It was quite exasperating as she had taken Jonah to obedience classes recently and he had embarrassed her by being the naughtiest dog in the class, although he was the eldest. She had put so much work in and then along came Richard, and had them both eating out of his hand and obeying his every command in next to no time! They seemed to recognise him as the alpha male in this pack. She had to admit that he certainly did exude a natural strength and assertiveness – he was brought up to be a Plantagenet after all, and you couldn't get much more assertive than that!

She drove the car slowly to their villa and parked it nearby while they unloaded their provisions and luggage. They had brought quite a lot of food from home to save purchasing it all from the supermarket at the Village. They unpacked and took the dogs for a walk, exploring the area. She had always found it nearly impossible to find her way anywhere here – all the villas looked exactly the same and she had never had a good sense of direction. But with Richard it was a totally different story. He always seemed to know exactly where he was and where everything else was in relation to it - he unfailingly found the quickest route anywhere instinctively. In fact he was bemused by her failure.

"You're so good at finding your way," she said, smiling.

"Compared to you I am, at least!" he teased. He had become much more relaxed and the lighter side of his personality had come to the fore, lately.

At night, the paths and roads were very dimly lit and she got lost all the more. He, however, could even spot a rabbit hundreds of feet away in the dark. She guessed he was used to dimmer light and that was the reason.

The next day they were on their way to the Outdoor Activity Centre where the field archery took place. He carried his longbow and a quiver full of arrows; she just had her money and valuables in a money belt. Their session was booked for 10.30am and they arrived a few minutes early. The archery took place in a large area of fenced-off woodland, with 3D models of various wild woodland animals dotted around. Basically, you had three shots at each 'animal', one from each of three wooden pegs embedded in the ground and you scored five points if you hit the model animal at all, ten for an arrow that hit within a small target marked on the animal – the 'kill' zone – twenty five for a hit just outside the centre of the target and fifty for the inner ring.

The place seemed to be deserted. Rose was just about to use her mobile to phone someone and say that their tutor hadn't arrived, when he suddenly appeared. He was a young man in his early twenties.

"Hi, I'm Kieran" he said, smiling. "You're the only two booked in today. I hope you don't mind. It'll mean you get to go round more than once, I expect!"

"No, that's great!" said Rose. "Oh, by the way, Matt here wondered if it was alright for him to use his own bow and arrows. He belongs to a re-enactment group and also a local longbow club – they make all their equipment in the authentic medieval way."

"Well, we wouldn't normally allow it, but as it's just the two of you I can't see that there would be any harm in it," he said. "I'll just have to explain the rules to you, safety and such like, and then we'll get you kitted up. Matt, do you have your own arm guard and finger tabs or do you want to use ours?"

"I have my own thank you," said Richard. "Do you not have any moving targets?"

"No, I'm afraid not," Kieran said. "Most people find it hard enough hitting the stationary ones."

Privately he thought Matt must be a bit of a dick. He'd seen these cocky types before. Most of them brought state of the art, expensive bows with fancy sights and counterweights on them and then scored lower than anyone else. He kitted Rose out and demonstrated how to draw the bow and aim, release the arrow and what to do safety wise.

They walked off to the first target, a wild boar. "How strange!" Rose thought, remembering that Richard's chosen emblem was a white boar.

"You should aim a bit low here as the target is quite close," he instructed and demonstrated by shooting an arrow which hit pretty close to the centre of the animal.

"After you, Milady," said Richard gallantly and Rose stepped up to the peg. She remembered how to use the bow as she had done archery at Center Parcs before and had originally learned as a student, about nine years earlier. She concentrated and drew the bow carefully, aimed and released – the arrow just skimmed over the top of the boar. Her next arrow skipped under it, but the third hit it squarely in the body. She was quite pleased with herself. Surely Richard's medieval bow would not be as accurate as a modern one?

Richard took an arrow from his quiver with an understated flourish and drew the bow, releasing the arrow in one fluid movement. Thunk! It hit the boar dead centre. She turned to congratulate him, but thereby missed his next shot, which he had loosed even quicker than the first and which hit almost touching the first shot. This was immediately followed by the third which was just above the other two, still in the 'kill' zone. Kieran looked stunned.

"Great shooting!" he said generously and they went to fetch their arrows.

"I've been shooting all my life," said Richard as they approached the target. All of his arrows were in the fifty score zone.

"It shows," said Kieran. "You've scored more with three arrows than most people do over the whole course!"

Richard just smiled modestly and pulled his arrows from the target. They were deeply embedded in the rubber as his bow was far stronger than the bows they normally used.

He kept up his immaculate record throughout the whole circuit and seemed to get a bit bored after the first round. So, partway through their second circuit, Rose stood a little closer to Richard as he shot and nudged his elbow, ever so slightly, just as he released his arrow. It was enough to make it swerve, missing the target area narrowly.

He whirled round in astonishment, his eyes flashing with anger and shock.

"You touched me deliberately!" he frowned, looking more amazed than annoyed. Evidently no one else had ever dared nudge the King as he loosed an arrow!

"I just thought I'd make it a bit more difficult for you – it's getting boring," she returned, defiantly.

At that, he threw back his head and laughed aloud.

"You are a remarkable woman," he said. "Yet I think you are simply vexed that you are beaten!" His blue-grey eyes sparkled with amusement.

"Matt, would you let me try your bow?" asked Kieran. "I've never shot a longbow."

"Gladly," said Richard and proceeded to instruct the instructor for the rest of the session.

"At least it's stopped him being bored," Rose thought. She realised that if it were anyone else she would have been furious that they were so smugly good at everything, but Richard was never arrogant about his skill, just brushed it off in a charming and modest way. Nevertheless, she was determined to find something he was rubbish at!

"That was fun, wasn't it?" she said as they made their way back to the villa.

"A bit tame compared to what I'm used to," he grinned. "It's a pity we weren't allowed to shoot the rabbits and squirrels. I could have had a hat made for you for the winter!"

Rose looked across at him, wondering if he was serious or just teasing her again. She wasn't sure whether to be appalled or flattered.

"Rose, speaking of squirrels, I have noticed that those of your time are quite different from those I am familiar with. Ours are smaller, redder and have tufted ears. How is it these large grey ones come to be here?"

"The greys are not native to England, but were brought over here from America. There are still red squirrels in a few places in England, but mostly the greys have invaded and taken over the country."

"I know the feeling!" Richard said. "I had the same problem with certain 'Greys' trying to take over England!" He was of course referring to Edward's queen, Elizabeth Woodville Grey and her numerous brothers, sisters and children, marrying into the nobility wherever they could engineer it.

"But America hadn't been discovered in my time," he continued. "Where is it? Can you tell me more of it, please?"

Rose explained that America was a huge continent, lying to the west of Britain and that its southern part had been discovered by Christopher Columbus, financed by King Ferdinand and Queen Isabella of Spain.

"It wasn't long after you...er...the battle of Bosworth, that he discovered it," Rose continued. "1492 it was. Apparently his brother, Bartholomew, had come to England to see whether the King would grant him funds to finance the expedition but Henry Tudor said 'No'. He was always a skinflint, it seems," she laughed.

Richard nodded, looking thoughtful as they arrived back at the villa.

My Prayer

"Do you mind if I visit a local church?" Richard asked. He couldn't get used to the fact that very few people worshipped regularly anymore and then usually only once a week. He still felt uncomfortable if he didn't visit a church or chapel and pray every day. He would always mutter little prayers of grace before meals and Rose had noticed and asked him to say them aloud, which he appreciated and she enjoyed as well. She thought it lovely to say 'Grace' before food, not least because she felt that blessing the food gave it a more wholesome aspect somehow. She remembered reading about how water crystals appeared more beautifully patterned under the microscope when they were spoken to with love, compared with not being spoken to at all or being insulted and scolded. If water did this, why not other foodstuffs? After all, water made up a high percentage of most foods.

She would also often see him cross himself, particularly if he saw something which he considered lewd or blasphemous (which was quite often in what he referred to as 'These godless times'). He had, however, reduced the frequency of this gradually, she guessed as he became more used - or inured - to the weird ways of mankind these days.

She occasionally went with Richard to worship, partly because she loved accompanying him anywhere and partly because she relished the peace and serenity of the churches. She went with him this time. The local Catholic Church, St Thomas', really was pretty and felt cosy and holy. She had always loved visiting churches and cathedrals and, although she wasn't herself religious (she thought of herself as spiritual rather than being affiliated to any specific religion) she respected his views and quite enjoyed the ritual of the services.

This time, it was a more personal thing, as there was no service scheduled, and it was only the two of them who were present. He knelt in front of the altar and clasped his hands together; he was always very serious about his worship. She did the same. She didn't know what he prayed for but she prayed that, if he got back to his own time, he would somehow survive Bosworth.

After they had come out, curiosity got the better of her and she said: "Dickon, may I ask you a personal question?"

"You may ask but I don't promise I will answer," he smiled.

"What do you pray for when you kneel down in front of the altar in a church or chapel?"

"I pray for many things. For my beloved son, Edward, who died so young and his gracious mother, my wife, Anne, who was also taken from me too early. I pray for all the dear people who have been taken by God, I pray for their release from purgatory and that they will pass through the gates of heaven. Those such as my dead parents, my brothers, Edward, George and Edmund.

And also for Richard Neville of Warwick and his brother John Neville, Montague. Warwick was a great man, just misguided by his pride. I loved him as a son loves a father. And John was torn between his loyalty to the King, my brother, Edward, and to his own brother, Warwick. After the battle of Barnet, where they died, we found that John had worn Yorkist raiment under his armour to show his divided loyalties. I wept for him and Warwick – it should have been so different."

"Did you want to be king?" Rose asked, taking advantage of his unusual loquaciousness.

"No, not at all," he replied. "I fully intended to support Edward V as king until Bishop Stillington came to me and revealed that Edward had made a previous marriage with another noblewoman - Eleanor Butler, formerly Talbot. This meant all his children with Elizabeth Woodville were bastards and couldn't inherit the crown, so I was the next in line and it was my duty to take the throne. I also realised that not to do so would likely result in my early death and the deaths of my family."

He shook his head in a gesture of disbelief. "It seems taking the crown didn't prevent any of those deaths after all, not even my own. What a waste of time and effort!" He sighed heavily, running his hand through his hair to draw it back off his face. "I'm sorry, Rose. My mood has become morbid and mournful. What do you suggest to change it to one more congenial?"

"How do you fancy line dancing?" she smiled. He returned her smile, his eyes twinkling again.

"I don't know the name of this type of dance, but I think myself able to dance many different steps, so perhaps I could learn it easily enough," he said.

"Come on then!" she laughed. The line dancing class was great fun and certainly lifted the mood. Richard struggled a little, but persisted and managed to, finally, get through a few songs without going wrong. He loved the cowboy boots belonging to his neighbour in the line and by the end of the night he was a little bit tipsy, having drunk more wine than usual because of the exertion making him thirsty. To her amazement, he put his arm around her as they returned to their villa. She slipped hers around his waist. It felt comfortable and cosy, snuggled up against him like that and she noticed her heart racing.

"Oh my God!" she thought to herself. "You're really falling in love with him, you fool, Rosie!"

Even as she admonished herself, she knew it was too late. She knew that it was probably the fact he had trusted her with the tragedies he had suffered when so young that had been the final nail in the coffin of her indifference. She had always found vulnerability, in an otherwise strong man, to be very attractive. She found herself wondering what it would be like to kiss his generous lips. At the same time her rational self was shouting: "No Rosie! You'll only get hurt all over again!"

"Do you know what?" Richard was saying, his speech ever so slightly slurred. "You are a very special woman, do you know that? I don't usually tell people much about my feelings. But I feel I can speak to you about anything. I think you are my best friend, my soul friend. But it's not physical, is it?"

She hesitated a second or two and then whispered: "No, it isn't," her heart slowly breaking.

Well, being his friend wasn't so bad. She could live with that. She would have to.

The next afternoon, they went pony trekking. She enjoyed watching him ride, liked the way he looked into the distance, his eyes narrowed against the sun, the way his muscles tensed under his shirt as his strong hands pulled on the reins. She quickly looked away, blushing, when she realised she had been imagining those hands caressing her body. Suddenly he leaned out of the saddle and picked a wild rose that was growing in the hedgerow, presenting it to her with a flourish.

"My Lady Rose, please accept this flower, your namesake and my family's emblem, as a token of my esteem!" he said, in mock seriousness. She felt tears pricking her eyes. If only he could really be her knight in shining armour.

"Now, I'll race you back!" he laughed, kicking his horse into a canter and then a gallop, before she could manage a trot. She laughed too and thought that she should at least be thankful that he enjoyed her company and could confide in her to the extent he did. She vowed that she would never betray his trust by revealing those confidences - she would adopt his own motto - Loyaulté me lie: Loyalty Binds Me.

The next day she got him to have a facial, though he stubbornly refused to try waxing.

"It is natural for a man to have hair on his body. I will not go against nature. But I will submit to a facial, since you seem to think it is even more relaxing than a massage, and I find those very soothing," he said.

She had continued to treat his scoliosis, and he had continued to do the exercises required of him. She wasn't absolutely sure, but she thought she could detect a very slight improvement in the degree of curvature. He certainly reported that his pain was greatly diminished and she was happy for that. She found the treatments a little more difficult since she had recognised her forbidden feelings for him. It made her want him even more to see and feel his naked skin on the treatment couch and not be able to act on her inclinations. But she managed to keep a professional distance and was glad that he seemed to be improving.

They went to the Spa together and both had a facial. He enjoyed sitting in the warm chill-out room afterwards and kept touching his face in fascination.

"You were right!" he said. "I actually fell asleep while my facial was going on! It was mostly a very pleasant experience. Although it was alarming when the girl, Holli, put a cloth over my face and covered it with some kind of paste. I couldn't see or open my mouth and thought I would surely suffocate, so I sat up, gasping. I think she was a little shocked but she was very understanding and let me continue without my mouth being covered, which was much nicer."

She smiled at him and he grinned back.

"What shall we do this evening, after church?" he asked.

"Do you fancy ten pin bowling?" she asked and explained how the game worked. He enjoyed the game even though Rose just beat him in the first round. He came back stronger in the second, though and ended up winning by one point.

They had been drinking beer while they were playing and Rose had a bottle of Calvados in the villa, which they opened later. This time they were both slightly drunk and Rose, buoyed up by Dutch courage, said she was glad he felt she was his best friend. "But it's not enough," she whispered shyly, her eyes lowered, as they sat at the kitchen table, where they had been playing chess.

Only Love Can Hurt Like This

"You want to be more than friends?" he whispered. She nodded miserably, sure he was going to say that was all they could ever be. Instead he lowered his beautiful head to hers and gently kissed her lips. She felt exhilarated and afraid at the same time. His lips were warm and soft, and then she felt his tongue gently probe inside her mouth. She returned the kiss, her heart thudding, stroking his wonderfully silky hair. She thought she had never felt such joy and yet such trepidation in her life!

He slid closer to her, cupping her face tenderly with his strong fingers and then suggested they move to the large corner sofa. There, he leaned onto her, his kisses becoming more passionate. She could feel her body responding to his, as she slipped her arms around his back, under his shirt, caressing his warm, hard muscles.

"You smell wonderful!" he breathed. Rose felt as if she was in a dream and sighed with pleasure. All at once she felt him tense and he pulled away abruptly, his face stricken and pale, his chest heaving.

"What's wrong?" she said, the dream fading as fast as it came.

"Your perfume, it reminded me of Anne. Oh God, Anne! Rose, I'm sorry, I can't. I forget myself. 'Tis too soon after losing her. It wouldn't be fair to you in so many ways. I do care for you, but I am still affected by Anne's death. My emotions are yet in turmoil. It is too soon for me to get involved with another woman. I feel it would be dishonouring her to...I'm so sorry. I got carried away in the heat of the moment - it's unlike me to lose control like that...I'd better get to bed."

He turned and went into his room, closing the door softly.

She sat there wondering how her life had been changed from ecstasy to agony in a few seconds. Now she had spoiled it all – he would surely not want to be friends with her any more after this. She felt angry at herself and at him, and vaguely impressed at the same time by his strength of character. She had basically offered herself to him on a plate and he had refused her. God! She felt so ashamed. Tears streamed down her face as silent sobs wracked her body.

The next morning she looked, horrified, in the mirror at her puffy eyes and face. She cringed when she remembered how brazen she'd been, but she couldn't prevent herself reliving over and over again the memory of his lips on hers. She remembered every word he had said to her, both the wonderful ones and the ones that had broken her heart.

As for now, she was embarrassed to face him. She was sure he would be distant and aloof.

In this she was wrong. He looked straight at her when she entered the living room area, anxiety all over his face.

"Rose, I want to talk to you. About last night. I want to apologise for trying to seduce you like that. I was wrong and I hope I haven't spoiled our friendship. I couldn't bear to lose that. You are the only friend I have here. Please forgive me. I was in my cups and my self control was not of its usual strength. I should never have kissed you like that. Rose?"

"There was no harm done, Dickon. It was a beautiful kiss. I don't regret it – I will always treasure the memory of it. You haven't spoiled anything. Anyway, it was me who started it. And of course we can still be friends, of course we can!"

He came to her then and took her in his arms, clasping her tightly to him in a great bear hug. She felt safe and warm there in his comforting embrace, and closed her eyes for a few seconds, savouring the moment.

"We will always be friends, Rose," he breathed.

I Don't Want to Miss a Thing

On their return from Center Parcs, they continued their research about the Battle of Bosworth. Rose tried to collate all the research they had amassed so far.

"OK", she said. "Here are some of the factors which might have affected the outcome of the battle. First: That you didn't punish Margaret Beaufort and her supporter, Reginald Bray, for conspiring to overthrow you and put her son, Henry Tudor on the throne, or in other words, that you failed to stop her continued plotting but simply put her in the custody of her husband, who was himself suspect."

"Well, as she was a woman I found it against the chivalric code to punish her as I would have if she were male. I had to trust her husband, Lord Thomas Stanley, to keep her under control and prevent her communicating further with her son. I had no choice as he was one of the most powerful and influential Lords in the country, along with his brother, William, and I hoped, by rewarding them, to keep them on my side. But I suppose I could imprison her in a convent and consider how to stop the Stanleys taking part in the battle."

"Good! The next thing we have discussed before; you granted Stanley's request to take home leave just before the invasion of Tudor and took his son, Lord Strange, hostage for his compliance - this didn't work either, unless it prevented him taking part at all - but he certainly didn't fight on your side. It may have even made him decide to support Tudor because of your threat to his son's life."

"Ye-es! Perhaps I will arrest the Stanleys and keep them under lock and key until after the battle."

"OK. Next is that Percy, the Earl of Northumberland, deliberately failed to notify York of your need to muster your army and that he delayed his march to the battle. Then he pleaded tiredness to avoid taking a direct part in the battle. His inaction meant the York contingent arrived too late to take part."

"That's typical of that imbecile! He always resented my popularity in York and the North of England. I will ensure that someone else is sent to York to muster the men and speak to Percy about the consequences of failing in his support of his King. And if they still fail to arrive on time, I will delay until they come."

"Just be aware that Percy reported that there was plague in York - that might have been true to some extent, so there may have been fewer men available anyway."

Richard nodded.

"Next item: Rhys Ap Thomas, the Welsh chieftain, failed to keep his oath to hinder Tudor's approach through his territory. He had sworn that Tudor would enter England only over his belly but he used a ploy of lying down in a ditch so that Tudor could walk over him and thus defeat the oath."

"Treacherous cur! I will suggest he keeps his oath and perhaps offer him more in the way of reward if he does...and punishment if he does not."

"Now, it is known that you led a cavalry charge against Tudor, which failed for one or more of several possible reasons:

1. That the charge was impulsive and/or desperate. The desperation might have been because John Howard, Duke of Norfolk, had been killed, possibly by an arrow when he unwisely lifted his visor, and the battle had started going awry.

2. That Tudor's pike-men used a formation unknown to you at the time.

3. That it failed because you lost your horse for one of the following reasons: it was killed under you; it lost a shoe and went down; it got mired in the marsh and fell."

"Fine. I will warn Jocky Howard about opening his visor, though he should know this. I will double and triple check Surrey's shoes and scout out the ground before the battle to avoid the marshy area. I doubt the charge was impulsive - I always plan my battle strategies carefully and I had indeed thought about including a charge in the plan. So, I won't act out of desperation - I am forewarned now. I can research on the Internet how to counteract a formation of pike-men such as you describe. Anything else?"

"Couldn't you just take a machine gun or two with you?" Rose suggested, facetiously.

He frowned in concentration. "No, I want to win fairly," he said, taking her comment seriously. "In any case, we shouldn't rely on being able to take something from this time back to the past. What if it just disappeared when I got back?"

"I was only joking!" she said. "Although, you did bring your bow, arrows and dagger with you to this time, didn't you? I suppose archaeologists would be quite perplexed to find the remains of an ancient machine gun at the battle site! In any case, we don't even know yet whether you can get back yourself, do we?" she added, rather hoping that he would have to stay.

"No, we don't, do we? That's the next thing we need to research - for all I know Tydder may have invaded and be king of England since I left. In any case, I thank you Rose, for all your help in this - I wish I could endow some honour or gift to you in return for all your support. As you know, I cherish loyalty in people above all else." And he gave her that precious, warm smile that showed his dimple and instinctively held out his hand. She blushed and knelt before him taking his hand and kissing the ring in the mediaeval fashion.

"The honour is mine, Sire, and my loyalty is yours always," she whispered.

Rose was of the opinion that he should change as many of the different elements they had mentioned as he could, in order to give himself the best chance of success and Richard agreed.

As for their mutual attraction, Richard and Rose had reached a tacit understanding. They both knew that there was a special bond between them but, on Richard's part at least, it was one of friendship, not romantic love. Rose thought she understood his reasons for denying the obvious attraction between them and blamed his fierce piety, knowing that his upbringing, background and faith compelled him to do what he thought was right - in this case, honouring his dead wife - even if, now and then, she wished and hoped she could convince him differently. He was extremely stubborn and once he had set his mind to something, he was not easily persuaded or deterred. This was an excellent quality in a lot of ways, but extremely frustrating if you happened to disagree with him.

In any case, for the time being she appreciated the degree of intimacy and friendship that he allowed her, which was considerable, when she considered his private nature and the way he guarded his thoughts, often only revealing them to direct questioning and even then probably not fully. Often she would catch herself looking at him, wondering what he was thinking about. His eyes were like deep mysterious pools of murky water, hiding thoughts which could at times be as bright as a summer's day or swiftly become dark and dangerous, like a storm cloud. She was sure that sometimes he brooded on his powerlessness in this modern world; on his lost wife, Anne and their only child, Edward, both dead much too young; on his responsibilities and obligations as King; and most of all, on whether he would be able to get back to this own time and put all his plans into action.

Chapter Six - October 2014

Thank You For the Music

October 2nd 2014

Richard woke on his five hundred and sixty second birthday, feeling thirty three. Rose was already up for a change and there was a pleasant air of expectancy in the little house.

"Good morning, Dickon!" she said. "I'm making you a special breakfast. And I have a few little surprises for you as well."

"Mmm! It smells good," he said, sitting down at the table and pouring himself a large glass of beer. He downed it in one and refilled the glass.

Rose brought his breakfast over. It was a full English and included black pudding and fried bread, neither of which Richard had had before.

They made casual conversation as they ate. They had been trying to work out how they might be able to get him back again to his own time. They had decided to try it on the same date he'd appeared, but one year later, 22nd June, 2015. He had been learning all he could about the Law of Attraction and agreed it could have played a part in his travel through time. As they couldn't guarantee there would be anyone on the other side to draw him through, they had deduced that they both needed to think about sending him back, both of their minds focusing on the same end. Rose knew it would be a hard task for her to 'wish' him away, but she had to try for his sake, if that was what he wanted.

That meant they had over eight months to work out how he might manage to change history, assuming he managed to get back at all. They had discussed also whether, if he did get back, it would be to the time he had left or whether time would have continued in the fifteenth century as fast as it had passed in this one. Perhaps, as he had mentioned previously, he would get back and the Battle of Bosworth would have already been fought without him!

His eyes suddenly rested on a large parcel on the sideboard.

"What's that?" he asked, eagerly.

"It's your birthday present," she said. "You can open it once you have eaten your breakfast."

He started chewing faster, as eager and curious to see what it would be as a young boy. Eventually they had finished eating and Rose was brewing some tea.

"Go on then, you can open it now," she said, as excited as he was.

It was a strange shape, but he didn't wait to try and guess what it was, he just peeled the wrappings off carefully, folding them for future reuse.

Inside was a large box and inside the box was a musical instrument.

"It's a lute!" he exclaimed. "How did you manage to find an authentic lute? They aren't used these days are they?"

"You can get anything on EBay!" she laughed.

He took it out of the box and began to tune the strings carefully, then started strumming and plucking them. The sound was lovely, different from a guitar or a mandolin but with a little of each in there somewhere.

Then he began to sing along to it, a haunting, beautiful melody with his low tenor voice forming a counterpoint and blending perfectly with the instrument's own sound. Rose didn't know the tune but loved it straight away. Seeing him so happy made her suddenly feel tears pricking her eyes. She had grown more than fond of him during these past few months. She felt she knew him better now, even though he didn't always reveal his inner feelings. It felt as if she had always known him, somehow.

They also had a lot in common, considering the 'age' difference. He naturally preferred less crowded places and, although she had been born in London, in the Inner City area, she did also. They both enjoyed art and music – she was good at art and he, music, but they each appreciated the other's skill in their separate fields. They both had an affinity with animals, although he was a lot less soft-hearted about them than she, because of his upbringing, of course. She remembered him laughing at her when she had asked him to change the TV channel during a nature programme in which a baby antelope was about to be eaten by a cheetah.

"It's nature, Rose. All creatures kill to survive, even men, perhaps especially men," he had said, but humoured her and, grinning, turned it over.

She had also made him a birthday compilation of tracks she thought he would like on a small iPod. There were tracks meant to inspire and encourage him as well as some she knew were favourites of his. She had included 'The Glory of Love' in memory of that first car journey when it had played so appropriately, there was Chad Kroeger's 'Hero' to give him inspiration and courage in what he had to do, 'The Silence' by Alexandra Burke, which she felt applied to him – he rarely gave much away about his feelings - and 'Songbird' by Eva Cassidy, which they both loved. There were also several classical pieces, which she knew he would appreciate, since classical melodies were still his favourites: Grieg, Holst, Strauss as well as some more modern ones such as John Williams and 'Gladiator' by Hans Zimmer. She had also included songs by a Mediaeval-style folk group, The Legendary Ten Seconds, who had written two whole albums about Richard III himself and they were quite good too! She had added several choral pieces, definitely his favoured type of music, 'Benedictus' being a particular preference. Finally she had put on all her own favourite tracks, an eclectic mix indeed!

She wondered what would be happening this time next year. Would he be gone? If so, would he have been able to change history and defeat Tudor? Would he still be stuck here and would that make him happy or sad? She suddenly realised that she secretly hoped he wouldn't be able to leave. She wanted to hang onto him, keep him to herself; she didn't want to share him, not even with England, his greatest love!

But that was a selfish thought. She had to try and change her thoughts so that she could help him get back, if he really and truly wanted to return there. Maybe he would change his own mind and want to stay here in this new and exciting world, play his lute and become a musician – who knew what would happen? She resolved to wait and see what he wanted and comply with that. If she truly cared for him, which she did, she should put his wishes before her own.

She looked up at him again, as he played his lute, singing and looking as joyful as she had ever seen him. Hopefully, he would see that he could be content here, and then maybe she could be happy too. Because she knew, if he managed to go back, she would never be truly happy again, that there would always be something important missing from her life. Belonging to the Richard III Society wouldn't be enough to fulfil her obsession any more. For they had a soul link – it was surely because of that that he had arrived here in the first place. Their connection had drawn him to her through the mists of time.

"Come here, Rose! Let me teach you how to play," he said.

She went to him gladly, knowing that she would be lucky to pluck a few right notes from the lute – music was not her forté, although she could appreciate a good melody and skilful musicianship.

He sat her on his lap, his arms around her, gently moving her fingers on the strings of the instrument, as he plucked them. She decided it was pointless worrying about what might happen in the future, or what had happened in the past. She should just enjoy him in the present, every day that he was here, and savour and remember each magical moment she spent in his company.

They played the lute together for a while, not very well, but with great enjoyment and laughter. He was a good teacher, more patient than she would have thought, considering he was supposed to have the Plantagenet impatience and temper. She had seen his temper in action, now and then, but his impatience seemed to be directed more often at himself than others.

The previous night, she had offered to cut his hair for him, as it was getting quite long and unruly, and he had agreed, as long as it remained at least chin length.

He had a shower and washed his hair first, using the coconut shampoo he preferred. He was quite fastidious about his appearance, and the clothes he had chosen on their shopping trips were always smart and understated. He had good taste, although he had a definite preference for gold jewellery and purple colours.

He sat meekly in front of her now, a towel around his shoulders, and she combed his hair through gently, measuring out the lengths and trimming about an inch or so from the ends. She surreptitiously kept a lock, putting it in her pocket to hide it there. She didn't know why she wanted it, she supposed just as a memento of him for when he left. When she had finished the cut and dried his hair, she showed him the effect in the mirror and he pronounced himself satisfied with the results.

"Sit back for a minute and I'll do an Indian Head Massage for you," she said. He looked up at her suspiciously.

"What is that? It sounds like it could be a kind of torture," he frowned.

"No, it's nice, you'll love it," she said and he allowed himself to be seated sideways on the chair. She began by rubbing his back, through his clothes, softly at first and then more vigorously, warming his back. He groaned with pleasure.

"Mmmm! You have magic fingers, Rose – and they are always so warm!" he purred.

She laughed, moving her hands to his shoulders and neck, kneading and softening his taut muscles. Then on to his head, massaging his scalp and forehead, pressing certain points on his face and ears and stroking her fingers through his hair. She used different kinds of moves, some were like raindrops falling, some squeezing his hair and tugging it gently.

Finally she smoothed down his shoulders and pressed on his knees and then his feet to ground him again.

"How was that, Sire?" she asked finally.

"Reem!" he replied. He had heard the expression on one of the reality TV shows and used it all the time now. He never ceased to surprise her, the strange things he liked about modern life. He enjoyed the reality shows because he said they were about "real people with real problems and emotions". It seemed to be true that he genuinely cared about ordinary people.

Hot Stuff

For the evening, they had booked a table for a meal with a few of Rose's friends. They had met Richard before and knew him as her distant cousin from Yorkshire. Surprisingly to Rose, none of them had seemed to suspect anything out of the ordinary, dismissing any faux pas he made as being because he was from the sticks (anywhere outside London and Essex, from their viewpoint).

Richard had been shocked at the mode of dress of some of the people Rose introduced him to. For example, one of her friends, Jan, often wore clothes that seemed to be much too small for her! The first time they had met, he had stared wide-eyed at her legs, revealed up to the thighs by a micro mini dress and emphasised by high stiletto heels that made her a good three inches taller than him, crossed himself and averted his eyes. When he had questioned Rose about her later she had simply said: "Well, she's an Essex girl!" He wondered at first if 'Essex girl' was a euphemism for 'whore', but Rose went on to explain that many ordinary people wore revealing clothes these days. He looked sceptical.

"YOU don't," he said.

"Well, I have been known to. I suppose I haven't really felt like dressing up to the nines since my divorce. And to be honest I have deliberately toned down my dress so as not to offend you."

"Really?" he said, arching one eyebrow. "Well, I thank you for your tact, although you have aroused my curiosity now!"

She had promised she would wear something a little more fashionable this evening on his birthday celebration. She had found a dress that she loved, which was pretty and feminine without being too sexy. He might be curious, but she didn't want to dress too over the top. He was a man she felt would be more impressed by subtlety. The dress was cream with a pretty flower pattern and reached just above her knee. The neckline was discreet and the sleeves were elbow length. She wore shoes with a small heel, not too high. When she appeared that evening dressed thus and wearing more than her usual minimal amount of makeup, he stared at her in delight, his blue eyes shining and twinkling. He leapt to his feet and swept her a formal bow, taking her hand and pressing it tenderly to his lips.

"You look reem!" he said, which kind of spoiled the romantic, mediaeval scenario she had begun to imagine!

They were going to a local curry house. She had warned him how spicy the food was, but he had seemed eager to try it and she had to admit he was quite daring in what he was prepared to attempt. He wasn't reckless but he was curious, and she liked that he was willing to try something once or even twice before deciding whether he liked it or not. He had, for example, persisted with the coffee, and was now a confirmed coffee drinker, even enjoying it on the stronger side. And it wasn't only food and drink where he was adventurous. She remembered him insisting on trying out the zip wire at Center Parcs, after he saw someone go whizzing by across the lake. He had loved it too, pronouncing it "Exhilarating. Almost as exciting as battle!"

Arriving at the curry house, they entered and Richard gazed in wonder at the exotic flocked wallpaper and multiple mirrors.

"I love this!" he said, smiling broadly. It was typical Indian curry house décor.

"Don't you have curry houses in Yorkshire then?" asked Jan's boyfriend, Harry.

"Not where I come from – it's only a tiny place," he replied. "I've led a sheltered life." He winked at Rose, his eyes twinkling with amusement.

"But you must have had curry before, though?" Harry persisted.

"Oh, yes, of course!" Richard said, convincingly. Rose hoped he wouldn't give himself away when he tasted the food!

In fact, Richard behaved impeccably. He ordered the same as Rose, trusting that she would guide him and not betray his ignorance by ordering something too hot. She ordered Chicken Korma and Onion Bhajee with Lemon Rice. He ate it with gusto as if he had been eating it all his life. He did turn a little red in the face when he took a rather large helping of the hot pickle, but otherwise she was very proud of him – and not a little surprised.

However, a few hours afterwards, when they were back home, he went missing for some time and she suspected he was in the bathroom.

"Rose, you didn't warn me that the curséd stuff would burn all through my body!" he lamented.

"Curséd? I thought you had enjoyed it? You did eat it all, I seem to remember," she replied.

"Or course I did, I was trying to blend in, and everyone else seemed to like the foul fare!" he said. "And perhaps you noticed I was drinking more than my usual quantity of beer – to try to quench the fire in my throat and belly!"

She laughed, then said: "Well I thought you blended in beautifully. No-one would have suspected you were suffering so."

"Well, that's because I have had a lot of practice. As King, I am expected to enjoy all sorts of strange concoctions and recipes at the various banquets I have to attend. They are very tedious. I hasten to add that the company tonight was far from tedious – just the fare left a little to be desired!"

Mars, The Bringer of War

Their painstaking research continued.

"Rose, I think we need to know as much as possible about what, according to your history, I did from June 22nd 1485, when I left my world for this one, and August 22nd, the Battle of Bosworth. I know you have told me that there are few surviving documents, but whatever we can find out should help. If I know something of what I did which resulted in my defeat at the hands of Tydder, I will be more able to change it," said Richard.

"Good thinking, Batman!"

"Sorry, I don't comprehend your meaning."

"Oh sorry, it's just a reference to a saying from an old TV series. Let me look up some of my old research – I'm sure I saved a lot of the documents I've viewed on-line. Here we are." And she pulled up a document folder containing about twenty references. "Let's work chronologically, shall we?

"OK, on Wednesday 22nd June you gave instructions to your Commissioners of Array that their men should be ready at one hour's notice. You thanked them for their assistance in the past in resisting traitors and you ordered them to ensure their men were properly equipped and paid. Captains were assigned and you told them to put aside any private quarrels and unite in your support to resist Tudor's imminent invasion. Had you done that before you came here?"

"No, I hadn't, but I remember that it was planned for later that day."

"OK, then we skip to Friday 24th June, when Lord Stanley requests leave to go back to his estates, saying he will be able to help you better from there. You hold his son, Lord Strange, hostage for his good behaviour and let Stanley go."

"How very generous of me!"

"Yes, too generous, I would say, in hindsight."

"Mmm. Hindsight is a valuable thing in this case."

"Right – I think you should refuse him."

"Perhaps I will."

"OK. Then you remain at Nottingham for the rest of that month and the whole of July, though there are gaps which are not accounted for. It is known that on 27th July you ask for the Great Seal from the Chancellor, which you receive on 29th."

"That is as it should be – I needed that to give official instructions."

"Fine. Then you are at Nottingham from 1st – 9th August – Tudor lands at Milford Haven in Wales on 8th. On 10th it is unknown where you were, but 11th-17th it seems you were mainly at Beskwood Lodge again, hunting. The next known location for you is on 20th when you arrive in

Leicester and spend the night in the Blue...sorry, White Boar Inn. On 21st you leave Leicester and probably set up camp on Ambion Hill. You may or may not have struck your spur on the bridge on your way out. There is a legend that this happened and that some old crone or witch predicted that your head would hit the same spot on your return."

"Nice!"

"Yes, I know! Then on 22nd..." she paused.

"On 22nd I die," he said levelly.

He remained silent for a while, contemplating...what? His own death? Those horrible accounts of how his body was savagely attacked and then horribly mutilated and displayed? He took a deep breath and continued.

"Can we go over again what is known about the Battle itself and any new research you've unearthed?"

"Of course. Well, it is now thought that perhaps the Stanleys' positions, which they reached and occupied before you arrived, forced your army to deploy partly on Ambion Hill and were cutting you off from Watling Street. When you charged for Tudor, you were bogged down in marshy ground, your horse may have either fallen or been killed there and then you were surrounded. However, that is just one theory – we have no eye witness accounts."

"What are the other theories?"

"Well, first of all your leader of the vanguard was John - Jocky - Howard, Duke of Norfolk, along with his son, facing up to Oxford. John was killed, possibly by an arrow through his open visor, and Northumberland, who was in the rear (at his own request) was ordered to reinforce Norfolk's men, who had started to retreat, but refused."

"Betrayal number one," he said, his eyes narrowed.

"Yes. Well, no actually, unless you're counting from the start of fighting. You had ordered Thomas, Lord Stanley, to join your army and he refused, saying he could keep an eye on Tudor better where he was. William Stanley had already been declared a traitor by you as he was known to have been in collusion with Tudor."

"These three are the three vital betrayals are they not? The two Stanleys and Northumberland?"

"Yes, that's right. If either of the Stanleys had shown their hand for you or if Northumberland had reinforced Norfolk's line, you wouldn't have needed to charge and things would probably have been very different."

"Anything else I need to know?"

"Well, I could tell you some of the more interesting theories and a few of the 'legends' that might or might not be true."

"Please do."

"OK. There is one theory that you intended to charge right from the start - that it wasn't a desperate or impulsive decision. This is because you had Juan de Salazar with you, who was experienced in cavalry charges. What do you think of that?"

"Yes, actually, I think that is more likely than an impulsive charge. I do have an impulsive side, but in battle it is always wise to have a plan and several contingency plans to fall back on should something change or go wrong. A charge has always been a dream of mine – to lead a cavalry attack to death or glory! Although I don't think it was a primary strategy. I would have had it there to use if a suitable occasion presented itself, and it looks as if it did."

"And knowing what you know now, would you still do it?" she asked, worriedly.

"Perhaps. I would have to weigh up the situation. But at least I have some foreknowledge now."

"OK, theory number two is that William Stanley was actually coming to your aid, when he joined in the battle."

He snorted.

"Not likely," he said. "He and his brother have ever been turncoats and they resented my intervention in a land dispute between them and the Harringtons, whom I supported."

"Still, let me explain further. I read one book - and it was a novel, but I thought the theory intriguing - which suggested that William Stanley was actually bringing his men into the battle to aid you. You had already attainted him for treason and he was thought to be observing the battle from a nearby hill, so he would have seen that your charge brought you close to Tudor. When you charged for Tudor, you nearly reached him – apparently you were only a sword's length away and fought like a demon."

"Yes, the exhilaration and blood lust can do that to you. Carry on," he said, looking pleased.

"Well, from his vantage point, Stanley would have seen you slaughtering Tudor's men right, left and centre and then he would have seen Tudor's standard go down – as you know, you killed his standard bearer, William Brandon, and unhorsed his bodyguard, John Cheney."

"Yes, I read about that on-line. I have to admit I am quite proud of myself for Cheney – he was bigger and brawnier than Edward, and I'm quite slight of build."

She smiled. How typical of a man to be proud of something he hadn't done yet!

"Anyway," she continued. "When he saw that standard fall, William Stanley must have thought Tudor was lost and you were victorious. Wouldn't it have been just like him to come in on your side once he thought you were winning?"

"Ye-es, well, that kind of behaviour was typical for both the Stanleys - they often supported different sides and always put their own interests first. But then, why did I lose, if that's what really happened?"

"Well, because your men, expecting him to betray you, started fighting his men and thereby gave Tudor's an opening, and they took it. It wouldn't be the first time a friend was mistaken for an enemy, would it? The guy I met from the re-enactors pointed that out."

"No that's right. At Barnet, Oxford's Star emblem and Edward's Sun in Splendour got confused and resulted in Edward getting a shock win over the Lancastrians. I see your point. Generally, though, the leader of a force shouts out the name of the man they are supporting: 'À Richard!' or 'À Tydder!' for example, but I suppose in the noise of battle, that may not have been heard. I will be sure to advise my men of this possibility and instruct them to ensure they listen carefully to the battle cry of Stanley."

"Then there are the rumours or 'legends' about the battle," she went on. "Apart from the old crone, that I already mentioned, which might have been added in hindsight, one was that you slept badly and had nightmares the night before the battle, because of your guilty conscience."

"I rarely sleep well – my back pains me at night sometimes, especially when I sleep in a different bed. And on the eve of a battle one is always beset by worries, doubts and fear. My 'guilty conscience' would have had nothing to do with it. Next legend, please!"

"There was a story that there were no chaplains in the camp, or that they had left the host behind and so you and your army could not be shriven that day, before the battle. It was said that you announced that if God was on your side you wouldn't need to be shriven and if He wasn't it would make no difference - something like that."

"Sounds like the sort of thing I would say!" he laughed. "But if the lack of the host or chaplains is true, that would not help the morale of my men, whatever I might say. So I will ensure they do get to be shriven before the fight."

"Thirdly, there is a story that John Howard found a note pinned to his tent saying: "Jocky of Norfolk be not too bold, for Dickon thy master is bought and sold.""

"Hmm! That is worrying," said Richard.

"Because it shows you were betrayed?"

"Not that, no, as it could have been just a ploy. More worrying is that someone had managed to get to Norfolk's tent without being challenged. It suggests a very clever enemy or a traitor in our midst. I indeed have much to think about. Thank you, Rose." And he gallantly kissed her hand.

Locked out of Heaven

On October 31st, Rose brought back a selection of sweets from the supermarket to use for the 'Trick or Treaters' who might knock on the door. She opened the packets and put the sweets in a large bowl near the front door. She was quite busy that day right into the evening. She was writing up her last notes of the day and had forgotten completely that it was Hallowe'en, when the doorbell rang.

She came out of her treatment room to answer it, but Richard had beaten her to it.

"Trick or treat?!" cried a group of three mini witches, giggling.

"What is this?" said Richard, frowning.

"It's just some 'Trick or Treaters', Dickon," said Rose, offering the bowl of sweets to the children. They took a handful each and ran off, laughing their thanks.

When the door was closed Richard stood there staring at Rose, his face pale and stern.

"What is the meaning of this...this abhorrence!" he said. "Those children were simulating witches, were they not?"

"Well, I suppose so, but they're only playing. It's all in fun - they only want to get a bit of chocolate. There's no harm in it, really, you know?"

"It is not a jesting matter. This is…this is…enticing innocent children to be heathen, to be godforsaken, to deny them Heaven!"

"Don't be ridiculous, it's nothing!" she exclaimed.

"It is against God's Holy Law!" he said, in his quiet voice of steel. "I will not endanger my soul for the sake of such frivolity. I forbid you to take part either, Rose, I forbid it! I have accepted many of your strange customs and taken part in some questionable practices, but here I draw the line."

He stood there with his hands on his hips, his expression sterner than she had ever seen it. She wanted to shout at him that he couldn't order her about in her world, that she would do whatever she bloody liked! How dare he expect to behave as if he owned her? He wasn't even her husband. She opened her mouth to start the tirade and he made that swift movement with his head, tilting it to one side, while his laser gaze melted her resolve. He was clearly daring her to disobey him. She was suddenly reminded of that celebrated Holbein painting of Henry VIII - Richard, too, emanated power, authority and steely self-confidence. How could such a relatively small man exude so much raw dominance? He was truly majestic! She lowered her gaze to the floor.

"OK," she had murmured.

It was all she could do to prevent herself falling to her knees in front of him! It felt so strange, the power he had over her, half frightening, half exciting. He nodded, as if her submission was taken for granted, then turned and went back in to the lounge and sat down at the computer to continue some research. She looked at his back, a little straighter now than when they had first met, and felt a tangible, physical longing to run over to him and submit to him in every way possible - his power over her was like a strong aphrodisiac and it surprised her, as she had never before been attracted to dominant men. He was wearing his favourite jumper, which contained colours she thought of as 'Scottish heather'; soft pastel and olive greens, purples, blues and dusky pinks combined. It always made her want to hug him, it looked so soft and inviting. She wanted him so much, but his rigid self-control stopped her from ever acting on it. Her dreams of him had no chance of being a reality and she felt cheated somehow - the one man she had found who ticked all the boxes for her and she couldn't have him.

Chapter Seven - November 2014

Requiem for a Tower

A few days later, at the beginning of November, Rose took Richard to the Tower of London to see the display of 888,246 ceramic poppies, 'Blood Swept Lands and Seas of Red', made to celebrate the centenary of the outbreak of the First World War. They travelled to Monument station in order to avoid the worst of the crowds, who had really taken the display, which was created by artists Paul Cummins and Tom Piper, to their hearts and came in their thousands to view the installation. The weather was chilly and drizzly, reflecting the sombre mood of remembrance of war. Richard paled a little as they crossed the main road. They had to wait in the centre island for the traffic lights to change and the cars thundering past both in front and behind them made Richard feel very uncomfortable and the throng of people pressing on each side of them was distasteful and alien to him. It had been fairly busy and loud in medieval times, but nowhere near as overcrowded and deafening as it was now. The noise of the traffic and the crowds on the London Underground were particularly disturbing to him. He also hated the garish lights, though he admitted that the city smelled sweeter now than it had in his own time.

However, once they were close enough to see the sea of scarlet poppies in what used to be the moat, Richard became engrossed in them and they spent a long time wandering around, admiring the installation and taking photographs (at least Rose did - Richard hadn't got around to learning how to use a camera yet!)

They stood staring at the ocean of red, a symbolic wave of blood representing the real blood shed by so many for their country. The area where there was a waterfall of poppies emerging from a window, 'The Weeping Window', was the most popular and many people were stopping to take photos, causing a bottle neck. This meant they had to inch along, waiting for the way to gradually clear in front of them.

Rose felt as if she couldn't breathe and began to panic. She had always been a little claustrophobic. She remembered testing herself as a child by tucking in the duvet at the sides and the bottom of the bed and diving head first down to the far end. She would then touch the end and turn around under the covers to emerge gasping. Her phobia wasn't usually debilitating, but on odd occasions she felt a bit panicky. Suddenly she realised that there seemed to be a lessening of the crush at her back and she was able to pause to allow those in front to move off, without being pushed from behind. She turned to see what had happened and Richard stood there, leaving a space in front of himself for her and somehow projecting a virtual force field around him which compelled the crowd to back off. She wondered whether he had used his steely gaze on those surrounding him. Whatever he had done, it had worked and she was tremendously grateful. She realised that he had probably had a lot of practice in preserving his personal space as a fifteenth century king. She met his gaze and mouthed:

"Thank you!" giving him a grateful smile.

After they got out of the crush, he took her arm and steered her off to the side, back around to where they had started. She was astonished how self-assured and in control he was, in a century that he had only experienced for a few months. They stood and contemplated the poppies and their meaning again. Richard thought that it was a wonderful idea to commemorate the fallen with a poppy each. And the scale of the loss of life in that terrible war was really brought home to them when they had seen the whole of the moat filled with a bright red carpet, beautiful and sad in equal measure.

"And you say that there is a poppy for every single man who fell in...what was it called? The Great War?"

"Yes, that's one of its names - it's also known as the First World War. And yes, there is a poppy for every one of the fallen in that war, 888,246 to be exact, I think. Wait until you see the Remembrance Sunday service - you'll love it!"

"I look forward to seeing it then," he said, smiling. "I might see if I can do something similar to remember our fallen, although we don't know the exact numbers involved. Edward estimated that over twenty thousand fell at Towton, our bloodiest battle, but our record keeping wasn't as efficient as yours is now.

"Well, I sometimes wonder whether that's such a good thing - it's a lot like Big Brother sometimes. Oh sorry, you don't know about that do you? It was a novel written about a totalitarian, controlling Government, where even forbidden thoughts are not allowed."

Richard chuckled. "Hmm! I can see how that sort of thing would be useful to a ruler!"

Rose rolled her eyes.

Inside the Tower, Richard acted as guide for some of the time, and was elated that most of the Tower remained as he had remembered it. He pointed out the areas he had frequented and told her what the different parts were used for. He explained every section of the massive fortress and the few areas he wasn't familiar with he avidly learned about from the guide. He showed Rose where the royal menagerie had been in his time and described how he and George had once sneaked there to see the lions and polar bear and George had nearly got his arm bitten off by the male lion! His stories were as entertaining as those of the Beefeaters, bringing his experiences of those far off times to life for her and she loved it because she knew they were true and because she just enjoyed listening to his melodic voice.

He enjoyed trying out the archery simulator but declared it was nothing like a real bow and arrows, when he failed to score as highly as Rose. He touched the stone at times, his eyes going distant as he remembered some long ago incident and then he would turn to her and tell her all about it. It was truly enthralling to be guided by one who was recounting stories at first hand.

When they entered the Wakefield Tower where the Lancastrian King, Henry VI, had been imprisoned during the reign of Richard's brother, Edward IV, he became very pensive.

Hazard

They decided to take the Beefeater tour – those Yeomen of the Guard were impressive in their colourful clothes - until one of them recounted the story of the Princes in the Tower, saying: "This is the Bloody Tower, previously known as the Garden Tower when the two Princes were imprisoned there. Richard III, their wicked Uncle, murdered them in order to usurp the throne and become King in their place."

Rose glanced nervously at Richard and saw him turn pale and narrow his eyes, but he said nothing.

Rose said quickly: "I thought that the Princes had been seen playing in the Tower grounds after Richard had become

King - wasn't he asked to take the throne by Parliament after Bishop Stillington revealed that the previous King, Edward IV, was a bigamist and so the Princes were illegitimate?"

The Beefeater looked round, amused. "Ooh! Looks like we have a Ricardian in the crowd!" he said. "OK, it's true that Richard became King before they disappeared, claiming they were illegitimate, but most people think that was a trumped up excuse. They did disappear on his watch, so I'd say he was responsible. I'll leave it up to you individually to decide whose side you are on. Now, let's move on..."

The crowd shuffled on, following the Beefeater, and Richard looked at Rose, a soft smile on his face.

"Thank you for defending me, Rose, but you don't know the whole story. You should know I am not the innocent man you think I am, you need to know the truth..."

"You can tell me later," she said hurriedly, worried he would say something she didn't want to hear. Oh God, surely she and thousands of Ricardians had not been wrong in believing Richard had nothing to do with his nephews' deaths? She suddenly felt uneasy and afraid.

When they went up to the Wakefield Tower, she did venture to ask him about the death of Henry VI. In the Tower there was a plaque stating that he was murdered as he was kneeling to pray.

"What was the truth about his death, Dickon?" she asked.

"Edward had him killed, of course. Henry had already been used once to depose him and he really couldn't allow the possibility of it happening again. It was regrettable, but necessary. I was in London at the time, but didn't know about it until afterwards. I don't know whether I would have done the same as Edward, but I could see why he did it. Henry was a dangerous focus of rebellion, although in himself he was a harmless old man who would have been better as a priest or monk than a king. He was an innocent victim, as were many others in those evil civil wars."

"And what about his son, Edouard of Windsor? There were rumours that he was murdered after the battle of Tewkesbury, as he was fleeing."

"So I have discovered through reading some of your books, Rose. And some even say it was I who did the murdering. As you know, I was at that Battle, but I didn't even see him. I believe he was killed while fighting in the field, but he may have been cut down while fleeing. I don't believe he was murdered. I saw his corpse afterwards and his mother, the Bitch of Anjou. I remember her tearing out her hair and screaming fit to wake the Devil – most unseemly for a former Queen. I have felt a little more sympathy for her since losing my own son. I realised then how she must have felt, but at the time I was still very young myself. I had become inured to battle scenes, bloodshed and violence early on, I suppose.

"They were bloody times, Rose! You are lucky that England does not have wars like that anymore, although I know there are other forms of violence which happen in this time - terrorism, for instance."

It was true that Richard's times were different, more ruthless and bloodthirsty. Did that mean he would have done things which nowadays would be considered legally wrong and morally evil, without a second thought? She still didn't dare ask.

They left the Tower as it closed, having just had time to see the Crown Jewels. Richard thought they were beautiful, but was sad that he couldn't show her his own original crown. He recognised the spoon that had carried the holy oil, though, the only thing left from his time, thanks to the ravages of Cromwell's Republic. He was still in awe of it, his eyes going dreamy as he looked at it within its glass case.

As they walked along the subway towards the station, Richard stopped suddenly, his head on one side, listening, while she continued a few steps ahead of him, turning round curiously to see what he was up to. As she did so two men came running up to her and grabbed her by the throat, backing her against the wall, her arm scraping across the rough concrete. She let out an involuntary shriek, her heart hammering in fear like a bird fluttering against the bars of its cage, her rib cage! One of them held a flick knife at her throat and the other shouted:

"Get your rings off!"

She began to comply, realising that they had not seen Richard, who had been a little way behind, hidden in the shadows. But not for long. His voice was like the coldest Antarctic ice when he ordered:

"Release the lady, knave, or by God you will rue the day you laid a hand on her!"

He didn't shout, barely raised his voice, but that voice was full of menace.

The second man laughed nervously, revealing a small diamond on his front left tooth. The first was more cautious and simply looked at Richard, his eyes narrowed. She followed his gaze and saw Richard advancing swiftly towards them, his jewel encrusted dagger in his right hand. Before she could even take a breath to tell him to stay back, he had elbowed the first thug in the throat, and swung the second round against the wall, the point of the dagger aimed at his eye – the tables were thoroughly turned now. The first thug, who was tall and thin with blond hair, was groaning in pain and clutching his throat where Richard had elbowed him. Richard was nose to nose with the second, who was shorter and stockier than the other man, but still taller than Richard.

"I suggest you leave right now and thank God that I am feeling merciful. If ever I set eyes on you again, you shall make meat for the ravens!"

Rose was flabbergasted by the sudden and frightening change in Richard. He had reacted instantly and decisively – no hesitation at all - and the look in his eye was so coldly terrifying that she felt shivers of apprehension go down her back. This man was living in her house!

The two thugs made off down the subway, their eyes filled with fear and loathing.

"Are you alright?" Richard asked, making the dagger disappear somewhere within his clothes.

"Yes, I'm OK. Just a bit shaken."

She wasn't sure if the incident made her feel more or less safe in Richard's company. How had he realised what was about to happen? How had he managed to take them both by surprise? And how had he resolved the situation without any blood being spilt? Especially her own! It might have ended in a wholly more painful way for her, if the second man hadn't hesitated as he had.

She wondered if Richard was a little more like the Tudor portrayal of him as a tyrant than she had hoped or thought. How did he know how to act so swiftly and so violently otherwise? She couldn't forget the look bordering on madness in his eye, the swift change from polite, affable gentleman to ruthless, violent savage. Not for the first time she wondered what she had got herself into.

On their return journey, he asked her what was wrong, picking up on her mood of confusion.

"I'm just a bit shocked about how you attacked those two thugs who tried to mug me," she said quietly.

"Why? Would you have preferred me to have stood aside and let them abuse you?" he asked, genuinely puzzled.

"Well no, I suppose not, but it's not usual for men to pull out a bloody dagger and...and..." she faltered.

"The dagger was clean, Rose, I always make sure my weapons are properly cleaned after use," he said, taking her remark literally. Her expression of horror must have made it obvious that that did nothing to reassure her.

"Are you afraid of me? You are, aren't you? I did it to protect you! You were in my company and I had a duty to defend your honour and your life."

"Duty! And would you have killed those men if they hadn't backed down?"

"Yes," he stated simply. "Rose, they were going to harm you. Would you have preferred me to do nothing and run away like a craven cur?"

She blinked, tears pricking her eyes, owing to delayed reaction and the realisation of the danger she had been in.

"I'm sorry. Of course you did what you thought was right. But these days the best course of action would have been to call the police. Also, you yourself might have got injured or killed."

"Don't be ridiculous. I'm a king, a general and a battle veteran. Do you really think two lowly cut-purses could better me? Besides I don't have a mobile phone, do I?" he said, grinning.

She couldn't help returning his smile – charming Richard was back. But she was unable to resist a parting shot.

"You didn't think Tudor could beat you either, did you?"

"Ooh! That's a low blow, Rose!" he said. Then: "Are we still friends?"

"Yes, we're friends," she said.

Remember

It was November 11th, Remembrance Day. Looking at Richard now, as he sat watching the TV, intrigued by the solemn ceremony being portrayed on the screen, Rose wondered again what the truth was about the Princes in the Tower. Richard had attempted to talk to her about it more than once, but each time Rose felt a terrible sense of panic and put him off or changed the topic of conversation. Eventually he had dropped the subject and now she wished she had let him tell her - at least she would know the truth. But what if he...? She couldn't bear to even think about it, but she knew that, like his return to the Middle Ages, it was something she would have to face eventually. Perhaps if she brought the subject up at a suitable moment? If there ever was one! Whatever, she knew that even if he confessed that most heinous deed, she wouldn't stop loving him and he would still have many redeeming qualities, like his sense of honour, chivalry, justice and mercy.

He sat relaxed on the sofa, his right hand absently stroking the soft, silky head of Jonah, who was looking up at him out of the top of his eyes, adoringly. Surely, if the rumours about dogs' ability to judge character were right, Richard could not have done something so evil? Both Jonah and Jubilee absolutely worshipped him, following him around like little lost lambs. Richard simply took it for granted and had been most amazed when Rose had protested that her dogs loved him more than they did her!

"Of course they love you, Rose, but they also take you for granted because you are so soft with them - you spoil them actually," he had said. "Dogs like to have a leader to follow - it makes them feel secure and protected and the leader gains their respect by being strong and…"

He had paused mid-sentence, narrowing his eyes a little as some stray thought interrupted his lecture.

"Hmm!" he'd said, frowning.

"What?" Rose had asked, unable to resist. He was so frustrating when he wouldn't volunteer what he was thinking.

"I just realised a fundamental mistake I have made," he'd mumbled, as if to himself. "I think, from the research we have done, that I have been too much like you."

He had looked directly at her then, smiling. She loved his smile and wished he would offer it more regularly. His eyes softened and the little lines at the corners made his face look altogether gentler and mellower - younger too.

"Yes," he'd continued. "I have decided that I must become stronger and more ruthless when I go back."

Rose was glad he had added the last bit - she was trying her best to make him more flexible, and softer!

"What do you mean, Dickon?" she'd asked, worriedly.

"Well, from all the research we have done, it seems that I have lost the respect of several of my lords and nobles. For example, we think, don't we, that Thomas Stanley blatantly disobeys me when I ask him to muster his men and aid me against the Tydder. Percy also, refuses to co-operate and disobeys a direct order from me to engage the enemy. And as for William Stanley - well, he openly colludes with the enemy, seeming to feel he is impervious to retribution from me. It can't be tolerated! I am their anointed King, even if some of them are resentful of that fact, and I must be obeyed without question. I have tried to win them over by being approachable, fair and just - generous too. And what do I gain from it? It seems I gain treachery, betrayal and a bloody death, not to mention the blackening of my name. Well, it will stop, as from now. When I get back there, I will make them wish they never even thought of betraying me!"

His voice had changed to the ice-cold tone he used when he was at his most angry and his face again showed only the hard, implacable determination that characterised most of the portraits of him that still survived into the twenty first century.

"Are you sure?" Rose had whispered, a little intimidated by his demeanour; she hated conflict and arguments.

"You see, Dickon, many of your supporters today love you BECAUSE you were kinder and truer and more just than most of the other kings of your time. They love that you were honest and generous and approachable by the common people. If you change..."

She'd left the sentence hanging and looked at him in anxiety. Ironically, Richard wouldn't be Richard if he changed into the tyrant of the legends!

"Don't worry. I shall still be those things, but only to those who have deserved such considerations; and I shall always be able to be called upon by the ordinary man for justice. I shall likewise ever be loyal to those who are loyal to me, but there will be no more second chances for those who wish only to destroy me."

Rose remembered this conversation as she gazed at him now, gently fondling Jonah's ears, a cup of tea in his other hand. She smiled - he didn't look very formidable at that moment! Just then, he seemed to feel her eyes on him and turned his glance up at her, his teacup mid-way between the table and his lips, his eyebrow raised questioningly.

"What are you smiling for?" he asked, looking at her from the corner of his eye, his tone suspicious, although his own smile revealed that he was only bantering.

"Nothing, really," Rose replied. "I just thought you looked very domesticated sitting there like that."

His eyebrows shot up and he sat upright.

"Domesticated! What am I, a sheep or dog?" he blustered indignantly.

"No, you're just my tame King!" Rose laughed, grinning at his bemused expression.

"You are a brave woman, Rose Archer, to speak to your Sovereign Lord in that insolent fashion," he said, mildly, turning back to the TV. Then: "Tell me more about this ceremony on the TV."

So she sat down beside him and pointed out the present Queen, the Dukes of Edinburgh, York and Cambridge and the Prince of Wales.

"He is so old!" he said, amazed. "The Prince of Wales in our day was always young. But then again, none of our rulers managed to reign as long as this queen! How long did you say she had been ruling? "

"Well, she doesn't exactly rule, she is more of a figurehead these days - she has no real power," Rose explained. "But she has been queen for over sixty years, nearly as long as Victoria. Her Prince of Wales was pretty old too."

Rose had told Richard about all the kings and queens who had followed him. In fact she now had a huge fridge magnet on her refrigerator, bought in York, with pictures of all the monarchs from William the Conqueror to the present Queen, and Richard was intrigued to learn about them all. Today, he mocked the bearskins of the guards, however, saying they looked ludicrous.

"What about the codpieces in your day, then?" retorted Rose, defensively. "And those stupid pointy shoes?!"

He squirmed a little and finally admitted that the codpieces and shoes of his age were more ridiculous than the bearskins. Rose grinned in triumph. She didn't often get the last word.

As the ceremony on the TV continued, Rose explained again about the poppies, the Unknown Soldier and the Cenotaph. He was rapt with interest and enthused about it animatedly.

"How marvellous that an unknown warrior represents all the soldiers who died in war!" he said. "It is a wonderful way of remembering them all and praying for all their souls. You know, your world has a lot of good ideas and customs that I might try to adopt once I get home."

He was impressed with the solemnity of the service and declared that he was pleased England could still preside over a ceremonial occasion so well. He listened to the one gun salute, the playing of the Last Post, watched all the participants lay their poppy wreaths on the Cenotaph and took in the prayer of the Bishop of London, joining in with the Lord's Prayer under his breath, in Latin.

His favourite element was the choir, which had, since the time of the Conqueror, been a part of the King's retinue, now performing that duty for the clergy. He had always loved the pure, clear voices of the pre-pubertal boys and had founded a superb choir himself, when he was King. As they sang 'O God, Our Help in Ages Past', Rose could see his eyes brighten as he swallowed the lump in his throat. She had to admit it was a very poignant and moving sound, as their sweet young voices sent their praises up to God. He listened attentively to the words of the National Anthem too, his face pensive. Finally he shook his head in regret at the huge numbers of dead from the various wars, remembered on that day.

"Will we never learn Rose?" he said, sadly. "War is not the answer."

"No it isn't," she agreed. "As Bertrand Russell said: 'War does not determine who is right, only who is left.'"

Poison

As Rose became more comfortable with Richard she ventured to ask him questions about more personal events.

"What actually happened when Edward IV died?" she asked him one day as they sat at a table outside the local pub, enjoying a drink. They had the dogs with them, tied to the leg of the table and were well away from any other customers. Luckily, the winter of 2014 was unusually mild.

"Well, of course it was Anthony Woodville - Rivers - who had him poisoned. But at the time I didn't know that, so I…"

"Wait a minute! He was POISONED!!!?"

"Well, yes, although I didn't have any proof, which was why it was never brought to trial. The Woodvilles were very clever at covering their tracks, you know. But Buckingham," Richard almost spat the name of the man who had betrayed him so cynically after having helped and encouraged him to take the throne. "Buckingham came into some information about the business via one of Rivers' servants who was unwilling to be a party to regicide. He told me about it at Northampton, where I had gone to meet the new King, Ned's son, Edward, and his uncle, Rivers. But, as Harry Buckingham had arrived after Rivers, he couldn't tell me straight away - we had to wait until Rivers retired for the night. But I'm jumping ahead, aren't I?"

"Do you want to go back to the beginning then?"

"Very well. I was in the North, occupied with keeping the Scots in line and governing Yorkshire on Edward's behalf, when I received a letter from Will Hastings. He was Edward's friend and probably the most influential noble in his government. The missive informed me of Edward's death and urged me to make haste to secure the Prince, because Edward, on his deathbed, had named me Protector of the Realm during the Prince's minority. I had a Mass said for my brother Edward in York and had everyone swear allegiance, along with myself, to the new King, Edward V. I wrote letters of condolence to Elizabeth, to Parliament and to the King himself. It was arranged through Rivers, who had been overseeing young Edward's household in Ludlow, that I should meet the Royal party at Northampton and adopt my role as Protector from then on."

"And what were your feelings at that time?"

He tilted his head sardonically. "You sound like one of those disaster reporters on TV who ask some poor victim, who is obviously devastated, how they are feeling!"

"Oh! I'm sorry, I didn't mean it like that!"

"I know, Rose, don't worry. I know you're interested in the facts of what happened... I felt numb, to be honest. Angry with the Court, which had been influenced so much by the Woodvilles. I couldn't weep then; I was just numb and hollow, as if all the life had gone out of me. Edward had been the centre of my world for so long, my lodestone. Yet I knew I had to carry on and honour him and his wishes. I had to do what was right by him in death as I had in his life. I felt it was the influence of certain people - including Hastings, incidentally - who had caused his health to decline through dissolute living, leading to his death. I didn't know then that it was murder, although his lifestyle doubtless left him more vulnerable to the poison.

"Edward had become very overweight and his health was affected by the amount he drank and the general debauchery at Court. The last time I had seen him he'd looked terrible. I had felt a horrible emptiness inside me, remembering how strong and healthy he had been in his youth, yet he was not even forty then - although he looked over fifty.

"I was also apprehensive about the Woodvilles. I didn't trust them because they were always very self-serving and…'up themselves' to borrow a modern phrase which sums them up perfectly!"

Rose smiled fondly at him. It was so typical of him that his duty to his brother's memory came first. Richard continued.

"Then I got a second letter from Hastings. He urged me again to gather an armed force and seize the Prince, because the Woodvilles would try to have him crowned before I could do anything about it, and then I would be powerless, leaving them in control. Hastings hated the Woodvilles as much as I did - more, maybe. He said they had two thousand armed men as a 'guard' for young Edward and that I should bring a like amount of men. By that time Buckingham - curse him! - had also written to me offering his support and a contingent of men. I accepted his offer, but told him only to bring three hundred men, and I did likewise. We arranged to meet at Northampton, where Rivers and the boy-king were also supposed to rendezvous with us."

"But they weren't there, were they?" Rose couldn't resist chipping in.

"Correct. When I and my three hundred arrived in Northampton at the best lodging house, the landlord told us that the King's party had travelled on through. I was just about to gather the men and push onwards to try to catch up, when we saw Rivers and a few of his men coming back along the road from Stony Stratford. He was all smiles and waved to us cheerily from a distance. We went into the lodgings and he said that, because of the great number of men they had, they had decided that Northampton would be overcrowded and to press on to Stony Stratford and stay there - he, Rivers, had come back to let me know."

"And what did you think about his story?"

"I didn't believe a word of it! To begin with, there were plenty of places to lodge in Northampton and it seemed strange that he had come back himself rather than send a messenger, if his tale were true. Also, the road to Stony Stratford passed through 'Woodville' territory; perfect for an ambush. But Buckingham hadn't arrived yet and so I played for time by going along with his tale. We ordered a meal and my men settled in for the night. Rivers was staying there for overnight as well and would accompany us to meet the King on the morrow, or so he said."

"What did you have to eat?"

He stared at her, incredulously.

"Rose Archer, I am telling you about an act of treason and you are only concerned with what I ate?!"

She looked uncomfortable and her cheeks glowed a hot pink.

"No, of course not, but...well, I mean, it IS interesting to me as you ate such weird things in those days!"

"Says the woman who likes food so hot it could blow your ears off and gives you the trots!" he retorted. "Anyway, I truly don't remember what it was, nothing special. I was too preoccupied with how to handle the situation with Rivers. Anthony Rivers was actually a very learned man, quite talented in writing and very eloquent, as well as a great knight in the lists. But he was also full of himself and ostentatiously pious. However, he was a pleasant table companion and a witty conversationalist. Just as we were finishing our meal, there was a commotion outside and Buckingham arrived with his three hundred men."

"What was Buckingham like?" Rose interjected. "Was he very handsome?"

"He was handsome in an effeminate way, I suppose. He was obsessed with his appearance and clothes. He was very charming - he could talk the hind legs off a donkey, and had a way of persuading you to his point of view, while letting you think the whole idea had been yours in the first place! He loathed the Woodvilles because he felt he was above them - well, I suppose many of us did, to be fair! But he was especially venomous about them, probably because he had been forced into a marriage with Elizabeth's sister, Katherine, simply because he was very wealthy and one of the two or three highest ranking nobles in the realm. Edward never liked or trusted him, and I see in hindsight that he was right about him, but I felt a bit sorry for him actually. He had been pushed out of favour by Edward, so I gave him a chance. I thought his lack of recognition at Court was Elizabeth's doing, but it turned out it wasn't - it was Edward's decision, I realise now."

Richard paused and took a long draught of his beer before continuing his tale.

"When he arrived at Northampton, it was quite late. As soon as Rivers saw him, he said he would retire as he was feeling tired. After he had gone, Buckingham sat down beside me and grabbed my arm - I hate that kind of thing! He told me, all in a rush, that he had reason to believe that Rivers and his nephew, Thomas Grey, had poisoned Edward. I was shocked. I disliked the Woodvilles, but I had never suspected them of murder! I asked him what made him think that and he told me that Edward had become ill, suddenly, about a week before his death, after a fishing trip. Everyone thought he had just caught a chill but he had not responded to the physicians' ministrations and had worsened, in fact. He had had a bout of stomach pains and vomiting that had gone on for about two days. After that he had roused and began calling for food and drink - and his mistress - only to suddenly succumb again, this time never to recover."

Richard took a handful of crisps from the bag in front of him, offering some to Rose, as he went on.

"A servant of Rivers had gone to Buckingham - their estates were not very far from each other - and told him that he knew that Rivers had arranged to poison the King, with the help of Thomas Grey who was at Court. As I said, Rivers had charge of little Edward at Ludlow, the Prince of Wales' traditional seat.

"The servant had seen Rivers give a powder to Thomas and heard them discuss the matter, thinking no-one was about. At first he had thought they were talking about giving Edward medication of some kind, but when the king got ill and died, he realised that their words could equally have applied to poison, so he told Buckingham. Buckingham didn't believe him at first, but he did some digging and found out that Grey had sent a letter to the North, advising us of Edward's death a full three days before he actually died! This would make sense if they had tried to poison him only for him to vomit up enough of it so that it lost its effect. They likely sent word of his death prematurely. Then they tried again a few days later, succeeding the second time.

"Not only that but Anthony Rivers had been acting very suspiciously - this again was reported by the servant. He had been consolidating and confirming his powers, particularly with respect to the Prince, young Edward, and his own right to raise an army. And he illegally passed on the Deputy Constableship of the Tower to Thomas Grey, which gave him access to the Royal treasure. Looking back, this seemed to anticipate Edward's death and aimed to give the Woodvilles an advantage. Buckingham was of the opinion that, because Elizabeth seemed to be falling out of Edward's favour, thanks to his 'merry mistress', Elizabeth Shore, the rest of the family were becoming less powerful too. At the same time, I was becoming more influential, being granted positions of ever increasing authority and power and they became frightened of losing their grip on Edward, deciding that their best course of action was to kill him. They already had the Prince under their influence and control in Ludlow, and they only had to have him crowned quickly, before I could take my rightful place as Protector, and they would effectively be ruling the kingdom through the boy-king."

This was an unusually long speech from Richard, but Rose was sitting there, more and more enthralled. Poison was something she had never considered!

"Buckingham convinced me that we should put a guard on Rivers' room as he thought he would try to sneak away early in the morning. However, he did more than that; he tried to assassinate me! In the night I heard movement outside my room and suddenly had a feeling of dread - my skin crawled and I broke out into a cold sweat. I was immediately wide awake, but I feigned sleep - I just pretended to stir in my sleep as a cover for searching for my dagger, which I always keep under my pillow."

"Yes, I'd noticed," laughed Rose. "I got a terrible shock when I went to change your bedclothes while you were in the bathroom and found it lurking there under the pillow!"

"Well, it's a good thing I had it then, Rose, or I would be a dead man now," he said gravely.

He paused for several seconds.

"OK, I know technically, I AM a dead man now, but you know what I mean. Anyway, I had my dagger and I waited until I could hear someone breathing beside the bed, then I struck - I couldn't see in the dark who it was, but when someone came hurrying because of the commotion, the intruder was revealed to be one of Rivers' men. He had a sword drawn ready to strike, but luckily I had caught him by surprise and my dagger had got him in the abdomen. He had a slow, lingering death but not before he admitted it was Rivers who had sent him to kill both myself and Buckingham. They had found out that the other servant had blabbed to Buckingham and already dispatched him. In the meantime, I sent my men to arrest Rivers and keep him under lock and key. Buckingham and I took our men and went off early to Stony Stratford."

"So the Woodvilles really had tried to kill you?"

"Oh yes! As you can imagine, I was furious, but I knew that I had to get the Prince under my control, otherwise I would be as good as dead, and so would my family. When we got to Stony Stratford, the new King and his retinue had just been about to start off for London. I knew that most of the men they had - about two thousand, you remember - were ordinary farmers and such like from Wales and so I acted as if nothing was wrong. I just rode in, announced that I, as Protector, was now in charge, arrested Richard Grey and two others of the new King's retinue and dismissed the men, telling them they were no longer needed.

"It was a bluff of course, but I am quite good at that. I once bluffed Thomas Stanley into turning back and allowing my men room to pass when he was standing in opposition to me with a much larger body of men than I had. I was only seventeen at the time and I had caught him travelling in the wrong direction. Instead of going towards Edward, who had summoned him to muster, he was going the opposite way - very suspicious. I hinted that Edward would hear of it if he didn't allow me to pass, and he gave way. I was shaking in my boots that day, but I learned an important lesson: that you couldn't show fear, or you were lost."

"So what happened then?" asked Rose.

"Well, Buckingham and I took the boy-king into the inn and explained that Rivers was under arrest because of treason against myself - his uncle and the rightful Protector. He hadn't even been told that his father had named me as Protector - those bloody Woodvilles! He was upset about Rivers, and very suspicious of me, but we managed to persuade him to come with us to London. We had all made obeisance to him in the proper way. He had no choice really - I was in control by that time.

"We took him into London in triumph and we had foiled the Woodvilles for the time being. The people cheered him - they had loved Edward and were quite willing to love his son - only many of them were very wary of how hard it is when a king is a minor. It always leads to unrest and conflict, I'm afraid. The country suffers and the people too, as the factions all vie to control the young King - it's a horrific scenario. As it happened that situation never came to pass because, as you know, I ended up taking the crown."

Lady Eleanor

"How was it that you decided to take the throne, then?"

"Well, I didn't decide, the situation was thrust upon me - personally I would much rather have gone back to Middleham and remained Lord of the North - that was power enough for me. But I did worry that Elizabeth Woodville and her clan would eventually try to eliminate me and my family from the equation. Before I had time to think on it, Bishop Stillington arrived to seek an audience with me in private. It was quite late in the evening and I was tempted to send him away until the morning, but then I decided it must be important for him to interrupt me at such a late hour. He had been given a lot of power and influence under Edward and had been loyal to the House of York, so I admitted him. When he requested that my friend, Frank Lovell, withdraw, I told him he could speak freely in front of Frank. I ordered some refreshments for us and he sat on a chair in front of me, trembling. I began to wonder what on earth he had to tell me!"

"What did he say?"

"Patience, Rose, I'm coming to that. He told me that he was party to a dreadful secret that he had kept against his own better judgement for many years. He said he couldn't live with it on his conscience any more, that it was a matter of state of the utmost importance. He finally got up enough courage to tell me that he had officiated at a secret plight troth between Edward and lady Eleanor Talbot, the widow of Sir Thomas Butler. This was before Edward had married Elizabeth Woodville-Grey - and that, too had been a secret wedding which he didn't reveal for five months. It was certainly in character. Of course, at the time I was nowhere near Edward - I was away at Middleham with Richard Neville, Earl of Warwick, learning to become a knight."

"Wasn't that just a betrothal though? Couldn't Edward just have had it annulled?"

"No, not at all, it was a legal marriage - a precontract. That means a previous marriage - before the one to Elizabeth. As long as he consummated it - and I think we can be pretty certain he did that - it was legally binding, rendering his later marriage to the Grey Mare bigamous and, more importantly, all his children illegitimate. The next in line to the throne after Ned's children was Edward, George's son, but he was barred because of his father's attainder for treason and in any case he was...not quite right in the head. It would have been a disaster for England if he had become King - Harry VI all over again."

"What did you do?" Rose asked.

"I just sat there, shocked, at first. My head was spinning - it was incredible! How could Edward have been such an idiot?! Then Frank said: 'Dickon, you do realise that, if this is true, you are the rightful King!'

"I felt a cold dread go through me, a heavy weight on me. Heaven knows, I had been worried about the Woodvilles' influence over young Edward, but this...this was impossible! The very thought of having to spend so much time at Court, which I hate, the responsibility and the amount of work involved, I didn't want it - I would have much less chance to be with my family...and then I thought about them and the danger they could be in if the Woodvilles had power. And Frank was reminding me of a conversation we had had when I told him what changes I wanted to try and get the new King to implement - I could do it myself! I could change England into the just, fair, enlightened society I dreamed of. And my family would be safe, or so I thought."

He sighed.

"Stillington convinced me of the truth of his words and I knew I had to do my duty. We informed Parliament of the news and they immediately requested that I take the throne. It all happened very quickly. It was confirmed in my first Parliament the next January by Titulus Regius. I was King and Anne, my Queen."

"Tudor ordered all copies of that document destroyed, you know?" said Rose.

"He did? How do you know of it then?"

"There was one single copy that was overlooked - otherwise your reputation would be even worse than it is. It shows you were recognised as King by official Parliamentary documentation."

Kings

"Tell me about your coronation. Was it a very grand affair?" Rose asked then.

"Oh yes! It was spectacular! Of course much of it was already arranged for Edward V's benefit. I simply had to change some of the details. But it became a double coronation – the first for 175 years - because, of course, Anne was by my side."

He gave a sad little smile, but didn't seem distressed at the memory.

"Is it true you both had to bare your bodies for the ceremony?"

"Of course. How else could we be anointed with the holy chrism? I tell, you, Rose, it was the greatest thrill of my life when that holy oil touched my chest, back and head – I could feel the power of God enter me then, like a warm, tingling glow. Then the crown was placed on my head – it felt heavy and solid. I remember catching Anne's eye – she looked terrified and excited all at the same time. She was so beautiful with her crown and sceptre and the royal ring on her delicate finger. Her cheeks were as flushed as they used to be whenever we..."

He stopped abruptly, glanced at Rose and then continued:

"Well, never mind about that. The procession to and from the coronation was magnificent; all the Lords and representatives of every noble family were present and rejoiced with us – or at least they made as if they rejoiced. When I think I allowed Margaret bloody Beaufort to carry Anne's train! And Stanley carried the Lord High Constable's mace. And of course Harry Buckingham presided over the whole thing – he loved it, as he had always adored being the centre of attention. Yes, I know in theory 'twas Anne and I who were the main players for once, but he came a close second. He always dressed flamboyantly and he was a veritable peacock that day, absolutely in his element. There was a long service and Mass; then we were presented to the people. After that came the coronation feast. Now that you would have loved, Rose!"

He took advantage of any opportunity to tease Rose about her love of food. She was used to it – her family always used to call her 'the dustbin', and say she had a 'stomach like an incinerator'.

"What exotic food did you have then?" she asked, humouring him.

"Well the first course consisted of fifteen different dishes – we had swan, wild boar's head (of course, in recognition of my personal device) and various fish courses. I remember pike and lamprey and trout and salmon, flavoured with various herbs and spices. There were roasted apples and milk puddings, and it finished with a stunning subtlety, in the shape of the palace of Westminster.

"The second course comprised sixteen dishes and there was so much that the poor fed better than they had for decades on the leftovers! There was venison, beef and mutton, chicken and pork dishes, syllabub and another subtlety of myself and Anne sitting on our thrones, the detail amazing, even down to the crowns we wore with the different jewels, all made of decorated marchpane.

"The third course had seventeen dishes, including a magnificent roasted peacock resplendent in its feathers – the tail displayed as in life. There were dishes of heron, sturgeon and rabbit, egret, curlew, partridge, pigeon, quail, snipe and a final subtlety of a white boar in my honour.

"The entertainment was the finest in the land, with my own choir as well as the best musicians – lutenists, pipers and harpists. There were tumblers and jugglers and short plays performed by mummers.

"It was a magical day, but very tiring. Anne especially was almost dead on her feet by the time we were at liberty to retire; we could barely attempt the final course of food."

"It sounds fabulous! I would love to have tasted some of those dishes that we don't have today. We tend to stick to very few varieties of meat and fish. In fact I am considered eccentric by most of my friends because I enjoy trying new dishes, and I love meat and fish the most."

"What is the most unusual dish you have tasted, Rose?"

"I think it's probably springbok," she answered.

"I have never heard of it," said Richard. "Is it now a native animal here?"

"No, it's from Africa," said Rose. "A kind of antelope – it can jump really high. I've also tried moose, kangaroo, ostrich, python and alligator. My favourite is moose, but ostrich is a close second!"

Richard looked at her curiously. "These are animals of which I have no knowledge," he said. "Pray, enlighten me?"

Of course, to do this, Rose had to explain about the countries that Richard knew nothing of, so to help her they looked them up on-line – 'Thank goodness for Google,' Rose thought, showing him her tablet, and Richard eagerly absorbed all he could about these strange creatures and their, to him, alien lands. Richard was always happy to learn about the modern world but he still fiercely defended the customs and practices of his own time, which was perfectly understandable, of course.

Senses Working Overtime

Their conversation about the food at Richard's banquet, as well as their shared love of trying new tastes, reminded Rose of a unique restaurant in London, which she had visited a couple of times before. She thought Richard would like it, so she booked a table for them on-line and informed Richard that she had a surprise for him; they would be eating at a very special place on the following Saturday evening. He asked what the place was and wanted to know what was special about it, but she refused to divulge it.

"I want it to be a surprise, Dickon. Suffice it to say that I doubt very much whether you have ever had an experience like it before!"

Intrigued, he tried to wheedle more information out of her, but she resisted, leaving him in a pretend sulk. He wasn't generally a sulky person, although he was often serious and earnest. She had come to know his traits and they only served to increase her admiration and love for him. It would be so much easier to accept that she would never be with him if he'd fitted the Shakespearean portrayal of him. Nevertheless, she was glad he wasn't that evil caricature of a tyrant. She was well aware, however, that he was a man, and had faults like any other. Also that his age had moulded him to a certain extent and that values and customs were very different then. They were violent and turbulent times in which he had lived and a man had to be more ruthless then than he would these days, in order to survive and thrive. She had seen his temper flare and cowered under his Royal gaze at times. He was a powerful man in his day and she well knew the old adage that power corrupts. She hoped fervently that he had not been corrupted by it, but she still didn't dare to ask him 'the question' – "What happened to the Princes in the Tower?" - being too afraid of what the answer might be.

As Saturday drew nearer, Richard asked her what he should wear. She knew he was trying to gather information about their destination, but he was left none the wiser when she replied:

"You can wear anything, really. Whatever you feel comfortable in – it doesn't matter."

"But if it is a restaurant does it not have a dress code?" he asked.

"No, not really. Look, I'm going to wear a smartish dress, but not anything too sophisticated," she replied. "Perhaps it would be better not to wear light colours," she added.

He narrowed his eyes at her, but she ignored him. He would have to wait and see!

They took the train to London from Rayleigh and then the tube, which he hated. He didn't like people invading his personal space, but she noticed he was adept at maintaining it somehow, as he had at the Tower of London - he just had that aura of being untouchable. They soon arrived at Farringdon and walked about five minutes before they came to a main road. It wasn't the best area in London, but not the worst, either. She led the way across the street and finally pointed out their destination. It was a restaurant/bar that appeared to have darkened windows. It was called "Dans Le Noir". Knowing that she was aware of how the bright lights still sometimes dazzled him and gave him headaches, he wondered whether it was a place with dim lights, mimicking a mediaeval ambiance. In this thought he was quite wrong.

They entered the place and a hostess took their names and gave them a key to a locker in which they were to put their coats, bags and also any watches and mobile phones. Richard was perplexed but intrigued. After a few minutes they were given a choice of four menus: Meat, Fish, Vegetarian and Chef's Surprise. She chose the latter and he had the Meat.

Then they were introduced to their waiter, who was called Jules. He was blind. In fact, all the waiters were. This was because the guests were served in pitch black darkness and the waiters had the advantage of being used to the experience and were thus able to guide them and serve them better. The experience of eating and drinking in the dark was supposed to enhance the diners' sense of taste by depriving them of their sight. It also served to enlighten ordinary people about what it would be like to be blind, therefore helping to increase awareness. In addition it offered employment to disadvantaged individuals in the community, which was great.

Richard was astonished, but keen to experience this new culinary delight. Jules explained what would happen. Rose must place her right hand on his right shoulder and then Richard should do likewise, placing his right hand on Rose's right shoulder. Jules would then lead them into the dining room in single file. They would pass through two blackout curtains, and thence be able to see nothing at all. He would guide them in turn to their seats, which would be opposite each other and there would be other couples on either side of them. Cutlery and a glass would be directly in front of them. If they needed to use the loo (which was thankfully not in complete darkness!) they should just call his name and he would lead them out to the cloakroom area.

Richard's eyes were shining with interest as they followed Jules into the darkened room. The waiter had been right: they couldn't even see their own hands in front of their faces! There was an excited hum of conversation in the room, and it sounded full, although they could see nothing. Jules seated Rose and then Richard.

"Are you there, Dickon?" asked Rose, as she felt on the table in front of her for her eating implements.

"Yes, I'm here," he replied. "Well, this is certainly different. I'm thoroughly intrigued!"

Jules arrived with a bottle of mineral water for each of them and told them to feel for their glass and place their finger inside it to ensure they poured the water inside and not outside the rim and to know when it was full! It took Richard a few minutes to realise he was trying to pour his out with the cap still on the bottle!

Then their first course arrived and, after trying out the best way to get the food into their mouths (often by hand), they proceeded to try to guess what they were eating. Richard immediately dispensed with the cutlery, as he was used to using his hands more anyway. There were a variety of flavours and Rose could taste what seemed like smoked salmon and some kind of sauce which she couldn't identify, but which was delicious. Richard thought his starter tasted like spiced sausage of some kind and he wasn't far off as they found out afterwards that he had had haggis.

The other couples around them were equally enthralled and excited and, perhaps because they couldn't see each other and therefore had no prior misconceptions because of appearance, they were more disposed to talk to each other. They spent the time while they were waiting for their next course trying to guess each others' ages, heights and occupations. Rose was curious as to how Richard would describe his occupation and was surprised when he said he was a musician.

"What do you play, Richard?" asked Dave, who was seated on Richard's right.

"Well, I used to play guitar," he said. "But, I have an interest in the Middle Ages, so I changed over to the lute and I have been playing that for several years now - I play that better than guitar now, in my opinion. And I like playing something a bit more unusual."

"That's awesome!" said Dave. "I only asked because I play myself - I play the flute. I really enjoy Mediaeval-style music too, we'll have to get together for a jam session."

"Sure," said Richard, not knowing what a jam session was.

"Really? That'd be so cool! Whereabouts do you live? I'm in Chelmsford."

"Oh, I know Chelmsford," said Richard. "We live in Rayleigh, so we're in Essex too."

"Perfect," said Dave. "We can swap contact details when we get back in the light."

"Great," said Richard.

Rose was surprised and a little disconcerted that Richard had lied so unashamedly and so convincingly. And she had thought honesty was one of his major character traits!

"Do you know how to play any instruments, Rose?" asked Gina, Dave's partner. "I play the violin and cello."

"I used to play the acoustic guitar a little, but I haven't done for years, and I really have no musical talent." Rose declared. "I don't read music and I can't even sing very well. My mother was a good singer and my grandfather could play the piano by ear but unfortunately, I have my grandmother's singing voice, and she couldn't sing!"

"Oh, your voice isn't too bad," said Richard, kindly.

"When have you heard me sing?" she demanded, amazed.

"Sometimes you sing in the shower, and when you're driving," he laughed.

She sat in the dark, open mouthed. She didn't think she had sung loud enough in the shower for him to have heard from outside the door and although she did often join in with the radio in the car, she had thought she was singing so softly that he wouldn't have heard her over it. The man had ears like a bat!

Their second course arrived and she thought hers consisted of three different meats. She wasn't sure what any of them were, but they were all delicious and there was apple sauce and pureed potato. Richard said he thought his was liver, beefsteak and ham. They eventually found out Rose had eaten bison, crocodile and impala. Richard again scored a hit with the ham and liver, although the steak turned out to be kangaroo steak.

They were also served a cocktail which, Rose thought, contained vodka and orange juice and something else she couldn't place. Richard was at a loss although he enjoyed it. Finally, the dessert course, which they all had, arrived. It consisted of two separate items: one was chocolate, which Richard recognised as he had become hooked on it the first time he tried it, the second was a mousse-type dessert tasting of a fruit, but Rose couldn't identify it. It was possibly passion fruit, she decided.

"It's not passion fruit, whatever that is," said Richard confidently. "It's raspberry."

"Raspberry? No, I'm sure I would recognise that, it's one of my favourite fruits."

She took another spoonful, carefully feeling for where it was located on the plate. There was still no light at all, meaning they could still see nothing.

"My God! You're right! Now you've said it, it's obvious! How strange that I couldn't place it."

Richard was frowning in disapproval at her language, but of course she couldn't see him.

"Perhaps it's because I am used to eating in dim light."

"Why's that then, Richard? Has your electricity been cut off?" said Dave.

"No," cut in Rose. "Until recently, he was living in a very dingy old place, with lots of dark corners and very old-fashioned lighting, weren't you? I think your theory is right. This experience in supposed to enhance your sense of taste, but we're so used to seeing our food, that that is how our brains have become accustomed to identifying it. I suppose it would take a lot longer than an hour or two to change the brain's way of functioning. Interesting, though."

Fantasia on Greensleeves

When they emerged, blinking, into the dim light of the corridor, they exclaimed in surprise at seeing each other for the first time. Dave, whom Rose had expected to be plump for some reason, was tall and skinny, with blond hair curling over his ears. Gina was small, chubby and blonde, not dark and slim as Rose had predicted. They decided to go to the nearest pub and have a drink together. They found they got on really well, being about the same age and happily exchanged contact details.

On arriving home later that night, Richard was grinning. He had arranged to meet up with Dave and a few of his friends the next week to try a jam session together.

"What is a jam session?" he asked Rose.

"It's when a group of musicians all get together and play, improvising the music and experimenting as they go along," she replied.

They took the dogs for a walk as soon as they got home and Rose was pleased that Richard had enjoyed the meal so much and also made a new friend.

The next week, they got into the car and drove over to Chelmsford. Richard had packed up his lute in its special bag and was eager to play with others again. Dave and Gina lived in a smart three-bedroomed house in Springfield, on the outskirts of Chelmsford. Dave had built a large summer house, with soundproofed walls in the garden and used it as a music studio. He introduced them to his other two friends, Alan and Santi. Alan was a tall, dark Scot and Santi a short, slim Spaniard who reminded Rose of Manuel from Fawlty Towers. They chatted for a while before they attempted to play together and found they had similar musical tastes. Richard nodded sagely when they asked if he liked Viking metal and New Mediaeval. Rose realised he was an excellent bluffer. It was rather a worry.

They got out their instruments, tuned them, and then Dave began playing a few tunes from iTunes through his speakers, so that they could all be reminded of them. Rose was impressed with how quickly Richard learned tunes that, although well-known to the others, he had never heard before. He joined in and his companions didn't seem to notice that he was tentative at first. Luckily, his ear for music was excellent. One of the tunes Dave had played was

Vaughan Williams' Fantasia on Greensleeves. Richard loved the tune and Rose wasn't surprised as it was supposed to have been composed around the time of Henry VIII, so the type of music and the mood were familiar to him. She loved this version too. The group ended up playing some neat music and Richard was very well satisfied with his trip. The other two, who played the piano and guitar, had said they were going to try to pick up some more Mediaeval instruments, if they could.

Over the next couple of weeks, they managed to find an old harp in an antique shop and a harpsichord, as well as pan pipes and a set of bagpipes online. Alan, the pianist, found he did well with the harpsichord and Santi loved the harp. Dave adopted the panpipes on occasion and they all took turns with the bagpipes.

They met up regularly to practise together, becoming more and more accomplished every time. In the end, they decided to form a band called the Middle Agers and got a few gigs playing local pubs and any gatherings with a Mediaeval theme. Richard had to bite his tongue at some of these, because they weren't all as authentic as they thought.

"It's great that I am earning some money, don't you think?" he asked Rose. "If I find I can't get back home, I could always fall back on my second choice career!"

Rose smiled, secretly hoping that would be the case, but torn because she had noticed his use of the word "home" when talking about going back and she knew that was what he really wanted. She still dreaded it. Every time it was mentioned or crossed her mind, she felt a cold feeling like an icy hand gripping her heart and squeezing until it seemed it must stop beating.

They had settled into a happy routine. Every morning they would get up, have a coffee and walk the dogs in the woods. Richard and she were both highly entertained by Jonah, who ran around like a mad thing, jumping over little bushes, brambles and branches. He was so full of joy at being free to run and roam wherever he wished for a while. Richard envied him that. In the afternoon, they would ride, provided Rose wasn't too busy with patients, and she would cook from scratch most evenings. Richard enjoyed helping her and often peeled the vegetables whilst watching TV.

Richard helped Destrier with their training every Saturday daytime and practised with the band one or two evenings a week, gigging at weekends, chauffeured by Rose.

Any spare time they had was spent researching on the internet and questioning every expert they could find about Bosworth and paranormal time travel.

Chapter Eight - December 2014

Hocus Pocus

In early December, they had arranged to meet Lynne again as she had told them that she had discovered something new.

They met her in the Roebuck, a Gastro pub in Rayleigh High Street, and ordered their food at the bar. Then they took a table at the window.

"So, what have you found out?" Rose asked Lynne.

"Well, I've been working on the theory that Richard was drawn here because of your powerful obsession with him, utilising the Law of Attraction."

"Yes, yes - we know that!" said Rose, glancing sideways at Richard and blushing furiously. He returned her glance accompanied by a mischievous grin.

"Well, there are several other examples of manifesting a person using the Law of Attraction, although they are mainly 'soul mate' examples," said Lynne. Rose blushed even more and Richard raised his eyebrows. "But all of these examples seemed to have an extra element - a catalyst of some sort," Lynne went on.

"Such as?" asked Richard.

"Well, as far as I can gather, the person who was 'transported' for want of a better word, saw a vision or apparition of some kind just beforehand. For example, one in Greece saw a white swan, another in Colombia, a black monkey."

"I saw a white boar!" said Richard excitedly.

"Did you?" asked Rose. "You never told me that before!"

"Didn't I? It must have slipped my mind...although actually I believe I did mention it in the first conversation we ever had. I said I'd been following a white boar that had led me a merry dance or something like that."

"Oh, so you did!" agreed Rose, wondering at his memory for details.

"Well, before you get too excited, there are other elements that seem to be required," added Lynne.

"Yes?" said Richard and Rose in unison.

"Well, firstly, the date is always significant in some way and if they return it is on that same date, if another year."

"What was the date you arrived on, Dickon?" Rose asked, while trying to remember herself. "Wasn't it June 21st? Well, that's the summer solstice, isn't it?! Could that be the significance, Lynne?"

Lynne wrinkled her nose, deliberating.

"I'm not sure, maybe it is, although I feel it should be a more personal association."

"It wasn't!" said Richard. They both looked at him.

"It wasn't what?" asked Rose.

"It wasn't 21st June, it was 22nd," he said.

"Oh gosh, you're right, it was the Sunday, wasn't it? Well is that date of any significance for you?"

"Not that I can think of at the moment," he said. They remained silent, feeling rather frustrated and each absorbed in their own thoughts.

"You said there were other elements - plural - didn't you, Lynne?" Rose said.

"Oh yes," said Lynne. "There's another common element. It seems that the person being transported has always been aided by a spirit helper or passed relative - somebody outside the world as we know it - who can decipher the way things will pan out and who has some kind of vested interest in facilitating the transfer."

"Ooh! I have never heard of anything like that before," said Rose. "Richard, do you know of any guide or spirit who could be leading you?"

Richard frowned. "I don't like this idea of a 'spirit' trying to contact me, but the obvious one who might be helping me is Anne...or Ned, possibly? Maybe they saw, in Heaven, what the future held for me and led me forward in time so that I could be forewarned and change the outcome?"

"Hmm!" said Rose. "That would make sense. Lynne, is there any way of finding out who it is who is helping or leading Richard?"

"Well, you're not going to like this," she began, her eyes on Richard. "In your day it would have been seen as sorcery or witchcraft, but if we…"

"No!" said Richard, his eyes blazing with a mixture of fear and anger. "I will have nothing to do with witchcraft! I forbid it!" His clenched fist hit the table with a loud thump, making both women jump.

Lynne glanced nervously at Rose. "OK, OK, we won't do it then. But I don't know how we can get any further forwards without it."

"What are you talking about exactly, Lynne?" asked Rose.

"Well, I was thinking about using a Ouija board?"

At this, it was Rose's turn to look horrified. "No way! I totally agree with Richard - I don't want anything to do with that kind of thing."

"Well, what about if we spoke to an expert in spiritual matters, a medium?"

"Do you know anyone?" Rose asked.

"Yes, I know several. It really isn't scary or evil, you know," she said, attempting to reassure them.

"What do you think Richard? Would you speak to a medium?"

"No, Rose, absolutely not! My faith forbids it expressly - contacting the dead is an abomination!"

"What do you suggest then, Richard? Only we really need to have some kind of plan or you'll never be able to get back," said Rose, secretly wishing that would be the case.

"I will pray, Rose. I will pray. That is the only solace and help I trust. I know of late my prayers have gone unanswered, but I will not lose my faith. In the past, God has guided me in my dreams. It's true that lately he has seemed to forsake me, poor sinner that I am, but Rose, you could pray, could you not? Would you? It seems that you are part of the reason I am here, so perhaps your prayers would be more effective than mine. What do you say?"

He regarded her seriously, his beautiful blue-grey eyes pleading with her. She could see the fear, the hope and the entreaty in those expressive eyes, as if he were allowing her to see inside his soul. She knew she would agree to do whatever he wanted, although she wasn't really religious. She wondered again what sin he had committed. But she would do as he asked. For him. Of course she would - she would do anything for him! He covered her hand with his, and she smiled up at him.

"I say 'yes' Richard. Of course I will help in any way you see fit. I'm not sure my prayers will be as effective as you hope, but I can only try. Perhaps we could pray together? What about you, Lynne? Will you join us and pray for guidance?"

Lynne took a deep breath in. She sighed and nodded. "Where and when?" she asked.

They arranged to attend the local Catholic Church, Our Lady of Ransom, that weekend and they drove there in the car, having picked Lynne up at her home which was about a mile away. They took part in the whole service as best they could. It was easier for Richard, although much of the Catholic service had changed for him. However, he did recognise the general method of it. They all crossed themselves and genuflected as they entered the church, and they each lit a candle, asking mentally for God's guidance, before taking their seats at the back of the church. They listened intently to the sermon and sang the hymns as best they could. Only Richard, however, received the host at the altar as Rose and Lynne were not confirmed Catholics.

At the end of the service, they remained in the back pew of the church as they had agreed before they went in. They waited until everyone else had gone and then knelt together, their hands clasped in prayer. They did not pray aloud, but each sent their heartfelt request for guidance in their own words, visualising them rising up to God from their own hearts. They also requested that God send them a sign, a clue to help them send Richard back to his own century. Finally they went back to Rose's little bungalow and chatted for a while before Lynne left for home.

Richard and Rose had a night cap before they retired for the night and Richard went to bed first, giving Rose a chaste goodnight kiss on her cheek and a swift hug.

"Pleasant dreams!" she called.

Dream A Dream

The next day, at breakfast, they discussed whether they had had any sign from God in their dreams. Rose had dreamed of a rolled up scroll, lying on a table and covered in neat writing. She couldn't make out anything of what it said, but saw a pair of strong hands take the document and throw it on the fire. Then she felt the door shut as whoever it was left the room. Immediately she moved forwards and grabbed the fire tongs, pulling the burning pages out of the fire and dousing the flames with a convenient pitcher of water. She knew it was she who pulled it out, but when she looked down at her hands, they looked masculine, strong and brown, compared to her own. The hands unrolled the manuscript and she saw the words, but they were written in the script of a Mediaeval hand and she struggled to understand them. She only knew the manuscript was tremendously important for some reason. That had been all she remembered dreaming.

"Can you not remember any of the words you saw, Rose?" asked Lynne when they met up with her later. "Or even describe or draw a copy? Richard might recognise something if you could."

Rose closed her eyes and tried to revisit the dream scene. Richard and Lynne waited patiently. After a minute or two Rose's eyes flew open.

"I just remembered this." She took a piece of paper and a pen and tried to make a copy of the one or two 'words' she had seen but was unable to decipher. Richard looked over her shoulder as she drew them. She felt his warm breath on her neck and her heartbeat quickened involuntarily. She hoped neither he nor Lynne had noticed her blushing.

"That is my name, Rose!" he exclaimed. "But I do not understand the significance of this."

"We will have to think about it some more and do more research," Lynne said.

Then it was Richard's turn. He said he had dreamed he had been in a monastery, a huge one, that was filled with smoky mist so that everything was blurred and unclear. He heard a voice say: "You are a loyal and honest man, Richard, but your faith has been sorely tested. You must have faith in me and believe that I work to help you and this stricken land of yours. Do you trust me?"

"Who art thou, I pray thee?" Richard had asked.

"Know simply that I am one who has wronged you, unwittingly, but who wishes to make redress. Do you trust me?" the unseen man repeated.

Richard had hesitated. How could he trust someone or something he couldn't identify?

"I want to, but I cannot trust by will alone - it is not a thing which can be forced. I will say this - that I wish to at least see your face before I answer."

"Hmm!" chuckled the man. "Honest as ever! Very well."

And the man waved his hand and the mist cleared. Richard looked curiously at his face, seeing honest, blue, wise eyes and finely chiselled features. The man was dressed as a noble, with a crucifix around his neck and a black robe around his shoulders. Then the mist descended again and the man disappeared in it.

"Who was it then, Richard?" asked Rose, enthralled.

"I have no idea, Rose. It was not anyone I know. I have never seen that man before in my life!"

"Well, what do you think it means?"

"Maybe he is the one who has instigated my journey here, as Lynne described. The catalyst who has made it possible?"

"But who is he?" said Rose. "You said he had wronged you. Can you not work out who it would be from that?"

Richard laughed bitterly. "There are so many who have wronged me that I fear I would never remember them all. But, nevertheless, I am sure I have never seen him before. I am adept at remembering faces. Also, the clothes were not of a style which was familiar to me in my time."

"Then perhaps it is somebody from a foreign land or another time. We have a bit more to go on, at least. What about you, Lynne? Did you have a significant dream?"

"Well, if I did, I don't remember it," she said, despondently. "I will try again and let you know if I experience anything, OK?"

The others agreed and said they would contact her again after Christmas to see if any further progress in their research had occurred. They were all going to be busy with the festivities until then. Richard and Rose returned to the bungalow in silence and were occupied by their own thoughts.

DNA

It was the morning of December 10th, Rose's thirtieth birthday. She felt rather depressed. She was thirty years old and what did she have to show for it? Seven years of marriage and a divorce. OK, she was gradually expanding her business as an osteopath, but it was hard. Her main regret was that she had no children. Yes, there was still time, but….well, suffice it to say, she could almost hear the sound of her biological clock ticking away - tick tock, tick tock, tick tock. She resented that women were pressured by time to start a family early. Men had it easy - they could father children almost until the day they died. Not fair!

She was lying in bed, unable to make herself get up and face the day - one day nearer to death! Goodness, why was she so morbid today? There was a soft knock on her door. She brightened immediately.

"Come in!" she called and Richard entered, carrying a tray on which was a latte from her coffee machine, a cooked breakfast and a glass of juice, and a tiny cake with one solitary candle on it. On the side was a single white rose in a thin vase of water and a small package. She was amazed - she hadn't even told him it was her birthday!

"Thank you, Dickon. How did you know?"

He grinned. "I have my spies! Actually, it was Lynne who told me - here are some birthday cards that came in the post today as well, and one from me."

He handed her several envelopes, including a pink one with her name written on it in his distinctive, Mediaeval hand. He had made an effort to modernise his handwriting and it was now a strange hybrid. She opened his card first. The picture was of a black Labrador puppy with a bunch of white roses in its mouth, some spilling onto the floor. She smiled and turned to the inside. There was a short verse and underneath it he had written: 'To Rose, who is my comfort and joy, my inspiration and counsellor and my dearest friend. Yours Richard xxx'

She read it again - did it say 'Yours Richard' or 'Your Richard'? She didn't ask, but chose to believe it was the latter. She felt choked with emotion, but managed a small wobbly smile as she opened the little packet. She tore off the paper and threw it aside, then took the little blue box and opened it carefully. It was a beautiful, round, golden locket with, again, a rose on the front of it.

"I thought you might like to put my picture in it," he said.

"Your picture! Why would you think I might want your picture in it?" she asked, teasing him.

"Because I am so handsome, of course," he said, mock seriously.

"You're very modest," she said.

"I'm just honest," he said, deadpan, though his eyes were twinkling.

Rose smiled and thanked him, privately wondering whether he was, in his subtle way, warning her that he would be leaving and that she would therefore need something to remember him by. She suddenly remembered that she had something even better than his photograph - a lock of his hair. When he left her to enjoy the breakfast and attend to her ablutions, she retrieved it, placed it inside and put the locket around her neck.

She had taken the day, a Wednesday, off work so they went for a ride in Hockley Woods with the dogs. They couldn't go too fast, because Jubilee was slowing down now, at her age. Rose had become quite an accomplished rider under Richard's expert tuition and her horse, Goldy, had grown more responsive along with Rose's skill so that they made a great partnership and she could now see why Richard loved riding so much. They chatted easily with each other as they rode and Rose tried just to take each moment with Richard as it came and not worry about if or when he would leave her.

When they got home, tired and exhilarated by their ride, they continued their research regarding Richard's return to his own time.

"Look, Dickon. They have done some more analysis of your DNA - they are now 99.999% certain that the skeleton is you!"

He snorted. "Well, that's a relief!" he said sarcastically.

"Apparently there is a 96% chance your eyes were - or are - blue and…wow! A 77% chance you had blond hair."

"Well, I believe I did as a child. I was quite fair until the age of about ten, and of course I do have blue eyes." He smiled and fluttered his eyelashes.

Rose laughed, then turned back to the news report. "They say, however, that there is not a match with your paternal DNA and that of the descendants of John of Gaunt, who should have the same DNA. That means that somebody's father down through the line of descent, wasn't the real father. Scandal! Can you shed any light on that?"

"There were always rumours - you know my father was rumoured to have been cuckolded by a French archer called Blaybourne, resulting in Edward. My mother even said as much when she was angry at Edward for marrying Elizabeth - she disowned him. But she did take it back later."

"Well, that wouldn't affect your DNA or the descendants they tested as they were not on Edward's line. There were at least two such breaks in the line, they say. There are nineteen links in the chain and the breaks could be anywhere - short of digging everyone up and testing them all, we'll never know! They say there was gossip that Edward III wasn't the actual father of John of Gaunt, so one of the breaks could be there."

Richard chuckled. "That would make Henry Tydder even more of a bastard!"

I Wish It Could Be Christmas Every Day

Soon after her birthday, Rose enlisted Richard's help to get the Christmas decorations down from the loft. He was keen to see how Christmas was celebrated in a time where religion was not as important as it had been in his. He thought the lights were magical and he liked the idea of the Christmas tree - he was a nature lover himself and approved of all those aspects of Christmas such as holly and mistletoe, which had also been used in the Christmas celebrations he knew. He also liked learning the songs - they mainly listened to Classic FM because they played the more traditional carols and religious choral songs that Richard loved, but occasionally they listened to Christmas songs from the popular radio stations or TV and he did enjoy some of those songs too. After a while he was singing along with them - he remarked to Rose that he felt his lungs were more powerful since she had begun treating his back.

"Yes, that would make sense," she said. "Your spinal alignment affects your ribs, which are integral to your breathing efficiency."

He was very disappointed that fewer people celebrated Christmas with a Mass than in his time, but Rose said she would be happy to accompany him to Church. They both really enjoyed the service at the Catholic church and Rose suggested that he try an Anglican service to see what he thought of that. He was rather suspicious, but finally agreed, and they attended the Christmas Eve carol service at Holy Trinity Church. He enjoyed it, but thought the service was a watered down version of a Catholic ceremony and wondered why no-one was dancing along to the carols, as that is what the word 'carol' meant in his time! After the service they were given mince pies and mulled wine - he was astonished to find no meat in the mince pies, which was the way they were made in Mediaeval recipes, but he savoured the mulled wine and ended up talking about the meaning of Christmas to the priest, who was very impressed with his knowledge.

He was eager to find out what kind of food modern folk ate for Christmas too, and when Rose said that the most traditional meat was turkey he was perplexed, as he had never heard of it. She showed him pictures and videos on Google and when he discovered that they originated in the Americas, he was even more interested.

"Potatoes, tomatoes, avocado, sweet corn, peanuts, chocolate, vanilla - many of my favourite tastes from the modern world originate there. I will be keen to taste this fowl," he said.

Rose had no close family left who lived anywhere near her - most of them were still in the London area - and, although several of her friends, including Laura and Lynne, had invited her to celebrate Christmas with them, she thought she would rather spend this special Christmas with her Royal guest. She asked him if he would prefer to be in a large group or just celebrate with her and he eagerly chose the more intimate day, with Rose and the dogs.

"It would give me immense pleasure to share Christmas with you," he said. "I have known so many pompous, overblown celebrations these past few years that it would be a relief to relax in the company solely of someone I care about, for once. I would be delighted to help you prepare the food too - I have rarely had the opportunity to do that either."

She smiled at him and he returned her smile, his blue eyes crinkling at the corners and his dimple as charming as ever. She was glad - Christmas was her favourite time of year and if she had him all to herself, it would give her a unique memory of him to cherish after he had gone.

They shopped for goodies and presents in the weeks leading up to Christmas and he was as good as his word in helping her to prepare the meal. She cooked the turkey on Christmas Eve and he peeled and chopped the vegetables while she made the giblet gravy and prepared the jelly as well. She laid the Christmas table with the place settings, crackers, decorations and a centre-piece the night before and, after he had gone yawning to bed, she stayed up late, wrapping presents.

The next morning, while Rose continued the preparation, Richard took the dogs out for a walk and returned to a veritable feast! They had Coquilles St Jacques for starters, turkey and all the trimmings for main, followed by Christmas pudding (home made in October to a secret family recipe) with brandy butter, and lemon and raspberry jelly. They drank Champagne and pulled their crackers and Richard was enthralled with everything. He particularly enjoyed her pudding and had second and third helpings.

After the meal they opened their presents. Rose had bought him chocolate Brazil nuts and a blue cashmere scarf which enhanced the colour of his eyes. She also gave him a white rose enamel pin from the Richard III Society and a painting of himself that she had done in secret whenever he was out (which happened more frequently now he was used to modern ways), depicting him wearing the crown that had been made to go on his coffin at his re-interment. When she had found out that it would have fitted his head, had he been alive, she thought it was a shame she would never see him wear it and so decided to paint him thus, using some of her photos of him and a picture of the crown. He was enchanted by it and proclaimed her every bit as skilful as the artist who had done his portrait a couple of weeks before he had left Mediaeval England.

"I don't know about that," she had replied, modestly.

"Well I do - you are very talented, sweeting!"

And he came over to her and kissed her full on the lips. She was so taken aback that it was over before she could enjoy it, but it made her blush nevertheless.

"Now open your presents," he urged, as excited as a little boy.

She picked up the two packages that he had handed to her one at a time and found that the first contained perfume, a floral one called Flowerbomb, which she loved immediately. She put some on and sniffed it appreciatively.

"Is it suitable?" he asked anxiously. "I asked the shop assistant to help me choose."

"It's perfect!" she smiled, taking up the next gift. This turned out to be a pair of leather driving gloves, which were ideal as she had been complaining her hands were cold when she first started the car.

"There's more!" he said. "Wait a minute." And he slipped into the kitchen and she heard him open the freezer. He came back with a small parcel, wrapped in Christmas paper and very cold!

"What on earth is this?" she laughed. "A snowball?"

"Open it," he said.

She did so and nearly screamed and dropped it when she saw what was inside but she managed to control herself and simply said:

"I'm none the wiser - what is it, Dickon?" The package contained several long, slimy eel-like things, frozen solid. They were the ugliest things she had ever seen!

"They're lampreys, of course," he said, with obvious delight. "You said you had never tasted them, so I decided you should. I know how you like to try new things. It was the devil of a job to get them though - I had to send to Canada for them. Apparently they are endangered in England now."

"Wow!" she gasped. "Well, I shall look forward to tasting them, but I don't have a clue how to cook them."

"There are recipes online - I checked," he said. "It's usual to bake them in a pie. I think they are cooked with wine, nutmeg and different herbs; you will love them Rose, just as I do. Did you know that the town of Gloucester, of which I am Duke, of course, has always sent a lamprey pie to every new monarch? They traditionally come from the river Severn. In fact, your present Queen has even had them sent to her, on her coronation and her twenty fifth, fiftieth and sixtieth anniversaries."

"No, I didn't know that," she laughed. "Maybe we should cook them for New Year."

"As you wish," he said, bowing his head in agreement. "There is one more present. I hope you will like this one." He looked worried and she felt very anxious; what on earth would this be? How could he follow the lampreys for weirdness?

"I have to go next door to get it," he said and marched off to the adjacent bungalow, leaving Rose open mouthed in surprise.

He was back in only a couple of minutes with a large package, which he put down on the floor in front of her. As she opened it, the lid was forced off and a little furry face emerged, yapping. It was a miniature dachshund, not a puppy, but very small.

"I hope you don't mind, Rose. He needed a new home and...well, I know you love dogs. It was one of the neighbours who asked me if I thought you would be interested. If you're not, I will return him."

"No, that's fine, Dickon - he's gorgeous - as long as the other dogs get on OK with him."

"They have met him before; once when I took them for a walk I took them to meet him. I think they will be OK."

"What's his name?" she asked.

"It's Hunter and he's two years old," he said. She cuddled the little dog, who yapped again and licked her face. She put him down and went over to Richard. "You are so thoughtful, your gifts are personal and wonderful, thank you!" she said and leaned in to give him a peck on the lips, as he had done to her.

To her shock, he pulled her close and kissed her fully, gently, but lovingly, his tongue pressing against hers in a way that made shivers of desire thrill throughout her body. He wasn't demanding and didn't fondle her or try to take it any further and she was too afraid to force it in case it all went wrong again, so she just followed his lead and returned his kisses in the same gentle, loving way. She could feel his love for her in the slow deliberate way he kissed her - it was no drunken fumble. Surely she wasn't mistaken? They clung together for several perfect minutes, just kissing, not urgently, not passionately but perhaps as loving friends. She wasn't sure if it was going to lead anywhere, when suddenly the little dog, Hunter, started yapping and trying to climb up her legs, interrupting them and breaking the spell. Richard put her gently away from him and smiled at her.

"Merry Christmas, Rose!" he whispered.

"Merry Christmas!" she replied.

Chapter Nine - January 2015

Red Red Wine

Rose was on cloud nine after Richard's behaviour towards her at Christmas but, in the cold light of day, she had been unable to broach the subject of their feelings for each other and so it had remained tacit.

The following week, on New Year's Day, they collaborated in the making of lamprey pie, following an old Elizabethan recipe online and laughing as they struggled to gut the lampreys and remove their spinal cords, which were, apparently, poisonous. The pie had turned out well and the sauce the lampreys were in had been amazing. Rose liked jellied eels, being a London girl, and lampreys, she thought, were somewhat similar. They were extremely tasty and Richard had almost swooned when he took a bite of the pie. He'd closed his eyes in ecstasy and groaned with pleasure. Rose thought his present had been more for himself than for her!

Their routine continued on into the New Year and one evening they were chatting companionably and drinking wine with their home-cooked dinner. Rose had taken to cooking a lot more from scratch now that Richard was staying with her. Ever since her divorce, she had relied on takeaways and frozen meals most of the time; there hadn't seemed much point in cooking for just herself. It was only now that she had begun thinking about cooking real food again that she had realised how much she had missed the taste. This evening, her offering was spaghetti Bolognese. She watched with interest as Richard, with a puzzled expression, tried to copy her as she twirled the spaghetti around the fork, while holding it against the spoon. Each time he tried to lift it to his mouth, it slipped off the fork, dangling down dangerously near to his new, white shirt. He had just bought a few shirts, quite conservative in style and colour, but smart and expensive – even in this new world he was unerringly drawn to the best of everything.

Suddenly, with a swift, smooth motion, he drew out his dagger – the same one he had kept on his person or nearby since she had first met him – and sliced through the long strands of spaghetti with impatient, stabbing movements.

"Damn the proper etiquette!" he mumbled under his breath as he stuffed a huge spoonful of sliced-up spaghetti and Bolognese sauce into his mouth. He gave her 'that look', head slightly tilted, gaze of steel, that dared her to comment. She said nothing.

"A man could starve around here," he added after swallowing his first mouthful. Then, more mildly: "Mmmm! This is delectable! Pity the mode of conveying it to the mouth is so troublesome."

"Wait until you try Chinese and chop sticks!" giggled Rose, imagining the scene.

She poured him some more wine, which was a good, deep-red Rioja, and ventured one of her 'burning questions'.

"Richard, can I ask you something?"

"Oh dear! I know, as soon as you call me Richard instead of Dickon that it will be a difficult or sensitive question. As always, you may ask, though I don't guarantee that I will answer."

He took a large swig of the wine.

"Will you tell me a bit about your brother, George? What was he like? How did you actually get on with each other?

And was he really executed by drowning in a butt of Malmsey wine?"

Richard swirled the wine around in the glass, watching the light catch it and reflect the dark red liquid, like blood. He sighed softly.

"George was an enigma. He could be the most charming person you could ever wish to meet. He was a faithful husband to Isabel. He loved his children as much as any man. He loved his brothers too, I like to believe. I certainly loved him, but I didn't always like him. He was so completely different from me, we didn't ever really understand each other. He had a cruel streak and he was obsessed with being King. He could never accept second place in anything.

"I remember when we were children. He was three years older than me and much bigger and stronger, so he could beat me at most games and physical activities. He would never let me win to encourage me – no, he had to be the victor, always. There were a few things I could sometimes beat him at though: archery, hawking and chess. I would win those more than half the time and he hated it! He would sulk for hours whenever I triumphed. It was quite funny really. But George in a sulk wasn't a pretty sight!"

"Why do you think he was like that?"

"I don't really know. Perhaps because he was neither the eldest son nor the youngest. Edward and I were at each end of the family, so to speak, and we therefore had more of a defined role. Edward was the heir, the King, the one with the power and I was the youngest and smallest son, in some ways Mother's favourite. Perhaps he felt I usurped his place as the spoiled younger son."

Rose raised her eyebrows at his choice of the word 'usurped' and realised he, too, had noticed it when he hesitated and took another gulp of Rioja to cover his discomfiture.

He continued: "George was like Edward in some ways – they were similar in looks, though George was not as tall nor as handsome. You could tell they were brothers though, whereas I was the odd one out, really. They were both fairly stocky and fair – they both had almost blond curls and light blue eyes. I was, well, you can see – smaller, slighter in build and my hair, though it was fair, was not as curly and I had darker blue eyes. It bothered me for a while; I felt like the cuckoo in the nest. It was Mother who reassured me. George had knocked me down while we were play-fighting and sat on me, calling me a runt and a changeling. I had run to Mother - I must have been only about nine years old – and asked her if it was true, was I a changeling? It would explain the differences in my appearance. She told me that, on the contrary, if I could see myself beside my father, I would realise that I was a miniature version of him, a true Plantagenet. Of course, my father had been killed about a year earlier so I couldn't compare us and I had forgotten what he looked like. I don't think I had known until that moment how that whole question had been worrying me. After that I grew in confidence as I grew in size and soon George gave up trying to beat me. I trained so hard that I soon became as strong as him and I was faster so I bested him quite often."

"What about the question of Anne and her inheritance?"

Richard's face clouded over for a moment at the mention of his dead consort.

"George was abominable about that! He had always been greedy both for wealth and power. After his marriage to Anne's sister, Isabel, and the death of their father, Warwick, at the Battle of Barnet, he thought if he could keep control of Anne he might get his hands on all the lands previously owned by Warwick, as well as their mother's estates. He was so furious when he found out I wanted to marry Anne that he hid her in the cook-house belonging to a relative of one of his retainers. They actually made her do menial work! Poor little Anne. I was beside myself with rage when I finally tracked her down. At that moment I could have killed George, right there on the spot!"

He paused, his eyes gazing into the distance at some scene from the past. He shook his head, sadly.

"George was an idiot sometimes. If he thought I was just going to give her up and go away, he didn't know me very well. He took it for granted that Edward would always forgive him anything. Well, Ned did forgive him for joining forces with Warwick and deposing him. I suppose George thought if Edward had forgiven him for treason once, he would do again. In that he was sadly wrong. At the time, I couldn't understand why Edward was so implacable - George's offences at that time seemed much less than those Ned had forgiven before. However, little did I know that George had been shouting his mouth off about Edward and Elizabeth's marriage. It all became clear later, when Ned's pre-contract with the Lady Eleanor Talbot came to light. He and Elizabeth could not allow George to make it known and so he had to be silenced."

"So poor George was killed to keep Edward's little secret?"

"Exactly. He was found guilty of High Treason, despite my pleading for his life - Edward was never going to reprieve him, whatever I had said. It's a bit of a comfort actually, knowing that it wasn't my lack of eloquence that doomed George - I'd always partly blamed myself, you see."

"And the Malmsey?"

"Yes, it's true! Edward allowed him the favour of choosing the method of his dispatch." He snorted. "Typical George to choose to drown in a butt of wine. At least Edward let me forgo the duty of announcing the verdict - I don't think I could have done it, and then I might have been found guilty of treason too. Apparently, George was allowed to drink himself into a stupor first and was then drowned."

Richard sat motionless, his expression like stone, gazing at the table. The only clue that he was feeling any emotion was the slight, shiny brightness in his eyes and the muscle working in his jaw as he clenched his teeth.

"How awful," Rose said and reached over to give his hand a squeeze. He allowed it, but only for a few seconds before he gently removed it from her and picked up his glass for another drink.

"So the Shakespeare and More versions were wrong then?" Rose asked, watching his reaction carefully.

His head whipped up from contemplating the table and he looked right into Rose's eyes, his gaze almost burning her it was so intense.

"Do you ask me if I murdered my brother, George?" he said in his softest, most dangerous voice. She knew he was angry because he felt she had betrayed him by even asking the question.

"Richard, I'm sorry if I've upset you. It's so difficult for me because the values and customs of your time are so radically different from ours. I only want to understand you better."

"Then let me clarify for you. More and Shakespeare were wrong. I was not dissembling when I pleaded for George. I didn't hate him and I didn't see him as an obstacle to the throne. I was nowhere near the Tower when his execution took place and I didn't speak to Ned for months afterwards because I was so upset that my only two remaining brothers had so set against one another that the one had killed the other! I took George's children in and treated them as my own. I had Masses said for him and oversaw his respectful burial in Tewkesbury Abbey, alongside his wife. And I categorically did not murder him! Does that satisfy you? Have you finished toying with my memories and emotions now?"

His voice was cold and hard - his tone cruel.

Rose was now trembling in distress, tears starting to sting her eyes. She turned from the table and ran out into her bedroom, flinging herself onto the bed and sobbing her heart out.

Kiss From A Rose

She didn't hear the door open a minute or two later and started as she felt a tentative touch on her shoulder.

"I'm sorry, Rose," he whispered, gently stroking her cheek with his index finger. "Forgive me - I forgot myself. Of course you need to know what kind of man I am. You seem to know my heart so well at times that I forget you have not long met me and expect you to read my mind. It hurt that you even countenanced the idea that I could have murdered my own brother!"

Rose turned her head away from him and sniffed, wishing she had thought to pick up a box of tissues. He held out one of his elegant laundered handkerchiefs. It was pure white and spotless. It immediately disarmed her.

"I can't use that! It's brand new," she said.

"Take it, please."

She took it tentatively and wiped her eyes and nose. He sat down beside her and put his arm around her, folding her in towards his shoulder. He stroked her hair and sighed, rocking her like a child. She was angry with him but this display of care set her off weeping again.

"Ssshh, sshh, sweetheart," he said, feeling her shudder as she tried to hold in her sobs. She glanced up at him through her wet eyelashes and was shocked to see the brightness of tears in his eyes too. She clung to him, feeling his strong chest against hers, his arms embracing her warmly and she gasped as she heard herself whisper:

"I love you, Dickon."

He smiled and held her closer.

"I know, I know," he said, as one would soothe a child.

After a long pause he said: "You know I can't marry you, don't you? And I will not dishonour you. A king has no choice in his bride - if I get back and if I can change history and win at Bosworth, I shall have to marry a foreign princess. I wish…"

He sighed, releasing her and made to get up but she suddenly grabbed his face and pulled him back towards her. She took him by surprise and suddenly they were kissing. She shyly pressed her tongue to his and then withdrew. He tasted of Rioja, warm and oaky and she sensed his desire kindle as he kissed her in return. His kiss was bold and yet tentative, matching his personality: both self-assured and vulnerable. Their lips and tongues slid against each other and their breathing grew ragged and desperate. Christ! It had been so long!

"The only thing I care about is whether you love me," she said, softly, her eyes pleading. "Say you love me, in Medieval English?" she begged.

She felt him freeze, heard his sigh and saw his look of pained regret.

"I...", he hesitated, then looked away.

"You can't say it!" she said, "You don't love me, do you?"

"I can't answer that," he said, his eyes stricken with pain for her. "I don't want to mislead you or hurt you any more than I already have. I won't say something unless I really mean it. You are a beautiful lady and I do care about you, so much. But there can be no future for us. I'm so very sorry."

He groaned, then continued:

"I feel so…confused. You arouse me and yet something holds me back, it doesn't feel right. Perhaps it's because you are married still in the eyes of the Church."

"But I'm not a Catholic. And I was so young when I married, I didn't really understand what I was doing."

"But you made a vow, didn't you, Rose? 'Til death do us part'? My Church doesn't recognise divorce, so you are still married and we would be committing adultery. I have enough sins on my conscience. I'm so sorry."

And with that he turned and left the room.

If You're Not the One

So here she was, crying over him again. She wished with all her heart and soul that she did not feel the way she did about him. He consumed her, his face haunted her dreams, his voice echoed in her head and she thought of nothing else. She had noticed that, whoever was in a room, however nice they might be, they were eclipsed as soon as he was there; like the sun, the York Sunne in Splendour, he was all she could see. The yearning in her heart was a physical pain and she gasped for breath as she sobbed and sobbed, unable to move or do anything else. The pillow was wet and her nose was blocked, which made her feel even more miserable. She knew with dismal certainty that her eyes would look like an ugly alien's tomorrow and she would have to face him. She would have to know the shame of rejection and worse, sense his pity.

She knew he wasn't hurting her on purpose. If he didn't love her, it wasn't his fault - she couldn't force him to love her and she didn't want to. She wanted him to want her spontaneously and naturally. She knew he cared and she had felt his arousal when they had kissed, but something was holding him back. Was it really his religious views? She wished she could read his mind, just for a little while, so she could work out what he was afraid of or what compelled him on his lonely path. If he wasn't the right one for her, why did she feel this emotion so strongly? It was almost as if he were a drug that she couldn't set aside, no matter how much damage she knew it was doing to her - she was on course to self-destruct.

Suddenly she wondered what he had meant by the words: "I have enough sins on my conscience." Could he have been referring to the Princes? Had he had them murdered after all? Perhaps she had had a lucky escape. But no, surely a man with such a conscience could not have done that. He was so wonderful in so many ways – did she even care about the mystery of the Princes anymore? After all, things were so different in his day.

It wasn't very long now before they would be going back to the Major Oak to try to find a way for him to return. The thought of him leaving panicked her. He had been with her for over half a year now. At first the time had passed quite slowly, but she remembered holidays where the first half crept by but as soon as the mid-point had gone, the remainder sped past, and the same rule seemed to apply now. There were fewer than six months left now. She felt split in two. She wanted him to remain with her forever, and so half of her wished that the portal would not work, that their quest to change history would remain thwarted as it had the last time they were there at the Major Oak. And yet she knew he was desperate to return, and the part of her that loved him unconditionally wanted only for him to be happy and therefore wished for him to find the portal and return to fulfil his destiny in his own time.

She knew he was finding it hard to cope with the pressure of modern life, too. Strange though it might seem to a modern person who thought Mediaeval life was dangerous and violent, for someone who was used to it, it was slower paced and much less stressful. But if he succeeded in going back, she didn't dare to think how she would cope without him. She had been obsessed by him before; now, her obsession was all-consuming and she feared she would be destroyed by its power. She could only hope that her love for him was so strong it would form an unbreakable link that would bind them together in some small way, transcending time itself.

Chapter Ten - February 2015

The Riddle

When they next spoke to Lynne, she told them that she, too, had now had a significant, recurring dream. She said that she had seen a man, with a beard, led to the block and beheaded. He went to his death with dignity and resignation, placing his head on the wooden block and then pausing to rearrange his beard so that it hung over the edge of the block. She didn't recognise the man, but tried to describe him to Richard, to see if he did.

"He was well-dressed, obviously not a commoner. He had a longish beard and his hair and beard were both brown. He was of medium height and build."

"It could be Buckingham? I wasn't present at his execution, so I can't say what he did. He did have a beard and his hair was brown. Brown and curly. How old was he? Buckingham was some years younger than I."

"No, it can't have been him, then – this man's hair was straight, and he was older. I'd say he was in his fifties or sixties."

"Hmm. Hastings perhaps. It can't have been Collyngbourne as he was hung, drawn and quartered," said Richard, frowning.

Lynne glanced at Rose, appalled. Richard, seeing their expressions, looked at them sideways, his eyes narrowed.

"He deserved it," he growled.

"Wasn't he the one who wrote that seditious poem about you?" asked Rose.

"Yes," he said slowly. "I suppose you are going to repeat it now, are you?"

"Not if it gets me hung, drawn and quartered!" Rose retorted.

Richard chuckled.

"Actually, I rather liked the poem. That wasn't why he was executed – he had been colluding with Henry Tydder."

"What was the poem then?" asked Lynne curiously.

"It went something like: 'The Rat, The Cat and Lovell, Our Dog, Ruleth all England Under an Hog!' Is that right, Dickon?" said Rose.

"Yes, more or less. Dick Ratcliffe was the Rat, Will Catesby the Cat and Frank Lovell was the dog, because that was his device."

"And who was the Hog?" asked Lynne, innocently.

"I was the Hog, my personal device being the white boar."

"Oh yes, I've seen Rose wearing that emblem," said Lynne. Richard raised his eyebrows appreciatively. Rose blushed, of course.

"Anyway," said Rose, changing the subject. "Could it have been Hastings that Lynne saw then?"

"Again, I didn't see him 'headed. The description might fit, although he was unlikely to have been as calm as Lynne suggests. His execution happened with little warning: the last I saw him he was shaking in his pointed shoes."

Lynne was looking worried.

"So why was he executed and why so quickly?"

"Will Hastings was very powerful and influential with Edward, my brother," Richard began. "He hated the Woodvilles because they had as much, if not more, influence than he. So when he realised they were trying to seize power by controlling the new boy-king, Edward V, he sided with me and urged me to take control of the King, as Protector of the Realm. He expected to be able to influence the new Edward as easily as he had the old. However, after I took control and brought Edward to London, I had Harry Buckingham by my side. Harry was full of himself, having at last been given some of the power he always thought he had deserved, and Will realised that he was never going to have the influence over the King that he'd grown accustomed to. He was jealous of Harry, in other words. Also he realised that many people wanted me to take the throne - even before the pre-contract of Edward's was discovered, which rendered the princes illegitimate - because I am an experienced leader and lord. So he changed sides and started plotting with the Woodvilles to overthrow me as Protector. I had been told of this by Catesby, who was then Hastings' lawyer, but couldn't accept his treachery."

"Wasn't he executed without a trial?" asked Rose.

"Yes and no. Don't forget that I was still Constable of England and had the authority to judge wrongdoing and pass sentence, provided I was satisfied that there was sufficient evidence of guilt. There was, so I made the decision there and then."

"But why didn't you wait until Parliament approved it?"

"I felt guilty, disloyal to Edward. Although I never liked Will because I felt he'd led Ned into wanton, dissolute behaviour and I didn't approve, I knew Ned loved him. Executing Will, even though he had clearly committed treason, felt like betraying Ned. I knew if I didn't do it immediately I would change my mind. Afterwards, I had him buried next to Edward at Windsor. Ned always did say he wanted to be buried beside his best friend."

"But what was it that he'd done, how did he commit treason?" said Lynne.

"He was using Elizabeth Shore to pass messages between Margaret Beaufort and Elizabeth Woodville, who was in the sanctuary of Westminster with her children, including Thomas Grey, her son by her first marriage. I think Elizabeth had promised Hastings he would be made Chancellor again if he helped her, and power was always too hard to resist for Will."

"Who was Elizabeth Shore?" said Lynne, becoming interested in the complicated power struggle that was The War of the Roses.

"Elizabeth Shore? She was a court harlot. She was Ned's favourite mistress and when he died, she split her time and attentions between Hastings and Thomas Grey. She was a clever little thing, very intelligent and pretty. She had what you would call charisma, especially around men."

"Weren't you tempted by her charms?"

"Yes, I was, as a matter of fact. She offered herself to me after Ned died – she was very attractive and I might have succumbed had my marriage to Anne not been so happy. But I would never have betrayed Anne. When I took my vows, I meant them and Helen of Troy herself would not have been able to seduce me to break them. I take a vow seriously and 'tis a pity some others did not."

"Isn't she the one who did penance in her nightgown, walking barefoot through the streets of London with a candle?" asked Rose.

"Yes, I made her do that as punishment for her part in the conspiracy. She got off lightly in my opinion. However, the Londoners loved her and felt sorry for her. None more so than my solicitor, Thomas Lyneham, who later even asked my permission to marry her!"

"Yes! And the document in which you replied to that request still survives. You were very tolerant of her, really, weren't you?"

"Yes, maybe I did have a soft spot for her. I respect intelligence."

"Nothing to do with her physical attributes then!" Rose teased. Richard just gave her his warning stare.

"So, was Hastings a priest or something?" asked Lynne.

"No, not at all. He was a dissolute, corrupt, power-hungry womaniser."

He paused.

"OK, actually, being a priest doesn't necessarily preclude those character traits," he continued. "I know a good few clerics who are more worldly than most ordinary men."

He shook his head sadly.

"Why did you think he was a priest, anyway?" he asked.

"Well, the man I saw had an air about him like a priest, I think. I may be wrong but it was the impression I got."

"If that's the case, then he is nobody I know or knew. I never executed clerics – or women."

"Maybe you should have!" mumbled Rose, under her breath. There was nothing wrong with his ears. He looked at her sharply, his lips pursed.

"I will not endanger my soul by killing women and priests – it is not my way, nor was it Edward's either. But I take your point. I will have to find another way of controlling Bishop Morton and Lady Margaret Stanley – not to mention her errant husband, Thomas, and his brother, William."

Unfaithful

"So what did Buckingham do to be executed?" asked Lynne. "Didn't you just say he was your closest ally?"

Richard sighed. "Yes, he was...at first. He came rushing to help me take control of the young King, Edward, and supported me when I arrested the King's uncle, Anthony Rivers and others in his retinue. He encouraged me to take the throne when he heard about Edward's bigamy, and he made a fantastic speech pleading my suitability and right to be King, before Parliament. He did all my bidding and advised me well for the first few months of my reign until we discovered the Hastings conspiracy and I put Morton into his hands for safe-keeping. I believe he was gulled by Morton - a wily fox if ever there was one - into believing he had more right to the throne than I did. Why not go for the top prize? It was ironic really that I, the rightful King, was reluctant to take the crown whereas those like Harry Buckingham and Henry Tydder, who had no rightful claim to it, were desperate to get their grubby little hands on it!"

"I have often thought that, even today, the people who are interested in becoming politicians are ambitious for power and are the very people who are the worst for the country and that those who would be great for the country wouldn't want to be in power," said Rose.

"It was ever thus," smiled Richard, ruefully. "So Buckingham joined a planned rebellion against me, started in the county of Kent - the Southerners still do not trust me, because I am from the North. Not only that but he...he," Richard hesitated and sighed again.

Then he continued: "He betrayed me in a terrible, most ungrateful way. I was completely shocked and realised that I didn't really know him at all - he was a man who couldn't keep faith with his Sovereign Lord, the very Lord who had rewarded him to the skies, but it wasn't enough."

" 'The most untrue creature living' that's what you called him, isn't it?" said Rose.

"Yes, I did…and he was," he said, his head bowed and his eyes bright with unshed tears. Rose didn't want to upset him, so she changed the subject back to their quest.

"Well, we are no closer to identifying this man in your dream," she said to Lynne. "Can you remember anything else you saw or heard in the dream?"

"Nothing much. I saw the executioner - he was weeping and - yes - he called him by his name: Thomas. Then, this Thomas said something just before he died, something like 'My beard has not committed treason against King Henry.' "

"King Henry? Henry Tydder!" shouted Richard. "It was someone he executed?" He began to wrack his brains to try to think whom of his followers might have been executed by Henry Tudor.

"You must know better than I, whom Henry executed," said Richard to Rose. "After all, it was after my time!"

"Let's see – there were quite a few of them. He executed William Stanley, Perkin Warbeck, probably your natural son, John," she glanced at Richard as she said this. "The Earl of Warwick, George's son, then there were some straight after Bosworth – because he tried to date his reign from the day before Bosworth, so that all who fought for you could be punished as traitors, did you know? These included Catesby. But I can't remember him executing a priest. I'll have to check it on the internet."

They agreed to keep in close contact with Lynne and let each other know of any breakthroughs.

When they got back home to the bungalow, Rose had a couple of patients and then they had a cuppa and some cake, and settled down to surf the web.

Rose typed in 'Thomas, cleric, beard, executed by Henry Tudor' and hit return.

"The results are confusing – there are several possibilities," she sighed. "I don't think it was Henry VII - more likely Henry VIII - he had more people executed as well, so it's likely it was him. Now as to who this priest was - maybe Thomas Cranmer. He was Archbishop of Canterbury under HVIII and was executed…oh no, it can't be him he was executed by Bloody Mary, not Henry! So we're back to square one. The trouble is there were many Thomases in those days and a lot of them were executed as well!"

They finally gave up for the time being.

The Silence

Lynne phoned Rose a few days later. "Rose - this mystery is driving me mad! I wish Richard would let me use the Ouija board."

"Well, he won't consider it, so there's no point in moaning!"

"I suppose not," she said. "But I still haven't had another dream."

On the fourteenth of February there was a red envelope on the doormat, addressed to Rose.

"It's a Valentine's Day card!" Rose said, excitedly. She opened it quickly, tearing the envelope off and throwing it on the coffee table. Richard picked it up and put it in the recycling. The verse read: 'Broom is yellow, Roses are white, Will you be my Valentine Rose tonight?' but there was no signature. Both the card and the envelope were printed, obviously by an online company, and sent directly from them so there was nothing to identify the sender. Rose recognised the allusions to Richard in the verse, of course, and Richard was the obvious candidate. He was acting nonchalant and said nothing, so Rose decided to wind him up a little.

"I wonder who it's from?" she said. "It's been ages since I received an anonymous Valentine card: how exciting! Maybe it's from Tony, my colleague in Westcliff. Or it could be from one of my Ricardian friends, maybe Stephen or Brian..."

She watched Richard's reactions carefully. He frowned slightly and fiddled with his ruby ring. He still didn't say anything, didn't even acknowledge Rose. Was he acting moody to throw her off the scent? Or had something else upset him?

The next day they went to see a 3D film. Richard had a problem understanding the concept at first, not surprising really, and he kept dodging flying debris, water and blows from the film for the first few minutes. But once he had got used to the strangeness of it he thoroughly enjoyed it.

"What wonders you have in this century!" he said. "That was as real as life."

"Yes, the effects are getting better and better, it's true," said Rose. "They even have 4D effects these days, when the seat actually moves and smells are wafted into the cinema."

Richard raised his eyebrows and shook his head in disbelief.

He was acting rather oddly, at times unusually attentive and at other times silent and brooding. Rose wasn't sure why. He was always courteous and gentlemanly but it was as if there had been a subtle change. He could be solicitous and caring - he had even volunteered to massage her shoulders when she had groaned that they ached after a particularly tough workout with Maria that morning. Yet just when she thought they were back to their previous easy companionship, he would become moody for no apparent reason.

When they arrived back at the bungalow, the phone was ringing. Richard picked it up and said, "Hello?" then looked puzzled and laid the receiver back down into its cradle.

"Who was it?" said Rose.

He narrowed his eyes. "I don't know…they hung up."

"Never mind - it was probably one of those fake survey people," she said.

"Rose…I…oh never mind," he said. "Would you like a glass of wine?"

"Mm! Yes, please," she replied.

She tried to make conversation but it was hard going. She was worried because they normally chatted comfortably for hours and she didn't like this change for the worse. He seemed withdrawn and depressed, but when she pressed him for the reason he denied it and clammed up.

Torn

Lynne opened the door and Rose went in, a worried frown on her usually cheerful face.

"What's up, Rose?" asked Lynne, immediately sensing Rose's mood.

"It's Richard - he seems down and distant lately - he hardly talks to me. I thought it best to leave him alone for a while - don't they say that men like to be alone when they are worried or miserable? They don't like to be pestered about the reason, but it's hard not to; I feel responsible for him as he's staying with me."

"I'm surprised. The last time I saw you, you were getting on fine - it was me he was annoyed with. When did this mood start?"

"I'm not sure exactly - well, actually yes I do remember - it was Valentine's Day. I got an anonymous card - I'm sure it was from him, but he acted as if he knew nothing about it, so I teased him a bit. I pretended it might be from various men I know."

"What makes you think it was from him? Was it in his handwriting?"

"No, it was printed - you know how he loves printing - it would be just like him to get one ordered online. He's getting quite good on the computer now. No, I think it was from him because there was an obvious Yorkist reference in the rhyme. Who else knows enough to mention the White Rose of York and broom - the common name for the plant the Plantagenets were named after?"

Lynne looked down, then licked her lips and said: "How about a cup of tea. That'll make you feel better."

"Wait a minute - what do you know? Was it you who sent the card? I didn't think you were a practical joker."

Lynne sighed. "No, it wasn't me - it was Laura. She rang me about a week ago and happened to mention that she'd sent it to play a joke on you - she doesn't believe Richard's really who he is; she thought you were playing a joke on her when you met her in Nottingham that time, so she said she was going to 'get you back'. I reckon your Dickon is jealous, if he thinks the card was from another man."

She put the kettle on and took out two mugs from the cupboard.

"He isn't 'my' Dickon - we are only friends. You know that, Lynne."

"Rubbish - it's obvious he adores you and you are head over heels in love with him."

"Lynne! That's ridiculous," she said, blushing despite her protestations. "Anyway, even if he did feel something for me, nothing can come of it - he has made that clear. He has to go back and marry a foreign princess."

"That's if we can find out how to get him back there, don't forget! Who knows? He might end up stuck here or he might decide he likes it better here. Believe me, he definitely has feelings for you - I've seen the way he looks at you, when you're busy doing something else and are unaware."

Rose couldn't help her heart leaping at the thought that Lynne might be right. On the other hand, she knew Richard wanted to go back and defend England. She took the cup of tea that Lynne held out to her, thanking her and taking a sip. She had certainly given her something to think about.

"Listen, Rose. Changing the subject slightly, I am going mad trying to find out about my dream. There were lots of Thomases in those times and so many who were executed, too. There was Thomas Cranmer, Thomas Cromwell and Thomas More - all executed by the Tudors. Cranmer was burnt at the stake by Mary, so he's out as the man in my dream. Cromwell and More were both beheaded by Henry VIII, but neither had a beard in any of the portraits I've seen. I was going to give up when I found a reference to More saying, at his execution, that his beard was innocent of any crime. It must be him, Rose! He must have grown a beard later."

"Thomas More! But it's his fault that Richard's reputation was so maligned. He influenced Shakespeare and started the whole sorry web of lies. Anyway, he wasn't a priest or cleric."

"No, but he was a very pious man - like Richard. In fact, he was later made a saint. And he was known for his integrity...like Richard. He was a lawyer, so interested in justice, too. He seems to have quite a lot in common with Richard. He even owned Crosby House, the place that Richard used to rent while in London, apparently. He is the patron saint of statesmen, lawmakers and people who have difficult marriages."

"But he wrote the History of Richard III which led to his character being defamed and besmirched! Why should he be trying to help Richard change history?"

"Well, that is the question, isn't it? It doesn't do us much good to know it's More who is helping Richard, if we don't know how or why. We need to speak to him."

"You mean the Ouija board, don't you?"

"Yes, I do! In fact, I've asked three of my spiritualist friends to come around tonight and try to contact More. I won't tell them about Richard - I'll make up something about my dream as the reason. Why don't you stay and join us?"

Rose paled.

"No, I can't. I feel really uncomfortable about it and Richard would go crazy - as far as he's concerned it's witchcraft or the devil! But I must admit I'm rather curious now and, of course, I can't stop you consulting it if you want. Will you call me and let me know if you find out anything relevant?"

"Yes, of course I will."

Rose nodded, feeling torn, as she left Lynne's house to make her way home.

Road To Hell

Lynne and her friends Kim, Frances and Angela were seated around the table in Lynne's dining room, a red candle flickering nearby and a glass of water in front of each of them. The 'spirit board', as Lynne preferred to call it, was in the middle of the table, an upturned shot glass placed in the centre. Lynne had a pad and pen in front of her to record their results. They had been trying for nearly two hours, but had only got nonsense so far. They had decided to have one last attempt. They held hands first, making a circle and Lynne asked her spirit guide to keep them safe and not allow any negative energies into the circle. There was upbeat, rhythmic music playing, which Lynne thought enhanced the energy available in the room for the spirits to use. They each placed one finger on the shot glass.

"Is there someone there who would like to speak with us?" Lynne asked. Nothing happened and she repeated the question, adding: "Please use the energy of the music to communicate with us. If there is someone there, make the lights on the EMF meter go to yellow or red, or make the candle flame flicker, please."

The EMF meter was on the table beside the board. It was a small device with a green light glowing to show it was working. It was meant to detect disturbances in the electromagnetic field, believed to occur when spirits were present. They had checked to make sure there were no power lines, mobile phones or other electrical equipment nearby which could affect it. As Lynne finished speaking, the candle flickered slightly and the lights on the EMF meter lit up into the yellow area. Kim's eyes widened in excitement.

"Thank you!" said Lynne. "Please can you move the pointer to the 'yes' position, if you are willing to talk to us?"

The shot glass remained still for what seemed like an age, but then gradually started to slide across to the word 'yes',

"Thank you. What is your name, please?"

The glass moved slowly, painfully and spelled out T-H-O-S.

"Do you mean Thomas?"

'YES'

"What is your last name?"

'M-O-R-R-E'

"Welcome, Thomas. First of all, have you been appearing in our dreams?"

'YES'

What message do you have for us, please?"

'H-I-S-T-O-R-I-E-   O-F-R-I-C-A-R-D-U-S-N-O-T-T-R-U-E'

Are you saying the history you wrote about Richard III is not true?

'YES'

'I-N-O-T-P-U-B-L-I-S-H'

"You didn't publish it?"

'N-O-N-E-P-H-E-W'

"Your nephew published it?

'YES-S-H-O-U-L-D-E-H-A-V-E-D-E-S-T-R-O-Y-E-D'

"Do you mean you should have destroyed the manuscript?"

'YES'

'M-O-R-T-O-N-T-O-L-D-M-E-L-I-E-S'

"Do you mean John Morton, Archbishop of Canterbury?"

'YES'

"You lived in his household, didn't you?"

'YES-R-I-C-A-R-D-U-S-G-O-O-D-K-I-N-G'

"You think Richard was a good king?"

'YES-B-E-T-T-E-R-T-H-A-N-T-Y-D-D-E-R'

"Better than Tudor?"

'YES'

"Are you helping to change Richard's reputation?" She couldn't ask directly whether he had helped to transport Richard to the future.

'YES'

"Why are you helping Richard?"

'G-U-I-L-T-M-A-K-E-A-M-E-N-D-S-M-Y-F-A-U-L-T'

"How can we help you?"

'H-E-G-O-B-A-C-K-D-E-F-E-A-T-T-Y-D-D-E-R'

"How?"

'F-O-L-L-O-W-W-H-Y-T-E-B-O-R-E'

"When?"

'J-U-N-E-2-2'

"Will he win?"

'U-P-T-O-H-Y-M'

"Do you want to say anything else?"

The glass slid to the word 'FAREWELL' and then off the side of the board. The EMF meter subsided to the single green light again.

Her three friends stared at her in bemusement.

"What was that all about?" said Frances.

"I think it was St Thomas More who wrote about Richard III in Henry VIII's time. He was the source of Richard's bad reputation, Shakespeare and all that. You remember Rose, my friend from school. She is an obsessive Ricardian and had a dream about him. I don't understand all this either, but I'm sure she'll know what it's all about."

Kim, Angela and Frances were obviously not convinced. Kim opened her mouth to say something.

"Well, it's been quite a long evening - let's do this again in a couple of weeks, eh?" Lynne said, hastily, ushering them out.

She was sure her nose must have grown an inch that evening.

Chapter Eleven - March 2015

Bad Things

Rose picked up the phone to find it was Lynne, who was in a state of excitement.

"The Ouija session went really well. We contacted Thomas More and he confirmed he is helping Richard. I have done some more research based on what he said. You know that history he wrote, well, he didn't actually publish it - he never finished it. It was his nephew who published it after Thomas died; he was a bookseller. Also, More was influenced by Morton - Richard's deadliest enemy - the one who plotted with Margaret Beaufort to put her son, Henry Tudor, on the throne. More was brought up in John Morton's household for a good while and basically Morton blackened Richard's name. It was only when More researched Richard's reign more thoroughly after Morton's death that he realised the version of events he'd been given was biased and factually incorrect – that's why he never finished the history. He never intended for it to be published and he realises he should have made sure it was destroyed. After he passed over, he was made aware of the wrong he'd done, by allowing its survival; it meant his nephew could publish it. That must have been your dream, by the way - you saw that manuscript he tried to burn, but his nephew rescued it without his knowledge. He feels guilty and responsible and he can't move on until the wrong he did Richard is put right. You have to tell him."

"I've been thinking about that. Richard expressly forbade it and you know how pious he is – he will be mortified! How can I tell him what you've done?"

"But he needs to know, so that he can get back home and change history."

"Well, I think he is going to try to do that anyway - was there anything else?"

"St Thomas More wants Richard to win at Bosworth, so he's giving him a second chance. He said Richard was a better king than Tudor. To make amends he led Richard here, helped by your Ricardian obsession drawing him through, to find out as much as he can and then return to re-fight the battle with hindsight. He needs to go back on the same date he came, 22nd June. The Major Oak must have been chosen because it was present in both times and in Richard's vicinity. I found out the significance of that date, by the way; it's Thomas More's saint day in the Catholic Church. He used the apparition of a white boar, Richard's own cognizance, to lure him there. He knew Richard wouldn't be able to resist following that!"

"No, I suppose not. So does he have to follow it back?"

"Yes, on the same date in 2015, and, hopefully, he will arrive back on the same day he left."

"OK, Lynne, thanks for letting me know all this. I'll think about telling him when he gets back from training with Destrier."

She replaced the receiver and wrote a few notes to remind herself what Lynne had said, and then went to make a coffee. She nearly jumped out of her skin when she saw Richard sitting quietly on the sofa! How had he crept in so silently?

"So what is it you're...thinking of telling me?" he asked. His voice was mild but she could sense the underlying tension. She decided to tell him everything.

When she had finished, Richard was stony faced and silent. He looked at Rose coldly.

"I forbade you to use that…abomination, didn't I?"

"I didn't use it, Lynne did!"

"Yet you didn't try to stop her. You have colluded with her behind my back. You've betrayed my trust." His eyes were hooded, defensive, hurt. She reacted instinctively, lashing out to justify herself.

"That's unfair!" she shouted. "I listened to her because we seemed to be stuck in our research and I thought it might help you get home. I let her do it for you; I don't even want you to go back, you…idiot!"

Tears filled her eyes and she turned to leave the room.

"I didn't give you permission to leave!" he snapped, furious.

She halted mid-stride and turned to face him, trembling with a sudden welling of emotion, a mixture of anger and fear.

"Go to Hell!" she spat. "As far as I know you deserve to - the cruel, dreadful things you've done! And you've never even mentioned what happened to those boys!"

She gasped, her hand covering her mouth, shocked at what she had said in anger. She knew it was unfair since she had equally avoided the subject - but it was said now and she couldn't take it back.

Don't Speak

Richard was staring directly into her eyes, so that she saw his expression change. His face paled and his eyes looked wounded…tortured, even.

"Don't, Rose," he whispered, a whisper more forceful than the loudest shout. "You don't want to know."

"I need to know!" she said, looking straight back at him, their gazes locked, his dark grey-blue eyes and her green ones searching, probing, resisting, struggling, neither willing to back down.

"Ask then, Rose," he sighed finally, lowering his head and running his hand through his dishevelled hair. She noticed it was trembling. He sounded defeated, broken. She was shocked that he had backed down first; his gaze, so often of unbreakable, irresistible steel had given way to hers.

She was afraid then even more, wondering whether she should allow him to remain silent, but she knew she would never have any peace unless she knew the truth, or at least his version of the truth.

"What happened to them, Edward and Richard, the Princes?" she blurted out. "Did they die? Who killed them? Were they spirited away somewhere? To what place? And what became of them or their bodies?"

"I...I don't know how to begin this," he said, his face agonised and his eyes brimming. "I can't...I've tried to bury this in my mind for so long, I don't know if I dare let it out again."

He turned away from her forthright gaze to look at the window and the garden beyond. He was fiddling with the ring on his right hand, twisting the circle of gold around and around, then began pacing up and down, up and down, like a caged tiger.

"I knew that the boys had been a focus of rebellion - they had already been the cause of an attack on the Tower, and I had only just been crowned. I had to stop it happening again. It is hard to be a king. The decisions you have to make can be...heartbreaking, and dreadful. Buckingham, who I thought to be my friend, who was so charming and eloquent, whispered in my ear that they had to go. If they remained, another rebellion might succeed and then I might be deposed. It would be a disaster. He knew just what to say to persuade me - he played on my sense of duty, my love of England, my hopes for peace. There's no excuse though - the decision was mine and mine alone. It was I who caused the deaths of two innocent boys."

He turned back to face her, finding her staring at him in shock, appalled and stricken. He took two steps forwards and grabbed her hands in his before she could recoil.

"Rose, listen to me! You need to know the whole story - you asked for it, didn't you? I'll tell you the way I knew it to happen."

"I don't know if I can take it after all, maybe I don't want to know the gory details...!"

"It's too late now. Anyway, I think you're right - you should know. Edward and Richard, the two royal bastards, were in the Garden Tower - it's now called the Bloody Tower, of course. After the rebellion, I had forbidden them to go out into the grounds. They were moved to an inner chamber with my own guards keeping watch. But the situation couldn't remain thus forever. It wouldn't have been fair on the boys, locked away like that. So I decided to have them taken away to Sheriff Hutton with the other children, who included George's son, Edward, Earl of Warwick. Then Harry Buckingham said he had a better plan. He would have them sent to Burgundy, to my sister Margaret and kept there in secret, until the realm was secure and they could return. He remained in London while I continued on the Royal Progress. He had a letter of authority with the Royal Seal allowing entry to the Tower to visit the boys. But, Rose, he intended to kill them! I was stupid, in hindsight, to trust him - I didn't really know him at all!"

"Richard, don't. I can't bear it!" Rose said, tears forming in her eyes. He ignored her pleas, continuing his story, now pacing up and down again.

"The Constable of the Tower, Robert Brackenbury, wouldn't let him in on the first day, despite the seal. He was a very wise man. But Buckingham went back again the day after with several henchmen and forced Brackenbury to let him enter. The two boys were smothered in their beds, their bodies disposed of secretly - I don't know where they are, Rose! Buckingham came to me in Gloucester and told me what he'd done. I can't tell you how distraught I was. He was totally unrepentant - said I'd thank him one day and that he had done it for me - killed those beautiful boys! I was so angry, he grew afraid and left before I had the wits to have him arrested.

"Then I got a message from Brackenbury, saying the boys had gone, that Buckingham was responsible. I wrote back expressing my horror and thanking him for his loyalty. I got another letter by return that amazed me. Brackenbury said that, after that first day when he turned Buckingham away, he had become suspicious and brought the two boys secretly, by boat, out of the Tower and hid them away somewhere in London. He had substituted two boys of similar age and appearance, placing them in the Tower in the place of Ned's sons. He wrote the first ambiguous letter to gauge my reaction; he had suspected I hadn't ordered their deaths. He said he would show me where he had hidden Edward and Richard, but not tell me for fear of his communication being intercepted. He feared the two substitute boys were taken and killed. Buckingham had already confirmed this to me, believing they were the two sons of Edward."

"So the Princes were still alive?" Rose asked, enthralled.

"Yes, they were kept for a while at the estate of James Tyrell, who later moved them to the custody of two separate associates of his on the continent. But two other innocent children were dead. It was all my fault for trusting Buckingham and I suffer the guilt of it every day. What greater sin can there be than the killing of innocents?"

"It wasn't your fault, Dickon! It was Buckingham who did it. Was that why he rebelled against you?"

"I don't know for sure. He had seemed to be trying to impress me by 'helping' me to make the throne secure. Perhaps he thought I would be so obligated to him that he would have power over me to rise even higher. When I reacted with horror at what he'd done, he fled and it may be that it was then that he let Morton, that wily old fox, whisper in his ear that the way was becoming clear for Buckingham himself to be King. He definitely wanted power and wealth. Perhaps he thought I was so displeased that I would execute him - and I would have. I did eventually! However, by the time I had found out the truth of it all, the rebellion of Buckingham and the Woodvilles had failed and he was captured."

"Is it true he begged to speak to you once more before he met his death?"

"Quite true, yes. I refused. I couldn't bear to see his face again and in it the reflection of my own guilt. As it turned out it was well that I didn't for he had managed to get hold of a dagger and I suspect he would have tried to assassinate me as well as those two poor boys."

"So why didn't you say that the Princes were actually safe? You could have shown them publicly."

"If I revealed the boys' whereabouts, they would again be in danger and my rule would again be threatened. I decided to accept both the guilt and the benefit of Buckingham's act. If I kept quiet, yes, I would be blamed, but people would think that there was nobody left to front a rebellion. After hearing of Tydder's plans to invade, I had decided to reveal the boys were alive after I had secured the realm completely by defeating Tydder at Bosworth. You know what happened there, so it seems I never had the chance to do that. But I accept the blame for them anyway. I accept my reputation as a murderer, even though it wasn't the murder of Ned's boys that I was responsible for - mine was the guilt for the killing of those two substitute boys. My crime was not less because those boys were not of royal blood."

"But, Dickon, it was not your crime, it was Buckingham's. You mustn't torture yourself about something that you were unaware of and totally opposed to!"

"It was my fault, though. They were in my care, my responsibility. I can't help feeling this. I have been shriven for my sins again and again, but I still don't feel worthy of forgiveness, Perhaps I do deserve to die and be dishonoured at Bosworth."

A single tear slid down his cheek.

"Listen Dickon, I'm sorry I asked you to stir all this up in your mind again. It was an awful thing, but you are not to blame! I think the best way to make recompense, if you can't overcome your feelings of guilt, is by being the best King you can be, by showing the English people justice and fairness, by treating all equally under the law, by being firm with corruption and lenient with crimes driven by poverty, by showing your courage, your generosity and your piety. You are a good, honest man, Dickon. And you will continue to be a fine king. We have to get you back there," she finished.

She went to him then and put her hand on his shoulder, lifting his chin so she could look into his eyes.

"What you have said has not changed how I see you," she said. "I know you now, I know the worst of you and I still love you."

They hugged each other tightly and she rocked him gently like a mother, their embrace warm and one of eternal friendship.

Requiem

It wasn't long after this traumatic time that Richard's re-interment ceremony at Leicester Cathedral was due to take place. Richard decided he would go, despite his misgivings, as his curiosity would not be denied. Once they had found out the schedule for the week, Rose had booked them in for an extra night, so they could stay in Leicester for the reveal of his tomb. She had changed hotels, though, because she had reserved places on the Fenn Lane Battlefield Guided Tour for ten o'clock on the Friday morning, so the hotel she chose for their Thursday night stay was the Royal Arms, which was only five minutes from the Bosworth Battlefield Heritage Site, where they would meet the bus. This was a must see for Richard. He was hoping to scout the lay of the land to give himself an advantage over Tudor, but Rose warned him that, firstly, there was still dispute about exactly where the battle took place and, secondly, the landscape would doubtless have changed a lot since 1485.

"Less forest!" he said, grinning.

"Less marsh, as well," said Rose. "And that could be the vital aspect of the battle."

She had also arranged for them to attend various concerts, and activities, to Richard's bemusement. They had decided to watch the Sunday procession on TV in Rayleigh and drive up to Leicester on the Tuesday. This would give them time to pay their respects, as Richard's coffin would lie in Leicester Cathedral for the following three days. The actual re-interment was on the Thursday. Rose had entered two different ballots to win tickets for the ceremony in the Cathedral, but hadn't held out much hope since there were only six hundred places and thousands had applied. As expected, she didn't get chosen for that, but she was very pleased to have received two tickets for Geoffrey Davidson's Middleham Requiem Concert, narrated by Sir Timothy Ackroyd at St. James' Church. Richard was looking forward to that on the Thursday evening.

On Sunday 22nd, they spent most of the day in front of the television, watching the slow, stately progress of Richard's coffin, as it made its way first to Fenn Lane Farm, where a short service was performed and earth from three places significant to Richard were put together in a matching wooden casket. The three earths had been taken from Fotheringhay, where Richard was born, from Middleham, where he lived, and from Fenn Lane, where he had died. Both the casket and the coffin were made by Michael Ibsen, the man whose DNA had been used to identify Richard's remains. He was a cabinet maker and had chosen English Oak from the estates of the Duchy of Cornwall, probably the best quality wood in the land, from which to make the items. The oak had begun to grow about one hundred and fifty years before and had been lovingly stored for five years before being chosen for the honour of enclosing the mortal remains of the last English King to die in battle. The grain of the wood was especially beautiful and the planks used had been cut so the grain was exactly symmetrical.

"There is a specially consecrated rosary inside, you know?" Rose told Richard as they watched. "It belonged to the historian, John Ashdown-Hill, and he had it modified with a white enamel rose and a replica of the Clare Cross. It was blessed at Clare Priory in Suffolk," she added.

Richard smiled and nodded. His eyes, however, remained fixed to the TV as he watched the journey of the coffin. There were several stops along the way; a beacon was lit at Bosworth and a twenty one gun salute by cannons occurred - Richard loved this! He was also touched by the arch of roses made by students at Bosworth Academy in Desford and representing the thousands or people who went missing in Leicestershire over the last year, Richard's connection being that he also was missing and had then been found. All along the way, thousands of people lined the roads and threw white roses on the coffin as it passed, flanked by two horses bearing 'knights' in shining armour. Richard was profoundly moved to see how many people cared enough to be there and wait for hours, just to catch a glimpse of his coffin. He loved all the ceremony and the service of Compline, which was televised live. He was very pensive that evening.

On the Tuesday, they set off for Leicester and made quite good time, arriving around lunch time. They checked in to the Travelodge, which had once been the White (and then the Blue) Boar. They had adjacent rooms again; Richard was now used to the routine in such establishments. He recognised nothing about the site, but did find some places in Leicester that he had known, such as the Cathedral of St Martin's, which had been a Catholic parish church in his time, but it had been promoted now to a Cathedral. He told Rose that most of it looked very different from the church he had known and he was rather perturbed that it was no longer Catholic.

After a quick lunch, they queued up to pay their respects to his remains. He was very edgy the whole time they waited, about two and a quarter hours. A gospel choir in the Cathedral gardens was singing: 'Going to see the King', which entertained them while they queued. The florist was arranging donated flowers into a display covering the ground at the front of the Cathedral; Richard shook his head in amazement at the sheer number of flowers. Rose herself had bought a bouquet of a dozen white roses before they left Rayleigh, and written a message on the card.

"Is that for me?" Richard asked, his straight eyebrows raised and his blue eyes twinkling.

Rose didn't deign to answer, but rolled her eyes at him. After the snaking queue had reached the front of St Martin's, they were finally invited to enter, with a certain amount of trepidation on Richard's part. As they entered, one of the florists took Rose's flowers, in order to incorporate it into the display outside.

There had been so many people wanting to pay their respects that the Cathedral had had to remain open for longer hours. This meant that the ushers had to do their ushering faster than they would have, in order to allow as many as possible to pass by the coffin. It was displayed on two trestles and covered with a specially commissioned pall which was hand embroidered with people who would have been important to Richard on one side and people who had played a part in his rediscovery on the other. The crown commissioned by John Ashdown-Hill was displayed on top of the coffin and there were candles burning constantly. There were also floral displays all around. It was a respectful and sacred atmosphere.

There was a steady stream of people trooping solemnly past the coffin and silently taking flash-less photographs. Rose wanted to take a couple too, but there wasn't time to do that and also say the prayer that the historical Richard had requested people should say for him. She felt rushed and unable to say the prayer the way she wanted. All of a sudden she felt an overwhelming wave of emotion and couldn't prevent tears forming in her eyes as she moved away from the coffin. She turned to present-day Richard and immediately saw that his face was pale and he was sweating, even though it wasn't that warm.

"Are you OK, Dickon?"

Richard raised his hand to his head and began to sway. Rose swiftly grabbed his arm to prevent him falling to the floor and a helper came to their assistance, leading them into a side area reserved for prayers and contemplation.

"What is it? Are you unwell?" Rose asked, her voice lowered.

"I feel strange; as if I'm not really here - I started to feel odd when we approached the coffin, and the closer we got the worse I felt," he mumbled. "It's easing a little now."

"Hmm! I wonder if it was being in close physical proximity to your own remains," Rose said. "Perhaps it's creating some kind of temporal strain - you'd better stay as far away from the coffin as possible."

They remained in the quiet place for a few minutes and Rose lit a candle for Richard while saying his Latin prayer. She was bemused to find she couldn't stop crying and Richard was still looking decidedly peaky. As she said the prayer under her breath, the colour seemed to return to Richard's cheeks and he glanced up at her.

"Thank you," he said softly and they got to their feet and made their way out of the Cathedral. They both felt better once they got out into the fresh air.

That evening, they had a meal in the nearest gastro pub and then made their way to the Catholic church, the Holy Cross, where a concert of Mediaeval music was being performed: Concert for a King. It was free to attend, although they had had to book in advance, and Richard knew almost all of the songs and tunes. After their strange reactions to being near the coffin, the reminders of his previous life seemed to restore Richard's spirits and he eagerly chatted to the main musician in the interval. They wandered to the front of the church where a magnificent floral display had been commissioned which took the form of a 'Tree of Life' created from dozens of white roses, each in their own little glass vial and with broom planted around it. It was breathtaking. They were also given a white rose each for donating a few pounds to the Cathedral fund. Richard gave his to Rose, who decided to keep them until they went to the Battlefield site. They took their seats in the pews for the second half and when they finally left, Richard's mood had lifted; he was grinning all the way back to the hotel.

On Wednesday, they had arranged to meet Laura, who had travelled over on the train. They met her by Richard's statue, in front of the Cathedral and decided to have a look at

St Mary de Castro Church, which had existed in Richard's time and had been the beneficiary of a small annuity of ten shillings from Richard, in payment for keeping a certain lamp burning constantly. He refused to say what the significance of the lamp was, he just smiled, his eyes distant and bright, focused on the past.

They had a perfect cream tea in Mrs Bridge's Tea Rooms round the corner from the Cathedral and after that Laura had to go back. She nudged Richard as she left, saying:

"How's it feel to go to your own funeral, then?"

"Odd," he replied, deadpan. "It actually made me feel quite ill when I approached the coffin."

Laura paused, frowning, puzzled, eyes narrowed. She opened her mouth to say something else and then closed it again. Then she hugged Rose and left, turning round to stare at Richard again before she disappeared around the corner.

They were standing right beside the statue of Richard, which had been restored by Leicester in preparation for the re-interment. The statue had been cleaned and its sword repaired and then it had been moved from the park, where it had originally been located. The weather had been excellent so far; bright and warm with fluffy little clouds, like errant sheep, floating across the blue sky and the statue stood proudly in the sunlight, covered in garlands of white roses with more strewn around the base of it. Richard read a few of the cards attached to the flowers, and Rose saw his eyes were bright with tears. She reached for his hand and squeezed it. He turned and smiled ruefully.

"I am moved by the love that is still felt for me, even after more than five hundred years. Look at this card - 'Propiciare animæ famuli tui Ricardi. May you rest in peace at last, Richard, Our True King. Christine'. The Latin is from the prayer that I requested the priests say for my soul after my death. And look - someone has placed a white stone on here which says 'R.I.P. Richard from Helen T - L.M.L' - that must stand for my motto, Loyaulté Me Lie. These people have found out so much about me. It is touching but strange too. I marvel that I am still remembered at all."

Rose gave him a quick hug and he smiled a little more normally.

It was now time for them to go to the Richard III Visitor Centre to see what new exhibits there were about the King whose last hours were spent here in Leicester, as well as the five hundred years after his death. There was a huge copy of Richard's likeness from the National Portrait Gallery at the entrance and he took a photo of Rose standing in front of it; he was becoming quite good at using the camera. Inside, some of the centre was impressive, (such as the story of the dig and the animated introduction), some things mediocre (Richard's life story and how he became King) and a few things disgraceful (such as the Nazi version of Richard as portrayed by Ian McKellan), but it was all interesting. Richard was nothing if not a conversation starter, and one of the topics on everyone's lips was the new version of the reconstructed head which had blue eyes and fair hair. He looked at it in amusement and Rose gestured to him to move on as its accuracy was such that he looked like its darker haired twin! When they finally came to the area which exhibited his former grave site - the now famous car park - Rose showed him that the floor was glass so that you could walk around over the actual dig. Happily, the grave itself was protected from people walking on it by glass walls. Nevertheless, Richard shuddered as he approached the area and peered at the projection of his own skeleton as it had been when it was found. He turned and glanced at Rose, his eyes expressing a mixture of horror and fascination. After that they went to the gift shop and saw the myriad of Ricardian goodies available to buy, from pens and notebooks to ties and tea towels, books and mugs. Richard shook his head in wonderment as a stream of tourists from all over the world queued up to pay for their plunder.

That evening they made their way to the Bosworth Heritage Battlefield Site where there was to be a lecture on Arming King Richard.

"But why do you want to go to this? Surely you know that I can tell you whatever you wish to know about my armour?" Richard asked, completely bemused.

"Humour me, please!" Rose replied. "I think you will learn something."

As they took their seats, Richard noticed an unassuming young man seated at the side of the area facing them. He was wearing leg armour and an arming doublet, and various pieces of harness were hanging up or placed on a table.

"Do you recognise him?" asked Rose.

"No, should I?" said Richard.

"He is your 'body double', laughed Rose. "His name is Dominic Smee and he has an almost identical scoliosis to yours."

"Really?" said Richard, interested now.

They listened to the lecture and Rose found it fascinating, although Richard seemed more interested in observing Dominic. Rose was particularly impressed when Dominic showed a photo of the view he had from inside the helmet - all he could see was his horse's ears, basically. And he still had to wield a lance and try to hit a target, while galloping along. She had new respect for Richard's military prowess when she tried on a helmet and could barely see anything. Not only that, but her hearing was muffled as well - it was extremely claustrophobic - and Richard had to wear that, ride, and use weapons, all while the enemy was trying to kill him!

Dominic had also told the eager audience that Richard would have lost about three inches from his height because of the scoliosis, making him approximately five feet five inches tall. Rose looked at Richard appraisingly and nodded in agreement; that was about right!

Dominic was very approachable and happily answered questions after the lecture. He chatted with Richard for several minutes about the problems of living with scoliosis and Richard was delighted to find someone else with a similar condition.

"It makes me feel less...singled out, I suppose," he told Rose later. "And isn't Dominic a nice young man?"

As they were near the Royal Arms Hotel, where they would spend Thursday night, they decided to eat their evening meal there. The food at the Royal Arms was excellent and the portions very generous, which was always a positive for Rose. She hated those nouvelle cuisine meals where the food looked like a work of art but left you feeling as if the meal hadn't yet begun! Richard was also used to substantial meals, although he didn't overeat - he was conscious of what had happened to his brother, Edward, who had become fat and unhealthy through dissolute living. Richard was very active, so burned a lot of calories and could therefore eat larger portions.

They drove back to Leicester and spent another night at the Travelodge and the following morning they got dressed, Rose in black and Richard in a deep blue (he had refused to wear black for his own reburial). After breakfast, they made their way to Jubilee Square, where a big screen had been mounted high, so everyone who didn't have an invitation to the Cathedral could see the service live. They had brought two fold up chairs and despite the weather being gloomy and drizzly, sat there and watched the long, solemn ceremony. Rose had tears in her eyes at a few points in the service, such as the reading of the poem, 'Richard', written by Carol Ann Duffy, the Poet Laureate, and read superbly by Benedict Cumberbatch. Especially poignant was the line about granting Richard the carving of his name, which he would now have. Richard found he was moved most by the respect shown to him by these modern people and the love that he still managed to inspire in many of them, people who had never even met him. He especially liked the Catholic part of the service and the authentic Mediaeval re-interment section, which had been similar to the one he and Edward had used to re-inter their father and Edmund, their brother, who had both been killed at the Battle of Wakefield. He sat with lowered head and prayed. Rose wondered whether he was praying for his own soul's repose or those of his family. Not long after the hand-made coffin was lowered reverently into the prepared grave, the sun finally emerged from the clouds and the weather reverted to the cheery sunshine they had enjoyed up until then. It was as if, now the solemnities were over, the celebrations could begin.

Pensive, they made their way to a nearby restaurant and ate silently, both lost in their own thoughts.

The evening, though, was even more moving and special for Richard, because it was time to go and listen to the Middleham Requiem. An additional bonus was the presence of the current Duke of Gloucester, also called Richard, and the man who had been the Mediaeval Duke of Gloucester craned his neck to observe the modern Duke curiously. Then it was time for the concert to begin. It had been written especially to commemorate Richard by Geoffrey Davidson and had only been performed three times before. Rose had never heard it either and, although their seats did not have a great view, being quite a way back, this did not detract from the beauty of the music. They both sat entranced, both with tears in their eyes when the duet between 'Richard' and 'Anne' after the death of their son was performed. Richard could not speak at the end, but grabbed Rose's hand and squeezed it gently, turning to her with his face a contradiction - he was smiling but his eyes were swimming and his jutting chin was just the slightest bit wobbly. Rose knew exactly how he felt - the sadness within the music contrasted poignantly with the joy he felt at being remembered through such a beautiful work of art. It was a perfect end to a special and unique day.

Afterwards, they drove to the Royal Arms Hotel, where they were going to spend Thursday night. The next morning they were booked on a guided tour to Fenn Lane Farm, which was where the experts now thought the Battle of Bosworth had actually taken place.

"Oh joy!" said Richard, sarcastically. "I can't wait to see the place where I will meet my death!"

Rose rolled her eyes in exasperation. They both knew the visit might help him plan his strategy when and if he returned to 1485.

Fire

They had a fantastic breakfast at the Royal Arms before checking out and driving over to the Bosworth Battlefield Heritage Site, where they were to meet the bus. Their guide was a very affable and knowledgeable man with the added bonus of being a staunch Ricardian. As the bus passed along the lanes, he pointed out the sites where the various armies at the Battle had been, as far as they had been able to ascertain. Richard's had probably been camped on Ambion Hill, about where the Battlefield Site was now. William Stanley's army was to the east and Henry Tudor's further south. The actual battle was now thought to have been fought on the area near Fenn Lane Farm and they stopped there and got out of the bus. Rose had brought the white roses they had been given at the Concert for a King and they stood with the other tourists in an attentive group as their guide explained just what it would be like to have been hit by a cannonball.

"The cannons were fired horizontally aiming for the opposing soldiers and if you were a victim the first thing you would see would be the flash as it fired and then you would basically be smashed into lots of little pieces. Then your fellow soldiers would hear the 'boom' of the firing."

The group were listening, appalled and enthralled, and Rose glanced questioningly at Richard, who nodded, confirming the horrific truth of it. Rose suddenly felt sick, thinking of the terrible things throughout his life that Richard must have seen - and done?

The guide then described the narrative of the battle and Richard was hanging onto his every word, storing away the information for future (or past) reference. Apparently, the Duke of Oxford had pushed Richard's general, Norfolk, back for a great distance by using a tight formation and making his men keep to it no matter what. Then Richard had seen Henry Tudor to the east in a small group, going towards Stanley's army, probably trying to urge him to join in on his side. The Duke of Northumberland had failed to engage when ordered, either by choice, through fear or prevented by the marshy terrain. Richard had thought to end the battle quickly by initiating a charge with his close household knights straight at Tudor. If he could take Tudor out, the battle would be over and a great deal of bloodshed would be avoided.

But there had been a marsh between Richard and Tudor and Richard's horse was thought to have foundered in it, throwing Richard off. Or perhaps he had dismounted deliberately. Before that he had unhorsed Tudor's champion, John Cheney and killed his standard bearer, William Brandon, but as he got to within two sword lengths of Tudor, Stanley made his move. Richard was betrayed, his helmet cut off or removed, and he fought on alone, surrounded by his enemies, crying: 'Treason! Treason!' and defending himself courageously until hacked down from behind. The guide pointed out the likely area where Richard was killed and the hill, now called Crown Hill, where his crown was probably presented to the victorious Henry. Richard's jaw was tense and his eyes hard and angry as he heard this, but he remained silent. Rose, too, kept quiet, her mind imagining Richard's terrible death which had actually happened, in all probability, right here. It was a sobering thought and she allowed him his private thoughts. It must indeed be strange to view the place where you were thought to have died. She stepped forward and placed the two roses reverently in the nearby hedge, since they were not allowed to walk onto the field, which was on private land.

When they got back to the Battlefield Centre, they decided to see the exhibition and Rose was lucky enough to have her own personal guide - Richard himself. He told her which cannonballs would have been fired by his army and which by Henry's - the archaeologists would have been insanely jealous of Rose had they known! Of course, he hadn't fought the battle yet, but he knew which size cannon he had. He also played with the interactive 'arm the knight' activity and did it in French with no mistakes at all. He pointed out coins minted in his reign and identified a ring as belonging to one of his squires.

They went outside and over to the huge sundial, made to commemorate the fallen of Bosworth on both sides. It was also covered in white roses and messages. Then they walked around the perimeter of the site, watched the sheep and patted a pony, silent in easy companionship. Rose told him that near Ambion Wood, one of her Facebook acquaintances had apparently seen the ghosts of four knights in armour mounted on their destriers, the leader, who wore a crown on his helm, raising his hand in salute. She wondered if it had been Richard's ghost.

"How does it make you feel walking around here - do you get any weird sensations?"

"Not really, Rose - it just seems rather surreal. I confess I do not recognise the landscape, although I have surely passed this way a few times. But you are right that there seems to be little to help with our research here."

"Let's go and see King Richard's well," said Rose. "It looks like a very peaceful place to me, from photos I've seen. It is where you were supposed to have taken a drink just before the fighting started."

So they wandered to the site of the old well and stood there looking at the mass of white roses that had been thrown inside in memory of Richard. Because of the re-interment there had been a dramatic increase in the tourists visiting the site and bringing flowers.

"Thank you for inviting me to come here. I may not have learned much to my advantage concerning the battle, but this is worth…so much. Knowing that my memory remains fresh in people's minds and that so many love me still is truly precious to me."

They had lunch at the Tithe Barn on the site and then made their way back to Leicester for the final time - the tomb was going to be revealed and they wanted to see it before they left. Rose was dubious about it - she had seen the design and didn't like the modern nature of it - she felt it should look more Mediaeval. But Richard had an open mind. They had to queue again, but not for as long as before. After about an hour they were ushered inside - it wasn't so rushed this time. Richard was very wary in case he started to feel ill again, but, although he went a little paler than usual, he managed to pass the tomb with no obvious ill-effects. It was by itself in the ambulatory, made specially to house it.

As they approached, Rose whispered to him: "I hate it - it looks like a slab of cheese on a cheese board - like it's been sliced by the wire as well!"

Richard could see her point. The large rectangular block of Swaledale fossil stone lay on the black plinth which had his name and device - the white boar - carved into it, along with his dates and, at the front, his motto and the English Royal coat of arms, from his time. On top of this the creamy yellow stone was positioned and it had a thin cross incised to a depth of about halfway from side to side and top to bottom. The stone was the colour of cheese and the cross could have been the slice marks of the cheese wire. But Richard had moved to the front and crouched down. At first she thought he was praying, but then he pointed out that, in that position, you could see the altar with the cross on it directly through the axis of the cross incision.

"That is amazing!" he said, excitedly. "And the stone itself is beautiful - look at the wonderful imperfections and fossilised creatures in it. And it's from Yorkshire so my bones have part of my home with me, along with the earth inside the tomb. Also, do you see? From a slight distance it looks as if the stone on top is floating - it's really a clever design, Rose."

Rose wasn't convinced, but she was glad he liked it - it was his tomb after all.

"Wouldn't you have preferred that one I showed you on the internet, that the Looking for Richard project commissioned?" she asked him.

"It was beautiful, too. I would have liked that one, yes, but this is lovely as well. It has all the necessary information on it, it has my motto, my device, my name and my Royal Standard. And I am laid to rest in the centre of my beloved England. I am content with that," he said. "In any case, I'm hoping all this will change after I go back, if I succeed."

They saw his funeral pall up closer and the lovely crown that John Ashdown-Hill had commissioned and that Richard thought was perfect.

When they emerged into the daylight, they saw that some of the eight thousand ceramic dishes with candles, which they had noticed scattered throughout the gardens and in the neighbouring streets (and even hanging from the tree next to Richard's statue!) had started to be lit. The smoke from them made everything look misty and the scent of them filled the air. Jubilee Square was massed with them in bold patterns and there was a depiction of a horse in the centre.

They wandered around looking at the fire sculptures and Richard said: "And this is all because of me. It is unbelievable, truly unbelievable."

They had a meal in an Irish pub and then made their way to the car park. But as they passed behind the Cathedral there was a loud bang and Rose realised that the firework display had begun, so they stayed and watched it all. It was pretty spectacular and they had quite a good view as the display exploded around the top of St Martin's. Richard had seen fireworks before but, he confessed, nothing as impressive as these. He revelled in the loudness and the colours. As the show came to a conclusion, the church bells began to peal - Richard's peal, composed especially for the occasion. He smiled as they made their way back to the car and was still smiling and talking about their trip when they arrived back in Rayleigh some three hours later.

Chapter Twelve - April 2015

Weight of the World

It was a few weeks after the re-interment and Richard's and Rose's lives continued as before. Richard would ride, train, play with the Middle Agers and explore modern life. His gym and Pilates training had noticeably improved his fitness levels. Then one day in April, on returning from a shopping trip, Rose had found Richard sitting at the computer desk, his forehead resting in his right hand, elbow on the desk. She had assumed he was researching on the internet, when she heard music playing: a choral piece, the various voices intermingling and sweet. It sounded as if it had been recorded in a cathedral, perhaps it had. She knew that, despite the variety of new forms of music that Richard had discovered since his unexpected arrival and his willingness to embrace most, if not all, of them, his first love was choral music. She started to go to him, opening her mouth to tell him what she had bought, when she heard a strangled sound coming from his bowed form. She recognised with shock that he was weeping and as she watched, she saw him brush his hand over his eyes, rubbing away a stream of tears. He was sobbing softly and almost silently, his shoulders quivering and his hair falling forwards, leaving his face in shadow. Then, she heard him mumble something, at first incomprehensible and then, as his distress grew and his voice became louder, she heard: "Anne, oh Anne! I miss you so. What would you do if you were here? What would you advise me to do? I can't bear living here anymore! I hate the noise, incessant noise. I detest the crowds and the dizzying speed of everything. I am trying to cope, but I miss my old life. I feel so alone. I don't even know if I will be able to get back, but I must…I must!" he sobbed, his voice muffled and choked.

Then he seemed to pull himself together a little and fell on his knees suddenly, his long, slender fingers clasped in an attitude of prayer. He turned his face up toward the heavens, his eyes closed, and said: "Sweet Jesu, please have mercy on a poor sinner. I know I have done wrong in my life and you have rightly punished me, but I repent of my sins and I beg and beseech you, sweet Lord of Heaven, to convey me back to my home, my time and my country so that I can try to govern England in a fair and just manner. Please hear my prayer, Jesu Christ, Our Lord. Amen."

He crossed himself and remained there, slumped in a kneeling position, his head bowed so that his thick, glossy hair fell forward, obscuring his face.

Rose lowered her head, biting her lip in distress at seeing him so distraught. She had been so selfish! Of course he must be desperate to get back home and all she had been trying to do was hold him here. Her heart felt empty because he had called on Anne and not her. Then she remembered that it was around this time of the year that Anne had died. Anyway, what did she expect? He hardly knew her after all. They were friends, but he had been married to Anne for over ten years and they had shared so much, so many experiences both happy and tragic. She realised yet again that if she truly loved him (which she did), she must put his happiness first and do her utmost to help him return to his own time and world.

She didn't want him to know that she had witnessed his distress - she respected his privacy too much and felt ashamed at the thought of how mortified he would be if he became aware of her eavesdropping. So, she withdrew back into the hallway, as silently as she could and then opened the front door again, making sure she made enough noise so that he would hear her. She called out to him cheerily, asking if he could help her to bring the shopping bags in and heard him clear his throat and call back to her:

"Of course I will. Anything for my favourite Lady!"

She could hear the slight tension in his voice, noted the air of embarrassment and sadness that seemed to surround him like an invisible veil, but he was hiding it well. She wondered seriously whether she would have noticed if she hadn't seen his agony for herself a few minutes earlier. He set to with gusto, covering his recent emotions with action - he may have been a King, but he was also a typical male and considered it a slight on his masculinity to carry any fewer than three carrier bags in each hand! Rose felt responsible for his happiness or lack thereof and, as they worked together putting the shopping away, she was pondering the best way to alleviate some of his pain.

"Would you like a treatment today, Dickon?" she asked eventually. "How is your spine feeling?"

"It feels better than it has done for years, thanks to you. I have been training three times this week and it has held up well. Although it always was easier being in harness." He paused, his eyes unfocused and dreamy, looking inward at some memory of his other life.

"A penny for them?" Rose smiled. He looked at her with a puzzled frown. "Your thoughts - a penny for your thoughts. It's a saying we use when someone is obviously thinking about something other than what is going on at the time."

"Hmm," he grunted, and she thought he was going to ignore the question, but then, after a thoughtful pause he said:

"I was just thinking about the banquets we used to have at Middleham. They were lavish, Rose - you would have loved them!"

His eyes twinkled mischievously. He had soon realised, after living with her for only a week or two, that Rose loved her food.

"We had some wonderful times there - Anne, Ned and I," he murmured wistfully. His eyes were again fixed on his image of the past and he chewed his bottom lip disconsolately. Suddenly he turned away and walked stiffly into the kitchen, saying over his shoulder:

"I'll make a cup of tea, shall I?"

The Proud One

Rose went to the cupboard and took two large brandy glasses down from the shelf. She retrieved the Calvados she had been saving for next year's Christmas pudding (she was unconventional when it came to recipes and food) and opened it.

"Why don't we have something stronger?" she suggested, pulling out two chairs so they could sit at the dining room table. "See what you think of this, Dickon. It's my favourite spirit. I first tasted it when I spent some time in Caen, in Normandy, as a student. It's apple brandy. Did you ever have anything like this at Middleham?"

She poured the aromatic amber liquid into the glasses, filling them to just below the midpoint. She took one and offered the other to Richard, swirling hers in her hand to elicit the wonderful appley fragrance of it.

"You are supposed to swirl it, sniff it and then swig it!" she smiled. "The Normans down it in one - I must say it is very warming on a cold winter night! À ta santé!"

She held her glass out towards him and he dutifully clinked his against hers, a custom he enjoyed.

"À ta santé aussi, Madame!" he said, bowing in a courtly fashion.

"Mmm!" he groaned in delight. "That is the most delicious drink I think I have ever tasted. We had nothing so refined and pure at Middleham. We would sometimes drink fermented apple juice, but this is like the nectar of the gods in comparison! May I have some more, please?"

She poured him another glass and he sighed in satisfaction as he sipped it this time, savouring each mouthful.

"Didn't you have such drinks at Court either?" she asked.

"We did have eau de vie, very rarely," he replied. "But spirits were more often used for medicinal purposes than drinking for pleasure. I suspect if we had had such a wonder as this, many more people would have suddenly developed mysterious illnesses! But in any case, I very rarely went to Court when Edward was King. I couldn't bear all the superficiality or the backstabbing, sometimes literally, that occurred there."

"Is it true that you hated Elizabeth, the Queen?" Rose asked.

"Well, I certainly disliked her. I thought it was wrong of Edward to marry her because it put our country into turmoil. She was such a greedy, selfish woman. That marriage also started the conflict between Edward and Richard Neville, the Earl of Warwick, Anne's father. As you know, Warwick was a very powerful man and helped Edward get the throne in the first place. He was known familiarly as "The Kingmaker". I knew him very well, as Edward sent me to his estate at Middleham to learn the art of being a good noble knight - he was like a second father to me after my father had been killed; I was so young when it happened I didn't remember much about him. Warwick was a very proud man and of noble blood himself. He was also my mother's brother's son."

Rose frowned in concentration, trying to follow the relationship.

"Yes, I know the convoluted relationships of the noble houses of my time are confusing to you in the here and now! He was my first cousin in other words, although quite a lot older than me. I learned such a lot from him and I grew to love the North, where I was based - at Middleham. And, of course, it was there that I first met his daughter, Anne, my beloved wife and consort."

Richard took another sip of the Calvados and licked his lips. He looked down at his glass, swirling the liquid so that it caught the light. Rose knew the story of Warwick and Edward, but it was unusual for Richard to be so voluble and she didn't want to interrupt his flow. She was also hoping she might learn something new, straight from the source, instead of from second or third hand accounts, distorted by time. Besides she just liked hearing him talk. His voice was clear and low, and he spoke confidently and fluently, using eloquent gestures to emphasise points. It gave her a good excuse to stare into his eyes and enjoy the animation in his expressive face.

"Richard Neville was shocked and humiliated when Edward announced his marriage to that woman. He had been negotiating for Edward to marry the French Princess, Bona of Savoy. He couldn't bear losing face like that - his pride was his undoing, really - and then later he felt that Edward was acting on the advice of Elizabeth and her family, that she and the Woodvilles were gaining influence over Edward and he was losing his. So he decided to try to oust Edward and place my other brother, George, on the throne. Thank God he didn't succeed - I'd hate to think what the country would have become under him! Please don't misunderstand me, I loved George dearly, but we were so different in character and I never really felt I understood him. He was so self-serving, vain and frivolous. He had a jealous, sniping side too, always was envious of Edward. It was invariably 'me first' with George."

He sighed heavily, perhaps remembering George's eventual fate.

"It must have been hard for you, caught in the middle of them all like that," Rose said, encouraging him to continue.

"Mmm. Oh yes, it was a terrible dilemma for me. I loved Richard Neville, Anne and George, but Edward was my King and I loved him most of all, then at least. I suppose I looked up to him from an early age. Do you know, after my father was killed and George, Margaret, our sister, and I were sent to stay with another family, Edward came to see us every day. He must have been busy as he was preparing to do battle for the throne, but he never missed a day. He brought us wonderful gifts and told us amazing tales of the battles he had fought and the sights he had seen. It's what made me resolve to be his loyal right hand man and follow him into battle as his rock. That's when I decided on my motto 'Loyaulté Me Lie'."

"Yes, 'Loyalty Binds Me'," Rose translated. "Were you never tempted to change sides and support Warwick then?"

"Never, for one moment. I pride myself on keeping my word and that had been long given to Edward; I was always his man. So I had to make the sacrifice and give up Anne, leave Middleham and go back to Court. I could understand Warwick's frustration with Edward but I was ashamed of George. How could he go against us - he was our brother! I remember feeling so uneasy through all of that terrible time - Edward and I ended up having to go into exile in Burgundy for a few months and we had no money and no support from Charles of Burgundy, even though he was Margaret's husband. I thought we would never get back to England again and I despaired at times - I missed England very much. It was only when Charles realised that Warwick had again changed his plans and was now supporting the old King Henry VI, that he decided to help Edward get the throne back. Because Warwick, who had been the most vehement hater of Margaret of Anjou, Henry's Queen, had gone so far as to ally himself with her by marrying Anne to her son!"

He shook his head sadly and downed the rest of his drink.

"I hope I'm not boring you," he smiled, looking directly into her eyes.

"Not at all," she said. "It is fascinating to hear it all from your own lips. You must have been devastated when you heard that Anne had been married to the Prince of Wales - another Edward, wasn't he? Why were there so many Edwards, Richards and Margarets in the mix?"

Richard chuckled, a sound she loved. When he laughed it was always with an air of slight embarrassment as if he was trying to hold it in, making it seem even more merry and natural. It was as infectious as the 'flu and she joined in.

"We'll call him Edouard, then, shall we? Yes, I have to admit I was jealous of him for a while and very angry with Warwick. He had wanted me to marry Anne, as George had married his other daughter, Isabel. That was the most tempting part, I really did want Anne, but my duty to Edward and the country had to come first or I would not only have been betraying my King, but myself. My personal feelings had to be put aside for the sake of my honour and my duty."

"You are nothing if not a true, chivalrous knight, are you?" Rose said. "But you got your reward in the end, didn't you? You did get to marry her."

He grinned. "Yes, I did. George was tempted back to us, when he realised that Warwick had discarded his plan to make him King. Edward and I defeated first Warwick and his followers and then Margaret and Edouard. Warwick and Edouard were both killed."

"Can I ask you something, Dickon?"

"You can ask," he said, "Although I do not promise to answer!" His favourite rejoinder.

"Who actually killed them? "

"I don't know who it was who killed Warwick - Edward had ordered that he be taken prisoner, not killed. Perhaps it was better thus. I don't know if Edward would have had the stomach to have had him 'headed. I certainly would have found it…difficult to have presided over it, as I would have had to, as Constable of England. Johnny Neville was also killed and he had Edward's colours on under his mail. I think Edward felt very guilty about that. Johnny was always loyal to him, sometimes even against his own brother, Warwick, but Edward pushed him too far and took him for granted. In the end he chose family over a loyalty that wasn't rewarded. I was saddened by both their deaths - I liked and admired them. I think it was then that I realised that Edward wasn't infallible, that he made mistakes just like any other man."

He shrugged and reached for the bottle of Calvados.

"May I?" he asked politely.

"Of course Dickon, you know I said to treat my home and things as your own," Rose said, holding out her own glass for a refill. The bottle was nearly empty. Richard smiled warmly.

"You didn't tell me anything about the death of Edouard," she said.

"Ah yes!" he continued. "We were both in the same battle, at Tewkesbury, but he was not anywhere near my wing and I never saw him alive. I suspect that George may have killed him, just to take out the heir to the throne, in the hope that he might still one day come to power. I was not involved despite what some say today. But I would have killed him if he had been there in front of me at the battle - it is kill or be killed in a war situation and if you hesitate you are lost. I might well have also killed him if I had caught him fleeing the field, as some say he did. I can't categorically deny it, I might have. It is the way, in battle. The common soldiers were often spared by Edward, but Edouard was one of the nobles who led the enemy forces and would therefore have been executed anyway, if he had survived. As it is, I don't have his death on my conscience, at least."

Rose asked: "And Anne, had she and Edouard...I mean, they were married weren't they? Was it consummated? Because a lot of historians think Margaret of Anjou wouldn't allow it until the throne of England was secure and it never was, so…"

She realised she was gabbling, and her face had coloured bright pink under his reproachful gaze.

"I don't think that is any of your business, is it?" he said simply, pursing his lips.

Bad Boys

Rose thought long and hard about how she might help Richard. She didn't like to see him so gripped by melancholy; his mood had not really improved since she had caught him weeping. There was now rarely any of his previous infectious enthusiasm nor eagerness for action and the smile, which illuminated and transformed his face, was merely a distant memory. Instead, he was either morose and sullen, withdrawn and lethargic, or falsely cheerful. In the latter phases his smile never reached his eyes, which stared often into the distance like a sailor desperately seeking land. She had tried to bring the subject up but he was evasive, denying there was anything wrong. Remembering what she had heard him say about the noise and bustle when he had been unaware of her presence, she wondered whether a trip away somewhere more peaceful might be in order.

Then she had a brain-wave - she contacted her Norwegian friend, Torstein, again and explained her predicament, confiding the truth about Richard to him and asking if there was any chance they could visit the Jostads for a week or so. She wasn't sure whether Torstein believed her tale but, if he didn't, he was much too polite to say and readily agreed to welcome them to his home for as long as they wished. Now she just had the problem of obtaining a passport for Richard!

After mulling it over for a day or so, she remembered Mike Scaletta, one of her regular patients. He always boasted that he could get anything for a price. It had been he who had listened politely to her comment that Ellie, her now deceased aunt who'd been in constant pain from rheumatoid arthritis, had complained that the Government should allow sufferers to have a small amount of cannabis and then, the week after, had given her a small package with a wink, saying: "For your Auntie. Plenty more where that came from - just let me know."

When she had opened the package she found a small, brown, shapeless lump of something, about half an inch in diameter. She understood, with a shock, that it was a piece of cannabis resin! She had thanked him politely but had thrown it away as soon as she could, hiding it among the other rubbish.

Mike was lying face down on the couch a few days after she had spoken to Torstein, and she cleared her throat in an embarrassed way before saying: "I was wondering whether you would have some advice for m...a friend of mine. She has a boyfriend who has no identity documents and he needs to get hold of a passport urgently. Where could she obtain one, do you have any idea?"

He wasn't fooled by her attempt at dissembling.

"Have you got an illegal immigrant boyfriend then, Rosie?"

"Yes, something like that!" she replied, rolling her eyes in exasperation as she worked on his shoulder.

"I always knew you liked bad boys," he joked. "How soon does he need it and how much dosh does he have?" he asked, completely unphazed.

"Well, he needs it by the end of May, I suppose, and he has a little bit of money saved, not a massive amount." She didn't want to be swindled out of a fortune.

"Can you get a passport-sized photo of him to give me by early next week? Make sure his eyes are visible and he isn't smiling - you know the score, don't you? I should be able to manage it. It'll cost you four grand though, is that alright?"

"I'll have to check with him, but it should be OK. And I'll make sure the photo is done properly. Thanks, Mike."

And it was that easy. She got Richard to have a passport photo done in a booth, making sure it would pass the rigorous inspection, and gave it to Mike along with a brown envelope stuffed with cash from the proceeds of the sale of Richard's rings and brooch. (She had made sure it was a brown envelope, as tradition required). Three weeks later, a perfect British passport was hand-delivered to her by Mike. She opened it to see Richard's photo staring back at her, his expression serious and wary, probably because of the flash - he hated flash photography! For a passport photo, it wasn't actually bad. Then she saw the name on the passport and smiled with satisfaction - Richard Broom. That would do nicely! She had paid an extra five hundred pounds in order to choose the name on the passport. They thought it best to keep 'Richard' but the surname Gloucester or Plantagenet might have attracted too much attention, so she had come up with the idea of using the common name for the planta genista - the plant that the name Plantagenet had come from originally, the broom plant! Richard thought it sounded fine. Mike had even arranged it so that the passport looked as if it had already been used and put it in a worn leather holder.

Chapter Thirteen - May 2015

Flying Theme (E.T.)

Thus it came about that she and Richard were waiting in the Departure Lounge at Stansted airport for a flight to Norway. Their return was booked for two weeks later - Rose hoped that two weeks away would restore Richard to his former, happier self and help him feel more relaxed and at home. She loved Norway very much and wanted to share it with him. Now she was anxious in case he didn't like it. But she put that out of her mind, as there was a very big step to take before it came to that - the flight itself. When she had first told him that they were going to Norway for a break, he had reacted with astonishment.

"We are going where? You want us to go on a long ocean voyage? The English Channel is tricky enough but the North Sea is absolutely treacherous! Are you demented? How is that going to be a 'nice break'?"

"No, Richard, you don't understand - it will only take two hours to get there - we're going to fly."

He'd stared at her in shock. His eyes were wide open, she could see the whites surrounding the dark blue-grey irises, and his mouth was open too. The fine eyebrows pulled together in a frown as he'd closed his mouth, his face even paler than usual.

"What? Fly?! Oh Sweet Jesu, on one of those noisy aeroplanes?"

"It's just science. The laws of aerodynamics. We fly with hundreds of people, all together in the aeroplane - it's a bit like a big car with wings. You like driving don't you, so you'll love flying too."

He continued frowning and began to chew his lip, obviously turning the whole concept over in his mind.

"What are aeroplanes made from? Wood? Feathers? It must be something light, to fly. How can hundreds of people all fly at once? Please explain, Rose."

Rose did her best, but physics wasn't her strong point. In the end they Googled it, of course. He was dumbfounded at the technology that meant a heavy, metal, gigantic structure, containing many people, could actually fly safely, and still marvelled that human flight was actually possible at all. Eventually, he stated firmly that he would have to try it out for his own curiosity's sake, but Rose sensed that he was more than a little afraid at the thought. She told him the statistics, changing it a little, so he could relate to the concept.

"More people are killed in battle than die in 'plane crashes," she'd said. "For example, how many men died at Towton? Didn't you say about twenty thousand?"

"Well, I wasn't actually present at that battle, as you know," he said. "But I think it must have been more than twenty thousand. Edward described it to me - it was literally a bloodbath."

"Wow!" she gasped. "It doesn't bear thinking about, does it? I can't even imagine what it must have been like, fighting in such a battle."

"Well, I can tell you what fighting is like generally, if you wish," he had offered. "That's if you have the stomach for it." he'd added, with an evil grin.

"Your age was so bloodthirsty," Rose had sighed. "There was death everywhere, wasn't there?"

He had become serious then.

"Yes, indeed. Many more people died of disease and infection - in fact most of the battlefield deaths were from later infections rather than clean kills. One thing that I might be able to do if...when I get back would be to promote hygiene - I will research it more to see what we can use in my time, as we don't have antibiotics."

"You could use maggots or leeches to clean the wounds - they are known to help with infection," Rose had put in. "Also silver is anti-bacterial, that's why the nobility were often healthier than the poor - they had silver plates and utensils."

"Yes, thank you, I will bear that in mind."

"But there was also plague, death in childbirth - of both mother and baby, executions. It must have been terribly traumatic for you as a child - for all children, I suppose."

"Yes, but it was 'normal' for us, so I would suppose we became inured to it after a while, as I said before. It is a much harder life in all ways. And yet, I miss it..." he had added, sadly.

Now they were waiting for their flight to be announced. It was an early flight, giving them ample time to travel by train from Oslo to Lillehammer, where Torstein would pick them up. Then he would take them up into the mountains, the most peaceful, lovely place she had ever known.

Rose had offered to get Richard a sedative from the doctor's to help with his first flight. Since the fear of flying was so common, even amongst modern folk, she was sure he would be gripped with it at some point, but knowing him as she did by now, he would doubtless try his best not to show his emotions. She worried that he might have a panic attack or worse. However, Richard had flatly refused.

"Do you think I am a child, Rose? I have fought battles in treacherous conditions, suppressed the Scots, been exiled - twice - to the continent. You have explained how it works and I trust you. I will not be afraid."

"But it is all so strange to you. It would be entirely understandable if you felt a little nervous," she said, trying to play down her worry.

"Thank you for your concern," he replied, politely. "I give you my oath that I will tell you if I become afraid or nervous - will that do?"

"Yes, Dickon, that will do!" Rose smiled.

About ten minutes later, they announced the flight. She had noticed that Richard had visited the loo a few more times than normal - he was just returning from that direction now.

"Good. There you are. They're calling us to the Departure Gate now. Let's go!"

Richard smiled back at her even though he looked whiter than usual - "A whiter shade of pale!" Rose thought. On an impulse she grabbed his hand, hoping to reassure him by her touch. She had always been a 'touchy-feely' type of person, to which her profession bore witness. Richard wasn't; he didn't recoil, at least, but gently withdrew his hand from hers saying: "Let me get the luggage."

She smiled ruefully - she might have known he wouldn't allow personal contact between them in public. He had, at least, been discreet about it though.

She led the way and he followed, pulling their cases behind, the wheels whirring like crazy as he strode along behind her.

They had to wait again at the Gate, and she watched him surreptitiously, noting his hands gripping the book he was pretending to read (he'd not turned the page for nearly twenty minutes) and the nervous tapping of his foot against the shiny floor. She tried to imagine how he must be feeling - having come from a world where the fastest thing was a horse to a place where huge metal machines actually flew in the sky while others whizzed about on roads and rails! She found she couldn't. She thought it was a miracle that he had accepted the twenty first century as well as he had.

She looked over his shoulder to see what he was reading. It was 'Bosworth 1485 - Psychology of a Battle' by Michael Jones. He was the author who believed that Richard had acted out of duty to his family and country and that he had planned his cavalry charge as part of his battle strategy. He also believed Richard had murdered the Princes in the Tower! Soon they were called to board.

They hadn't had any trouble at all so far with Richard's fake passport and they didn't now either. They were waved on board the plane and Richard, who was slightly ahead of her, turned to glance over his shoulder at her, his eyebrows raised and his mouth formed into an expression of…excitement? Anticipation? It was certainly not fear. She was amazed at him. If she was judging his demeanour correctly, he wasn't scared at all! She went ahead of him onto the plane to show him what to do and he acted as if he did this every day. She asked him if he wanted to sit near the window and he did. She talked him through what would happen and he listened dutifully and it was fine. The only time he looked alarmed was when the plane's engines roared and it accelerated along the runway. His face was a picture as they ascended and the land below them diminished into the distance, looking like a child's toy farmyard beneath them. He was entranced by the clouds as they flew through them and even liked the food!

"This is incredible, Rose! I am so privileged to be able to experience this - it's a miracle. I still think I must be dreaming. And apart from the speed, how much more comfortable it is than being on a leaky, rolling ship, swimming in vomit and horse shit…Oh, sorry for my language. I'm just a little excited."

She had explained to him in their first week together the differences in the power of curse words in his time and hers. In Mediaeval England, bodily functions were normal and had little power to shock, whereas words involving God, Jesus or other religious themes had much more impact. Nowadays the opposite applied. It was interesting.

Norwegian Wood

It was only about two hours and they were coming in to land at Oslo - Rygge airport. Richard was beaming as they taxied into the bay and they soon headed out of the plane. After a free bus ride and two trains (changing in Oslo) they finally arrived in Lillehammer. Rose looked out of the window and saw a familiar, tall figure waiting for them, his arms folded. Torstein had an open, handsome face and warm, blue eyes, with slight laughter lines surrounding them. When he smiled, he showed even, white teeth and his blue eyes sparkled. His physique was strong and athletic from the exercise he took hiking in the mountains, skiing in the winter and everyday work in the garden and chopping wood. He was a language teacher and his English was near-perfect. As he saw her, the smile appeared and he waved and started striding along the platform towards them.

He hugged Rose and kissed her on the cheek, then turned to Richard, who solemnly proffered his hand to shake. Torstein was about the same age as Richard but was very tall, towering over his Plantagenet guest in a way that brought to Rose's mind an image of how Richard must have looked next to his brother, Edward.

"Welcome to Norway," Torstein said politely. They thanked him and then Torstein led them out to his car. He asked how their journey had been and made polite conversation about the weather for a while, as was to be expected when English and Norwegian people got together. Those countries were both obsessed with it! Richard was just as used to this as the others, being English too, albeit his time zone was different.

"Do you notice any difference in Richard's accent and speech, Torstein?" Rose asked. Torstein and Rose always chatted about language and could spend hours discussing small points of grammar. It was a side to Rose that Richard had not seen before and he listened, fascinated.

"No, I can't tell the difference," Torstein smiled. "Where are you from then, Richard?" he added, including Richard in the conversation.

"I was born in Northamptonshire, but I love Yorkshire and lived there most of my life. I also have estates in other counties, but Yorkshire is where I feel at home."

"I have never been there," Torstein commented. "What is it like?"

"The hills and dales are beautiful and the landscape is wild and awe-inspiring," Richard replied. "You really feel close to God in that environment. You must come to visit us at Middle…well, you must visit Middleham, where I used to live," he corrected himself. "And thank you for allowing us to spend some time here. I am looking forward to finding out about your country - I have never had the opportunity of visiting it before."

"I thought we could go up to the cabin tomorrow and spend tonight at Gausdal," said Torstein, looking at Rose for approval.

"Sounds perfect," she replied.

It took about an hour to reach Torstein's house in Gausdal. It was at the end of a winding road and had a huge garden, which was unenclosed. As most houses in Norway were, it was made of wood and consisted of a single storey, but had a huge cellar underneath the house proper. There were three bedrooms, one of which was used as a home office and a huge open-plan, L-shaped lounge diner. The walls were natural wood panelling, decorated with photos, paintings and a tapestry or two - similar to the arras which were common in Mediaeval grand homes, Rose thought. The kitchen was to the side of this with a separate shower room and toilet. Norwegians rarely bathed, preferring to shower. There was a huge rock in the middle of the garden and several mature trees, mainly birch. Torstein kept it neat and well-tended. But the best thing about the garden was the veranda from which was a breathtaking view across the valley. After they had deposited their cases in the hallway, Torstein made some coffee and they sat on the veranda drinking it, with some Norwegian cakes. Rose looked at Richard and he smiled at her - he seemed to be feeling more positive already with the change of scene.

That Thing You Do

Rose had just visited the loo and, on returning, tried to get Torstein's attention through the veranda window. He had assumed that she and Richard were a couple and had placed their cases in the one room.

"Torstein!" she said in a stage whisper and beckoned him into the house. "Torstein! You have put our cases together in the room - we aren't together, we're just friends," she said.

"Oh OK, then I will get out the sofa-bed later - Richard can have my room and I will sleep on that."

"No! Torstein, I won't hear of you giving up your room - I'll be happy to sleep on the sofa-bed."

"No, I insist, Rose, you are my guests, aren't you?"

"But we kind of invited ourselves and you have been generous enough already, letting us stay. I won't let you…"

"I'll take the sofa-bed. End of discussion," said a quiet voice of steel.

Rose looked at Torstein and he at her, then they both turned to the slim figure standing by the veranda door, staring at them with eyes like chips of ice and lips pursed in determination.

Torstein opened his mouth to protest, Richard gave that 'I dare you!' tilt to his head and Torstein closed his mouth again, looking away in a slightly confused and embarrassed fashion.

"That's settled then," Richard said and withdrew gracefully to the veranda.

"How does he do that?" asked Torstein, bewildered.

"He was born to it. He's the King!" Rose laughed.

"You're serious?" asked Torstein. "I thought you were, you know, winding me round?"

"You mean 'winding you up', said Rose. "No, he really is the King of England - well, he was five hundred-odd years ago. Let me explain…"

And they went outside again to join Richard, and Rose, with Richard chipping in here and there, explained how she thought Richard had been drawn into the present day. To his credit Torstein listened intently, nodding now and again and occasionally raising an eyebrow, but he didn't laugh once!

After their short rest, they unpacked just the things they needed for the night and the next day, as they would be driving up into the mountains to the cabin in the morning. Richard left his things in the room Rose was using as there wasn't a wardrobe in the dining area, where the sofa-bed was. Then they all went to the supermarket to buy provisions for their stay at Nysetra, Torstein's holiday cabin. Richard had found supermarkets a bit confusing at first, but he had soon got used to them and could see how practical they were. He did say they were a bit soulless though, and Rose had to agree. They went around picking out the items they would need up there. They took breakfast items, juice, milk, veg and other basic foodstuffs…and a lot of beer. Then they went to the Vinmonopol and bought some wine and spirits. Richard insisted on paying for the booze, which was very generous of him.

"What is the exchange rate for Norwegian currency?" he asked, frowning, at the checkout. Rose told him and his eyebrows shot up. "Is this total correct? It seems much more than it would be in England."

"Oh, it is!" Rose smiled. "Norwegians pay an awful lot of tax on alcohol. The Government see it as a way to try and stop them drinking so much."

"Does it work?" Richard asked.

"No," put in Torstein, his eyes twinkling. He lowered his voice. "We still buy a lot of it, but most Norwegians make their own liquor too, you know?" He tapped the side of his nose, conspiratorially. "The tax makes a good extra income for the Government though!"

Richard raised his eyebrows and nodded thoughtfully.

Back at Torstein's house, they put the shopping away and ordered a pizza for dinner. While they were waiting for the delivery, Torstein showed Richard the house and garden. He loved the stove heater which was at the heart of most Norwegian houses. He also liked the garden and the view.

"It reminds me somewhat of Middleham," he remarked. "The landscape is not the same, but it has the same…I don't know…atmosphere...ambiance…feeling. So peaceful and beautiful and you can see so far into the distance. It makes you feel small and insignificant and that is comforting somehow. It is as if your problems become diminished in the vastness of the landscape."

"Yes," said Torstein. "I feel the same when I am up in the mountains, you know. I quite enjoy walking there in silence on my own."

"I feel like that when I look up at a starry night sky or a cloudy sky," put in Rose. "It's because the magnitude of it makes you feel minuscule and inconsequential and that makes you realise that your concerns are also small and negligible in the grand scheme of things. Maybe you are a bit more important though, Dickon, as you are King of England, so your problems concern a whole country."

He sighed and she immediately wished she hadn't reminded him of that. She quickly changed the subject.

"How about a game of dominoes or cards after dinner?" she asked.

"Yes, why not?" said Torstein, as Richard nodded. Then the doorbell rang and their meal had arrived. Richard had only tried pizza once before as Rose rarely ate it, and pronounced the Norwegian version tasty and filling. They washed it down with a bottle of rosé wine.

They had a relaxing time playing cards and then dominoes and Richard proved himself to be as competitive at playing games as he was on the battlefield. Their last game was Black Lady, like a trump game where the aim was to lose as many tricks as possible, since any hearts or the Queen of Spades (The Black Lady) in your trick gave you negative points. There was the added element that each suit in turn was trumps and so you had to get rid of those as fast as possible to avoid them winning the hand. It was a game partly of skill and partly of luck.

"Like a battle, really," said Richard. "But who is the Black Lady, do you suppose? Margaret of Anjou? Elizabeth Woodville?"

"No, Margaret Beaufort!" said Rose. "You need to neutralise her in some way, Dickon."

"Yes, I will," he replied. As they played on they became more and more tipsy, as Torstein had opened a bottle of Jägermeister and it went down smoothly and easily.

Finally they played a word game called 'Consequences' where they each had a long narrow strip of paper and wrote down a different part of a made-up story each round, before passing the paper on so that the end stories were mixtures of all three. The results were hilarious, although Richard had a propensity to put in a lot of beheadings and violent deaths! Oh well, it was natural that he would, with his turbulent upbringing and dangerous existence, Rose reasoned.

"We'd better get to bed, I think," said Richard, finally. He was the 'early to bed, early to rise' one and had begun yawning about an hour before. So they cleared up the debris from the pizza and drinks and retired for the night.

In her room, Rose couldn't sleep straight away. It was still early for her, so she sat up reading for a while. She pictured Richard in the lounge next door and wondered whether he was comfortable on the sofa-bed. She was tempted to go and offer her bed again, thinking of his scoliosis, but she knew as soon as the thought occurred, that he would refuse. He was very proud, even more than most men, and would see it as a sign of weakness to take the softer bed. She imagined him in the bed beside her and moved the second pillow so that she could hug it and imagine it was him. She closed her eyes and tried to relive their kisses from those times when Richard had, rarely for him, almost given in to his bodily desires. Eventually she drifted off to sleep.

Mountains

The next day they got up late (which was seven thirty a.m. for Richard and ten for the others). Richard had already done the washing up from the previous night when Rose and Torstein surfaced. He was sitting out on the veranda looking at the view and drinking a cup of black Norwegian-style coffee. He had now become a veritable coffee addict and liked it strong, which was just as well, since the Norwegians pride themselves on their coffee. They had a quick breakfast and then packed up their things and set off in Torstein's car to the cabin. Torstein put on a CD of a mix of songs that

Rose had sent him for Christmas one year and they ended up singing along with a few of them. Richard and Torstein chatted about Torstein's family, Norway, his work and many other things. Richard showed a genuine interest, remembering things that had been discussed previously and asking intelligent questions. It revealed a lot about the kind of King he was, approachable and diplomatic. Rose had let Richard sit in the front seat with Torstein and watched them chatting amicably from behind them in the back seat. She was pleased that her two favourite men in the world were getting along so well. The drive to the cabin took just over an hour and she loved it - the views from the car window were lush and sometimes awe-inspiring!

Torstein lived in the huge valley, Gudbrandsdalen, on the eastern side of the country. It was a fertile part of Norway and there were lots of small farms, including Torstein's father's, located on the side of the great valley, where the river Lågan ran, dividing it into two. He raised sheep, which were allowed to roam freely up in the mountains in the summer and were brought into the great barn for the winter. They all had a special tag attached to their ear, which indicated ownership and all the lead sheep had a bell around their necks to make it easier to find them again in the autumn.

They stopped off at the farm for a short while, Torstein's mother serving them more coffee and homemade cakes. Richard politely tried to make conversation, but she didn't speak English, so he ended up repeating his comment while resorting to gestures to try to get his meaning across. Rose translated for him and he turned to her in astonishment.

"You speak Norwegian? I had no idea you had so many talents. But I didn't hear you speak it when we were at the airport or on the train. Why didn't you use it then?"

"Well, most Norwegians seem to speak perfect English and it's just a lot easier to speak that - they like to practise it. Anyway, if I try to start a conversation in Norwegian, they usually reply in English. It's quite frustrating."

"It's a beautiful language," he said, turning back towards Gudrun, Torstein's mother. Then, to Rose: "How do I say that in Norwegian, Rose?"

"Norsk er et vakkert språk," she laughed, as he tried to copy the alien words.

They all laughed at his struggle, but he actually hadn't done too badly, presumably because of his facility for French and Latin. Gudrun was delighted and coyly thanked the handsome Englishman.

After bidding his mother and his brother, Nils, farewell, Torstein drove them up the steep, winding road, towards the mountains. He stopped at times, at Rose's request, for her to take photos of the landscape. There was one particular place that had, she felt, the best view in the world. There was a steep field with a few trees, leading downwards from the road, and in the distance, the other side of the valley spreading out below them. In between was a steep slope of land with houses that looked like toys they was so far away, but they provided the perspective to appreciate the scale of the landscape. They all got out to have a look.

Richard smiled at Rose.

"It reminds me of Yorkshire - the Dales!" he said.

"I thought it might," she replied, returning his smile. "That's one of the reasons I brought you here. I mean obviously the Yorkshire Dales are still there, but Norway is less crowded than England, more like Yorkshire was in your time. There are many parts of the landscape here that are different from England - well, you'll see - but there is a 'feel' of traditions that are no longer there in England, making it seem like travelling into the past - well, I feel that anyway."

They got back in the car and it wended its way slowly along the unmade road, passing a toll gate, for which Torstein had a pass. The terrain was now a bit rougher and more rugged, with fewer trees and more scrubby bushes. After a few more minutes, Rose recognised the small cluster of buildings that belonged to Torstein's family. There was a gate with a steep lane leading past the first couple of cabins and Rose jumped out of the car as soon as Torstein had stopped, to open it for the car to progress through. He drove past the first cabin, greeting his cousin, Johan, as they passed by, and then drove round the side over the gently sloping field to park just below the fourth cabin along. This belonged to Torstein, and he and his father and uncle had built it themselves. It was made especially for him, when he was about eighteen. Rose had stayed here numerous times and seen the landscape lush and green in the summer and covered in snow in the winter: it was always beautiful.

They grabbed their luggage and shopping from the boot and trudged up the hill to the front door of the cabin. Torstein had already unlocked the door and left his coat in the hallway and Rose followed close behind. Richard brought up the rear, carrying his case and several shopping bags.

As Rose entered the cabin she took a deep breath. She loved the smell of Torstein's cabin! It was woody and welcoming and, for her, the essence of Norway - she felt immediately at home whenever she entered the little wooden house, and her mind travelled back to other happy times she had experienced here. Of course, many of these had been spent with Matt, her ex. It might have made her feel sad to remember those times, that were no more, however Rose wasn't the sort of girl to dwell on the past. She would rather remember those times as they were then, joyful and care-free. She looked forward to other happy times to come.

"Well, this is beautiful!" remarked Richard as he put his bags down.

"I suppose it isn't as posh as some of the places you have owned, is it?" said Torstein, modestly.

"It's a lot cosier though," smiled Richard. "It's very welcoming and full of light. I tried to make Middleham a lighter place, by enlarging the windows, but glass was very expensive in those days and it was hard to keep those huge castles warm. Stone is much colder than wood, too."

Torstein showed Richard around and allocated him the left-hand one of the three bedrooms, with Rose's in the centre and his own on the right. His guests rooms had two single beds in each and a small wardrobe and bedside table. Torstein's was a bit larger and had a double bed and a wash basin, which they all had to share, taking turns every morning.

Apart from the bedrooms, the rest of the cabin was open plan, with a dining area to the left as you entered the cabin, a pantry to the right and a lounge area in the far left corner. There was a small kitchen with a gas hob and fridge, both run on gas canisters, located to the right of the lounge area with a separating wall and a central open fire hearth. The bedrooms were on the right of the kitchen. There was also a large loft where people could sleep if more guests were staying. A trap door in the floor of the kitchen revealed a larder for booze and soft drinks, and a fold down table was available if needed. There were two large plastic containers in the kitchen, one red and one yellow, both containing water. Torstein explained to Richard that the yellow one had drinking water and the red one had water that was only for washing. They each had a large ladle for removing the water, with a curved end which fitted over the side of the bucket, to stop them sinking in the water. It was a typically Norwegian simple, practical idea.

The cabin had a large veranda with a table for outdoor dining and there was a solar panel which powered the lights. Rose remembered when they had had to use oil lamps and candles after dark - not so different from Richard's time. The toilet was an outside one, a little hut on the side of the hill. That should really make Richard feel at home! Its door was fastened with a simple hook on a piece of string which slipped into a u-shaped pin. Inside was a wooden bench with two holes each with a lid. Rose had at first wondered why there were two holes. Did Norwegians like company when they were answering nature's call?! It was only a few years later that she had found a possible reason, after inadvertently drinking some 'Hjemmebrent': the home made, illegal 'moonshine'. She had been so ill she had needed the second hole to throw up into while using the other one for its original purpose!

After settling in, they sat on the veranda, drinking beer and chatting. The only other noise they heard was the sound of the sheep bleating and their bells jingling as they trotted about, freely grazing on the hillside. A person couldn't fail to relax and chill out in such a place - no internet, no TV and minimal mobile phone signal only aided that. The lack of technology seemed to make time pass slower and gradually one's mind and body adjusted to that and seemed to give a sigh of relief - peace!

Torstein suggested a walk - he loved partaking of the Norwegian National pastime and his long legs meant he left the others behind in no time. At least Rose had Richard's company on the way. Torstein paused to let them catch up periodically and then pointed out different landmarks and views. They were out for about an hour and a half and were ready for 'middag', the main meal of the day, when they got back. They cooked some chops and potatoes with a special Norwegian 'saus'. It was delicious.

They passed the evening drinking, talking and playing cards again. Richard retired to bed much earlier than the other two, as he had been up longer. Torstein and Rose stayed up for a good three or four hours after, catching up on all their news, and drinking. It was getting light again by the time Rose's head hit the pillow.

Earth

The next day, Torstein asked Richard if he would like to go fishing for trout. He jumped at the chance and the two of them planned to leave mid-morning after a cooked breakfast. Rose demurred, pleading that she would get bitten to pieces by the mosquitoes.

"They love me, unfortunately," she said.

Anyway, she had promised Torstein that she would paint a mural for him on his white, sloping chimney breast above the open hearth. They had agreed it the year before and for this visit she had remembered to bring brushes with her and

Torstein had picked up some acrylic artists' paint from the art store in Lillehammer. It would be a nice way to thank Torstein for his hospitality...provided it turned out OK! She had told Torstein to choose a photo from several she had brought with her as ideas for the mural. They were all landscapes, some lush, some rugged, some snow-covered. She had said that if he liked more than one and couldn't choose between them, she would try to combine them to make a unique picture. Torstein had chosen a view of a local area, with a long path winding away through the countryside and disappearing over a hill in the distance. There was a lake on one side and a typical Norwegian wooden fence with the slats laid diagonally. He had asked if she could incorporate some mountains in the background.

When the men had left, laden with rods, bait and all the other paraphernalia of fishermen, Rose first cleared the breakfast things and washed the dishes, then began designing the layout of the mural. She had to stand on a chair to reach. The time flew by as she painted, getting her jeans and T-shirt redesigned in the process of creation! The picture was coming together by the time the others returned. They had caught five fish - two large ones and three smaller, so they had their dinner for the evening.

They cooked their plunder on the barbecue on the veranda, after Torstein had smoked the fish with herbs in his 'smoke box'- a little metal container designed for the job. Rose had never tasted fish so good and Richard declared that it was as good as lamprey!

They passed the next day in the same way and by the afternoon, Rose had finished the mural. She was quite pleased with it and Torstein was delighted. She knew he wasn't just being polite later that evening when, his speech slurred from drinking a bit too much wine, he had said:

"Rose, I can't tell you how much I love that painting. It is even better than I thought it would be. I want to thank you for it - how can I ever repay you? You know, you will always be welcome in my house."

She smiled and told him, honestly, that it had been a pleasure. She had to admit she liked her work being praised - who wouldn't? Richard didn't say anything - she had noticed he was rather quiet and hoped he wasn't becoming depressed again.

Most of their days were spent walking and exploring the surrounding countryside. Sometimes they would drive out to somewhere that Torstein thought they would like, such as the huge pothole called Hell, the house that had belonged to the Norwegian writer, Bjørnson, or the Viking graves. Richard gradually became more and more at ease and seemed happier and calmer, although he was still quieter than he had been when Rose had first met him.

One day they climbed up to a small local mountain peak known as Nårkampen. When they reached the summit, they stopped and had a picnic, looking down from above. It was as if the whole earth was spread out beneath them. On the top was a large cairn of stones, which had a small box on the side of it, containing a visitor's book and pen. They all signed it, and dated it. When it was Rose's turn, she noticed that Richard had signed it Ricardus Rex and dated it 1485.

She gave him an exasperated look. He just grinned.

Dancin' Away With My Heart

Richard was clearly intrigued by Norway; it seemed to be a combination of the fairly primitive and the ultra-modern, but the primitive parts must have reminded him of home. Even in Gausdal, Torstein wasn't so ruled by the TV and internet as most English people were and it did make life move at a slower pace somehow, which Richard was more familiar with. He liked the little wooden cabins - they were cosy and welcoming. But the open-plan layout created a feeling of space and light too. In fact he, too, felt at home there. The Norwegian people had a wonderful character as well. They were fiercely patriotic, but not in a warlike way; they were open-minded and tolerant, but took their promises seriously. They were honourable people, which Richard could identify with, being one himself. He and Torstein got on tremendously well, and they had a similar teasing, dry sense of humour. Rose despaired at times. They could both tell her something as if it were true, with a deadpan expression, and it would turn out to be a complete 'wind-up'. It was hopeless when they joined forces.

Then, one night, after they had played their usual cards and dominoes, all the while downing copious amounts of Jägermeister, Torstein suggested putting on some music. Rose had her mini speakers and iPod with her, so she rushed to find them, banging her knee on a chair and nearly tripping over the rug in her haste - nothing to do with the alcohol, of course! She set the little system up and put it on random. There was quite an eclectic mix of fast and slow tracks, classical and pop, English and Norwegian songs. When 'Macarena' came on, Torstein got up, with some difficulty, and asked Rose to show him how the dance went. It was funny how confident he became after a drink or two - he was usually so reserved. She explained the moves and tried to demonstrate, but they ended up getting hopelessly tangled up and giggling like schoolchildren. Then a slower one came on and they stayed there, swaying, scarcely able to move without overbalancing. Torstein's speech was slurred as he said: "It is such fun to dance, isn't it?"

He suddenly turned to Richard. "Richard, Richard, come and dance as well," he urged.

Richard started to shake his head when Rose went over to him and, the alcohol having robbed her of all her inhibitions, grabbed his hands and trying to heave him up onto his feet, said: "Come on, Dickon, dance with me! Don't be an old fuddy duddy!"

"Perish the thought!" he laughed and got up, standing there with his arms spread in a gesture of confusion. "What do I do?"

The music had changed to a rather slow song and Torstein had decided it might be a good time to withdraw to the loo and had disappeared.

Rose, suddenly shy, took Richard's hands, placing one on her waist and holding the other, in a classic ballroom hold. He kept her at arm's length until she stepped close.

"We dance closer together for slow dances," she said.

Then she put his other hand on her waist and moved hers to his neck, starting to sway. He followed her lead, his breathing becoming faster, his eyes locked to hers. It was so sensual and intimate, the lights dim and the music romantic, the rest of the world blocked out. His lips naturally found hers and the kisses she remembered, the warm, loving, slow kisses began, confirming his love was as strong as hers. But why wouldn't he say the words? Then, miraculously, as if he'd read her mind, he whispered: "Thou knowest I love thee, Rose?"

She smiled into his neck - he had said it in 'Mediaeval speak'!

"I know, and I love thee," she replied. But they both knew they would have to part before very long. Rose couldn't speak, she just wanted to enjoy this perfect intimacy. She knew he wouldn't let it go any further, but perhaps their relationship would be spoiled if it did. They clung together, swaying to the melody, encased in a love that could never be, a white rosebud, nipped off before it could bloom. They stayed there a long time before finally parting for their separate beds.

All too soon they had to go back to England - they still had things to do regarding the Battle and Richard's plans to change the outcome, and time was passing.

As they said 'Goodbye' to Torstein and he hugged them both in turn, they felt sad to be leaving this beautiful country. Richard felt almost like he was leaving his home for the second time, and wondered whether he would ever come back to this lovely place. He had been told by Torstein a lot about the rest of the country: the Northern Lights, the midnight sun and the fjords, among other wonders, and he wished to see them, but knew he wouldn't be able to if he managed to return to his own time, as he sorely wanted; he would be too busy governing England. This made it all the more poignant a goodbye for him. However, Rose, too, felt sad at leaving, as she always did when she had to leave Norway. It was her spiritual home, of that she was sure. Although she had been born in the inner city of London and lived most of her life in towns and surrounded by many people, she loved the open spaces and peace and quiet of beautiful Gudbrandsdalen and wondered whether she might one day live there.

Chapter Fourteen - June 2015

Kissing You Goodbye

They made their way into the Major Oak clearing, Richard leading Rebel. He was dressed in the clothes he had been wearing when he arrived, the new helm attached to his saddle. He still had one ring. It wasn't one of his own - those had all been sold. It was a small locket ring which Rose had given him and it contained a small lock of her hair. They were both preoccupied with their own thoughts and said nothing for several minutes.

Then they both started speaking together.

"Rose, I just wanted…"

"Richard, can I just?… You go first," she said.

"No, ladies first," he smiled.

"I…I…I don't really know how to start. It's been such an honour to have you here and to get to know you, and I…"

She paused, aware she was gabbling as usual. Hold it together Rose, for God's sake, hold it together, she told herself. She immediately lost control and flung herself into his arms. He allowed her to hug him, taken aback by her emotion.

"Oh, Dickon, I'm going to miss you so much - how can I ever hope to get over you - I'm so in love with you!" she sobbed, trembling. "I'll never be able to get back to normal life. I'll never stop thinking of you."

And she buried her face against his shoulder. He held her, leaving Rebel's reins wrapped hastily round a branch and gently stroked her hair.

"Rose, you have to be sensible. I love you too, you know that, and I will miss you, of course. I will think about you every day of my life. But I'm a king and you know that a king has no choice in the direction his life takes. I have seen how England suffers under the Tydders and I have to try to stop it. It's my duty, isn't it?"

"Then take me with you! I don't care how hard it would be! I don't even care if I hardly see you - at least I might now and then. What have I got to keep me here? I have no children, my parents are dead, husband's gone. Please let me come with you?"

He sighed and said nothing for a few seconds, weighing up the consequences. Then he hugged her even closer and said, gently, but firmly: "It can't be, Rose. What if I still die at Bosworth? You will be left stranded in a time you know little about. And if I survive, I wouldn't be able to marry you, you know that. I would probably marry Joana of Portugal. I have to do what's right. Edward married for love and look what happened to the country. Plus, it would be torture for both of us to see each other and yet not be able to be together."

"I could be your mistress, I wouldn't mind, really. I understand you have to marry a foreign princess."

"I would mind, though. I would not dishonour my wife in that way. I remained faithful to Anne the whole time we were married and it would be the same for Joana or whomever I marry. It's best if you try to forget me or just accept that I love you very much and know that the memory of this time will sustain me whatever happens. It wouldn't be fair to you or my future wife if you came with me. You can see that, can't you?"

"But all kings have mistresses don't they? It's normal. Please Richard, I beg of you!" and she fell to her knees, grasping him around the legs.

He felt awkward and torn. He loved this emotional, spontaneous girl, but duty would always come first for him and it would be selfish if he took her with him, knowing that.

"This King will not have a mistress. I will not change my mind. You have to be brave. Besides have you forgotten there are no flush toilets in my time?"

She tried to giggle, realising he was trying to lighten the mood, but it emerged as a strangled sob.

She scrambled up.

"Well, will you at least come to this place every year and see if we can meet up just for a few hours, minutes even? I have to have some hope of seeing you again, or..."

He must have seen how stricken and desperate she was and worried then for her soul if she really couldn't bear to live without him. He didn't want that on his conscience.

"Very well, I agree to do that."

She felt a great weight lift off her at his words. At least she would have something to look forward to, to aim for. Provided he survived the battle, of course.

"On your oath?"

"I swear, yes."

"Will you kiss me one last time?"

He nodded and drew her into his arms, his lips finding hers unerringly and she tasted his sweet breath again, clinging to him as long as possible. His tongue found hers and his beloved lips nibbled gently at her own, tender and soft. He held her face in his hands and stroked her curls and she caressed his hair in turn and revelled in its silky softness. She was surrounded for a minute or two with the scent of him and trembled in his power. She felt as if the whole thing was a dream, unreal. It had all gone too fast and she wanted to hold him for just one more minute, one more second.

Then he broke away and looked right into her tear-filled eyes. His were also moist, but determined.

"I have to go - look! The boar, the white boar!"

She turned and looked where he was pointing, but saw nothing. He gave her one more swift kiss and mounted Rebel in an elegant bound. He galloped off towards the tree, turning once to wave his hand. He was heading straight for it and she was just about to scream that he was going to crash right into it when he simply vanished.

Chapter Fifteen - June 1485

Wind of Change

Richard almost made Rebel swerve at the last minute - if it didn't work, he and Rebel would likely both be badly injured, riding headlong into the tree. But he held his nerve and kept his eyes open. The tree was looming in his vision, solid and heavy and hard. Then it was gone and he was galloping into a glade surrounded by thick forest, by the forest he knew. Everything seemed greener and lusher than he remembered. And so silent, peaceful. He saw the white boar on the path ahead and followed it into the press of trees. As he urged Rebel on in order to keep up with it, it suddenly vanished and just a few hundred feet ahead on the path he saw Frank Lovell and Rob Percy and the others he had left behind a year ago.

"Sire! We have found you at last - we thought we had mayhap missed you, you were so far ahead of us. What was it you were pursuing, Your Grace?" asked Percy.

"And did you catch it, My Lord?" put in Lovell, his eyes twinkling in merriment.

Richard couldn't stop grinning, he was so pleased to be back. Their earnest, familiar faces were the best sight he had seen in weeks, excepting Rose's smile. And yet it seemed they had not even missed him.

"'Twas a pure white boar I chased, fellows, but I'm afraid it eluded me."

"Forsooth you jest, Sire - 'twas doubtless a reflection of yourself!"

They all joined in the laughter. Then Frank said: "My Lord, you seem…different." He narrowed his eyes, scanning Richard from head to toe. "What has happened to you, Sire?

Your countenance appears…less strained…happier? You appear to have lost some of the burden of your grief, Your Grace. Was this White Boar a faerie animal, some sorceress disguised as your cognizance?"

How typical that his best friend, Frank Lovell, should notice the change in him. It was inevitable, he supposed, after a whole year. Perhaps he would have to try to convince Lovell later of the truth of what had happened to him.

"Hunting works always as a rest for the mind, Frank. And there was certes a white boar - it was exhilarating to chase it, even though I failed in its dispatch. But you are right, I do feel as if a burden has lifted. I have been thinking whilst I rode and I have a new battle plan. Let us retire to the Lodge and discuss our strategy."

They rode along, chatting happily and making jokes. It was as if Richard's change of demeanour was contagious and everyone seemed to feel more positive. When they arrived at the Lodge, they gave their horses into their grooms' care and strode inside the main building.

Beskwood Lodge was a timber-framed structure with a tiled roof and thirty eight rooms, including a Great Hall. As they entered, their nostrils were assailed by the smell of roasting meat and baking, mixed in with beer and the herb-scented rushes on the floor. Richard went straight to his usual room and was divested of his clothes by his servant of the body, who then helped him to settle into the bath. He luxuriated in the warm, scented bath, closing his eyes and wondering if his strange experience was real or rather a dream. The man soaped his shoulders and back, then suddenly paused.

"What is it, John?" asked Richard, noticing his hesitation.

"'Tis nothing Your Grace, just that…your back, Sire! It looks…much better than it did when I dressed you this morning. 'Tis impossible, yet my eyes do not lie!" He stopped, lowering his eyes when he noticed Richard's frown. "I apologise, Your Grace. 'Tis none of my concern, of course. Please forgive my impertinence, Sire."

"There is nothing to forgive. Your eyes do not deceive you. All you need to know is that I have discovered a method of improving my affliction by exercise. I ask your discretion regarding the apparent speed of the cure."

"Of course, Sire. My discretion is absolute," he said, bowing his head in respect.

"Thank you John," he smiled then, glad that John had remarked on it, because that was proof that his experience and, in particular Rose, had been real, not just a pleasant dream.

After his bath, John dressed Richard in his formal clothes, as they were having a small feast of sorts that evening. He wore black as he was officially still in mourning for Anne. He liked the texture of the clothes he wore, but remembered how strange and smooth the clothes of the twenty first century were and he certainly missed zips and Velcro, having to wait for what seemed like an age for John to fasten his points and doublet. He set his dagger at his belt, happy to be able to wear it openly again, and walked down into the Great Hall. Everyone made their obeisance to him as he entered. He gestured for them to rise and seated himself at the top table, with Rob Percy and Frank Lovell either side of him. They had several courses: venison and pheasant and…lamprey! His mouth watered already and he reached for his knife and fork - smiling to himself as he realised there would be no forks for many years yet. Or...well! He would have a word with his smiths, after the battle.

After they had eaten and drunk their fill, Richard rose and signalled his henchmen to follow him into a secluded chamber on the first floor, which was the most private place in the Lodge. He, first of all, signed the letters of instruction to his Commissioners of Array, asking for their men to muster at short notice: it seemed like déjà vu.

"Right, my men. Now I will unveil to you my new plan. Do not be dismayed or surprised because it is a radical and unusual one. I have my reasons, even if they may seem obscure at the moment."

He had their full attention now.

"This is what I intend to do..."

Chapter Sixteen - July 2015

You Ruin Me

Rose had been on the verge of a nervous breakdown for weeks. She simply could not come to terms with losing the man she felt was her soul mate. It had been awful when she and Matt had divorced, but this was a hundred times worse! Matt was still around and they had separated gradually, allowing her to acclimatise to being alone. She had had Richard with her constantly for over a year and now he had been ripped from her world, taking her heart with him. Actually no, he had left her heart behind. It would have been better if he had taken it for then she would be dead and not feeling this pain. She sensed her heart gingerly, afraid to know…yes, it was broken, crushed, damaged beyond repair. The only way she could function was to build a wall around it like a suit of armour around a valiant knight. But then no one would be allowed in and she would have to live the rest of her life alone; that could be a long time.

She wondered whether she would see Richard after death. He would be dead now of course, even if he had survived Bosworth. Maybe she could take an overdose and join him. But she soon discarded this idea. She wasn't the type to despair like this and anyway, Richard wouldn't approve.

She knew that, in his world, Bosworth had come and gone, but she didn't know what had happened. She had expected everything to change, the world around her to be transformed if he had won at Bosworth, but she had noticed nothing out of the ordinary and hadn't dared to look online.

She carried on with her career, throwing herself into it and taking comfort from the fact that she was helping many with their physical pain. She went out with friends, but her heart wasn't in it. She drifted along, existing rather than living. All the joy had gone from her life. Richard had brought her so much happiness while he was here, but she wasn't sure the pain she felt now was worth it. She knew no other man would ever match up to him.

The night finally came that she didn't cry herself to sleep. It was a long, slow climb back to contentment, but she took it one step at a time. It was about four weeks after Richard had gone and she was driving home from a shopping trip in Southend, which was about five miles from Rayleigh. She realised that she felt a bit better. At last she felt ready to do an internet search to see if anything had changed. She was still full of trepidation and her hands were shaking when she typed 'Richard III' into the search engine.

'Richard III (2 October 1452 – 22 August 1485) was King of England for two years, from 1483 until his death in 1485 in the Battle of Bosworth Field...' It was all still the same.

She couldn't read any more and her positive mood vanished like a thief in the night. He had failed. Nothing had changed at all and he had died at Bosworth, again! She felt as if she couldn't go on herself. It was not just that he had been killed, as he would be dead now anyway after five hundred plus years! But to realise that he had known what was in store for him and still led the heroic last charge, still been cut down and humiliated, still had his reputation blackened by the Tudors, felt like a knife twisting in her gut. Not only that, but if he had died at Bosworth, he wouldn't be able to meet her at their rendezvous next June. It had been the one thing she was looking forward to and now that was cruelly snatched away from her.

She went to the bathroom cabinet and took out the tub of paracetamol. Her hand was shaking as she opened the lid and prepared to end it all, tears coursing down her face. Just as she brought the tablets to her mouth, she heard his voice. It was as clear as if he were right there beside her.

"Do not endanger your soul, Rose. You know this is wrong. Do not do this!"

She shook her head, she was going mad now! She raised her hand to her lips again.

"I said 'No' Rose! I forbid it!"

His voice was steely quiet and she could picture in her mind how he looked, his head tilted, daring her to disobey.

She dropped the tub in the washbasin and went next door. She sat on the bed and buried her head in her hands. Eventually, she picked up the phone and dialled Lynne.

She came over straight away and was wonderful. She made her a cup of hot chocolate and listened to her, sobbing and incoherent, as she told her about the internet search and Richard's failure. She asked her about the voice she'd heard in the bathroom - was it really Richard? Lynne said there was no reason to think it was anyone else - perhaps he was watching over her. She let Rose talk about Richard for hours and just nodded and sympathised in all the right places, she dried her tears when Rose couldn't hold them in any more and then she gave her a huge hug before she left.

"Are you sure you don't want me to stay - just to make sure you are OK?"

Rose smiled. "Thank you, but I think I'll be alright now. You've been fantastic!"

Rose closed the door after Lynne and put the catch on. She patted the dogs, who had been rather put out by all the disruption, and went to bed.

She dreamed of Richard on his horse, in his armour and charging into battle. She called out to him, but he didn't seem to hear her…

Chapter Seventeen - August 1485

Past the Point of Rescue

When Richard saw that Lord Howard had fallen, he groaned in frustration - hadn't he warned him not to raise his visor? Idiot! However there was no time to worry about him now - Howard's men were on the verge of fleeing in panic.

He took a deep breath and forced his racing mind to remain calm. He sent two urgent messages to his commanders. One was to Northumberland to reinforce the demoralised men. However, he was doubtful whether Percy would obey, despite Richard having threatened him with dire consequences for disloyalty and promising him great rewards if he stayed true; William Stanley's army was watching from his left flank and Percy wasn't about to commit suicide by crossing in front of it. The second message was to Lovell, who was leading the York men, also telling him to engage the enemy.

He had sent Lovell to York, knowing Northumberland would be likely to 'forget' to send for the York contingent, but Lovell had returned with only eighty men, York being cursed with the plague. And they had only just arrived in time for the battle. He doubted eighty extra men would be enough. He had successfully kept Sir Thomas Stanley out of the equation by imprisoning him at Pontefract temporarily, but there was still the notoriously fickle William Stanley, who had stayed hidden beyond Richard's reach until today, and who would not commit to either side until he saw a clear winner emerge.

Richard had to be that winner or all would be lost! His honour, his crown, his very life was at stake. In any case, he refused to flee like a snivelling, craven coward, perhaps only to end his days under the executioner's axe, or forced to live once again in exile away from his beloved country. No, he would be courageous and execute his defiant charge, attempting to take his enemy by surprise. He would either fail (again) but as the King he was, with honour and courage, or triumph over the upstart Tydder, finally ridding himself of the last Lancastrian pretender. He still had a few cards left to play.

He called his squire over and bade him find out from the scouts exactly where Tydder was positioned. The squire hurried off to do his bidding and Richard turned to his household knights: his loyal followers, his faithful friends and most true lords.

"You can see that the battle is not going as expected - Northumberland is keeping back and Stanley will not commit. We must act decisively if we are to prevail - I will not flee, but will live or die as the rightful King of England. I intend to attack the Tydder directly, a bold, but dangerous strategy. I do not ask you to accompany me; you have served me well and faithfully and I hereby absolve you of further obligation. But I would be pleased to have those of you who will, to support me in this endeavour - who is with me?" he roared, the golden crown shining on his helm and his sword raised in the air. His huge white destrier, White Surrey, snorted and stamped his hoof, for all the world as if he knew what his master had said. He waited, wondering if he would be forced to do this reckless deed alone. But he needn't have worried - there came an immediate, deafening response from the three hundred or so closest to their Lord.

"À Richard! À Richard! We are with you, Your Grace!"

His heart swelled with pride and he had to fight to contain the emotion threatening to overwhelm him - these men were effectively putting their lives into his hands. They trusted him, yes, they loved him. If he did die today, he would die knowing he was loved.

At that moment the squire returned and spoke to Richard, pointing over to the east, where it could clearly be seen that a group of mounted men were making their way towards William Stanley's army. The banner of Cadwallader, the Red Dragon, was flying but there were but a handful of men around it - he could see a mounted figure in the centre of the group - it was Tydder. There was no time for delay.

"For England! For St George and for honour!" he bellowed and spurred White Surrey into a canter and then a gallop, not waiting to see whether the men had followed him - for once he had to trust. White Surrey responded magnificently - he was truly a fearsome beast and the fastest destrier Richard had ever known - he soon outdistanced the men, who had indeed all followed their beloved King.

Richard had commanded his blacksmith to double and triple check Surrey's shoes, and he was confident that the eventuality of him losing a shoe was all but impossible. As soon as the enemy group realised what was happening, they seemed to hesitate, as if unsure whether to continue or return to the safety of their army. In that moment of hesitation, Richard galloped madly through the intervening ground, his horse sure-footed and swift. He had sent his scouts on ahead to ascertain where the swampy terrain was and had ensured his route was well away from it. He had his battle axe in his hand, and his helm with the golden circlet atop it shone in the sunlight.

He reached the group way ahead of his entourage and immediately began to hack his way mercilessly towards the Tydder. His way was barred by the huge figure of Sir John

Cheney, the giant of a man whom Tydder was using as a bodyguard - what a coward the man was! He didn't allow White Surrey to even break stride, but urged him on even faster and aimed his axe at Cheney's head. The blow missed, but not by much, crashing into his shoulder and chest, injuring his arm and knocking him clean off his horse. Richard galloped on and felled Tydder's Standard Bearer, William Brandon, easily, swinging his axe with deadly accuracy, not even stopping to see the colours fluttering down into the mud.

He galloped on, slicing limbs and smashing skulls and then he saw that the man he had marked as Tydder, could not be him - he was older, much older. With dismay he realised that this was a trap! God's bones! He had forgotten that possibility. Tydder was no fool and his general, Oxford, was a wily tactician. They must have counted on him going for a heroic charge, just like his father Richard of York at the battle of Wakefield, who charged into the enemy in an attempt to rescue his beleaguered household. He reined Surrey in savagely, the horse whinnying as he slid in the dirt, but he kept upright.

His eyes swept the field, searching for the real Tydder. Suddenly the battle seemed to stand still around him and he felt his gaze drawn to a lowly herald, standing in the midst of a group of young soldiers, dressed in a dirty brown tunic and old leather armour. As the man glanced at him fearfully, he recognised the man in the online portraits he'd seen of Tydder: those odd eyes were unmistakeable - it was him! He turned Surrey, with his knees, yelling at the top of his voice:

"Tydder is here! Follow me! À York!"

He swung his axe, felling the enemy guard which had hastened to defend Henry as soon as they realised that their plot was revealed. Tydder was now just a few yards away. He was petrified, Richard could see. And so he should be. He had no armour on appropriate for a nobleman and he was skulking among his servants, trying to hide while his Uncle Jasper, for that was who the decoy must be, was the true warrior. Richard spat on the ground in disgust. His men had, by this time, caught up and he turned proudly, yelling his encouragement to them and then he was face to face with Tydder. He saw the terror in the eyes of the cur as he tried to find a horse in order to flee Richard's righteous anger. Richard heard him yell desperately at a passing knight:

"A horse! A horse! My riches for your horse!" The man rode on, not even recognising the pretender. "Halt! I command it!" he cried, sounding like a petulant child. Richard was almost upon him now and he was defenceless.

At that moment, he heard a thunder of hooves and wheeled around to see Stanley's forces galloping down the hill to join in the fray. To his horror, he heard the cry "À Tydder!" begin to sweep across the oncoming men. There was no more time left - it had to be now! He spurred White Surrey forwards in one more swift charge, yelling at the top of his voice, while drawing his sword - his battle axe had become embedded in an enemy's breastplate.

Tydder was now fleeing at a run and Richard urged his horse even faster, intent on his prey. White Surrey almost stumbled, but recovered and carried Richard right up to Tydder. But he couldn't bring himself to kill a fleeing man. He was a chivalrous knight, not a murderer. He brought Surrey round Tydder, blocking his escape and Tydder halted his flight - he was gasping for breath.

Richard's knights had surrounded Tydder and Stanley's men were still approaching. Richard ordered his friend,

Frank Lovell, to arrest Tydder and he immediately approached him, holding a length of rope. But as Lovell made to take hold of Tydder's arm, the sneaky knave pulled his other hand out of his tunic holding a dagger and lunged at Frank, a look of hatred on his twisted features.

Richard acted instinctively to defend his friend. He didn't hesitate, but swept his finely balanced sword around with venomous force in a sweeping arc, taking Tydder's head clean off! The earth became red with the fountain of blood flowing from the headless corpse, which had fallen to the ground with a thud. He leaned down from the saddle and grabbed the Tydder's head, the eyes still frozen in fear.

"The Tydder Bastard is dead!" he yelled, his voice hoarse with emotion.

The cries around him suddenly changed to "À Richard! À York!" Stanley's men changing their coats even as they arrived at the scene.

"Sire, thank God you have prevailed - we saw your courageous charge and rushed to help - but I see you didn't need it!" said Stanley, kneeling before the bloody but triumphant King.

"Hmm!" muttered the King, fixing Stanley with his cold stare, head slightly tilted. He turned and saw Tydder's army completely in rout now - he was victorious, as he always knew he would be.

Chapter Eighteen - August 2015

Halo

It was two weeks later when Rose was standing in Rayleigh High Street looking at the Church. There was something wrong with it that she couldn't place. It was the sign, with its name; they had put up a new one. She went over to look more closely at it. That's odd, she thought. The sign said "Holy Trinity Catholic Church". Someone was going to get into trouble; it wasn't a Catholic church, it was Anglican. She saw Mrs Campbell, one of her patients and a regular church-goer, leaving the Church and called over to her.

"Hello, Mrs Campbell. Who made the boob with the sign? The sign-writer or the person who ordered it?"

"Boob? I don't know what you mean, Rose. What boob do you mean?" she said, her bird-like features drawn together in concern.

"Well the Church isn't Catholic, it's Anglican, isn't it?"

"Anglican? Never heard of it! It's always been Catholic as far as I know - certainly for all my lifetime."

And she gave Rose a weird look, turning to go on her way.

Rose stood there, her brow furrowed in puzzlement. She had been on her way to visit Lynne and have a chat, so she went back to the car and drove along Eastwood Road. As she passed the park, she started. She was sure she had read the name of the park wrongly, It was called King George V Playing Fields, but she could have sworn she had read 'King Richard III Playing Fields'. Her mind was obsessed! It must have been a trick of the light. She drove on and turned into Tudor Road, where Lynne lived. That was rather unfortunate, the name of her road. She had made sure Richard never knew what it was - he might have been offended.

"Oh no," she thought. She must have missed the turning - this road was called Gloucester Road. She drove out again, but ended up lost. She felt stupid - she had been to Lynne's house countless times! In the end, she gave up and rang Lynne.

"No, that's right - Gloucester Road. What's the matter with you Rose? I've never even heard of the name Tudor - it sounds weird!"

Rose felt like she was going insane. What was the matter with her? She finally found Lynne's house and asked if she could check something on the internet. Her hands were shaking, yet again. She typed in the words: "Richard III" and waited for the page to load. When it did, she saw this:

'King Richard III became King of England and France and Lord of Ireland when he stepped into the breach after the children of the previous King, Edward IV, were found to be illegitimate.

He defeated the upstart would-be usurper, Henry Tudor, at the Battle of Bosworth Field and went on to reign for over twenty years.

After Bosworth, Richard executed Lord Thomas Stanley and his brother William, as well as the Earl of Northumberland as they had all committed treason by attempting to set a trap for him at Bosworth in order to help Henry Tudor. Tudor himself was killed by Richard, personally, after a dramatic and courageous cavalry charge. Tudor, who was masquerading as a common herald, fled when Richard discovered his deception and was beheaded in the act of fleeing by the furious king. Tudor's scheming mother, Margaret Beaufort, was sent to a convent for the rest of her life, deprived of all her lands and riches. Bishop John Morton was imprisoned in the Tower but was killed trying to escape - some said it was deliberately set up by Richard.

Richard is a controversial king, many believing he was too ruthless for cutting down Tudor while he was in the act of retreating and for executing the Stanleys and Northumberland after the battle, others pointing to his subsequent enlightened reign and his restraint in not executing Morton or Margaret Beaufort.

The Henry Tudor Society was formed in the mid-twentieth century with the aim of rehabilitating Tudor's blackened reputation as a coward and its members maintain that Tudor was not fleeing but had surrendered and that Richard murdered him in cold blood. They claim that Henry would have been a better ruler than Richard, but are seen as a deluded fringe organisation, not taken seriously by real historians.

Richard III's achievements:

He was the first monarch to swear his oath of allegiance in English.

Richard reformed the bail system and brought in the "innocent until proven guilty" premise.

He promoted trade in printing and books and was the first monarch to encourage women to read and write.

He introduced the first lending libraries in London and York, run by the monasteries, which gradually spread to other cities, towns and countries.

He founded the chantry chapel at York Minster, as a family mausoleum.

He funded Christopher Columbus' expedition to the Americas and some of his extended family were thought to have joined Columbus and explored the world with him.

He had his laws printed in English so his people could understand them and stamped out corruption in the courts.

He resisted the religious reformation and is the main reason England is still a Catholic country today.

He was an accomplished musician and is credited with composing the famous Mediaeval song, Greensleeves.

He built a beautiful chapel, begun by his brother Edward IV, on the battlefield of Towton, the site of England's bloodiest battle, and paid for priests to pray for the souls of the fallen on both sides.

He initiated the custom of using flowers to represent each fallen soldier - white roses for the Yorkists who fell and red for the Lancastrians.

He was the first English monarch to knight a (converted) Jew and later began a policy of non-discrimination against other religions. However, Catholicism was firmly the official religion of England.

He started the custom in England of using knives and forks to dine with.

He brought in greater taxes on alcohol, which eased the pressure on the Royal exchequer.

He helped control disease by insisting on strict hygiene measures in his physicians and the use of silver as an antibacterial. He promoted measures to control hygiene regarding cooking and food preparation, leading to better health.

He defeated the Scots, yet made a lasting peace with them, giving them autonomy, which they still have today, and marrying his eldest daughter, Joana, to James IV of Scotland.

He founded the Council of the North while the Duke of Gloucester and brought similar bodies to other parts of England, after his succession.

He was a conscientious and active king, who always kept fit and ate healthily.

He invaded and conquered France in the year 1499 and married his son, Edmund, to the daughter of the defeated French King and thus annexed France to England. To this day, it is still a possession of England.

He travelled extensively and met and became patron to Leonardo da Vinci, whose famous portrait of Richard's wife, Joana, commonly known as Mona Joana, hangs in the National Portrait Gallery. Richard is credited by Da Vinci for awakening his ideas for flying machines and other innovations. Richard commissioned Da Vinci's famous Last Supper painting and owned an extensive art collection himself. One of the most mysterious works of art he owned is a small painting on paper of Richard mourning his first wife Anne, whose ghost is comforting him. It appears to be signed Rose, but the artist remains a mystery and it has been claimed that the painting is a later forgery, since the pigment and paper used are thought to have been unknown in Richard's time.

By marrying Joana of Portugal, he united the houses of York and Lancaster, ending the Wars of the Roses and bringing peace and prosperity to England. His niece, Elizabeth, married Manuel of Portugal on the same day, and later became Queen of Portugal when Manuel (the Lucky) succeeded his cousin, Joan, known as the Perfect Prince.

Personal life: Richard married Anne Neville in 1471 and they had one child, Edward, who died aged ten. Anne died not long afterwards, probably from tuberculosis. His second wife was Joana of Portugal, a pious and gentle lady with whom he had five children, Richard (later Richard IV of England), Joana, Edmund, Anne and Rose.

He brought peace to the realm and justice to the common man. He is immortalised in numerous statues around the country and in many churches and educational institutions which he founded and patronised.

He is thought to have died in the year 1505, on a hunting trip, but his body was never found. He is the only English monarch not to have a known resting place. His son, Richard IV, continued his father's policies and had seven children, ensuring the Plantagenet dynasty was secure, surviving to the present day in the person of Queen Elizabeth II of the House of Plantagenet.

Richard III is known today as Richard the Just, or Richard the Wise, and his reign is considered the point in history when the Middle Ages ended and the Renaissance began. He ushered in modern thought and is recognised by most historians as England's greatest and most enlightened King.'

As Rose finished reading, she realised she was weeping uncontrollably in relief and joy. Now she had only to wait until next June...

The End?

Author's Notes

Richard was known to be hunting from (what was then known as) Beskwood Lodge just before the Battle of Bosworth. He was in the vicinity of Nottingham on June 22nd 1485.

Royal Rebel is made up, although Richard was known to have many horses.

I remember reading a quote from More that Richard was thought to wear armour under his clothes, but More suggested it was because he was afraid of being attacked and referred to it to illustrate his supposed paranoia. I do not know if there is any evidence that he did wear armour under his clothes but, if he did, I have surmised from the experience of Dominic Smee, who had an almost identical scoliosis, that armour might have supported Richard's back and that could be the reason.

There are some autobiographical elements pertaining to Rose. I am an osteopath, which lent itself well to the subject of Richard's scoliosis and I also paint, and speak French and Norwegian, so these parts of Rose's life are based on fact. I live in Rayleigh in a bungalow and I have the three dogs as does Rose in the story (but also a husband, John!).

Richard's playlist is actually my own, which I used as scene titles.

Because of the different calendar used in Mediaeval times, the dates in 1485 and 2014 when Richard left his time and appeared in Rose's would be different. (Since the introduction of the Gregorian calendar, the difference between Gregorian and Julian calendar dates has increased by three days every four centuries - at the moment it is 13 days). I have ignored this and used the same dates for the sake of clarity.

The places in the story are all real and I have visited most of them, so they are, by and large, as accurate as I could make them.

Evidence has now been found which suggests that Richard was seeking the hand in marriage of Joana of Portugal very soon after his wife, Anne's, death or maybe even just before she died. This contradicts previous accusations that he was seeking to marry his niece, Elizabeth of York.

Richard's scoliosis was severe and it is very doubtful whether osteopathic treatment would be able to lessen the degree of curvature. However, I have taken the optimistic view that Rose may have been able to effect an improvement in mobility and a reduction of pain.

Rayleigh was known for its hunting forests in the vicinity - there was a bear baiting pit but it was later than Richard's time. However, he would have known the Holy Trinity Church (if he had visited Rayleigh). There is no evidence known to me that Richard ever did visit Rayleigh, but equally, no evidence that he didn't!

There was indeed an actual episode of Pointless which asked the questions set out in the story when Richard finds out about his fate at Bosworth. The battle was known as Redemore or Sandeford at the time it took place, but I have used Bosworth for clarity.

Destrier, Making Fifteenth Century Re-enactment Glorious and B.O.A.R.s also exist and can be found on Facebook. I had to use some artistic licence regarding Destrier's training. They only train in the winter months, but as Richard arrived in the 21st Century in June and needed to take part in the re-enactment of Bosworth in August, I had to invent some summer training. Other than that, I have tried to stick to their actual method of working.

The video of Merlin, the bullfighting horse, is on You Tube.

The three best armourers in the world are thought to be English, Swedish and American, but because of Richard's time constraints I have changed the American one to German and I also changed their names. The cost of a full harness can be in the tens of thousands of pounds.

The runaway horse scene is based on a real incident which happened to me.

The visit to the Proms is accurate for the concert date and content, but it didn't actually take place at the Albert Hall, which I used as being a more iconic venue.

Richard was a book lover and had his own book collection. He would have known William Caxton who was in London during Richard's lifetime. Richard's first and only Parliament made laws taxing foreign traders but exempted books and printing.

The mention of the ghostly music at Fotheringhay was reported in Secret History: The Truth About Richard III and the Princes by John Dening and R.E. Collins.

There is a theory that Richard's son, Edward, may have been buried in Jervaulx Abbey, though his actual resting place is unknown.

Barley Hall, extant at the time, may possibly have been visited by Richard, but there is no evidence to prove this.

The Middleham Jewel replica is on display at Middleham Castle, but it is unknown to whom it belonged.

The idea of Richard having wanted to be a lutenist arose when I misunderstood a post on Facebook, but I liked the idea - it is known he enjoyed music and he did 'collect' his own choir.

The theories about the battle have all been suggested previously by various authors.

His itinerary before Bosworth is taken from John-Ashdown-Hill's The Last Days of Richard III.

The theory that Edward IV was poisoned by the Woodvilles is proposed in Secret History - The Truth about Richard III and the Princes by John Dening and R.E. Collins.

The Coronation food is invented by me, but based on known Mediaeval dishes.

'Dans Le Noir' is real and located in Clerkenwell, London.

My Norwegian friend is a teacher, does live in Gausdal and has a cabin in the mountains in Gudbrandsdalen.

The poppy display in the Tower was real and there on the date specified.

Edward IV's mistress, generally known as Jane Shore, was only called Jane in later times; her name was actually Elizabeth. Richard's solicitor, Thomas Lyneham, did indeed request to marry her and Richard's letter about this still survives. He comes across as amused and affable.

The re-interment of Richard III took place on 26th March 2015 and I attended Leicester at the time, staying at the site of the Blue Boar, where Richard was supposed to have spent his last night in Leicester before leaving for the battle, though this is conjecture. It is also theorised that it may have been called the White Boar until Richard's demise, again unproven.

There is a lot of bitter dispute among Ricardians who disagree as to where Richard should have been re-interred. It has become a modern War of the Roses: York vs. Leicester. As a relative newcomer to their ranks, I feel I shouldn't really comment and I actually am fairly neutral on the question. I can see valid points on both sides. Richard certainly did live for most of his adult life in the North and definitely favoured York, granting them tax concessions, having his son invested as Prince of Wales there and commissioning the building of a large chantry chapel at York Minster. He may have intended to create a family mausoleum there, but there is no written evidence for this. Equally, he may have changed his mind after he became king, possibly choosing Westminster (where his wife, Anne, was buried) or Windsor, where his brother Edward was interred. However, Westminster is apparently full up and the exact location of Anne's burial has been lost; Windsor would have needed the Queen's consent, I believe, and she has stayed, very sensibly, out of the argument. In Leicester's favour are the legal rulings which upheld burying him in the Cathedral of Leicester and the fact that Richard is now laid to rest in the centre of his beloved England. To be fair in the story, I have had Rose being pro-York and Richard being happy with Leicester. Of course, nobody today actually knows what he would have thought about it. I do feel that the most important things for him would have been that he was buried with the proper religious solemnity and that he was remembered.

The movements of Richard and Rose are those of myself and Lynne, my sister. I was the one, in fact, who felt faint and 'weird' while in the proximity of Richard's coffin, and I had to sit for a while in the side area, where I was able to say Richard's special prayer, in Latin, for him.

I also won tickets in the ballot for the Middleham Requiem Concert, which I attended, accompanied by my sister and not Richard, sadly (no offence to you Lynne)!

The research concerning Richard's DNA with respect to his paternal line and probable colouring was revealed whilst in the creative process, so was incorporated into the story and is accurate as far as I can ascertain.

All theories mentioned by Richard or Rose are actual theories about events for which there may be no, or very little, evidence. Historical events mentioned did happen, except those during and after the 'second' Battle of Bosworth, and the private scenes between Richard and his friends in the forest and at Beskwood Lodge. The actions of the Stanleys and Northumberland at the Battle and the tactics of Henry Tudor are chosen from many different theories.

There is also a speculation from a novel that William Stanley might have been charging in on Richard's side.

The 'facts' about Richard's long reign are my own imagination, although some of them are real, such as the founding of a chantry chapel at York Minster, the chapel at Towton, the laws regarding books and printing, his edicts regarding bail, justice for all and stopping the corruption of the judicial system and swearing his coronation oath in English and having his laws in English.

The supernatural time travel part of the story is my own invention. Perhaps...

Richard's Playlist

For those of you who would like to re-create Richard's playlist (even though the songs and lyrics are not necessarily relevant to the plot - just the titles relate), here is the list of the tracks I used as scene titles:

Alone - Gary Puckett
Bring Me To Life - Jai McDowall
Baby What a Big Surprise - Peter Cetera
Drive By - Train
Soap (I Use The) - David Gates
Rude - Magic
Try - P!nk
I Vow To Thee My Country - Katherine Jenkins, The Prague Symphony Orchestra
Finding Beauty - Escala
Don't Know Much - Linda Ronstadt ft Aaron Neville
Somebody That I Used To Know - Gotye
Feels Like Home - Jai McDowall
Amazed - Lonestar
Grenade - Bruno Mars
Everything I Own - Bread
Strong - Robbie Williams
True Colours - Maggie Reilly
I'm Too Sexy - Right Said Fred
Heart of Gold - Neil Young
The Best - Tina Turner
Handy Man - Jimmy Jones
Hero - Chad Kroeger
Read All About It - Emeli Sandé
Music - John Miles
Englishman in New York - Sting
Need You Now - Lady Antebellum

It's All Coming Back To Me Now - Celine Dion
The Armed Man - Karl Jenkins
Glorious - The Pierces
What Doesn't Kill You (Stronger) - Kelly Clarkson
Little Arrows - Leapy Lee
My Prayer - The Four Seasons
Only Love Can Hurt Like This - Paloma Faith
I Don't Want to Miss a Thing - Aerosmith
Thank You For the Music - Abba
Hot Stuff - Donna Summer
Mars, The Bringer of War - Holst (The Planet Suite)
Locked Out of Heaven - Bruno Mars
Requiem for a Tower - Escala
Hazard - Richard Marx
Remember - Bryan Adams
Poison - Alice Cooper
Lady Eleanor - Lindisfarne
Kings - The Pierces
Senses Working Overtime - XTC
Fantasia on Greensleeves - Ralph Vaughan Williams
Hocus Pocus - Focus
Dream a Dream - Charlotte Church
DNA - Little Mix
I Wish It Could Be Christmas Every Day - Wizzard
Red Red Wine - UB40
Kiss From A Rose - Seal
If You're Not the One - Daniel Bedingfield
The Riddle - Nik Kershaw
Unfaithful - Rihanna
The Silence - Alexandra Burke
Torn - Natalie Imbruglia
Road to Hell - Chris Rea

Bad Things - Jace Everett
Don't Speak - No Doubt
Requiem - Karl Jenkins
Fire - The Crazy World of Arthur Brown
Weight of the World - Lemar
The Proud One - The Four Seasons
Bad Boys - Alexandra Burke
Flying Theme (E.T.) - John Williams
Norwegian Wood - The Beatles
That Thing You Do - The Oneders
Mountains - Lonestar
Earth - Hans Zimmer
Dancin' Away With My Heart - Lady Antebellum
Kissing You Goodbye - The Pierces
Wind of Change - Scorpions
You Ruin Me - The Veronicas
Past the Point of Rescue - Hal Ketchum
Halo – Beyoncé

Bibliography

If you want to find out more about the real Richard III, these are the main books I have used for reference:

The Battle of Bosworth - Stephen Lark
Bosworth 1485: Psychology of a Battle - Michael Jones
Secret History: The Truth About Richard III and the Princes - John Dening and R.E. Collins
The Last Days of Richard III - John Ashdown-Hill
The Third Plantagenet - John Ashdown-Hill
Eleanor the Secret Queen - John Ashdown-Hill
The Mythology of Richard III - John Ashdown-Hill
Richard the Third: The Great Debate - Paul Murray Kendall
Good King Richard? - Jeremy Potter
A Trail of Blood - Jeremy Potter
The Maligned King - Annette Carson
Richard III: The Young King to Be - Josephine Wilkinson
Royal Blood: King Richard III and the Mystery of the Princes - Bertram Fields
Finding Richard III: The Official Account of Research by the Retrieval and Reburial Project - Annette Carson
A Glimpse of King Richard III - Matthew Lewis
The Wars of the Roses - Matthew Lewis
The King's Grave: The Search for Richard III - Philippa Langley
The World of Richard III - Kristie Dean

If you want to read more fiction about Richard, I recommend:

The Sunne in Splendour - Sharon Penman
Loyalty - Matthew Lewis
Honour - Matthew Lewis
Fortune's Wheel - Rhoda Edwards
Some Touch of Pity - Rhoda Edwards
The White Queen - Philippa Gregory
We Speak No Treason Vol 1: The Flowering of the Rose - Rosemary Hawley Jarman
We Speak No Treason Vol. 2: The White Rose Turned to Blood - Rosemary Hawley Jarman
Summer's End - Frances Irwin
By Loyalty Bound: The Story of the Mistress of King Richard III - Elizabeth Ashworth
The Killing of Richard III - Robert Farrington
Tudor Agent (Wars of the Roses II) - Robert Farrington
The Traitors of Bosworth (Wars of the Roses III) - Robert Farrington
G - Loyalty Binds Me - Christopher Rae
G - God and My Right - Christopher Rae
The Worm of Conscience - Carole Parkhouse
The Devil in Ermine - Isolde Martyn
The White Boar and the Red Dragon: A Novel About Richard of Gloucester, later King Richard III and Henry Tudor - Margaret W. Price
A Rose for the Crown - Anne Easter Smith
The Seventh Son - Reay Tannahill
The 'Laurence the Armourer' books:
On Summer Seas: The Fighting Plantagenets - Richard Unwin

A Wilderness of Sea: The Rise of King Richard III - Richard Unwin
The Roaring Tide: A Tale of High Treason - Richard Unwin
The Adventures of Alianore Audley - Brian Wainwright
Roan Rose - Juliet Waldron
Crown of Roses - Valerie Anand
The 'Cicely Plantagenet' Books:
Cicely's King Richard - Sandra Heath Wilson
Cicely's Second King - Sandra Heath Wilson
Cicely's Lord Lincoln - Sandra Heath Wilson
The Rose of York: Love and War - Sandra Worth
The Rose of York: Crown of Destiny - Sandra Worth
The Rose of York: Fall from Grace - Sandra Worth
My Lords Richard - Margaret Davidson
Treason - Meredith Whitford
The White Boar - Marian Palmer
Desire the Kingdom: A Story of the Last Plantagenets - Paula Simonds Zabka
The King's Niece - Liz Orwin
The King's Wife - Liz Orwin
Blood of the White Rose - Ellie Huncote
The King's Dogge: The Story of Francis Lovell - Nigel Green
Under the Hog: A Novel of Richard III - Patrick Carleton
Virgin Widow - Anne O'Brien
No Sanctuary - John C Hayes
White Rose - John C Hayes
The Last Plantagenet: A Story Connected with the Princes in the Tower - Toni Richards
The Dreams of Kings - David Saunders

These are a little more quirky:

Sacred King: Richard III: Sinner, Sufferer, Scapegoat, Sacrifice - J.P. Reedman
The Court of the Midnight King - Freda Warrington
This Time (Richard III in the Twenty first Century) - Joan Szechtman
Loyalty Binds Me (Richard III in the Twenty first Century) - Joan Szechtman
Rings of Passage - Karla Tipton
King Richard's Bones: A Royal Ghost Story featuring King Richard III - Elizabeth Aston
The Adventure of the Bloody Tower: Dr John H. Watson's First Case - Donald MacLachlan
The Plantagenet Mystery - Victoria Prescott
Hate is the Other Side of Love: The Duke of Buckingham and Richard III - Mallorie Meldrum

And of course the book most closely associated with Ricardians:

The Daughter of Time - Josephine Tey

I hope you join us!
If you do wish to join the Richard III Society you can find details of how to become a member on: www.richardiii.net

Printed in Poland
by Amazon Fulfillment
Poland Sp. z o.o., Wrocław